Fierce Gods

Col Buchanan is an Irish writer who was born in Lisburn in 1973, and now lives on the west coast of Connemara. In recent years he has mostly settled down, and loves nothing more than late-night gatherings around a fire with good friends. *Fierce Gods* is the fourth of the Farlander novels.

By Col Buchanan

The Farlander Novels

FARLANDER

STANDS A SHADOW

THE BLACK DREAM

FIERCE GODS

COL BUCHANAN

Fierce Gods

THE FARLANDER NOVELS

Book Four

PAN BOOKS

First published 2017 by Pan Books
an imprint of Pan Macmillan
20 New Wharf Road, London N1 9RR
Associated companies throughout the world
www.panmacmillan.com

ISBN 978-1-4472-1121-1

Pan Macmillan does not have any control over, or any responsibility for,
any author or third-party websites referred to in or on this book.

1 3 5 7 9 8 6 4 2

A CIP catalogue record for this book is available from the British Library.

Typeset by Ellipsis Digital Limited, Glasgow
Printed and bound by CPI Group (UK) Ltd, Croydon, CR0 4YY

Visit **www.panmacmillan.com** to read more about all our books
and to buy them. You will also find features, author interviews and
news of any author events, and you can sign up for e-newsletters
so that you're always first to hear about our new releases.

For my sisters

The Story So Far . . .

It is a time of war for the beleaguered *Free Ports* of the democras, that confederation of islands strung across the Midèrēs Sea. Surrounded on all sides by the *Mannian Empire*, the Free Ports hold out when most other nations have already fallen, offering the only lasting resistance to the Empire's domination . . .

On the front line of this conflict stands the fortress city of *Bar-Khos*, its mighty walls stretching across an isthmus that connects Khos with the occupied southern continent. Bar-Khos has been besieged by the Empire's forces for ten long, desperate years. If it falls, the rest of the Free Ports will likely follow. Defeat means the enslavement of them all.

Now, with the surprise invasion of an imperial army behind Khosian lines, attacking the city from the rear, everything hangs in the balance . . .

To the east, across the sea, lies the *Alhazii Caliphate* and its desert capital of Zanzahar. The Alhazii remain neutral in the war. Their power is founded on their monopoly of black powder, which they supply to both sides for profit. It is a monopoly based on their ancient trading partnership with the mysterious and advanced *Isles of Sky*, the location of which remains a jealously guarded secret. The Alhazii will do anything to stop the location of the Isles of Sky from becoming known. What they don't know, yet, is that a covert network known as *the Few*, which works behind the scenes to defend the democras of the Free Ports, has already uncovered their secret. Indeed soon, the Few should have navigation charts showing the way. Charts that could change the entire balance of the war – if only they hadn't recently gone missing . . .

Meanwhile, two moons orbit the planet of Erēs. One of them, a water moon, shows signs of life . . .

The Players

In the midst of this war, several people hold the fate of the Free Ports in their hands:

NICO CALVONE A young man returned from the dead; the son of Cole and Reese Calvone, and the recent apprentice to the old Rōshun assassin, Ash. Nico was recently slain in an imperial arena, far from his homeland of Khos. However, following a mission to the Isles of Sky by his Rōshun master and his father Cole, Nico was reincarnated by the strange technologies of the people of the Isles. He has since returned to Bar-Khos with his father, only to find that his mother has been kidnapped and enslaved by the invading Mannian forces. Together, father and son have set out to save her.

BAHN CALVONE A Red Guard officer and field aide to the Lord Protector of Khos, the famous General Creed. After a reckless show of bravery at the recent battle of Chey-Wes against the invading Imperial Expeditionary Force, Bahn was captured by the enemy. Along with other Khosian prisoners, he was secretly indoctrinated by Mannian priests to betray the cause of his own people. He was then allowed to escape. Bahn returned to the besieged city of Bar-Khos, unwittingly primed with his mission of treason. Not long after his return he received a surprise visit from his brother Cole, a brother who fled the endless war many years ago. Even more surprising is what Cole carries in his possession – charts to the Isles of Sky: a chance of changing the whole course of the war. Without explaining how he came by them, Cole asked Bahn to take the charts and to pass them to the relevant Khosian authorities. Something which Bahn has not yet done, even as the invading imperial army masses beyond the wall.

CHÉ A young man who was once an apprentice with the *Rōshun*, an order of assassin monks who offer protection to people through the threat of vendetta. Unknown even to himself, however, Ché was actually an infiltrator sent by the Mannian Empire, his mind manipulated so that he believed himself to be someone else. Upon deserting the Rōshun, Ché returned to the Mannian capital and became a *Diplomat*, an elite imperial assassin, and subsequently helped betray his previous companions in the Rōshun. He later joined the surprise invasion of Khos by the Empire's Expeditionary Force. It was in Khos where Ché finally deserted his own side. After a brief liaison with a young woman called Curl, a medico in the Khosian army, the ex-Diplomat was captured and imprisoned by the Khosians.

Coya Zeziké Famed Delegate of the League of Free Ports, and descendant of the even more famous philosopher Zeziké, whose teachings inspired the revolution of the democras more than a century ago. As a secret member of the Few, Coya Zeziké has travelled to Bar-Khos to lend what aid he can in their defence.

Shard the Dreamer A refugee from the occupied southern continent, and a native Contrarè. After fleeing with her family to the Free Ports, Shard made her home in the Academy of Salina, where, as a student, she helped develop the burgeoning craft of *rooking* – the craft of covertly accessing and subverting *farcrys*, a form of exotic technology which allow for distant communications through the medium of the Black Dream. By now though, Shard is much more than an expert rook. She has become a *Dreamer* too, able to manipulate reality by accessing the bindi itself, the cosmic code.

'If you cry freedom, start praying to your fiercest gods.'

NIHILIS, FIRST PATRIARCH OF MANN,
TO THE DEFIANT GREEN ISLANDERS.

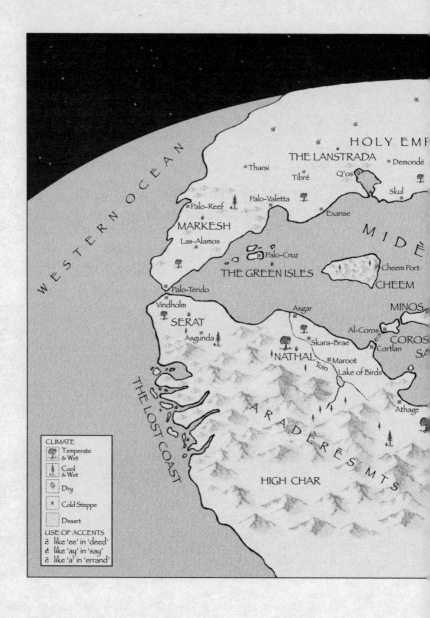

HOLY EMP

THE LANSTRADA
•Demondé

•Tharsi
Tibré
Q'os

Skul

Palo-Valetta

•Palo-Reef
Exanse

MARKESH
MIDÈ

Las-Alamos

Palo-Cruz

THE GREEN ISLES
Cheem Port

CHEEM

•Palo-Terido

Vindholm
Asgar
MINOS

SERAT
Al-Coros
COROS

Asgunda
Skara-Brae
Cortlan
SA

NATHAL•
•Maroot

Toin
Lake of Birds

A R A D È R È S M T S
Athage

THE LOST COAST

HIGH CHAR

WESTERN OCEAN

CLIMATE
Temperate & Wet
Cool & Wet
Dry
Cold Steppe
Desert

USE OF ACCENTS
ē like 'ee' in 'deed'
é like 'ay' in 'say'
è like 'a' in 'errand'

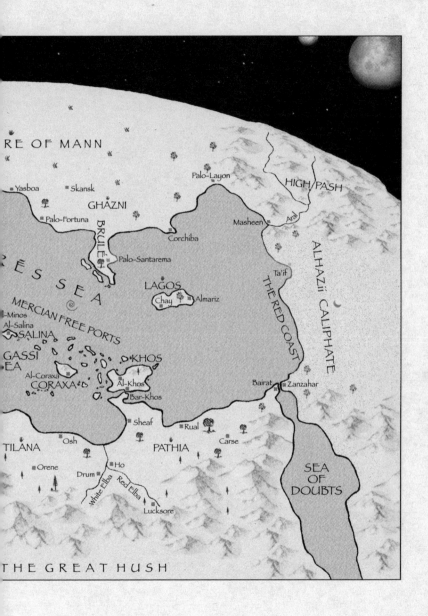

RE OF MANN

Yasboa   Skansk

GHAZNI

Palo-Fortuna

BRULÉ

Palo-Layon

HIGH PASH

Masheen Ard

Corchiba

Palo-Santarema

Ta'if

RÈS SEA

LAGOS

Chay Almariz

THE RED COAST

ALHAZII CALIPHATE

MERCIAN FREE PORTS

-Minos
Al-Salina

SALINA

GASSI
EA

Al-Coraxa

CORAXA

KHOS

Al-Khos

Bar-Khos

Bairat Zanzahar

Sheaf

Rual

Carse

TILANA Osh

Orene

PATHIA

Drum Ho

White Elba Red Elba

Lucksore

SEA
OF
DOUBTS

THE GREAT HUSH

The Woman Who Fell
from the Sky

'*Did I ever tell you about Horroco Pledge?*' rasped the woman through gritted teeth, clenched hard to stop them from clattering in the worsening vibrations of the descent. Already a sharp tang of blood filled her mouth from where she'd clipped the end of her tongue. '*Only man to take a Yukka ride to the planet and make it back again?*'

She had to speak, had to hear the sound of her own voice just to prove that this was still real – that she was really falling faster than a bullet through the upper atmosphere of the planet, tracing a trail of fire across the sky like a falling star.

Suddenly, a shudder ran through the protective Yukka shell all around her like a jolt of fear.

Ocean gasped, swallowing down more blood. Her lanky body jostled in the harness fixing her to the curve of the shell wall, and she gripped the straps even harder, feeling them digging into her flesh. Something cracked loud and spirited overhead, but Ocean dared not look up to see. She knew it was the thick outer casing of the husk starting to fracture in the heat.

'*Horroco Pledge,*' she rasped again, heaving for air through her flaring nostrils. '*One of those early hermit mystics, used to seek out the remotest islands of Sholos to live alone. Until even those islands were not remote enough. So the mystics turned their gazes to the planet overhead. They started hollowing out the Yukka seeds, and hitching rides inside them across the void. Hoping to find somewhere unpopulated, secluded, on that big fat planet of Erēs, even if they died in the attempt.*'

So startling, this primal terror gripping her body. Like she was a frightened child again, falling in a dream. Even her own throat seemed to have seized itself in a vicious chokehold, trying to throttle some sense into her as though there was still time for that, as though she wasn't fully committed. Her years of experience seemed as nothing in comparison to this present, pressing reality; wrapped in flames and plummeting to the surface of another world, riding the seed pod of a tree that had flung its spore in the wildest gesture of hope and life across the void.

A roar was pressing hard against her eardrums, the howl of scorched air through which she and the seed shell were plummeting. It was getting harder to breathe inside the hollowed-out husk, the oxygen thinned almost to nothing during the crossing, even with the tanks of blue-algae sloshing on the floor. But Ocean spoke aloud anyway, squandering what air remained on what seemed an even greater need just then – holding herself together through the shaking dignity of her own voice.

'*His pod . . . it came in too shallow. Skipped right off the atmosphere and ended up slingshotting all the way around the planet. He thought he was dead when his food and water ran out. All he had left was the supply of moondust he'd brought with him, hoping it might be a valuable commodity to the natives. So he ate it all and off he went, soaring in his mind while the pod shot off through the void, as alone as anyone has ever been . . .*

'*Hey, you even listening?*'

With a grunt of effort Ocean forced her neck forwards. She couldn't see the little swamp rat anywhere. He was no longer peering out from her pocket. Blinking the sweat from her eyes she gazed down at her juddering, suited body, and her legs ending at bare feet dangling just above the glowing floor.

Look y'all, I'm flying.

Ripping through the upper atmosphere of a planet!

Ocean bounced around in her harness like an underweight jockey, her eyes widening as she stared down at the fiery glow now rising from the floor of the pod, all too aware of what she was looking at. It was the Yukka shell's long-spent combustion chamber, which had first launched the mighty seed out of the water moon's atmosphere with Ocean snug inside it, being burned away in the heat of their rapid deceleration. Now, parts of the floor itself were thinning to a vague translucency which seemed to be barely holding back the yellow blasts of heat.

With a flash and a shudder the burning air pulsed even brighter, so that the space of the seed pod was filled with the flickering tones of flames.

'Old Horroco . . .' she gasped. '*He said – he said that when he was soaring like that, all alone through the void, high on moondust and waiting to die, he tried calling to the Great Dreamer, and even deeper to the Source itself . . . But he gained no answer to his pleas. Or so he thought, until a miracle of good luck happened, and he got snared by the moon's gravity so he made it back to Sholos. The only person ever to make a return trip!*'

Ocean grimaced at her own words. Even if she made it down in one piece, she was never coming back from this. She was never going home.

Sweat dripped from her face and fell spinning in slow motion towards the glowing roar of the floor. She felt movement across her shoulder. It was Pip, her friendly swamp rat, digging his claws into the impenetrable weave of her skinsuit.

'*Hey,*' she said to the little rat, its hair banded with dark green stripes like blades of grass. '*What happened to staying in my pocket?*'

The rat was going after a bug, she saw. A little moon bug that had caught a ride with them on their voyage, somehow hidden until now, sitting there on her upper arm with its silver carapace splayed open, beating its wings. Slowly, tenaciously, gripping on against the forces of free fall, Pip clawed his way towards it, his whiskers twitching.

'*You need to be doing that right now?*'

Her voice snagged the rat's ear, for Pip looked up to meet her eyes. He snapped his front teeth together, then carried on towards the bug.

Ocean reached out a hand towards him, seeing colours swimming across her blurring vision. For an instant she was struck with the sight of her hand shaking and swaying there in front of her – how her black skin turned bronze in the upward glow of the flames – and then she grasped the squirming rat and pulled him tight to her chest, tight to her heart, where his own tiny pulse raced in her grasp.

Another shock sent the shell of the Yukka pod lunging sideways. Ocean cried out aloud, though her shout was near lost in the angry growl of the descent.

Hard to believe the vibrations were worsening. She heard what sounded like a rip over her head, something forcefully separating. It was the worst of bad signs, the heat crisping the hoary outer shell and penetrating inwards, forming cracks where it was thinnest. It suggested she was coming in too steep.

With a deep exhalation she projected her inner eye out beyond the husk to take in the roaring brilliance of its exterior, almost too bright to look at in the surrounding darkness of night.

A jerk. A shudder. Part of the outer shell tearing off entirely.

'We're all right. We're all right. We're all right!'

At last Ocean dared to look up, only to see the split forming right above her head and running across the woody curvature of the shell.

'We're all right. We're all right!'

Screaming at a thousand lems a second through air growing ever denser, Ocean's voice juddered as though she was beating on her chest, the vibrations grown so bad now she was being shaken loose even from the straps holding her to the wall. She gripped harder to the harness and to Pip as she was thrown from side to side, her head rocking so violently she thought her neck would snap.

'Shit!'

Many of the seed pods didn't make it to the surface intact, coming in too shallow or too steep. Fifty-fifty were the considered odds for a Yukka rider's chances of survival. Sometimes the rider made it. Sometimes they didn't.

Dig deep, advised the disciplined core of her mind. *You've lived or died on a coin toss before.*

Hard to focus though with her brains being scrambled in her skull. Ocean's left arm and shoulder had somehow come loose, so that she was partly hanging free from her harness as she was thrown about, and coming looser with every heave. Pip squirmed in her grip to be free.

It was all clearly madness to her just then – this mission she had taken on, this insane feat of will and desperate chances. Any moment now the shell was going to crack apart and the flames would consume her in their hungry need for life.

But there was nothing she could do but hold on, and even as she thought that she was finished the roaring faded away just as quickly as it had come, replaced instead by a whine of passing air. Through the thin patches of the floor the flames were suddenly replaced by darkness. Around her, the vibrations became nothing but an occasional rattle.

She was through the upper atmosphere, having shed most of her velocity along the way. In moments the wobbling pod righted itself with a deployment of leaf vanes trailing behind its fall. Again she checked with her inner eye, and saw the vanes flapping above in ribbons that caught the light of the moons, slowing her descent even further as they unravelled themselves to catch the air.

She was still alive. She was going to make it.

*

Heavy, this world of Erēs.

Even with the superior strength of her Patched body, Ocean had the impression of moving through water as she struggled from the fresh-cut hole in the shell's top to emerge into a howling winter's night.

Freezing gusts narrowed her eyes to slits, blasting the great cloud of black hair on her head so that she felt the heft of it like never before. Below her, the seed pod bucked wildly in waves that tossed it this way and that, tilting sharply from one side to the other. In the moonlight its exterior looked scorched like some cauldron left too long in the fire, its hoary curved flanks still smoking. Steam hissed wherever waves crashed against them.

Ocean gasped against a spray of salt water. The bubbling backwash glowed with a green phosphorescence, and when she looked about she saw that the whole surface was shining with it wherever the waters broke. She gasped again as she cast the bundle in her hands over the side, so that it landed with a limp splash on a surging swell.

Instantly the object began to expand into the shape of a small boat.

Grinning from exertion, Ocean clambered clear of the hole on her long and shaky limbs with a sleek carryall dangling from her back. She clung on to the ragged edge for a moment, caught by the sight of white water racing towards her glowing with threads of green. She managed a curse before the wave washed her away in its bubbling riot.

Long moments of breathless scrambling for the surface, fighting against the drag of her carryall, the water, the colossal weight of the planet itself. For a desperate moment the woman found herself caught beneath one of the trailing leaf vanes of the Yukka pod, like coming up under a layer of sea weeds. But she didn't panic. Ocean had been born in the water, and if she was lucky she would die in it too.

But not today.

She broke the surface crying out for air, scattering water like beads of green fire. Just ahead of her, the little swamp rat squirmed over the crest of a wave with his long tail leaving an emerald trail behind him, obviously headed for the inflatable boat. By then the craft had fully expanded, its tiny wheelhouse visible above the bubbling swells. Ocean surged towards it too.

The soaked and trembling rat was watching her when she finally hauled herself over the flexing side. Ocean flopped into the pool of water on the floor. She lay there for some time, next to her sodden carryall, unable or unwilling to move, snug enough in the self-warming layers of her skinsuit.

When she lifted her chin to look at Pip again, the rat squeaked loudly.

'I hear ya,' she replied.

Ocean planted a palm on the sagging floor of the boat and forced herself upright. She tried to stand in the tiny boat but almost fell over the side for her efforts. Her balance was way off. She gave herself a few moments then tried again, clutching at the inflatable wheel of the boat to right herself, swaying on her bare feet.

Whoah. Big world!

*

At least there was some shelter inside the three flexing, transparent walls of the wheelhouse. Pip huddled out of the gale beneath the wheel, watching Ocean as she stabbed at the boat's power nipple until algae lights glowed to life across the instrument panel. Heat began to emanate from the veins running through the floor. At the back of the craft, a row of squid-jets started pushing out water against the swells.

She took a moment to catch her bearings, to centre herself, to bask in the weak light of the moons. Tatters of clouds trailed long and thin across the starry night sky. In all directions the far horizon was barely visible, even with the night vision of her Patched eyes.

My new home, she thought, knowing there was no going back now.

Strange, how normal it felt to be bobbing on the sea of an alien world. Yet Erēs was not entirely alien. Not even mostly so. It had been seeded long ago from the distant stars, just as the two moons above it had been seeded.

They were humans here just like her. And for all that this planet remained in quarantine, isolated from all the other worlds, they lived lives of hope and struggle just like everyone else.

Spray lashed across the wheelhouse. The boat's prow rose high on a wave. Ocean took a device from one of her utility pockets, then turned it this way and that until a flashing light on its side started to blink faster. When she pointed it directly east, the light stopped blinking and stayed fully on – locked on the signal of a distant transponder.

The signal of Juke, her hired accomplice on the planet.

'East it is,' Ocean declared, turning the wheel to bring them about.

She could only assume their calculations for the launch timing had been precise enough – that she had landed in the Midèrēs Sea as expected, right there in the Heart of the World. Ultimately, she had aimed for the Free Ports themselves, but such precision with the Yukka seeds was a matter of luck more than anything else. She could only hope the islands of the democras were close by.

With a last, lingering glance at the smoking Yukka pod, Ocean fed more power into the squid-jets and aimed the boat east into the prevailing waves, flexing her knees against the lifts and dips of the swell. She looked back again, though this time to the sky where the twin moons gleamed high and pale. She focused on the blue one, sweet Shilos, and all she had left behind forever.

Ocean pulled a face, then set off into the blasting winds of her new world, headed for the Free Ports.

CHAPTER ONE

Nico

Through the night galloped a zel bearing a pair of riders on its steaming back, foam snorting from its muzzle and lathering the black and white stripes of its flanks. The animal's lungs heaved like it was about to drop dead.

'Yah!' shouted the rider gripping the reins, whipping the zel for more speed. 'Yah!'

They raced down the shoulder of a hill following a muddy track in the darkness, barely able to see where they were going. Nico Calvone clung on to the back of his father's coat with a grip made icy from the winter cold, his clothes still soaking wet from the earlier rain, bouncing up and down so badly he was at risk of falling off. Snowy pine boughs lashed past his face. Clumps of mud and snow scattered from the animal's hooves as steam jetted from its nostrils.

His father was going to run the animal into the ground like this. But since scenting what had seemed like rotten eggs on the wind, Cole had whipped the animal's running lope into a full-out charge, and he showed no signs of slowing.

Over his father's shoulder, Nico glimpsed the Reach stretching before them from the foot of the hill, speckled with the lights of imperial camp fires. And there was Tume glittering in the distance, the city floating in a steaming lake whose black waters reflected the sister moons hanging above. A Khosian city that now lay in the hands of the enemy.

'Simmer Lake,' rasped Cole. 'We have to hope your mother hasn't reached Tume yet.'

'You're going to kill the zel like this!'

'No choice!'

It was fear that drove his father's breakneck pace down the hill. Fear of what would happen if they didn't reach her in time.

Days had passed since they had come across the belongings of Nico's mother on the road leading to their wild farm, way back on the southern coast. Reese's things had been scattered around a deserted handcart, and tracks of slavers had headed off towards the enemy-held north. Riding a pair of zels, Nico and his father had raced all the way to the Reach following their trail, losing one mount to exhaustion along the way. Now the other zel was about to drop too.

A ravine flanked the track on their right-hand side, dark and wide, flashing past dangerously close at times as the trail wound its way through the trees. As they rounded a turn Nico peered ahead, spotting something in front – a fire, burning brightly by the side of the trail, surrounded by the silhouettes of seated figures. Behind them he glimpsed a blackened cottage and a flag fluttering from the ruins of its porch, sporting the red hand of Mann.

'Imperials!' he hissed. 'A guard post!'

Cole lashed the zel even harder, leaning right over its neck so that Nico had to crouch forward too. In a full charge they thundered along the track towards the bonfire, where heads were turning now, a cloaked figure rising with a bottle in his grasp.

The cloaked soldier stepped out onto the track and held up a hand to stop them.

'Yah! Yah!' urged Cole, but it seemed that the sight of the soldier standing in their way was the last straw for the poor zel, for just then she cried out and faltered.

Nico nearly fell off as their mount reared up on her hind legs. He clung on as she collapsed to the earth beneath him, right there before the feet of the startled soldier.

In the rising steam of the animal's last breath, Cole and Nico sat in the saddle unmoving, like two fools trying to ride a dead zel. 'Gods damn son of a bitch,' panted Cole.

'Well what do we have here, boys?' cried the soldier in accented Trade, standing there gripping a bottle of wine, his other hand resting on his sword hilt beneath his thick grey cloak. Around the nearby fire sat his two companions. One was staring with drunken eyes while the other snored softly.

'You have any zels hereabouts?' snapped Cole impatiently as they climbed to their feet, looking about him. The imperial soldier tilted his head to one side, not liking Cole's tone. The soldier was middle-aged and overweight, his double chin bulging beneath his bearded scowl.

'Not since we ate them. What brings you out here in the middle of the night, then? Doing some scavenging?'

Hearing the suspicion in the man's voice, Nico joined his father's side with stiffened legs, his sodden clothes sticking to his skin. A pair of dogs were growling under a nearby tree. He could see something hanging from one of its boughs.

Nico observed the burnt-out cottage beyond the roaring fire, and behind it the black gulf of the ravine. He looked back towards the dogs that were jumping about under the nearby tree. His blood froze. From the boughs of the tree hung a pair of corpses – an old man and woman with whitened hair.

The dogs were leaping up to take bites from the spinning corpses' feet, which dangled as bloody strips of flesh.

'Just stragglers,' he heard his father say tightly. From the tail of his eye, Nico watched Cole slowly unbuttoning his longcoat for easy access to his blades. 'Don't suppose you've seen any slavers come through this way? We ran into some trouble back there. Got separated.'

'A team came through this afternoon,' piped his seated companion, a younger fellow swaying on a varnished dining chair. 'Had some fine women with them too.'

'Did you see a red-haired woman amongst them?' Nico blurted. By his side his father sighed.

'Red hair? Sure. Best looker of the lot. They wouldn't let us have a taste of them though, the bastards. Precious cargo.'

'How long ago?' asked Nico.

'I suppose that would have been this afternoon sometime.'

'You say you were with those fellows?' asked the overweight soldier, studying them closely. It was Cole he didn't like the look of. Something about the way Nico's father was leaning over the saddle of the fallen zel.

His hand was going slowly for his sword when Cole swung back with the longrifle and aimed it square between the man's crossed eyes. 'Easy,' Cole suggested. 'No sudden moves now. Nico. Grab his sword there.'

Nico drew the blade from the man's scabbard. The alcohol on his panted breath washed over him, hot and rancid.

By the fire, the younger fellow was still sitting there, blinking in confusion.

'On your feet, soldier!' Cole snarled at him and he jumped up like he'd been struck by lightning, toppling the chair behind him. The young man looked sober all of a sudden as he stared at the sword in Nico's grip and then at Cole's rifle.

'What do we do with them?' whispered Nico to his father.

'What do you think we do with them?'

'You don't have to do this,' said the big man with the rifle at his head.

'You really don't!' wailed his companion. 'Take what you want.'

'You think you deserve our mercy?' snarled Cole. He was truly angry now. 'You come here to enslave our people, and you think you deserve our mercy?'

For a moment they all just stood there, gasping their steamy breaths into the night. Their companion snored away on his chair.

The dogs were still snarling and leaping up at the corpses. The sight of them hardened Nico's heart. He knew what needed to be done. He grabbed at the younger man's cloak and shoved him towards the tree. 'You too!' he snapped at his companion on the track, jabbing his sword at him. 'Cut down those bodies. Give them a proper burial like they deserve. Maybe then, my father here will go easy on you.'

'Easy?'

'Maybe he'll make it quick.'

People will do anything, Nico reflected, if it means tasting a few more sips of air before their end. Working slowly, the drunken shambling pair of soldiers hacked down the bodies from the tree then kicked the dogs away with their boots.

'We don't have time for this, Nico,' grumbled his father, keeping his rifle aimed at them.

'We've time.'

They stood there watching in silence as the soldiers heaped rocks onto the two bodies stretched out side by side: someone's parents and grandparents. By the time they were finished they were both slick with sweat. The younger fellow bent over to vomit, moaning and shaking with fear. Cole marched up to him. He pressed the rifle barrel to the fellow's temple until he straightened, then planted it on his forehead and jabbed it hard so the soldier stumbled backwards, headed for the ravine behind the cottage.

'Please, you don't have to do this!' the young man pleaded, for he could see over his shoulder what they were headed for.

'Keep an eye on the other one,' Cole growled, leaving Nico standing there with his blade pointed at the fat man's armoured belly.

The big man licked his dry lips, eyes flicking this way and that.

'I have a wife, I have children!' hollered his companion through the gloom. They had stopped now at the very edge, and the man looked down and sobbed with fear.

'Yeah? So do I,' rasped Cole. He still had the end of the barrel pressed against the man's forehead. 'Now *jump*.'

'*Hist!*' cried the young soldier. 'Do something, will you?'

'Like what, Tylen? The lad has me at the end of a sword.'

'Please,' he called out to Cole, and Nico saw the fellow flinging off his cloak before fumbling to take off his armour. 'I'll take it all off. I'll walk away, I'll desert! Just please, *please*, let me get back to my wife and my children.'

'*Jump*,' said Cole with steel in his voice, and he prodded the rifle so the man tottered backwards over the edge.

'*No!*' he wailed as he toppled into the ravine.

Nico's heart was hammering away. His throat was dry. He looked to the remaining soldier standing before him. The man glanced down at the sword gleaming between them.

He's going to jump me. I should finish him now!

Nico had killed a man before, but that had been in the midst of action; not like this, in cold blood against an unarmed opponent. In his hesitation he saw the fellow's stare harden, and in a moment of slowing time Nico watched dumbly as the soldier knocked the blade aside and went for him, his hands grabbing for his throat. He was twice the bulk of Nico and they both went down hard, his foul breath pouring over him. Nico grabbed wildly for the knife in his belt.

A loud crack sounded above him as Cole rapped the man's skull with the butt of his rifle. The soldier slid off him, unconscious or dead Nico couldn't tell.

'Give me a hand here,' heaved Cole, and together they dragged him over to the ravine and rolled him over the edge.

Nico stumbled back towards the fire. It was like some awful dream of murder that he couldn't awaken from. The third soldier was still snoring drunkenly next to the flames. They grabbed him by the arms too and dragged him to the ravine, where they tossed him in after his companions.

Sweat was beading Nico's forehead. He walked back to the track without looking back; without looking at his father.

He could see clouds forming overhead, bringing with them a sudden breeze, stirring the pine trees all around him. Nico felt a few cool spits of rain.

Great, he thought, *more rain*; as though he hadn't just helped cast three men to their deaths.

His father grimaced as he looked to the north towards the lake and the distant lights of Tume.

'Let's go.'

CHAPTER TWO

Bahn

So tired was Bahn Calvone that dream time and waking time seemed to have converged into one bleak continuum, in which he existed in some kind of twilight world between them both. Phantoms played at the edges of his vision, thoughts twisted and crawled in knots of endless obsession.

He couldn't recall when last he had slept properly. Whenever Bahn tried to rest he was tossed this way and that by dreams that were as bizarre as they were disturbing. Dreams of leering monsters. Dreams of torture and breaking points. Dreams of a violent father, who in real life had never been anything but gentle.

No longer could he close his eyes without fearing what was to come. Even sleep, the final refuge, was now denied him.

Up here on the edge of the cliff the sea breeze blew at Bahn in fierce gusts, scouring his narrowed and red-shot eyes with frigid blasts. Yet his tears were mostly of his own making, cast from despair and exhaustion, fat drops spilling down his face and plummeting into the gulf of air below his feet.

Bahn was sweating slightly despite the breeze cooling his skin, as though he was still touched by lingering fever from his recent bout of dysentery. His Red Guard armour felt heavy today, his sword, his hobnailed boots, even his head with its dark moods and even darker thoughts, all bearing him down. Behind him swept his cloak, barely fastened at his neck, tug-tugging him back from the edge even as he leaned over it, swaying above the high and pitiless fall.

Down there, at the very foot of the cliff, were the countless tilted roofs of the Shoals, that notorious shanty-town clinging to the thin coastal fringe of Bar-Khos; shacks on stilts with planks strung between them, necessary for the tides that flooded the rocks during every storm surge. Smoke tussled amongst streaming clothes drying from lines. White water crusted the rocks along its edge.

It was hard to see anything with the tears smearing his vision, though Bahn was well past stopping them.

Let them flow, let him weep, demanded his shaking body.

Still, he had a hunger to see the world around him just then. A hunger like never before in fact, trembling here so close to the edge and the end. It was all he could do to keep clearing the endless tears from his eyes, like a field medico wiping desperately at a pair of arterial, bullet-sized wounds in his face.

He'd never understood those enemy prisoners who chose to be blindfolded before the firing squad; perhaps because Bahn had always held a slight fear of the darkness. To him it made more sense to want to see it all at your very end, turning your eyes to the sky and your heart to times worth remembering – not the premature blindness of your impending death.

Bahn blinked fast to take in the Lesser Bay of Squalls, and the squadrons of warships manoeuvring against each other in a prelude to battle. From the eastern harbour another Khosian convoy was making a break for it on the long Zanzahar run, several dozen ships headed for their sole remaining trading partner beyond the Free Ports, and their only source of black powder.

Turning his head, he looked westwards to the other side of the Lansway and the Bay of Calm, where skyships were circling each other in the air, cannons booming. Strings of enemy Birds-of-War swooped in over the more sheltered western harbour, dropping bombs amongst those vessels heading out to safety or fast returning from elsewhere in the Free Ports. A few enemy skyships circled the Mount of Truth, and the building on its flat summit that was the Ministry of War, where Bahn worked as a field aide to the Lord Protector, General Creed. Shells burst around the ships from the Ministry's defences, leaving puffs of dirty smoke that studded the air as they thinned into haze.

Bahn felt the concussions of the battles deep in his bones, though otherwise he was numbed to all that he saw. He gazed down towards the district of All Fools, sprawling between the two harbours across the throat of the Lansway, and then his stare roamed out along the land bridge stretching across the sea to the far southern continent.

Through the misty air the multiple walls of the Shield were barely visible today, dark forms rising across the waist of the Lansway to stand in the way of the Imperial Fourth Army, or what was left of it now, bogged down in Camp Liberty after their General Mokabi had been slain, his countless mercenaries flown or killed along with him. Beyond the foremost surviving wall, Bahn could just make out the muddy waters where the sea had flooded in around Mokabi's forces, killing a hundred thousand or more, and holding off any further attacks from the south.

After ten long years it was a strange sight to see the walls of the Shield standing in silence like that, now that the heavy guns had mostly been moved to the northern wall and the newer threat facing them there instead – the arrival, in the midst of winter, of advance forces from the Imperial Expeditionary Force, who had invaded the island from the sea.

He thought of his home to the north of the city, and his wife Marlee who had shared it with him for all this time. The mother of his children, a woman he still adored. Marlee would be in the local temple at this time of day, praying for the safety of everyone but most of all for her loved ones – her own side of the family, and those of Bahn's: Reese and Nico and even that crazy fool of his brother, Cole, still somewhere out there beyond the wall.

His only surviving brother, returned after all these years of absence. Only to run out again as soon as he'd gotten here.

What else should he expect from a brother who had never been there for Bahn when he'd needed him the most – those times in which the siege and the war had come close to burying him in their traumas? Cole had run off years ago to escape it all, his own mind near-lost in the tunnels beneath the Shield, fighting in the darkness as a Special.

Had his brother visited their mother upon his unexpected and brief return to the city? Bahn supposed there hadn't been time, and that he would have said so if he had. Still, he pictured his mother opening her door to fling her arms around Cole, hailing the hero son now returned to save them all with his charts to the Isles of Sky. So clearly proud of her eldest surviving son, while she barely tolerated Bahn's visits at all, the son who remained a lingering disappointment for refusing the path she had wanted for him, a path of monkhood.

It was just as well their father was long gone from this world. He would have beaten seven shades of blue into Cole if he had been alive upon his return, and Bahn would have enjoyed seeing it.

Except that wasn't right.

Their father had never raised a hand to them in his life, remaining a mild-mannered man to his dying day.

Why was Bahn now thinking otherwise?

I've lost my mind, said a voice in his head as though not his own. *I'm starting to believe I'm someone else.*

He had been this way ever since his captivity by the Mannians after the battle of Chey-Wes. Ever since the Mannian priests had drugged and tortured him, whispering thoughts into his breaking mind and planting suggestions he could no longer recall, save for one: report to a particular address in Bar-Khos, once he had escaped.

And he had escaped, Bahn and several other Khosian officers. Though only now did the truth strike home. The Mannians had allowed them to escape. They had wanted them to return to the city.

Bahn rocked on the balls of his feet, looking straight ahead again, swaying forwards over feet planted right at the crumbling edge of the cliff.

Do it!

He tried to think of his wife again, his daughter, his son, needing to clutch on to them for all that they meant to him, which of course was everything. But they were like drowning figures swept away in the welter of his thoughts, lost beyond his grasping.

Do it now while you have the strength to!

Bahn leaned forwards into the wind, blinking fast. A shape was hovering in the air directly before him. Bahn stared at it through his tears. It was a sea piper, its broad golden wings extended to catch the updraught rising from the cliff-face, close enough that he could see its bronze breast feathers ruffling in the breeze.

The bird was watching him, drawn in some way to his strange manner.

Swaying forwards Bahn leaned out further towards the animal, lifting his arms from his sides like wings. The sea bird drifted closer, piping out its sweet voice as though to stay him.

For a moment he was reminded of a different time and place, of bright song birds darting about on the breeze of a summer's day. A holiday with his family on his aunt's rice farm in the northern hills. His brother had been there, and Reese and their quick-tongued son Nico, along with Bahn's own wife and son. Vividly he recalled the burning days when multicoloured fish had flitted between the stalks of rice as though in play; indeed how the fish had toyed with them, darting in and out between their feet while the family ran splashing through the fields in increasing circles, laughing the joy of it into the summer sky.

It was them that he did this for, Bahn reminded himself now, steeling himself to jump.

'Are you all right, son?'

The voice behind him sounded old and frightened.

Bahn leaned back, clearing his throat.

Next to him an old woman appeared, nearly as close to the edge as he was. From the corner of his eye he glimpsed white hair beneath a tartan shawl. She carried a scrap of bread with her, and he watched her toss a morsel out to the sea piper, who snapped it up in its beak.

'Cold day,' she remarked, and was kind enough not to look around at his blustered condition.

'Yes,' he replied, suddenly shivering hard.

'I'm sure there are better days for it, son. Days other than this one.'

'Better days?'

'Aye. Better days.'

She tossed another lump of bread, standing there in the manner of someone not intending to leave any time soon.

Wiping his face clear, Bahn took a reluctant half-step back from the brink, feeling his strength draining away. He knew he wouldn't do it now, couldn't do it now. The moment was gone.

Instead he turned away with a grimace, heading back to the path he was so desperate to be free of.

*

Along the cobbled road Bahn marched onwards through the city heights, set upon this course now, his soldier's cloak tugging like a billowing side-sail, his boots inordinately heavy. There were few people about in the streets of this wealthy district, though Bahn kept his head down anyway, lost in himself, his thoughts a ragged sea with waves of bleak confusion washing away what was left of him, crashing around the stony hardness of his two eyes.

Now that he was facing the prospects of life again he had little interest in his surroundings. Yet he would have to, for he could barely recall the address of the villa he had previously visited up here, and so he forced himself to look about at the spectacle of mansions all around him, seeking anything that looked familiar.

Bahn had been born and raised in the city of Bar-Khos. Yet he had never walked through this district of Cherry Heights before this week. Here above the shanties of the Shoals, on this blustery hill overlooking the city and the sea, the wealthy Michinè patricians had built their mansions after tearing down the Pale Palace of the High King, survivors of a revolution that had swept their fellow aristocracy from the rest of the Mercian Isles.

Now though, it looked as though half of them were gone anyway, for behind the high walls many of the mansions appeared to be deserted, their windows boarded up and front gates wrapped in chains. Bahn caught sight of a house that he seemed to recognize, taller than all the rest with turrets like decorative watchtowers, and then on the opposite side of the road he spotted a mansion of pink stone.

This was it.

Bahn glanced back at last, remembering to check that he hadn't been followed, then stepped across the street towards the house. Suddenly he stopped in his tracks.

A fellow Red Guard was coming out through the iron gates he was approaching. Bahn squinted, seeing that it was the old staff sergeant Chilanos, one of the men he had been imprisoned with after the battle of Chey-Wes. He hadn't seen the man since their escape to Juno's Ferry together, where dysentery had claimed Bahn's body for the better part of a month.

'You made it then,' declared the old staff sergeant upon sighting him, and although Chilanos's tone was a pleased one, his eyes were as raw and exhausted as his own.

Perhaps he was suffering from nightmares too. The man had been tortured by the Mannian priests during their captivity, same as the rest of them. In the freezing cold they had been held in a pit with other survivors of the battle, while the priests had taken them one by one to be broken with pain and mind-altering drugs, feeding them bitter suggestions that even now Bahn could hear whispering through his blood . . .

'The others,' said Bahn. 'I hear they all made it back too.'

'Aye. Save for Bull. No one knows what happened to him. Maybe he didn't make it.'

Or maybe he deserted, considered Bahn.

A clatter of wheels sounded behind them and they turned as a rickshaw hurried past, both remaining silent until it was gone.

'It's good to see you well, Staff Sergeant.'

'And you, Lieutenant.'

They did not shake hands in farewell. Neither did they ask the other what they were doing there. They didn't need to. Old Chilanos pulled the cloak tighter about himself and stepped out into the wind. In moments, Bahn was alone once again.

Before him the gate lay open, leading through a well-kept garden to the house. He approached it slowly, pausing on the threshold of the front door as it opened in front of him into darkness.

The sky was close and bright over his head, a thing hanging in suspension readying itself to fall.

Bahn stepped inside.

*

'Sit down,' ordered the withered crone over her shoulder, croaking out the words as though she could barely muster the breath for them.

The room was hot and stuffy from the wood-burning stove squatting in its corner. Shutters sealed the windows from outside so the only light came from a thick candle perched upon the table top. Bahn loosened the scarf about his neck and sat down noisily in his armour. She was the same ancient woman he had spoken with the last time he had been here, drawn by a compulsion of his mind, though he could barely remember it now, just another fragment of waking dream.

Kira, he thought she was called.

With skeletal hands she tossed a bundle of sticks into the open stove, as though the room wasn't yet hot enough. Her bones creaked when she slowly straightened, then creaked some more as she shuffled around to face him in her loose white robe, tilting her shaven head forward, her withered scowl pierced in many places.

A priest of Mann.

Near the door a figure sat at another smaller table, his back turned, writing something into a notebook. He did not look their way. In the far corner a second man sat in the shadows, two eyes gleaming, watching on as the old witch Kira blew a fine white dust across Bahn's startled features.

Time slowed instantly. The thud of his heart was like a distant, monotonous thump against a door. When Bahn sneezed he lost all sense of himself for a moment, and when he came back his head was reeling, lost and confused. It felt as though his whole body was melting away. From the corner of the room something ticked away loudly, *tick tock*, *tick tock*. The sound of it was lulling him into a kind of waking dream.

'You know why you are here again, soldier?' she suddenly asked him, and she tilted up his chin so he had to look right into her eyes, black and bottomless. 'Shall I tell you?'

Bahn swallowed hard.

'It is time to begin the city's downfall, that is why.'

'But . . . my home. My family.'

'If you succeed, their lives will be spared when Bar-Khos falls. Your family will be free to leave. They may go anywhere they wish. Do you believe me, Bahn Calvone?'

Her eyes bore into his mind. Tick tock, tick tock.

'I— Yes, I believe you.'

She studied him long and hard, seeking the truth in him. But Bahn had nothing to hide. To lie was to know the truth in the first place, and he barely knew where his words came from any more, what was real and what was not.

'You are still a field aide to Creed, the Lord Protector?'

'I – think so.'

'Good. Then all you need do is follow your orders at the appointed time, and all shall be well.'

Tears were gushing from his eyes again. Bahn blinked at the old witch with his mouth falling open, gasping.

He thought of his brother again. He thought of the charts to the Isles that Cole had given into his care, now sitting at home within a drawer, neglected. Bahn wanted to tell her about them so that their weight could be taken from him, but a small core of self-preservation still remained inside him, just enough to prevail.

'And what – what are my orders?'

'Oh my child, you have the sweetest task of all.'

The old woman leaned towards him, and Bahn tried not to flinch as her rancid hot breath washed over him. Her screwed-up features hovered ever closer, two hate-filled pits for eyes amongst the wrinkles of her spite. Bahn knew then that the old woman was mad.

'You are the one who gets to be remembered most of all.'

CHAPTER THREE

Nico

It was raining hard in the heart of Khos, darkening an already gloomy wintry morning in the city of Tume.

The rain pounded against tarpaulins stretched as roofing across the steamy yard, loud and close and dramatic. At the edge of the yard Nico Calvone stood where it was least crowded, wrapped in a coat still wet from the night before and the day before that, just like the rest of his clothing.

Nico couldn't recall when last he had been so thoroughly soaked for so long. And so cold! Even standing next to a brazier of burning coals did little to thaw him out, for all that steam rose from his clothing to join the swirling miasma hanging above the crowd.

Midwinter on the island of Khos was no time to be travelling about like this. Nico should be indoors before a roaring fire, yet here he was in occupied Tume, surrounded by the enemy; cold, wet and hungry after their desperate ride here to the high Reach.

All morning they'd been searching the Mannian slave markets of the city for his mother. He had seen cage after cage of Khosian captives, men and women alike waiting miserably to be sold, but she hadn't been amongst them.

Nico ground his teeth together and tried to stay calm, tried not to think the very worst.

He looked for his father amongst the tight press of bodies, the officers and priests and camp followers of the Imperial Expeditionary Force, reeking of damp clothes and stale sweat, gathered here in the slave yard to buy some fellow humans. But he couldn't see him anywhere. Unconsciously, Nico rested a hand on the pommel of his sword for reassurance. One wrong word here, one mistaken step, and these people would be on him like wild dogs. At best, he'd be thrown

into one of the cages along with the other Khosian civilians unfortunate enough to have been captured.

He wouldn't let that happen, he'd already sworn to himself. He
would go down fighting first.

Flames crackled in the brazier. They kept snagging Nico's gaze, a
reminder of his previous captivity in the hands of the Empire and
the terrible things they had done to him.

Easy. Remember why you're here.

They were on the outskirts of the island city here. Around them
lay the eternally warm waters of Simmer Lake, bubbling with the
rotten-egg stench of sulphur. He'd never been to this remarkable
Khosian city before. And now it lay half ruined in the hands of the
enemy. Overhead, through the scudding rain clouds, Nico glimpsed
one of the moons shining pale and blue in the even paler sky. It
looked as though it was falling as the clouds raced past on either
side.

The image brought to mind the old farlander, drawn unbidden
from memory. Ash's fascination with the moons and the stars and
everything else up there in the sky, a fascination that Nico shared.

More memories of his previous life, slotting into place at random.
Since his resurrection they'd been doing that, Nico's memories
coming back to him, moments scattered by time but returning one
after the other, settling into the blank spaces of his mind.

What do you see? he'd once asked the old farlander around a camp
fire during their short time together, seeing Ash studying the night
sky.

Wonder, the drunken farlander had replied. *The beauty of all
creation.*

Nico remembered how he had scoffed like a careless child from
the other side of the hot coals at Ash's sentimentality, so unexpected
from the old assassin, drawing a scornful glance his way.

Cast a single glance around you, Ash had asserted. *Go on. Look from
any shore, from any piece of ground you stand upon, and you will strike upon
beauty, some wonder of the Great Dreamer. It is always worth remembering
how much beauty there is in this world.*

What about the rest of it though? Why is so much of life a nightmare too?

Why? The old man had blinked as though the answer was obvious. *Because all life is free will. So shit happens.*

But still, so much suffering!
Most of it we make that way.
But why?
Why? Because mostly we are insane.
Hardly. Not all!

No. But enough of us. Those who live in fear and greed and envy. Those who are not wholly human, but are fractured inside, separated from them-selves and everything around them. Who seek power and dominion over others.

Such people damage the world in their madness. They damage other people. And that damage lives on, creating ever more insanity. Sometimes even creating entire societies in its image.

Unless, somehow, it is stopped.

Still the blue moon kept falling through the sky to the west. It was the first time Nico had thought of the old Rōshun in days, since sensing the farlander's death in the breaths of the wind and the in-tuitions of his heart.

He grimaced, not liking the memory. Not liking the thought that Ash might have been right. That insanity could be infectious, passed on from one to another until whole nations could become insane.

Yet what was that at the front of the noisy yard, if not a valid-ation of Ash's words – that block of wood perched alone in the rain, with a woman, a young woman, shivering, naked and chained, standing atop it?

Looking at her again, Nico fought an urge to rush over and cover her with his sodden coat, and to help her away from this cruel place with what dignity remained to her. But instead he stayed rooted to the ground, still ruled by his reason. Just another dripping figure amongst many.

Smoke and steam hung in the air, trapped by the sheets of canvas stretched taut above the heads of the gathered people. Many smoked from wooden sookahs wrapped around their forearms, taking the occasional puff from stems at their wrists; an affectation common in imperial Q'os, he recalled, one borrowed from the Alhazii. Others took snorts of firesnuff or drank strong spirits. They seemed warm enough with the press of so many bodies. Yet the front of the yard, where the wooden block stood alone, had been left open to the ele-ments, as though these dealers and buyers in slaves liked it that way, having these captives exposed beyond even their sudden, shameful nakedness, standing there in the rain.

It was another way of breaking them, he supposed. Another way of stripping the captives of their remaining spirit, of rendering them something lesser than human.

Destroy a soul, rang the old Alhazii saying in his mind, *and you destroy a whole cosmos forever*.

If this wasn't insanity then he didn't know what was. In the charged atmosphere beneath the dripping canvas they were bidding on the woman with the same calm methodology as a cattle auction, clusters of people sniffing and clearing their throats in the damp air, faces clammy from excitement. Amongst them stood the craziest of all, a few white-robed priests of Mann. Wherever they moved the crowd parted in fear before them, their shaven heads gleaming with oil and their faces covered in silver piercings, surveying all with a cool appraisal, masters of their world.

Nico exhaled the fear from his muscles with a long and steamy breath. He was glad to be off to the side here, out of the stifling press where faces had loomed like impersonations of the living. Dabbing at his forehead with a dry hand, the young man took in the little silver-haired sea monkey where it was chained to a drum, beating out with webbed hands a fast and skipping heartbeat to the shivers and quakes of the naked woman on the block.

White smoke was drifting over the creature and into the rest of the space, cast from a row of incense burners and the beating fan of a young boy. Its stench cloyed at the back of Nico's throat, made him feel light-headed and reckless within his tingling skin. Something narcotic that loosened the senses. If the bidding was anything to go by, the smoke was having a similar effect on everyone else, their voices pattering faster and faster as the buyers worked themselves into a fervour.

Up there on the block, the Khosian woman sputtered in the freezing downpour and tried to wipe her face clear of rain, huddling and shivering in her irons before their hardened stares. She could be no older than he was, eighteen or so years of age, and the sight of her exposed body pulled strings within his own. But then he saw the misery in her face again, and all such desires fled him.

She's brave, Nico thought, seeing how she held back her tears.

They didn't seem to see her standing there though. Not a daughter. Not a sister. Not the river of life running through her. Only something to be purchased and subdued. Once again Nico fought an impulse to save her.

Where are you? he needed to know, casting about for his mother or his father. Disgusted with it all he looked away again, over the bubbling surface of the lake, where sure enough he struck upon something beautiful, just as Ash had said so: twin moons riding now across the morning sky, flanked by breaks in the clouds.

He blinked his tired eyes, spotting something else in the sky now, a flicker of fire coming closer. A pair of skyships, locked in a dog-fight, cannons growling and spitting flames, sweeping out above the lake. Nico watched as an explosion rocked the hull of the nearest vessel, lighting the underside of its great canopy of gas. He spotted a Khosian flag flying as the skyship turned away sharply, and sped with its thrusters blazing towards the south, trailing smoke and fire. Headed back towards Bar-Khos on the coast, he thought, the last line in the sand, where even now the majority of the Imperial Expeditionary Force was approaching the city walls.

No one seemed to be paying the air battle any mind. It was a world within a world here, this gloomy space beneath the canvas, lit here and there by a flaring lantern.

Faster still came the beats of the drum while the bidding intensified. The boy with the fan was yanking on the sea monkey's chain to make it drum faster, and waving the fan faster too to waft more of the narcotic incense into their midst. The smoke was starting to get to him.

Someone jeered in the crowd, shouting something at the naked woman. One of the slavers was slapping her flank with a cane to get her to turn around.

'Hey!' Nico shouted with his blood boiling over at last, though his voice was lost in the noisy bray of the crowd. 'Hey!' he yelled again, but then a hand grasped his coat fiercely from behind and yanked him backwards, kept on tugging him all the way to the rear of the crowd then clear of them entirely, until he was out from beneath the shelter of the awnings, and getting wetter.

'What are you playing at, you want to get us caught here?'

Cole's heavily scarred features scowled at him from beneath his wide-brimmed hat.

'Did you find anything?' Nico hissed back at his father, his voice near drowned by the downpour.

Cole nodded, wiping the scowl from his face. Behind him a tarpaulin flapped in the background, revealing the buildings of Tume through the sheets of rain, the Khosian city floating on its island of lakeweed.

'They had a red-headed woman here yesterday,' answered Cole. 'Sounds like she was a handful too.'

'Where is she then?' he shouted back, before casting about for a sign of his mother, looking again for a sight of her red hair in the far cages. Again his father grabbed a bundle of his coat in his fist.

'She's already been sold,' he growled with pain in his eyes, though his words sounded strangely flat as he spoke, as though detachment was the only way he could utter them. 'She was bought by a pimp yesterday, and taken south with a dozen others as pleasure slaves for the front.'

For a moment Nico shut his eyes and focused on his breathing, just like Ash had once taught him. It was all he had just then to master his sudden, impotent rage.

'They're taking her to Bar-Khos?' sounded his strangled voice in his ears.

'Right back where we started. Your mother's taking us on a big circle. We need to leave now.'

In a way he should hardly be surprised. This whole awful nightmare ride through the occupied Reach had been a wild fling of the dice from the beginning, borne on a desperate hopelessness that neither of them had yet to admit.

In their haste they had run both their zels into the ground. And now they would have to hurry south again, back towards the front lines of the war, in the hope of saving her before she reached the imperial forces besieging the city.

'This is your fault,' Nico spat, rounding on his father, unable to hold it back any longer, and he felt himself stepping over a line that could not be recrossed.

'My fault? How is this my fault?'

A curious sensation, standing off to his father like that, chest to chest, shaking with anger. Cole's own cheeks flared red but Nico only glared back at him, past caring, wanting it this way.

'Yes, your fault for running out on us. Your fault for making us fend for ourselves in the midst of a war. That's why we're both standing here now, isn't it, because you're a coward who ran away?'

His words struck a ringing silence.

Somehow he expected his father to lose his temper, even to strike him, like he had that one time before, years ago, on the night before Cole had left. Indeed he hoped for it, so that this time he could have the satisfaction of striking him back. But it seemed that Nico hardly knew this scarred man any more. For his father only turned and walked away through the pouring rain, head down.

'Sure, walk away,' Nico yelled after his back, wanting to drive the knife home. 'You know it's true. If she dies it's on you, all of it's on you!'

And then he clamped his mouth shut, realizing he couldn't take back the words.

CHAPTER FOUR

High Priest

It was growing light on the Mount of Truth, a new day rising. Far below Kira dul Dubois, the streets of Bar-Khos were already filling with activity and muted noise: street markets going up, refugees rising from their alleyway shanties, couriers galloping past jams of carts, soldiers marching for the northern wall. The first puffs of smoke rose from the city's many chimneys. Bells rang out and dogs barked at low-flying skyships patrolling overhead.

Such a strange and thrilling feeling to be standing there just then, the Mannian High Priest thought to herself with a sly satisfaction.

To be here on this hill on the southernmost limits of the enemy city, surrounded by a population who would tear her limb from limb if they discovered who she was; even as the Imperial Expeditionary Force amassed before their northern wall in the newest chapter of the siege.

What a thrill, Kira thought, to be so close to the Bar-Khosian Ministry of War too – that brick building standing on the hill's broad crown above her. Headquarters of the Lord Protector himself, General Creed, and the Bar-Khosian defences.

Kira barely noticed the stiff sea breeze tugging at her cloak and hat, causing the trees of the hill's parkland to thrash their branches like angry sticks. Despite the weakness of her ancient body, the disguised priest stood impervious to the gusts and the frigid air. It was nothing like the winter they were going through back home in the imperial capital of Q'os, where ice and snow had locked the great metropolis in their grip for months. Nothing, too, for a Mannian priest hardened by years of regular Purgings.

She had heard of the Mount of Truth from her people's ten-year-long siege against the Shield – a hill that stood on the southern edge of the city, affording a view over the mighty southern walls that rose one in front of the other, boxed in on either side by smaller seawalls. From here, in the thin light of early morning, Kira could see how the surviving walls of the Shield stretched across the Lansway, that narrow bridge of land connecting the island of Khos with the southern continent – one of the few remaining frontiers of the Empire.

Just beyond the ruins of the furthest walls, just beyond a flood of dull seawater that covered a good portion of the Lansway, lights glimmered from what remained of the besieging imperial forces here in the south. Forces hunkered down around the rubble after ten long years of siege had ended in calamity.

By all accounts it was a mess down there. Even now they were fishing bodies out of the flood waters.

A reported two hundred thousand mercenaries had gathered on the isthmus as winter had closed in, drawn by General Mokabi's call of riches and plunder if only they would storm the walls of the Shield once and for all. But once again the Khosians had shown themselves to be as wily as they were stubborn in the defence of their homeland. Just as they had lost their foremost wall to Mokabi's unstoppable forces, they had sprung a trap against his insanely huge army, flooding a section of the Lansway with seawater right in the middle of the assault. Tens of thousands of mercenaries had drowned as the sea had rushed in at them.

A hundred thousand, some were even claiming.

And General Mokabi himself, ex-Archgeneral of Mann, had fallen too, his corpse found mangled and broken by the side of a road. Murdered like a common soldier in the night; Mokabi, hero of the Empire, conqueror of the southern continent and architect of this latest invasion of the island.

Rōshun had been responsible, her people were reporting. The very same order of assassins who had waged vendetta against her grandson, Kirkus, next in line for the throne, until they'd killed him. The same order of assassins supposedly wiped out by an imperial commando raid that she herself had initiated in retaliation.

Yet here they were again, these assassins, these Rōshun, wreaking their revenge by joining the Khosians against the Empire. No doubt they were behind the nightly assassinations of officers that had been happening in the forces to the south, and would no doubt start occurring within the imperial forces now gathering across the northern plain.

Kira found herself glancing about with a sudden paranoia, as though silent killers might be closing in on her position. But it was only her heightened nerves at play, she knew, the jumpiness of an infiltrator lurking in disguise amongst an enemy people. For all her bravado, Kira had been this way since first arriving in the city over a week ago, brought here under the cover of darkness on a small skyboat to the sanctuary of their rented cliff-top mansion.

Her stomach would curdle at the thought of being captured by the enemy. Yet in a different way she would relish these fears, welcoming the fact that they drew her from her depression, made her feel alive once again. So alive in fact that she had insisted on coming out on this dawn walk to the Mount of Truth, even though it had involved a ride in a covered cart across the city.

Only her trusty Diplomat and bodyguard, Quito, had accompanied the High Priest up the sloping paths of the hill. Quito lurked nearby against a tree trunk, his head turned in the opposite direction. The bald-headed man was gazing northwards towards the smaller, singular northern wall of the city; no doubt taking in the plain beyond filled with the hazy smoke of imperial camp fires, where a dark smudge was the thousands of infantry marching in from the north-east.

Noisy cannon fire was being exchanged between the two sides this morning. The Expeditionary Force had managed to dig in some heavy guns, and were finally returning fire on the city. Knocking on the front door, as it were.

From the vantage of the Khosians, the situation must look dire indeed. Their northern wall was nothing like the giants down in the Shield. If a single one of its gates was to fall, the imperial forces had a chance of storming the city.

Yet Kira knew the situation was not so straightforward as that.

The success of this invasion had always been reliant upon Mokabi attacking hard from the south at the same time, putting the city's defenders under enough pressure that the Imperial Expeditionary Force to the north could break through the single wall there, and take the city from behind. But Mokabi had been late to launch his attacks on the Shield, and with the Lansway now flooded and the general dead, the southern campaign was stalled.

Now the Imperial Expeditionary Force was alone in this endeavour, and without hope of further reinforcements while the sea route from the island was blockaded. Its supply lines back to the Empire were stretched to near breaking, since everything had to be brought in by air. They were largely scavenging what food they could from the Khosian countryside.

Even worse, the imperial force itself was commanded by two generals who openly loathed each other, and had only recently been locked in a petty civil war for control: Archgeneral Sparus, the Little Eagle, and the younger General Romano, the new prime contender for the Empire's throne.

Really, it was all hanging on a knife edge. Yet still the imperial army was expected to take this fortress city of Bar-Khos by itself – with a little help from Kira on the inside – before the crippling elements of winter ate them alive.

These damned Khosians were a frustrating breed, and surprising too in their temerity. Up on the interior of the island, on the plateau of the Reach, their phalanxes had attacked at night, cutting through the vastly larger Imperial Expeditionary Force like wolves attacking a startled herd. And they had almost broken that herd, after its leader, Sasheen, the Holy Matriarch of Mann – Kira's very own daughter – had been slain.

Slain by one of her own, in fact. By a Diplomat, an imperial assassin, charged by Kira to do the unthinkable, to kill her own daughter in the event that the Holy Matriarch should try to flee from battle – something no war leader of the Empire could ever be allowed to do. Something Kira had never believed her daughter would do.

Sasheen.

Her pride. Her flawed jewel.

Kira felt a chill of emotion washing through her, a bleak dread like no other. Suddenly the thrill of her situation was gone, and in its place was nothing but the awful vacuum of loss.

She had never known such loneliness as struck her now, two thousand laqs from home, her closest family gone.

Where are you, Sosay? she thought, calling out to her old friend and accomplice. Sosay had been her one and only true friend in life, tighter than a sister since childhood, when they had run wild together through the streets of Q'os.

But Kira had killed Sosay too, years after the Mannian coup when they had risen high within the ranks of the order. She'd murdered her with a knife to the heart one night for her lack of devotion to the faith, and for Kira's own bitter jealousies.

Is there anything left of you watching over me? Spitting at me for what I did? Well, look at me now!

In a roar the breeze gusted even harder, making the living world seem larger all around her.

I'm lonely, Sosay.

So stupidly, wretchedly lonely.

Kira shuddered, ashamed at such wistful thinking. As a true devotee of Mann, the High Priest knew that there was nothing beyond the moment of death. Her old friend Sosay was bones and dust and memories in her head.

Such loneliness though! That was real enough, and she could feel it unravelling her inner composure, bringing a smattering of tears to her eyes.

'I must speak with my mother,' Kira muttered under her breath. 'Mother will understand.'

The priest shivered and wrapped her arms about herself, then started down the grassy slope towards the thronged streets far below.

'Mistress Kira. Where are you going?'

She stopped with a start, then turned around to see her bodyguard standing there watching her coolly from beneath a tree.

Kira wiped a tear from her eye. Looked back down to the city.

'My mother,' she panted, suddenly confused. 'I must seek her out.'

'But, Mistress,' said Quito gently, taking long strides closer. His sharp features loomed above her. 'Your mother is long in the grave. And she lived in Q'os. Not here.'

'I know that,' Kira snapped at him, blinking fast. 'Don't you think I know where my own mother lived?'

Quito sighed in that patient way of his.

'Take a deep breath,' prompted his knowing voice. 'As though you really need it. Yes, like that.'

He was good for her, this Diplomat, this trusty bodyguard. Kira dul Dubois breathed deeply until she settled into herself again, remembering where she was and when.

The war.

Boom, boom, boom went the heavy guns of the northern wall. Kira looked on with anger uncoiling now inside her like a creature seeking something to strike. Somehow, just then, her grief and confusion was all their fault, these stubborn Khosian fools who would fight to the bitter end even as the city fell around them. Everyone responsible for her losses was right here in this doomed city: the Rōshun; General Creed and his forces. And still they battled the Empire as though they were going to win this thing, as though they were going to live.

They mock us in their defiance. They mock our destiny. They mock our rightful dominion over this world.

'You know what Nihilis commanded,' Kira remarked to the waiting figure of Quito. 'When the Holy Patriarch conquered the Green Isles after the people there resisted?'

'He took the men's eyes, as I recall.'

'No, that was Masheen. Where he took all their women and children as slaves, and left twenty thousand blind men stumbling about in the rubble.'

'It's been a while since I studied my history books, Mistress Kira.'

'When Nihilis had almost taken the capital of the Green Isles, he demanded that every male in the city older than ten should kill themselves within the hour, if the women and children were to be spared the sword.'

'I recall it now,' said Quito. 'Everyone ended up killing themselves.'

'Yes. We must be careful here. But we must make them pay for this ten-year stand against the Empire. We must make them weep for generations to come. When the Khosian traitors blow the gates from within, we will storm this city with fire and sword. We will kill them all, we will kill every living thing. The whole world will remember what we did here to mighty Bar-Khos after it fell.'

'Are you high, Mistress?'

Kira felt a smile creep upon her lips. 'A little, Quito. Can you tell?'

Her words were those of a playful young woman, yet they came out in the roughened, throaty drawl of an old crone.

Kira tightened her arms about herself, feeling the chill in her bones at last.

The Khosian traitors were primed and ready to go. Some would try to blow open the northern gates when the time was right. Another, the Khosian lieutenant called Bahn Calvone, would attempt to lure the Lord Protector outside with as many defenders as he could, before putting a bullet in his head. Kira could only hope that the man's conditioning lasted for that long. She had sensed a conflict still surging within him. Some remaining inner core of resistance.

The conditioning would hold, she knew.

The dice had been cast. Now it was only a matter of time before the city fell.

CHAPTER FIVE

Bahn

There was a point he reached, after he had gone so long without proper sleep, after his exhaustion had become a thing to be worn like an iron coat, when Bahn Calvone found the world beginning to still around him, as though it too could take no more without a pause.

Within a sudden cell of silence he sat there unmoving at the kitchen table, staring down at his hands resting on its scratched surface, twitching and shaking next to the pair of objects that were presently gripping his attention: a pile of unrolled paper charts, held flat by the leather tube they had come in, and a loaded pistol fitted with double barrels.

Like a choice to be made, one or the other, though in his numbness he could no longer recall why it was so.

He stared at the uppermost map that was unrolled before him – one of the charts that his brother Cole had given into his safekeeping before setting off to find his wife. Bahn gazed at the dark pencil marks, taking in the Aradèrēs mountains stretching across the very top, and the eastern coastline of the Great Hush coursing down the right-hand side, snaking all the way to the Isles of Sky – which did not appear to be islands at all, but rather another range of mountain peaks slightly inland from the coast. A deceptive name indeed.

It was the closest-guarded secret in the world, the location of the Isles, just sitting there on his kitchen table. Deep down, Bahn knew his people could change the course of the war with these charts. The Alhazii Caliphate would pay anything, do anything, to ensure they remained undisclosed to anyone else. Even, perhaps, if that meant taking the side of the Free Ports in this war.

So why did he sit here staring dumbly, doing nothing, when he should be rushing to the Lord Protector with them?

Whose side are you on? he demanded to know, but Bahn no longer knew the answer to that, or even fully understood the question. He felt like a ghost inhabiting a living body no longer his own. A body that fed him his strange thoughts and memories.

At least, he thought, he hadn't handed over the charts to the Mannian witch.

Not yet, anyway.

Once again Bahn looked to the loaded pistol next to his hand. He began to tremble even harder.

*

He was so lost in himself that he failed to notice his son bounding into the kitchen from the yard outside; not until the boy was shouting something before the table and Bahn looked up at last, surprised, to take in the sight of young Juno's frightened expression. It was as though his son stood just beyond a wall of heavy glass, for Bahn could hear nothing of what he said, could only see his mouth flapping away in ranting silence as his wide eyes fixated on the heavy pistol lying on the table.

Yet Bahn could hear other things now, if he cared to listen. Like the water clock tinkling on the far wall, a marriage present from Marlee's father from before the war. Or the screams overhead of his infant daughter Ariale, named after the flying horse of legend. Or the shout of a man running past in the street outside.

Bahn felt clammy all of a sudden, the air in the room grown hot. He could barely seem to catch his next breath.

'*Can't you hear them?*' came the ten-year-old's voice in a sudden flood of noise, and Bahn blinked at his son then cocked his ears to the wailing horns outside the house.

'Can't you hear them, Father?'

Yes, he could hear them now. Sirens calling defenders to the northern wall over the steady rumbles of cannon fire.

With a start, Bahn sat upright in his chair, and in doing so realized that he was sitting there in the full combat armour of a Red Guard, and that he was due to report in at the wall. He looked up as his wife Marlee appeared in the doorway, holding the screaming red-faced form of their daughter in her arms, trying to soothe her. Ariale's wail joined the horns calling the city to arms. Her eyes and nose gushed while her mother rocked her up and down, a hand held across the top of her tiny head, both of them exhausted.

His infant daughter always seemed to be falling sick these days. If it wasn't a bad cough it was the stomach flux, or this fever.

It's this war, he thought to himself darkly. *It weakens her. She can hear the guns and smell the fear on everyone around her. She smells it off me.*

'Did you fetch the healer like I told you to?' Marlee asked of the boy.

'Yes, Mother, she's on her way.'

He was a good boy, this one. Not like his brother's lad Nico, contentious and always giving off at the mouth. Bahn had a sudden urge to tell him how proud he was to have him as his son. But it was as though a glass wall still stood between them, a barrier he didn't have the will to pierce. Instead he looked down at the surface of the table again. At the two choices left in his life.

A thud sounded in the distance. Then another.

Suddenly the windows rattled.

'Oh no,' panted his wife, and in her arms Ariale ceased screaming.

'What is it?' asked his son.

'Bahn, it's starting! *Bahn!*'

Even as he sat there unmoving, Marlee was pushing their son beneath the table and crouching down next to him with a now-silent Ariale. The concussions were getting closer. The house shook, and then an explosion went off nearby and it rattled their home even harder, glass and pottery shattering everywhere.

'*Bahn, my husband, why are you sitting there like stone?*' cried his wife at his feet.

But even as the plaster dust rained down on him, Bahn's attention remained fixed on the two objects on the table, the charts and the gun, locked in the uncertainty of the moment.

'*Bahn!*'

Her voice broke through at last. Time to move. Bahn scrabbled for the charts and rolled them back into their leather case, then shoved the tube firmly into his belt. He staggered to his feet, pulling the pistol towards him, its double barrels scraping across grit.

Bahn swayed there for a moment, feeling sick.

'Stay there,' he said. And then he stalked from the room without saying another word, without even looking back at his family huddled beneath the table staring after him.

*

Crowds filled the streets of the city. A human river of noise and motion flooding down from the northernmost limits of Bar-Khos, where the sudden onset of shelling seemed heaviest, and where the smoke of many fires was rising now into the leaden winter sky.

A good downpour would help damp any flames, but it had stopped raining at long last, after days of dreary dampness. Wrapped in his Red Guard cloak against the chill, Bahn could taste the smoke in his mouth and feel the sting of it in his already reddened eyes. It was unsettling to be marching northwards towards the sound of the horns, which continued to blare in their calls to arms, creating a kind of disharmonious music when heard against the din of the concussions. For ten years Bahn had grown used to the siege-front being in the south of the city, where the mammoth walls of the Shield had held back the imperial ambitions for all that time. Yet now, with the Empire's invasion force massing against the northern wall, all had reversed itself.

Ahead, the northern wall loomed above the city's rooftops, blocking out much of the grey sky beyond. Bahn did not have far to walk from his house, which was located in one of the northern districts, a place he'd previously considered safe for its distance from the front. Now the shells were falling all along the districts behind the wall, distant crumples or nearer blasts of fire. The streets grew more deserted as he neared the defences, until most of the people he could see were soldiers in a hurry, natives of Bar-Khos like himself in Red Guard cloaks and armour, or Volunteers from the rest of the Mercian Free Ports, men and women dressed in brown leathers. They hurried along grimly silent for the most part, though some were shouting to companions up on the parapets above.

By the time Bahn reached the wall the horns were beginning to fall silent, though the Khosian cannon were deafening as they fired from the many turrets in reply to the enemy shelling. Bahn joined the press rushing up the nearest set of steps, and made the long climb to the very top, his boots scuffing on the wet stone, the weight of his armour and weapons like carrying a man on his back.

By the time he made it to the high parapet above, Bahn was sheeting sweat and rasping for air, and he doubled over to catch his breath, thinking he would be sick. He was still weak after his recent bout of illness. Too damned long spent lying on a cot in Juno's Ferry recovering from dysentery.

No time for such complaints now though.

The wind was strong and fiercely cold up here, blowing clear the smoke from the braziers and the many burning buildings behind. Bahn squinted at the lines of defenders standing along the battlements. Men and women wrapped in cloaks and the steam of their rapid breathing, every face turned to the plain beyond the wall.

Sweet Mercy, thought Bahn with a shudder, gripping the chill stone of a crenellation for balance as he took in the imperial army arranged against the city. In the space of a day, the advance forces of the Imperial Expeditionary Force had grown to cover the entire plain.

Tents were going up by their thousands, surrounded by spiked perimeters of ditches and earthworks. Across the plain swept a horde of light cavalry in a showy display of white banners bearing the red hand of Mann. Beyond them, heavy infantry marshalled into formation to the steady, distant throb of war drums.

Fifty thousand enemy fighters were the numbers Bahn had been hearing. After suffering bitter losses at Chey-Wes, the Imperial Expeditionary Force had been reinforced by troop ships from the island of Cheem, before the League navy had finally cut off their sea route, sinking even more enemy transports loaded with men.

'We should be taking the fight to them right now,' growled a young Red Guard to some others. 'While they're still digging in like this.'

Snorts rose from his companions.

'We're outnumbered five to one. What's left of our forces are still recovering from Mokabi's assaults in the south. And you want us to go out and meet the bastards on open ground.'

'Well it worked up in Chey-Wes. Our chartassa made mince of them.'

'Aye, lad, but our chartassa didn't face all that artillery back in

Chey-Wes. And that plain is no ground to be fighting on right now, it's like a damned quagmire after all the rain. Our phalanxes would get cut to pieces just trying to manoeuvre across it.'

Bahn tried to exhale the sense of dread in his belly. He reminded himself that he had faced this army before and survived – after they had invaded the island's wild eastern coast, and the Lord Protector Creed had indeed led a Khosian force against them into the Reach, despite the enemy's superior numbers. A stinging draw had been the result of that clash, though the leader of the Imperial Expeditionary Force, the Holy Matriarch of the Empire herself, had been one of the casualties. Afterwards, having fought a desperate rearguard action while his people made their retreat across a frozen lake, Bahn had been captured.

His captivity amongst the Mannians remained a horror even now. Recalling it made his flesh crawl and the dread settle even heavier in his belly. And here they were once again, against all expectations, in the midst of a Khosian winter: the Empire's forces come to take the city and all that meant anything to him.

'Where's your helm, Lieutenant?' It was one of the older Red Guards who had been talking, a fellow officer.

Bahn stirred, realizing what the man had just asked him. Wonderful, he thought. In his fractured condition he'd forgotten to bring his helm to the battlefront, even as the Empire's shells fell all around him.

From the corner of his eye he took in the middle-aged captain with a tartan blanket wrapped about his armour instead of a cloak. The fellow hardly seemed troubled by what was facing them. A fool then, a fool who believed this wall would be enough to hold back the monsters facing them.

'Cole's brother, aren't you?' he asked Bahn.

'My brother?'

'Aye, Cole Calvone! We met a few times at the All Fools Respite.'

Yes, he remembered now. But that was years ago, a different lifetime away, back before his older brother had deserted everyone who needed him, not least of all Bahn.

Just then, Bahn found himself looking towards the east, towards the foothills running all the way to the snowy peaks of the High Tell.

His brother had rode off days ago with his son that way, hoping to bring back their mother from the family farm.

They had yet to return, though. And now imperial forces swarmed everywhere he looked. If they hadn't been captured, they must surely be . . .

'I have no brother,' he heard himself say aloud.

'But—'

'I have no brother!' Bahn snapped, and he stepped past the bewildered man before he could say anything in response.

He realized he was still gripping the loaded pistol in his hand. Half blind with sweat and tears, Bahn looked for General Creed along the parapet, and spotted his standard flapping in the breeze further along the line – a raging bear.

His body moved of its own accord. The face of the old witch Kira leered as a projection of his own warped mind.

Not yet! You must remember the plan, my child. The plan!

No, I must do it now or not at all. I cannot stand this waiting.

The plan, you fool! You must follow your orders as instructed!

He snarled his dissent and gripped the pistol even tighter, hurrying through the press towards the Lord Protector's position, watched curiously by the captain from behind.

*

Bahn found General Creed exactly where he'd expected to find him, right at the focal point of the defences. In his great bearskin coat the Lord Protector of Khos was standing over the main northern gates themselves, his long black hair flying wild in the wind and his eyes thinned to slashes, surveying the Imperial Expeditionary Force on the plain with a spiteful calm.

It was the first time he'd seen the general since Chey-Wes, even though Bahn had been back for days now, having been instructed by his Mannian handler not to report for active duty until this morning.

Marsalas looked tired, but better than expected for a man who had suffered a recent heart attack. Around him were gathered a handful of his generals and Michinè noblemen, including the First Minister, Chonas, and around them his cordon of veteran bodyguards. Yet the Lord Protector towered above them all, taller even than Bahn remembered him to be. Perhaps it was only the sheer immobility of Creed's posture just then. How he faced down the winds, the falling shells, the massing forces of an empire like one of the stony sentinels adorning the wall itself, so that Bahn was drawn to him as he always was at such times as this, the frightened to the fearless, the boy to the father.

His gun hung heavy in his hand as he stepped closer. Seeing it, a bodyguard stepped into his path with a scowl, but the motion drew Creed's attention his way, and the general's eyes flared open in surprise.

'Bahn!' the general roared over their heads at him. 'You bloody bastard, is that really you?'

The bodyguard let him through only when Bahn put the pistol away. With a clash of breastplates the Lord Protector embraced him, while faces turned to observe the scene. Bahn stiffened, surprised by Creed's sudden show of affection. Though he was surprised even more by the words that Creed cast to the others, explaining how his favourite field aide had returned unannounced from the dead, today of all days. How it was a good sign.

Inwardly Bahn recoiled, like a sea creature flinching from salt.

'I prayed to the Way that you had made it,' Creed puffed as he held him out at arm's length for a full inspection, a towering silhouette blocking the sun with the Khosian guns blasting away behind him. 'For once the damned cosmos must have been listening!'

The Lord Protector had stopped dyeing his black hair, Bahn could see, so that it hung to his shoulders bearing streaks of white like the feathers of a pica bird. His voice too seemed different, somehow rougher than before. 'I held out hope, when I heard that other prisoners had escaped after Chey-Wes. Where have you been all this time?'

It felt like days since Bahn had last opened his mouth in speech. He coughed, clearing his throat of emotions.

'Juno's Ferry, General,' he said as normally as he could manage, while his voice sounded like a brittle stranger's in his ears. 'Laid up on my back. Took a while to find my way home.'

'Well you look terrible, Calvone, but you're still a sight for sore eyes.'

A heavy clap on his shoulder, just like old times. Creed's eyes wrinkled, sparkling, as though Bahn's unexpected reappearance was indeed a good omen of some kind, a sign of hope for them all.

Beneath his cloak, Bahn could feel the weight of the double-barrelled pistol hanging in its holster, and the leather tube of charts pressing against his side.

'Your family, they are safe?' asked the general, looking back towards the smoking city district where Bahn had just come from, remembering where he lived.

Bahn looked back too, and saw his family huddled under the kitchen table as the shells came down around them. He blinked quickly, wondering why he had walked out on them like that, barely saying a word.

'*General!*'

A shout drew Creed back to the forward crenellations, where officers conferred with him under the thunder of the artillery. Bahn approached the group of men, recognizing faces amongst them. A few nodded in welcome.

He stared out upon the Mannian forces once again, still spreading like a flood across the muddy plain before the city. The first contingents of the Imperial Expeditionary Force had arrived the previous day from the nearby Chilos. Now the main force was here, filling the air with a low and menacing murmur as they occupied the plain. Yet the Mannians were wasting no time in beginning their attack on the city. Already their heavy guns were dug into fortified positions, close enough to lob shells over the wall, and as they fired at Bar-Khos the city's own cannon were trying to dig them out again with spurts of earth and debris, trying to push them back beyond range.

He was looking at a classic artillery duel, like many Bahn had witnessed on the southern Shield. Firing from the wall, the Khosian guns had the advantage of height, but the Mannian artillery had a longer range to compensate. Just as well the whole northern face of the wall was fronted with a slope of earth, and the gates protected by a curling shield of freshly erected earthen berms.

'Is that the Little Eagle, do you wonder?'

The soldier beside Creed was peering through a spyglass just as the general was now doing. Bahn saw that it was Halahan, the old

Nathalese commander of the foreign brigade of fighters known as the Greyjackets. It was good to see him still alive and well.

'Aye, it's his standard all right,' answered the Lord Protector. 'And that's Romano over there to the right. Joint command of the army, our agents are telling us.'

'I hear he's an impetuous little bastard, full of his own arrogance.'

'He'll balance out the Little Eagle's usual caution. They're both opposites. If they work together effectively, it might be difficult to predict their moves.'

'You notice how their heavy guns still aren't targeting the wall, just the city itself?'

'Spreading fear,' drawled Creed. 'That will be the Little Eagle's decision. He likes to soften things up before he attacks.'

'He's the Archgeneral of an empire for a reason,' grumbled Halahan around the smoking pipe in his mouth. 'You can be sure he's brought along some tricks with him.'

'Mind games, I'll guess. He'll mess with our heads, try to break our spirit. What's he doing down there anyway?'

'Where is he?'

'Near their forward mortars now. They're loading them with something.'

'Looks like he's waving at us.'

'Sure he is.'

'Well he's holding up his hand this way.'

'No, he's giving the order to fire.'

Sure enough, a ripple of smoke erupted along the line of enemy mortar positions.

Bahn squinted, watching the projectiles arching up into the air towards them, oblong shapes that looked white and shiny in appearance, moving slowly enough to track their flights.

'He is, the bastard's waving at us,' said Halahan, watching the distant enemy Archgeneral through the glass.

'Incoming!' someone roared from nearby, for it was clear by now that the projectiles were all aimed at the gates themselves, containing Bahn and Creed and the rest of his field staff. The enemy had sighted the Lord Protector's position.

Bahn crouched with a hand on his head, wishing he'd had the good sense to bring his helm with him to the battlefront. He saw

Creed's bodyguards raising their shields to protect the general just as the projectiles started crashing down before the wall, landing wildly this way and that. Some of them skipped against the berms of earth protecting the gates. Others bounced off the slopes that fronted the wall on either side, before falling backwards to finally crack open upon the ground.

They looked like pupae the size of barrels, giant cocoons that were breaking open before the eyes of the defenders even as pale forms rose into the weak daylight, shaking as they unfurled what seemed to be cloaks.

The creatures sniffed the air and looked about them as though in shock at where they were. White heads turned slowly towards the crowds of defenders gaping down at them. More shells fell amongst their numbers, black projectiles this time, which released a white gas upon breaking open, quickly obscuring the creatures with mist.

A blood-curdling scream of pain sounded out. One by one the pale forms leaped away from the smoke and surged up the slope of earth, screeching like madmen. Others started clawing up the very gates below Bahn and Creed's position. Up the slope they were vaulting a dozen feet with every bound, using not cloaks but leathery wings stretched between arms and feet to sail through the air, moving so fast they were hard to follow. Rifles erupted in earnest anyway; shouts of panicked alarm. Above the gates they were scrambling up the stones of the wall now. Before anyone could stop it, one of the creatures leapt over the crenellations and onto the parapet amongst them, scattering men from the slash of its claws.

Bahn kicked himself away from the thing as the creature unfurled itself amongst the scattered bodyguards, dripping wet and shivering in the daylight like some newborn calf, frightened out of his wits by the alien face that flapped open with a scream of blasting air. Its head was a featureless, deflating sack of skin that flopped about like a rag doll, and it tottered on hairy legs hinged in the way of a goat, on claws that clacked and scratched against the stone of the parapet. When it dropped down on all-fours the head inflated again and a mouth lunged out from it, clamping onto the neck of a fallen man to suck feverishly at his blood. Behind it another creature was leaping onto the parapet, and another.

'Slin!' someone was yelling. 'They're firing slin!'

Above Bahn, a Red Guard still on his feet swung at the creature with his sword, catching it across a shoulder and causing it to recoil in pain. Claws lashed out and clove the man's face into strips, sending him sprawling even as Bahn regained his feet and drew his own blade with a desperate tug.

Before Bahn's eyes the creature bounded onto the wounded soldier, uttering strange and creaking clicks from the back of its throat while the bloody protrusion of its mouth latched onto the poor fellow's neck.

Bahn froze, horrified by the sight of the semi-inflated head beginning to enlarge with blood.

He had heard of slin before, in the exotic Tales of the Fish performed on the street corners of the city, stories of fierce parasite-carnivores from the far-off wastelands of the Skif. They were meant to be hard to kill. He braced himself then lunged with his sword, but the creature was faster than he ever would be and swept the blade aside, then leapt at him with its kicking legs, bowling him to the ground in a bundle of panic as his sword went flying from his grasp. The creature planted a heavy hoof on his chest, blood dripping from its maw.

Bahn gagged on the musky scent, gagged even more at the bizarre sight of the animal craning over him, gills flaring as it stared at him with a trio of black eyes that held a deep and vengeful intelligence.

The gun, you fool! The bloody gun!

Even as he tugged the pistol free a boot flashed past his eyes, deftly kicking the creature from his frame of vision. It was Creed, hacking with a hatchet, and beside him Halahan swinging with the butt of his rifle, followed by a wedge of bodyguards. Bahn staggered to his feet. Another creature was nearby. People reeled back from a sudden purple mist rising up around it, the slin flapping its winged arms to release its dark spores into the air.

Hooks suddenly caught in his throat. Bahn's eyes stung so that he had to rub them clear to see. Men were yelling all around him, stumbling sightlessly or launching themselves at the creatures in desperate recklessness.

The pistol came up in his shaking hands and he tried to get an aim on the monster. Blood sheeted from a toppling man as the slin bounded onto another soldier too fast for Bahn to track, so that suddenly he found the gun pointed right at General Creed's head instead.

Bahn paused for an instant, looking down the double barrel at the general's profile. His finger trembled on the trigger.

Not yet, you fool! Remember the plan!

But this was the only choice left to him. The only way to betray himself, and perhaps the other traitors in the city, before it was too late for them all.

For a moment Bahn heard and saw nothing around him. Instead he thought of that morning in the house, of how he had stared at his son without hearing what he said, or even feeling anything. Bahn knew that he was lost.

He squeezed the trigger and the gun went off with a bark of fire and smoke. For a long moment Bahn stood there with his eyes shut, knowing his life was over, wondering why Creed's bodyguards were not rushing him. When he peered out again, a strange hush had settled over the scene.

'Easy, lads,' Creed told them all, and the general was staring back into the city like the rest of the defenders. Bahn's shot had gone wild and unnoticed. Meanwhile the remaining slin were gone, vaulting across to the rooftops nearest the wall while riflemen fired after them and horns sounded out a general alarm.

'Easy,' General Creed said again. 'The Little Eagle's only playing with us. Only giving us his regards.'

Bahn lowered the pistol with a strange feeling creeping through him. A feeling of fear at his own self.

'General, a rider approaches!'

Again the defenders crowded forwards to the crenellations. From where he stood Bahn could see a Mannian rider galloping towards the city gate with a white flag in his hand.

The Empire was sending Bar-Khos an envoy.

'Now what can they possibly have to talk about,' muttered an old veteran by his side, loud enough to catch the general's ear. But the Lord Protector looked on in silence, suspicion pinching his features, and simmering anger.

Even as the Mannian envoy approached the gates, a collective howl rose up from the slin on the city rooftops behind them, a cry of fear, perhaps, as much as rage, though no less terrifying if it was.

Bahn turned to look back, thinking of his family again, of all that was to be taken from him if he failed in his mission of betrayal, and his gaze followed the shapes of the slin bounding south over the flat garden rooftops, seeking escape or easier prey, no one could yet know.

'What do you want?' Creed hollered down to the Mannian envoy, sitting on a zel just beyond the berms protecting the gates. The distant figure wore the white robe of a Mannian priest, and his zel was entirely white too.

'To speak some sense into you all,' rose the man's voice in reply.

'Should we let him in, Lord Protector?'

Creed was pursing his lips in contemplation, not liking this at all.

'Mind games,' Bahn heard the general remark to Halahan of the Greyjackets. 'What did I tell you? Now it begins.'

CHAPTER SIX

Coya

'*What in Creation is that thing?*' gasped Coya Zeziké, famed Delegate for the League of Free Ports, from the saddle of his startled zel.

Right over their heads a pale long-limbed figure was leaping between the rooftops, partially gliding on what seemed to be leathery wings. Coya craned his head to follow it, but lost sight of the creature as it thrashed through the greens of a rooftop garden.

Dark spores drifted down in its wake. Coya rubbed at eyes that were suddenly stinging with fire, and felt a cough tickle the back of his throat. Other people in the street were doing the same and shouting in alarm, their shouts joining others all the way to the northern wall that rose above the district behind them, where the heavy guns were momentarily silent.

'Slin,' declared his bodyguard ahead, calm as always. Riding in front, Marsh's steady stare was reflected in the rear lenses of his wraparound goggles, which allowed him to see behind; two magnified eyes gazing from the back of his head.

'You're joking,' Coya replied with a cough from behind his handkerchief. 'Slin?'

'You saw it yourself.'

'I can't say what I saw for certain.'

His bodyguard inclined his head by way of a shrug.

They cantered onwards, heading south along the city's main thoroughfare, the Avenue of Lies. Over the heads of the panicked crowds Coya could see the procession of cavalry and rickshaws they were trying to catch up with not far ahead, the riders armed and alert to the screams on either side of the street.

It felt like he and Marsh were riding in circles this morning. At the onset of the enemy shelling they had both set off for the northern wall, racing along side streets that were less thronged than the Avenue of Lies. But at the wall they found the shelling had suddenly stopped. Some kind of ceasefire was in effect while a Mannian envoy was allowed inside the city, an envoy who was being escorted south for a meeting in the Council Hall, even as fiercesome creatures vaulted the rooftops overhead, slaughtering Bar-Khosians indiscriminately.

They were slin all right, Coya saw now. Through a plaza full of scattering people another creature was bounding wildly, and Coya saw it clearly, its goat legs and winged arms, its rag-doll head flapping as though empty, its limbs of pink-white skin longer and thinner than any human's.

Slin, loose in Bar-Khos!

'What did I tell you,' said Marsh, and the bodyguard drew one of his pistols and cocked the hammer.

Coya had heard of them, as most people had. Creatures made famous by the Sans Elios Expedition into the far wastelands of the Skif, a merchant venture that had gone horribly wrong. The few survivors had recounted tales of the man-sized cocoons they had discovered and brought back with them in the hold of their skyship – creatures called slin by the natives. They told how the slin had awakened one night to gorge upon everyone they could reach, hiding in a veil of blindness cast about themselves while they preyed most of all on those who were sleeping – drawn, according to the natives, to the vibrations of their dreams.

Though these slin were hardly waiting for nightfall, Coya saw now, nor were they chasing after anyone's dreams.

In full daylight the creature in the plaza bounded onto a stone well and then onto the back of a fleeing man. Its wings swept forward to envelop his head and shoulders and then it began feeding on him, its mouth locked on the top of his skull, its own partly inflated head rippling like a blouse filling with wind even as the man kept on running.

Within seconds the slin leapt off him onto another poor soul, and its previous victim fell limp to the ground with the top of his skull missing, what remained of his grey matter running out of it like broth.

'Sweet Mercy,' hissed Coya, seeing the man's eviscerated features fixed into a twisted scream, like one of those famous paintings by Juminji.

He jerked at a sudden bang next to him. It was Marsh, taking a shot with his pistol, startling both their mounts. Marsh never missed with a pistol, and the creature screeched and hopped off into an alley so they lost sight of it.

'Good shot.'

Here in the northern limits of the city smoke was rising from buildings hit in the recent barrage. It was another cold day in Bar-Khos, not long past midwinter. At least it had stopped raining. Coya wore layers of wool and hemp, including a brightly dyed hat with long tassels covering his ears, a traditional Minosian garb and a present from his wife. That morning, Marsh had only rolled his eyes at the sight of it on his head, as though Coya intentionally donned the most conspicuous of clothing just to make his job more difficult. But Coya's real reason had been to cover up the bandages wrapped around his skull. Even now he still carried a portion of a crossbow bolt buried in the back of his brain, a recent wound gained during their mission into the Windrush forest. One that should have killed him outright.

A wound that might still kill him yet, though, for all that Shard the Dreamer had worked her magic on him, for all that it barely seemed to affect him, this shaft lodged in his brain.

Marsh thought he should be lying on his back somewhere trying his best not to die, at least until Shard or someone else worked out a way of getting it out. No doubt his bodyguard was right. A simple sneeze or a slap on the back might be enough to kill Coya now. Every time he moved too quickly he imagined he could feel the weight of the shaft slightly putting off his head's centre of balance.

His wound was just about all they had to show for their journey into the Windrush, in which they'd tried to gain the aid of the forest Contrarè in the war.

Even worse, that was hardly the extent of the bad news. Still, there was no sign of the charts either. Charts to the Isles of Sky no less, returned to Khos by the survivors of a skyship expedition sent into the Great Hush and beyond. An expedition which Coya himself, and some of his peers in the Few, had secretly arranged and supplied in hope of saving the Free Ports.

The location of the Isles of Sky, the only known source of black powder in the world. Not to mention all those strange devices of exotica, like farcrys and Rōshun seals. The Alhazii Caliphate had grown rich over the centuries through their monopoly with the Isles and its advanced technologies, and they would do anything to stop their location from being discovered. In the past they had declared crushing embargoes against nations seeking the Isles for themselves. Threats were cast even for researching lesser alternatives to the potent black powder of the Isles, like simple sulphurous gunpowders. And the Caliphate was famed for its deep-cover spies. They had eyes everywhere.

Yet with the surprise imperial invasion of Khos, Coya and his peers in the Few had considered the risk to be finally worth taking.

They knew the Caliphate had no interest in conquering the world like the Mannians; only in profiting themselves by supplying both the Empire and the democras in their long and bitter war of attrition. But neither was the Caliphate interested in being conquered. If their monopoly was threatened, they would negotiate. With the charts, Coya could make them choose a side at last.

Except the charts had gone missing before he had even gotten his hands on them. The skyship had been destroyed on its return journey from the Isles, and the survivors trapped on the other side of the Shield. When they had tried to return home during the chaos of the battle for the Shield – during General Mokabi's all-out assault against the southern walls – people had died while others went missing, the charts along with them.

It was enough to make a person tear their hair out in frustration.

Coya blinked at the startling passing sight of a burning building, where people worked in lines to pass buckets of sloshing water from a well, trying to save someone's home in this city where there were no longer enough roofs to shelter everything, so overfull was it with refugees and defenders. Soot stained their desperate faces as they worked. Fear carried in the children's shouts and the barking of the dogs.

For all his adult years, Coya had been fighting to keep the islands of the democras – *people without rulers* – safe from the threat of empire. Not only because he was the descendant of the philosopher Zeziké, spiritual father of the democras. Or because he was a League

Delegate and secret member of the Few. More than anything, Coya fought to protect what had become most dear to him, these people and lands of his birthplace, the Mercian Free Ports; this chain of islands that were as diverse in their cultures as they were fascinating for their rugged landscapes, all of them flourishing in a golden age of liberty and cooperation. Even here, on Khos, where the Michinè still held sway at the limits of the democras, Coya had come to the front line to lend what aid he could. For he knew that it was here where the entire fate of the democras would be decided.

If mighty Khos fell, breadbasket of the democras, the rest of the Free Ports would surely follow.

'We need those damned charts,' Coya Zeziké growled aloud, clenching his teeth hard.

*

A gust stirred the many strings of windchimes strung across the street, so that they clattered overhead as it blew along the Avenue of Lies – the main thoroughfare running north to south through the city all the way to the Mount of Truth, standing over the throat of the Lansway and the Shield. Coya was glad of the wool hat now. His bandaged head and ears were warm beneath it even in the bitter gusts. He was even gladder to be riding a zel and not hobbling around with his cane and crippled body. It could be tiring moving about at the rate of an arthritic old man.

The Avenue was thronged with carts and soldiers hurrying towards the wall, though they were making way for the phalanx of riders escorting the lone form of the Mannian envoy headed in the opposite direction – a white-robed figure riding erect on an equally white zel.

Further south, people lined the route to watch the Mannian priest pass by. Some screamed obscenities, others threw rocks or bits of rotten food which the Khosian riders had to deflect with their shields. Yet the envoy pretended to pay them no heed, instead giving a delicate wave in welcome as though he belonged there, as though this was to be their future.

'Coya Zeziké!' a voice called out from a passing group; Volunteers from the other Free Ports of the League, excited to see the famous Delegate and descendant of the philosopher Zeziké himself in the troubled city. Coya raised a hand towards them in acknowledgement, much like the envoy up ahead in fact, and Marsh swore aloud, picking up the pace as he forced his zel through the press. As his lifelong bodyguard, trained since a boy to protect the living blood of Zeziké, Marsh's constant nemesis was Coya's fame.

'Relax,' Coya told him. 'I'm here to be seen, remember? It helps with morale.'

Marsh was checking the buildings on either side, the windows and rooftops. 'Aye. A lot of good you'll be with a Diplomat's bullet through your head.'

'Please,' protested Coya, not wanting to think of such things. The man seemed in a particularly foul mood this morning. Maybe it was just lack of sleep from the Khosian heavy guns going off all night.

Marsh slowed to draw alongside him as they trotted up to the rickshaws tailing the procession. Sombre Michinè aristocrats sat in the backs of the rickshaws pulled along by pairs of sweaty men, their faces powdered white and their attention fixed resolutely ahead. In the foremost one Coya spotted Chonas, formidable First Minister of the Khosian Council.

'Ah, Delegate Coya!' declared the First Minister as he spotted him riding alongside. 'Come to take part in the forthcoming talks?'

'Talks?' echoed Coya. He looked ahead to the figure of the Mannian envoy, who was still waving his hand at the people's hostility while he grinned like some much-loved celebrity, full of teeth and bravado.

'The Empire has deigned to send us a Peace Envoy, here to negotiate with the Council on matters of the siege. Once we return to the chambers we will hold a session to order. You are more than welcome to attend, of course.'

Coya straightened a little further in his posture, as he always did in moments of anger, his crooked body momentarily forgetting the constant crippling pains it had known since birth. He called out loudly as he rode alongside the trundling wheel of the rickshaw. 'Peace Envoy, is it, while they sit an army outside the walls?'

It was forward of him, to speak so bluntly to the First Minister of Khos without the use of proper titles. Usually Coya ignored such nonsense, especially when it was aimed at himself, but they were in Khos here, last remaining seat of the old Mercian aristocracy.

As though to remind him of his proper place, the companion sitting by the Minister's side cast Coya a stony stare. Chonas though had other things on his mind.

'Indeed,' agreed the old fellow. 'One wonders whether such ironies are intended in these titles of theirs. Or do they really believe in the righteousness of their predations?'

'They make themselves believe. They tell themselves stories of how they're saving the world from itself by enslaving it.'

Chonas said nothing, reflecting on what Coya had said. Before the revolution of the democras, the Michinè of Khos had once been rulers of the island, subservient only to their king. They were hardly strangers to such grandiose self-deceptions themselves, though Coya kept his observations to himself.

'Where is the Lord Protector in all of this?' Coya asked. 'I don't see him anywhere.'

'Still up on the wall, I believe, discussing the defences with Tanserine. I think he disapproves.'

'He isn't the only one. What have we to gain here, talking to the enemy? They will only aim to divide us and weaken our position.'

But Chonas waved the remark aside. It wasn't like him to show such recklessness, and it was only then that Coya saw the fear in the First Minister's watery old eyes. He realized the man was grasping at any straw that he could. A dangerous state of mind for times like these.

'It never hurts to listen, young Coya. You of all people could learn from such advice as that.'

A grunt of agreement sounded from Marsh at his side.

'Velchum,' Chonas said to the stiff-lipped fool sitting next to him. 'I must speak alone with our friend here for a moment.'

'Sire?'

'Well hop to it then.'

The Michinè barely masked his displeasure as he stepped off onto the cobbles.

'You there!' coughed old Chonas to the bearers pulling along the small two-wheeled cart. 'Sing us a song if you will!'

'A song, sir?'

'Yes! Something stirring like one of those sea shanties from the Shoals. An extra coin for your efforts.'

Still pulling the rickshaw, one of the bearers cleared his lungs and started heaving out a song. His voice was terrible, entirely absent of tune, yet strangely the sound was hardly at odds with the general atmosphere around them, the boisterous crowds yelling at the envoy as they made their way along the Avenue.

They were passing the Stadium of Arms now in the centre of the city, an amphitheatre of white stone columns and arches, rising high over the commercial district around it. Soldiers from its soaring walls peered down at the passing procession, looking on in silence. On the rickshaw, Chonas leaned out over the side so he could speak more quietly with Coya.

'Any news for me on those charts?' he said beneath the driver's awful rendition of a song.

Coya tugged his zel even closer. 'You've heard then.'

'Of course I've heard. You've gone and lost them, is what I heard. It's all the network is talking about right now.'

'My dear fellow, I hardly had them to begin with, only the promise of them.'

'You have no idea where they might be?'

Coya opened his mouth then shut it again, irritated by the old Michinè's tone, as though somehow it was Coya who was responsible for their loss.

He took a deep breath to settle himself.

'The Rōshun say the charts were in the hands of a longhunter called Cole, a Khosian, when they met up with him south of the Shield. If he lives that's likely where they still are. Unfortunately there was no sign of him after the Rōshun re-entered the city, though admittedly everything was in chaos that night. That was the night of Mokabi's big attack and the flooding. They're still picking up the pieces down there, but there's no sign of the man amongst the wounded. He could be dead. The charts might be buried under three feet of mud by now.'

Chonas glanced back over his shoulder, checking to see that his powdered companion was still trotting along behind the rickshaw.

'Or he could be alive. He could have gone rogue with those charts in his possession, trying to sell them to the highest bidder.'

'Maybe. There are still too many unknowns.'

'Come now. Dealing in unknowns is what we do in the Few. It is our craft, is it not?'

For a moment Coya felt his youth in the face of the Minister's advanced years. For all that he was twenty-seven, he was still a youngster by this man's reckoning, who himself had been a member of the secret network known as the Few for longer than Coya had even existed; an organization that subtly guarded against concentrations of power throughout the League, and which most of his Michinè peers would have violently opposed had only they ever known of it.

But Chonas was one of those rare Michinè who supported the goals of the democras. Which was how a member of the Khosian nobility, that last diluted vestige of aristocracy remaining in all the Mercian isles, found himself working so closely with the descendant of Zeziké, the very philosopher whose ideas had led to revolution and the toppling of that old order.

'Make a guess for me,' prompted the First Minister. 'What is your intuition here? What are our chances of getting these charts? Are they really lost?'

Coya shook his head.

'There's nothing to be gained in believing so. I believe they're still out there in the hands of this man Cole, for whatever reason I don't know. But yes, they're still in play. They have to be.'

'What do you know of this longhunter then?'

'The Rōshun tell me he was Khosian by his accent. And that he had the way of a military man about him. An ex-soldier.'

'Wonderful,' grunted Chonas, chewing his false teeth together hard. 'Just who we need to be carrying the fate of Khos in their hands. A damned bloody deserter.'

CHAPTER SEVEN

Nico

'*Khos*,' spat the voice of his father as they jogged along the road, trailing threads of breath like misty scarves. Through the sheets of rain, his father peered about at the wintry landscape revealing itself in the milky light of a new day. 'Never thought I'd see this place again.'

He was talking to his son once more after a night of sullen running. Pretending that Nico had never said those things outside the slave market at all.

'I know the feeling,' Nico replied, peering out from the shelter of his own dripping hood as he ran, easily matching the hard loping pace his father had been setting throughout the long night, glad that the silence was behind them.

'Oh?'

'My time with the farlander, Ash. My memories are all over the place, but I remember, when things got really bad, how I longed to be back home like never before.'

Still his father avoided asking for more details, as though afraid of what he might hear. Not that Nico could criticize him for that. He wasn't any better. So far he'd asked little about his father's own life during his years abroad. He had barely even asked about Cole's voyage with the farlander to the Isles of Sky, where they'd hoped to bring Nico back from the dead; indeed where they had achieved just that. Too strange even to think about. Too unsettling by far.

Home, Nico repeated in his mind as though to sample its flavour.

Somehow it felt different to him now, the Khos he had known, the Khos he had left not so long ago on the heels of a Rōshun farlander, promised to be his apprentice. Perhaps it was due to this new body that he wore, identical to his old one save that it was a copy, a replica. He was truly seeing it all through new eyes. Though

FIERCE GODS

more likely it was the many burnt-out cottages along the road, and the occasional corpses lying on the ground, frozen in various contortions, strangely elevated as the rain washed away the surface of snow around them. Ordinary people caught in the jaws of the Empire's ambitions. Whole families slaughtered.

Such passing sights struck him hard enough at the time, though much harder than he knew. Later, in the dark of nights, Nico would see the corpses again in his mind, though more freshly this time, more sharply than when he'd seen them for real – he would glimpse the children amongst them, and the babes, and a morbid melancholy would take hold of him that would fade upon waking, given long enough, but which would never entirely leave him for the rest of his life.

For now though, emulating the hardened manner of his father, Nico bore what he saw without comment, while he was filled increasingly with a sense of death hanging like a dread promise across his homeland; this Mannian creed of anti-life writ in corpses strewn across the snow.

He knew the same would be in store for the people of Bar-Khos, if the city was taken. The Mannians would rape and butcher in their thousands and enslave the rest of the population; they would revel in their callousness towards those they considered lesser than themselves – the conquered, the defeated, the weak. After all, Nico had travelled to the distant imperial capital. He had seen for himself their naked cruelty, when they had burned him alive on a stake in the arena for all to watch, the very same arena that hosted the slaying of the poor and disabled for sport.

These scum had already conquered most of the known world. They had spread their fanatical dogma of exploitation for profit, of dog-eat-dog, of the *divine flesh*, around the Heart of the World, and now here they had come to Khos and the democras, to stamp out the last remaining resistance to their power.

If they were not stopped here, they never would be.

Onwards Nico ran through the rain and the early morning light, trying to shake the dark mood from his mind.

Last night they had raced along a road thronged with carts and travellers, rushing to reach the river crossing at Juno's Ferry, hoping to catch up with Nico's mother on her journey south to the slave pens of the front. By then, Juno's Ferry had fallen to the Imperials. Those Khosian soldiers unfortunate enough not to have escaped in time had met a fate worse than death, for they had been nailed to every tree in sight. Their croaks for pity assaulted Nico and his father from all sides as they stepped off the barge amongst a crowd of camp followers, having crossed the sacred, steaming waters of the Chilos.

Since then, they had carried on southwards towards Bar-Khos at the fastest pace they could maintain. But the main road was thoroughly churned into frozen furrows and holes, so that the route was choked in many places by wagons bogged down or broken.

When they had reached a lesser road that also headed roughly south, Cole decided they should take it instead, figuring that those transporting the pleasure slaves and his mother to the front would most likely have taken it too. Nico wasn't so sure about that, but he went along with his father's judgement anyway.

Riders came and went along the lesser road, imperial couriers bearing messages between the front and their stronghold of Tume back in the Reach. There was other traffic too, camp followers on foot and the odd squad of soldiers, though from what they overheard they were still far behind the lines here, with most of the Imperial Expeditionary Force now converging on Bar-Khos having rafted down the Chilos.

In the first glow of dawn, the road wound its way through a landscape devoid of life in these depths of winter, save for the crows wheeling over stands of trees, or a sudden hare springing from the verge into deeper grasses. Nico gazed at the ground flowing ahead of them, wanting it to lull him once more into a running meditation in which all his thoughts were effortlessly replaced by a deepening presence in the moment.

But his clothes were too wet for that, clinging to every movement of his body. And his hands so numb he could barely feel them, nor the tip of his nose.

It should be getting warmer the further south they came, but instead it seemed to be growing colder, until now the latest downpour was starting to turn to bitter sleet.

'Bad weather coming,' his father remarked with a glance to the west, as though the endless rain and sleet was hardly bad enough.

Nico grunted, chomping through a sausage as they ran, swallowing down chunks between breaths, filling a stomach cramped and sick with hunger. His father tore mouthfuls from a loaf of bread. Nico held out the sausage and they swapped so they could each have a bite of the other.

He squinted, seeing something move on the road ahead of them. But as they drew closer he saw that it was only an old scatterweed, a crazyweed some people called them: those balls of thorny branches that rolled across the landscape borne by the wind, feeding on the debris and fallen leaves they speared up and carried along the way. As he and his father approached the crazyweed it bounced off the bank of the road then veered with the wind so that for a time it accompanied them in their run, tumbling along at their side as though it had chosen to join them.

'How far ahead do you think they are?' asked Nico with an eye to the bouncing weed.

His father sucked in air before he could reply. He was growing tired.

'Half a day maybe. If we're lucky we should catch up with them tonight. Tomorrow at the latest.'

'I can't stop thinking what she must be going through.'

'Better not to, boy. You'll only torment yourself.'

'That's what I'm telling you. I can't help it.'

He'd been trying his best not to think about what his mother must be going through at the hands of her captors, for the thoughts had been driving him crazy. Yet every time he passed another destroyed hamlet or body lying by the roadside, it was a bitter reminder of how insane and dangerous these people truly were.

'Interesting terrain up here near the Reach,' said his father, from the blue yonder of his mind.

'Huh?'

'I always liked this part of Khos. Still enough trees to be partly wild. And with the Windrush so nearby. And the Chilos. Good country.'

Since dawn's first light his father had been unusually chatty. Indeed since the first stiffened corpses they had come upon, suddenly rendered visible by dawn so that Nico could see how they had been running past them all night long without noticing. Just trying to keep Nico's mind off the passing horrors, he slowly came to realize now, and his father's concern only made him feel worse for what he had said the day before.

'If you say so,' he responded, staring through the sleet at the passing trees and snow and marsh grasses, a white world broken by frozen streams and ponds. His father saw much more in a landscape than he ever would, Nico knew. He had knowledge of most wild things that lived and grew on Khos, intimate with the cycles and balances of nature. A true outdoorsman.

'I remember the first time I ever saw the lowlands of western Khos,' said Cole, his voice strained with exertion. 'Where they grow all those endless crops of grain, and chase away the travelling Greengrasses trying to rewild the land as a threat to their business. I remember looking across the world and seeing how all of it was farmland, just field after field enclosed within hedges, ditches, stone walls, and hardly a stand of trees worth mentioning. Everything tamed. Everything the same. My uncle owned a farm there. You never met him. He thought the lowlands were pretty. *Civilized*, he used to call them. I couldn't bring myself to tell him that what I saw was desolation, a barren plain empty of most of the life that once had been there, killed or driven away. A land stripped naked of its forests, subdued, put to work.'

'You're thinking of the wild farm again, aren't you?'

'Always. How was it when last you saw the place?'

'Thriving still.'

A grunt by way of acknowledgement. The pride and joy of his father's life, his wild farm in southern Khos, where their cottage was located in a rugged landscape bordering the sea and the foothills of the High Tell. Over the course of the years, with passion and infinite patience, Cole had grown a forest garden filled with beneficial and perennial plants, all working in balance with each other and needing little tending, providing year-round food and medicines, and a semi-wild home for all manner of species normally driven away by farming.

More a way of life than a farm, he had been keen to tell others. A way of *being*. Just like the travelling Greengrasses always claimed, those wandering monks of the Way who had passed these things on to his father and many others. The Greengrasses made it their life's work to spread the teachings of wild farming wherever they went in the Free Ports. They reminded people that they belonged to the land, not the other way round, teaching sustainable techniques of farming that went with the grain of nature, not against it. Practices that his father had taken to heart.

It was Cole's desertion of his beloved wild farm that had been the most shocking thing of all, even more so than running out on his family. Yet now he wanted to change the subject, perhaps for the same reason he didn't wish to speak about Reese, from guilt and the fear of what would become of them.

'When I saw the Alhazii deep desert for the first time,' Cole panted, 'it was a thousand times worse than that. The desert was once fertile land covered in forests of giant chiminos. Until the birth of some early civilizations there, a few millennia ago. They cut down all the trees. Salted the soil with over-irrigation. Eventually destroyed the land base itself along with their own existence. I knew all this from the Greengrasses . . . But it wasn't until I laid eyes on the Alhazii desert that I understood what the people there had done. What their civilization had created in its own image. All I could see was sand in every direction. A continent of dust where life had once thrived. And the people living there now, the desert-dwelling Alhazii . . . they seemed to have forgotten what it once had been like. Somehow they thought it was normal that they etched out what lives they could in this vast, dry lifeless graveyard of dead species. As though the Alhazii desert was only natural, not man-made at all.'

Cole blew the breath from his lungs and sucked down a fresh supply. It was wearing him out, this talking on the run. And he was starting to favour his left foot as though the right one was suffering. Still, it was impressive that he was still going, still loping along with the longrifle in his hand, when most men half his age would have dropped in exhaustion long before now.

'We'll have to stop and rest soon,' he said. 'No sense running ourselves into the ground like the zels.'

'But I haven't even hit my third wind yet.'

His father glanced across at him as though he was joking, but Nico meant it. For all the hours they had been running like this, he was merely tired.

'When did you get so fit, lad?'

'I don't know,' Nico lied, and then he shook his head in scorn. 'Since coming back with this new body of mine,' he admitted. 'I feel stronger in it. Definitely fitter. Like I could bound over a house or keep on running forever. I've never felt as comfortable in my own skin as I do now.'

'Interesting. Maybe they straightened out a few kinks.'

'Yes, I've been thinking that.'

'The pock marks are gone from your forehead. From scratching when you had the child pox.'

It mellowed Nico's heart to hear his father speak that way, to remember him as a boy; to have carried that memory with him for all this time.

His voice almost broke when he next spoke aloud.

'Why *did* you come back, after all this time?'

A long pause, Cole's expression lost within his hood.

'I felt a calling. It was time.'

You couldn't have felt it a little earlier?

Nico thought back to the wild farm too. The family cottage that had been his home, where he and his mother had lived on after Cole had deserted them.

'She missed you, you know. She never stopped missing you.'

His father glared with a single eye, then gazed southwards through the sleet. Despite his obvious weariness he pushed himself harder, spurred by whatever regrets lay on his path behind him, drawn onwards by some lingering remnants of hope.

'She's going to be fine,' he growled at Nico. 'You hear me? Your mother's going to be fine!'

*

With the early fall of twilight a fierce wind loosed itself from the plateau of the Reach behind them, bearing clouds thick enough to cast the world into darkness. It was a charged wind too, common in this season of storms, carrying with it the scent of lightning and causing the hairs of their bodies to stand on end. What was known on Khos as an Arcwind.

Soon the sleet was falling again, but this time with the added fierceness of the storm. Onwards they pushed, knowing that Nico's mother was still somewhere ahead of them on the road. It grew colder than ever. The sleet turned to snow. With conditions verging on a blizzard, blowing them this way and that, his father cursed aloud and shouted that it was no good, they had to get out of this weather. Cole led him from the road into the deepening woods, seeking shelter. He was like a divining rod when it came to things like this, and soon they came to a dead tiq tree standing tall and bare-limbed, with the trunk hollowed out at its base. Icicles hung from their nostrils by then. Nico could no longer feel his extremities.

It was like a dry cave within, a cave of knotted wood with a floor of old leaves and sticks blown in from the triangular opening, which they used to start their fire.

After a while they were both snug and warm inside, with the knobbly walls of the space reflecting the light and heat of the fire, making Nico sleepy for all that it was barely evening. They had been running for what seemed like an endless time.

A bare foot prodded his flank, stirring his gaze from the flames.

'Throw another log on the fire,' came Cole's weary voice from beneath the hat perched over his eyes, lying there against his backpack.

The fire crackled and hissed when Nico tossed another broken log upon it. The wood was damp and the smoke stung his eyes, but his skin tingled wonderfully in the heat.

'Those cone nuts are crisping up,' remarked his father without looking, twitching his nostrils.

'I like them that way,' Nico told him, and turned the spiky tiq cones over where they sat on the stones around the flames, turning dark. Even though he had already eaten some jerky from his pack, his stomach growled as he smelled the roasted nutty scent of them.

'You still hungry?' asked Cole.

'Starving.'

'Used to be a time we couldn't get you to eat.'

'What, when I was five?'

A smack of lips from beneath the man's hat.

Once more Nico's mind settled on his mother and what she must be going through right now. Nightmare images flared through his imagination. Feeling sick, he turned away from them by looking instead to the still form of his father.

It seemed to him that Cole had spent a great deal of time alone with himself over the years in which he had been gone; years living as a longhunter, he had said, much of them spent in the vast wilderness of the Great Hush. For as long as Nico had known him he had tended towards the quiet side, but now he barely spoke at all, not unless spoken to first, or when trying to take Nico's mind off something. Seldom did he hold his son's gaze for very long.

'You haven't asked me about Boon yet,' Nico ventured quietly.

His father slid the hat from his eyes and peered through the smoke at him with his steady blue gaze. Cole had been close to the family dog too.

'What about Boon?'

Even now it was hard to say the words. Nico recalled his heartbreak at the death of his lifelong companion, back when they'd been living rough in Bar-Khos. The tears had dripped from his face as he'd buried the old dog in the earth with his own two hands, stricken by the sheer awfulness of his loss.

'*What about Boon?*' his father asked again.

'He's dead. He fell sick in Bar-Khos. I buried him there.'

The news was enough to pinch Cole's expression into a frown, and to send him rifling through his pack for his tarweed and papers. Within moments he had a roll-up in his hand; he lit it with a metal spark-lighter and took a draw of smoke, exhaling as he stared at the flickering firelight with his forehead deeply furrowed.

'I'm sorry to hear that,' he said after a time.

Cole stared at the flames without focus, as though seeing into the past. Shadows softened the many scars criss-crossing his features, and Nico was reminded of how his father had once been a strikingly handsome man, before the war had robbed him of his good looks.

'Why did you leave us, Father?' Nico blurted suddenly, before he could stop himself. It was the only way he could ask such a question.

His father brooded some more in silence. The flames crackled within their circle of stones as the snow outside was hurled about in the gusts.

'I just couldn't take it any more,' he said. 'The siege. The war. If I had stayed any longer . . .' Cole winced, shaking his head. 'I would have ended up taking my own life, just to stop the pain of it.'

Nico's heart was beating fast now. He had witnessed the steady deterioration of his father over the early years of the siege. Each time

Cole had returned to the family farm in the stained leathers of a Special bearing even more scars than before. But he had never really known what was going on inside the man, how much those fresh scars must have reflected much deeper wounds too.

'What do you mean?' he asked him softly.

'It was a nightmare down there, Nico. Fighting in those tunnels under the Shield, year after year. It got to the point where I could hardly sleep in darkness any longer, not without jumping awake to the slightest of sounds. And when I was awake, the worst of memories would flood through me at any time. Friends I saw butchered to death. Friends I left to die, buried in rubble. I was falling apart.'

He looked to his son through another exhalation of smoke, eyes watering.

'But I'm sorry,' he said. 'I'm sorry I left you both behind like I did. You've every right to hate me.'

What could he say to that? How to cast aside all those years of anger he bore against this man who was his father?

'Hate is putting it a little strongly,' Nico offered, though he would go no further than that one concession. He wasn't willing to forgive him just yet. Not while his mother remained a captive in enemy hands.

Together they looked to the fire, their troubled stares swallowed by the flames.

Another memory came to Nico just then, another piece of his life falling into place. Or rather another piece of his death, for in a flash he relived the moments he had been staked to a roaring bonfire in distant Q'os, terrified beyond sense and reason, struggling to be free from an agony so consuming he knew he would go mad from it, willing to give anything to be gone from there and home again in Khos. In those terrible moments he had prayed for the old Rōshun to come and save him, but his prayers had gone unanswered.

'I died in the imperial capital, you know. They tied me to a stake on top of a bonfire, and they set it alight.'

'I know.'

Nico blinked hard, feeling the heat of the flames against his face. He'd barely had a chance to speak with Ash before they'd parted for the final time. So many questions remained unanswered.

Bending forwards, he plucked one of the cone nuts from the fire and tossed it from one palm to the other, letting it cool, faintly horrified by the lingering glimpses of his own blackening skin on the bonfire.

Was the crazy old farlander really dead, as his intuition suggested? It seemed impossible that such a force of nature could suddenly cease to exist.

Beside him, Cole was taking his beloved longrifle from its wrapping so that he could rub it down with a cloth. It was typical of his father to seek out activity whenever he was uncomfortable. Not so unlike Nico himself.

'You were living in the city?' came his father's subdued voice.

Nico exhaled long and hard. He placed the crispy cone nut back on one of the stones, his appetite momentarily forgotten.

'For a while.'

'How come?'

'I didn't like the lover my mother took in, so I left home with Boon.'

Cole slowed in his polishing of the rifle.

'A lover? What was he like?'

'Too young for her. And something of a bastard. Los was his name.'

His father grunted, eyes hidden in the shadow of his hat.

Outside, the gusts had abated for a moment, so that in the darkness Nico could hear something snuffling about near the entrance; a gruffan perhaps, seeking out snow lice with its long snout, even in this weather. Remarkable, just how sharpened his hearing was in this new body.

'You liked living there?'

For a moment he didn't know what his father meant, and then he realized he was talking about Bar-Khos.

He settled back, trying to recall his time living rough in the besieged city, letting the recollections come to him in whatever order they wanted, though what came to him mostly were memories of Boon, his companion and protector for all that time.

In his mind came the sight of Boon barking at the moons and leaping about on his paws just as Nico did, both of them dancing to the pounding music in the same wild fashion as all the other sweating youths around them. Youths tattooed and pierced like native Contrarè, crested with hair like travelling Tuchoni, as high as the moons they were all howling at, leaping at, crashing into each other to the band's beating drums, the thrum of jitars, the shrill racing cries of scroo pipes . . . Wolf dancing, they called it, those savage street youths of Bar-Khos, reckless and mad, raised in the rumbling midst of a siege. Wolf dancing to the full moons on the roof of a ruined city warehouse, howling their freedom while the guns of the eternal siege barked away like dogs of war.

Boon had loved every moment of it.

'Sometimes it was fun,' he recalled, smiling to himself, wishing that Boon was alive and here with him. 'When I wasn't starving, or just trying to find somewhere I could be alone for a while. The city is so packed now.'

His father was watching him closely now, as though trying to peer through the gulf of space that hung between them, trying to span the missing years since he had left.

'Like father like son,' he said with a shrug of his head.

'What do you mean?'

'You always were something of a loner. Same as me.'

Nico frowned, knowing it to be true. In his youth he had been closer to his dog Boon than he had been with those of his own age.

He recalled children taunting him outside the schoolhouse, accusing him of being a coward for having a coward father who had fled the fighting. And he knew they had been like that with him because he had stood alone.

'I can't help it,' he confessed. 'I always feel like a stranger in groups. An outsider. Someone looking in from without. Even when I'm amongst people, I'm not really amongst them.'

'Well, that's your curse and your blessing right there.'

'It's felt mostly like a curse, so far,' grumbled Nico, staring down at the flames in a reflective mood of past heartaches.

A dry snort of air from his father.

'Only because you haven't found your feet yet. Do you still go around worrying what other people think of you?'

'No more than anyone else does, I guess . . .'

'Well don't. You ever look at other people's lives? Hypocrites and narrow-minded fools the lot of them, and those who aren't will take you as you are. You just need to live the way you need to live, never mind the opinions of others.'

Nico prodded a log with his stockinged foot, prompting a crackle of flames. He looked out through the entrance of the hollow tree and saw movement out there, the furry back of a gruffan disappearing into the stormy night. Such a simple life, he thought to himself with a spark of envy.

'About all I can think of right now is what my mother is going through. And that girl we saw today in the slave market. How they're both hunkering down somewhere hungry and miserable and forsaken, if they're even that lucky, while we sit here talking in the heat and waiting out the storm.'

'You're too sensitive, son. You always have been.'

'What, like you?'

'Aye, like me. You'll break yourself against the world like this if you don't harden yourself against it first.'

'Great. That really helps me right now.'

Cole finished wiping down the rifle, or decided he'd had enough, for he placed it away again while he puffed on what remained of his roll-up, thinking to himself, searching for an answer.

He followed Nico's gaze outside.

'We stayed not far from here once,' sounded his voice beside Nico. 'Visiting my mother's sister, you remember? Bahn was there too, my brother, with his family.'

It took him a few moments of grasping, but at last a memory formed in his mind. 'Yes. They had a rice farm. They flooded their fields for the growing season. So?'

His father's eyes were gleaming now.

'You remember how we used to play in the fields with the rainbow fish?'

Nico leaned back from the smoke of the fire, images flaring in his head. Bright days of sunshine with the white heat bouncing off the water, brilliant sparkles dancing outwards from the ripples of their movements. All of them splashing through the flooded field chasing after the tiny rainbow fish that flashed between the rice shoots and their feet. His mother laughing in that carefree way that she had back then, made ever more giddy by the tickles of the fish darting in around her glittering anklets, her hair flaming against the sun.

'I remember. The fish kept the roots fertilized and clean of pests. They were almost tame. And clever too. They seemed to recognize different people. Even played with them.'

'Yes, but do you remember how you felt in those days? Carefree and full of joy?'

'Like a warm wind flowing through me.'

'Then hold on to that. In your darkest moments, when all the light seems to have gone out around you, remember back to that time. Remember that life is mostly good if you allow it to be, if others allow it to be.'

'But what of hope?' rasped Nico, and his voice – ground up by emotions – sounded older than his years. 'Right now some hope would be a bloody fine thing too.'

'You want hope?'

'Yes, I want hope!'

Cole leaned closer towards him. His eyes were glazed with fire. 'Tomorrow, we're going to catch up with your mother on the road. And one way or the other we're going to free her. By the time we make it back to the city, those charts I left with my brother will have made it into the right hands, and this whole war will be over.'

He settled a hand on Nico's shoulder.

'You mean the world to me, son. You and your mother. I promise all is going to be well, you hear me?'

Nico blinked tears from his eyes, wishing it could be true.

CHAPTER EIGHT

Coya

In the Council Chambers of Bar-Khos, the high glass windows had darkened with the blackness of night so that they hung like ominous portals over the assembly below, rattling with the strengthening gale outside. Oil lights had been lit in the great crystal chandeliers hanging from the ceiling, bright and trembling. Directly beneath them, a pool of water sunken into the floor shimmered with the reflected faces of the gathered people, all of them turned towards the bald-headed priest in his robes of white silk, arms crossed within the warmth of his sleeves as he spoke.

The Peace Envoy for the Empire stood alone on the floor of the Bar-Khosian Council Chambers with a dreamy look in his eyes, as though he was intoxicated on something, or mildly concussed, or perhaps simply the kind of man who tended to look elsewhere when he talked, for he gazed over their heads even as his steady voice addressed the crowded, silent chamber, reciting his speech from memory. Something about peace and reconciliation at the reluctant point of a sword.

By the water's edge, leaning on the ebony grip of his cane, Coya Zeziké stared down at the pool's surface only half listening to what the Mannian priest was saying.

Coya was contemplating other things as he chewed absently on one of the hazii cakes he carried with him everywhere to relieve his pains. Thinking of his wife in fact, back on his home island of Minos. Reminded of her by the subtle aftertaste of hazii weed on his tongue, of all things.

Rechelle's mouth had tasted of the herb the last time they had kissed, lying on her bed unable to rise from it, gazing up at him with her pretty features hollowed out with fatigue – his wife weakened dangerously by another late miscarriage.

Like a bringer of miracles, Rechelle had been the one to prescribe him the herb in the first place, releasing Coya almost instantly from a lifelong burden of physical agonies which had gradually been wearing him down to the point of immobility. Pains which hadn't gone away, precisely, but were blunted enough that he could live with them while maintaining the momentum of his life. Rechelle swore by the effectiveness of hazii weed for all manner of ailments, from pain relief to melancholy to those rare cancerous tumours of the skin and organs. A natural herbalist like her mother, she cast the weed into honeyed cakes or as a refined oil, and used it to help her family, friends and neighbours alike with that same warmth of heart he had fallen so deeply in love with; a woman he would always revere, his life companion and lover. Thinking of Rechelle now made him miss her with an ache that overcame all his others.

Standing over his cane, Coya swallowed down the rest of the dry cake in his mouth, exhaling nosily through his nostrils while the Mannian priest's voice droned somewhere just above the level of his thoughts.

Half a dozen steps away his bodyguard and lifelong protector glanced in Coya's direction, checking to see that he was still alive. Marsh swayed on the balls of his feet, bored as Coya was.

It seemed as though the Peace Envoy would never stop talking. And the more he talked the hotter he was getting, despite the chillness of the air, so that now the priest dabbed at his brow with a handkerchief. Even the Michinè ministers, used to endless dreary pontificating, were beginning to cough and shift about in their growing restlessness.

Once more Coya drifted away from it all, buoyed on the soothing tide of the herb, thinking of Rechelle.

His wife had been warned about the risks of trying for another child, that she could lose her own life in the attempt. But she had tried anyway, and indeed she had nearly lost her life in the process, when miscarriage had caused internal bleeding that even now, weeks later, hadn't entirely stopped. He should be at her bedside now back in Minos, reading her stories and tending to her needs, not here in these dank council chambers in the middle of a siege, risking his life again on yet another errand for the sake of the democras. What if Rechelle's strength failed to recover and she faded away before he could return? How would he ever live with himself, with the grief and loss and guilt of such a thing?

He wouldn't, he knew. Rechelle's loss would be the end of him too.

Coya shivered, frowning unhappily. It was cold in this large hall used for banquets and the visits of important dignitaries, even with the several hearths roaring with fires. No doubt a result of all the naked stone walls absorbing the heat, typically Khosian in their austerity, a few hangings thrown up here and there to counter the sparseness of the place, a few rugs and curtains.

The rectangular pool was an ancient feature sunken into the floor. Around its edges grew copper-leaf creeper vines and bushy dwarf trees rooted in the cracks of the flagging, so that it resembled a little oasis of life within a vault of stone.

Not all oases are mirages, Coya recited obliquely, recalling a saying of the desert Alhazii.

At one end burbled a gentle, natural spring barely disturbing the surface, the famed Spring of Awakening. Before the revolution, this hall had been used for the crowning of the old kings of Khos. It was here that the newly endowed kings had imbibed of the waters in order to gain a state of enlightenment from their divine properties; a ridiculous tradition, Coya thought, considering the behaviour of the average Khosian king back then.

In those days, long after Khos had been settled, and the native Contrarè driven into what remained of the Windrush forest, the settlers themselves had seen the land they now lived on taken from them by force, by their own rulers. Open common lands that had been enclosed into vast estates in which they had been worked like cattle simply to survive. A system that had survived for so long it had become what was considered as normal.

Such hypocrisies in this world, he thought with a minute shake of his head, and he looked to the priest still spouting his nonsense to the gathered Michinè ministers. Steal a loaf of bread and you could have found yourself physically branded a thief; yet steal a people's land and you were lauded as a king, a civilizer. Murder your neighbour and get strung up from the gallows; murder a dozen people, a hundred people, a hundred thousand people in the name of conquest, and your name became glorified in the history books.

The larger the crime, the more noble it seemed to become.

Coya smacked his lips together, glancing to the shallow waters near his feet. He was thirsty all of a sudden.

A few Michinè were watching him as he carefully bent down and dipped a hand into the surface of the pool. Expressions aghast, they looked on as he raised the holy spring waters to his lips and took a noisy slurp from them, washing down the last few crumbs in his mouth like some suddenly enlightened king of old.

The water tasted strangely bitter in his mouth.

Tasted like a lie.

*

'I will say it again,' echoed the voice of the priest through the long hall, finally piercing the space of Coya's thoughts. Up on the podium, the white-robed Peace Envoy was at last approaching some kind of crescendo, some kind of point to his speech. 'I will say it again, one last time, so you may remember these words when you formulate your reply. Should the people of Bar-Khos agree to open the city gates for the forces of the Holy Empire of Mann, and to accept our rightful reign, we swear to spare the lives of every man, woman and child.'

Coya grunted as he straightened over his cane; a young man carrying the burdens of the old, looking up from the water to stare hard at the imperial priest dictating threats to them in their own city.

It was just as he said it would be. The envoy trying to divide them with his words.

'And if we do not surrender?' called out Chonas, First Minister of Khos.

The envoy spread out his arms in a gesture of reasonableness.

'Then when Bar-Khos falls, it will be on your own heads what happens to your people.'

Their voices rose like a surging tide even as hail hammered the windows along the northern wall. Chonas held up a hand to try and settle their protests. He stood with most of the Michinè Council behind him, or at least what was left of the Council, for some were missing, feigning illness while they were rumoured to have already fled the besieged city by ship.

'You came here under flag of truce to tell us this?' asked Chonas, raising his bushy eyebrows high.

'I was sent here in the hope of speaking some sense into you, yes.'

More noisy protests sounded around the edges of the hall, where the rest of the gathering was comprised of citizens from the city Associations, those Khosian street societies which helped to keep the Council somewhat in check. Coya knew their presence here was a hard-won victory for the ordinary citizenry of Bar-Khos. It had taken a revolution and further decades of bitter struggle before they had gained a voice in the processes of power, a time in which the Michinè class had tried every possible means, including murder and subversion, to suppress their rise.

But now they were united, Michinè and Associations alike, in their hostility towards the lone priest standing in the centre of the floor, this supposed Envoy of Peace.

The Mannian was dabbing at his clammy bald head with his handkerchief again, looking flushed. But then he turned with everyone else, startled, towards a sudden commotion from the rear of the hall as someone flung open the double doors, injecting a rush of cold air along its length.

Behind it came the rap of hobnailed boots.

'Surrender or die, is it?' declared General Creed in his full armour and bearskin coat, striding past Coya's position, reeking of the smoke and blood of the day's action. 'Your people made that same promise to us ten years ago. Yet here we are, still standing.'

'Hear, hear,' agreed Coya with a rap of his cane upon the stone floor, gladdened to see the Lord Protector making an appearance. Yet the Michinè only frowned to see him here.

Again the priest opened his arms wide in a magnanimous gesture. 'That is hardly what I—'

'Enough!' Creed growled. 'What more do we need to hear from this man? Why continue with this charade?'

'Because we are not savages,' replied one of the Michinè as he stepped forward into the light, and Coya recognized him as Pericules, the new Minister of Defence. A man barely qualified for the position, save that his ailing uncle had recently passed it on to him.

'He has come here to discuss terms with us. The least we can do is engage with him on the issues at hand.'

'Give me one good reason why?' Creed asked, clearly as baffled as Coya.

'I'll give you fifty thousand good reasons. Encamped right now beyond the city's northern wall, threatening to overrun us.'

'*Pah*,' spat Creed in disgust, casting that aside with a throw of his hand. 'In this weather, in these temperatures, that army out there will already be unravelling at the edges. Diseases will be running rampant. Common illnesses from exposure and worsening morale. It's all empty bravado and he knows it is. We need only hold on to our resolution here and they are finished. Why do you think they have sent someone to parley with us in the first place? Because they care about saving lives? Or because they worry that they're facing defeat in the middle of a Khosian winter?'

'They did not seem to be unravelling this morning, when I gazed upon them from the wall,' said Pericules.

His words were not at all what Coya expected to hear from the Khosian Minister of Defence, particularly before a representative of their enemy. Perhaps it was only the man's inexperience betraying his fears to them all, or the usual Michinè belligerence towards the Lord Protector himself for being a common man. But then Pericules spoke on, and what he said stunned Coya into stillness.

'Come now. All of you. There is no one rushing to our aid here. We are alone in this. If we do not make these hard choices to save ourselves, who will?'

Enough!

In the flickering light of the hall Coya rapped the steel tip of his cane hard against the stone flagging, stunning the entire assembly into silence.

'My dear Pericules,' Coya said as smoothly as he was able. 'You are hardly alone here. The rest of the Free Ports support you whole-heartedly in the defence of your island. Or have you forgotten the thousands of Volunteers now shoring up your city's defences? Or the squadrons of skyships patrolling your skies? And all of those medicos and their supplies? And the League navy even now engaged with imperial forces off your shores, trying to keep your shipping lanes open? Need I go on?'

'Yet still the enemy shells rain down on our northern districts,' retorted Pericules, supposed Minister of Defence. 'Still our defences could be overrun at any moment. What good will your words be to us then, Coya Zeziké? Can we even take the chance of annihilation if another option is available?'

He sounded desperate, almost babbling. General Creed was glaring at the man with a mixture of disgust and suspicion. He tore his gaze away to look around him, meeting Coya's eyes at last across the width of the pool. Something of meaning passed between them.

They've bought him off somehow. The Empire has bought the new Minister of Defence to their side!

In his bearskin coat the Lord Protector took a step closer to Pericules. His voice was dangerously quiet for all that his eyes flashed with fury.

'You really think it worth discussing, our surrender to the enemy?'

Pericules licked his lips while he glanced to his fellow Michinè.

'I would hardly have expected such talk from our notable Minister of Defence, of all people.'

It was as though in that moment the whole gathering grew suspicious too. Coya felt the change in mood. Chonas and the other Michinè exchanged subtle glances of query, confusion, muted alarm. The people of the Associations muttered amongst themselves around the walls.

'Bahn,' announced the Lord Protector's voice. 'Open a window there, if you please.'

The chamber was deathly silent as a Red Guard lieutenant stepped out from the general's entourage. The officer crossed the room to the nearest high window on the southern side, where he paused and looked about him a little uncertainly, then fetched a chair and brought it back to stand upon. He strained to tug open the window's latch.

A stiff gust blew in against all their faces, bearing with it a few shots of hail that scattered across the floor like chipped diamonds.

It was a coincidence perhaps, or merely the fact they all held their breaths in the same instant of silence, that they heard just then the crash of a wave from far below the building, perched as it was on the heights of the city right on the edge of a sea cliff.

'You wouldn't dare!' erupted Pericules as the general came for him across the floor. The Minister backed away, horrified, and when he ran out of floor he splashed into the knee-deep pool, falling in his robes before struggling to his feet again.

'Help me!' yelled the man as Creed jumped down into the pool and waded after him. But no one moved, only watched on in grim uncertainty.

'Wait, no – *gghrrrrk*!'

Creed had seized him by the throat. Grimacing and blood-stained, he dragged the fellow from the water and marched him across the room straight for the open window. No one tried to stop him. Instead they looked on like a jury of the damned as the general roughly grabbed the smaller man, and with a great heave lifted him up over his head, defying his fifty-odd years.

'*No!*' screeched Pericules.

In a handful of steps, Creed ran at the open window and launched the Minister of Defence clear through it.

'You have our answer, priest,' he told the Mannian envoy, even as the screams fell away behind him.

For his own part the bald-headed envoy drew himself up to his full, considerable height, and stepped towards them. He was sweating profusely now, alarmingly so, like a waterbag stuck with holes. From the side, Coya noticed how unusually plump the fellow's belly was beneath his white robe, as though he carried a cannonball inside him, or was rapidly filling up with gas. How had he not noticed that detail before?

The priest's face seemed to have become a struggle for composure.

'I can't say I'm surprised,' sounded his strained voice as he came nearer, and the man started scratching at the inner wrist of his left arm as though bitten by a flea.

Even as Coya watched on, Marsh stepped close to his side, alert and sensing trouble. The priest was scratching so hard now that bloody welts were forming on his skin.

What's he doing there? Is he mad?

Marsh uttered a low growl, hand reaching for one of the pistols beneath his longcoat.

'Look after that wife of yours,' he remarked as he brushed past Coya in a hurry.

'What's that?' uttered Coya like a fool, even as his bodyguard and lifelong companion charged for the envoy in quick animal bounds across the flagging.

Marsh took a desperate running leap, firing the pistol in his hand at the same time. The priest screamed, tilting his head backwards to release a blast of blue flame from his open throat, another erupting from his belly.

Together he and Marsh tumbled into the pool with flames engulfing them, a roaring fireball spilling across the water even as the priest violently exploded, showering everyone in roiling fire.

CHAPTER NINE

Nico

'Is it them?'

'Hard to say from here.'

'It has to be. You said we'd catch up with them today.'

Nico's father pulled a face within his hood. Cole was crouched down on the side of the road next to him, peering through the freezing blizzard at the wagons circled up ahead, his scarred features whitened with patches of ice.

'I doubt they're the only slavers on the road today,' said his father in misty tatters of breath.

'But it has to be them!'

'You're the one with the miracle vision. You tell me what you see.'

But even Nico's superior eyes were having trouble making much out through the storm. Up ahead the wagons had been circled not far from the ruts of the road, and they were obscured by snowy gusts that ripped at the canvas awnings strung out between them, tearing away the white billows of smoke rising from a fire of wet logs. He glimpsed a figure moving within the circle, too indistinct to make out.

Another gust howled against them, so sharp it cut into Nico's cheekbones. The storm had raged all night and through the better part of the day, until now twilight was falling again and still there was no sign of respite. They had coped as long as they kept on running in the weak sun. But now, hunkered down in stillness, their extremities were starting to grow numb.

'We'll be good for nothing if we stay out in this much longer. We have to do *something*!'

'Easy,' said his father. 'We can't rush this.'

But that was exactly what they needed to do. Time was most definitely not on their side here.

'We need to get closer,' Nico decided, and he rose to his feet with the pack on his back.

'Hold on,' said Cole, but Nico ignored him as he bounded off into the woods

'*Nico!*' hissed his father after him.

*

The moons were rising up there above the storm. Nico couldn't see them, only the glow of their light in thinner breaks of the clouds. It struck him that by the Mercian lunar calendar it was nearly the turning of the old year into the new. Right now he should be snuggled up at home before a roaring fire, anticipating the feast to come with friends and family. Not out here in the raw elements trying to save the life of his mother.

We're coming! he called out in his mind as though she might hear him.

Beneath Nico's hood the curls of his hair swept wildly like the limbs of the trees. He had rounded the slaver camp so he could approach from behind, hopping so fast over the fresh surface of snow that even his father's long-legged stride had only barely kept with him. Now, approaching a low rise to the rear of their camp, he felt his father's sudden grip on his arm yanking him around.

'Hold up, I said!' Cole panted hotly into his face. 'We're not going another step until I know your head's on straight.'

'What do you mean?'

'If we get up there, and we spot your mother amongst the group – I need to know you're not going to do something stupid.'

'What am I, a child?'

'I mean it, Nico,' his father rasped, squeezing his arm hard. 'We have to wait for the right moment, you understand me? No matter what is happening down there, no matter what they might be doing to her, we have to be smart about this if we want to save her, you hear me, boy?'

'Yes, I hear you!'

'Then follow me and do what I do, nothing more.'

Into the worst of the gale Nico tramped behind his father up the slope of snow, his pulse throbbing in his veins. He could see snow lice leaping up wherever Cole's boots broke the surface, dancing with the snowflakes as they tumbled away together in mating pairs. When he glanced down he saw them jumping up from his footfalls too, little white bugs like seeds of rice.

A dream came to mind. An image from the night before provoked by the crisp whiteness of the surface. Nico had stood upon a snowy plain covered in the bodies of slaughtered lambs, thousands of bloody lambs lying dead and torn open, white and red, white and red, as far as he could see.

We're coming! he called out again to his mother as they surged up the hill.

*

They had dogs down there, whoever they were, for a few barks sounded from the circled wagons.

'Damn,' said his father with a scowl, his narrowed eyes snaring flakes of snow.

They lay on the crest of a hill with the storm raging over them like a rushing flood, looking down on the road and the camp and the many shapes huddled around its smoky fire waiting out the blizzard. Someone was playing a reed pipe against the roars of the wind.

'Can you see her?' asked his father, swiping a wayward snow lice from his cheek.

'It's still hard to make anyone out. They have captives, though. They're chained to the wheels facing the fire. Eighteen, nineteen of them.'

'How many guards do you count?'

'About a dozen.'

Cole rubbed the stubble of his chin. 'That's more than I was hoping for.'

'So what do we do?'

'Wait until they're all asleep. See how their sentries are deployed. Make our move then.'

'Wait around in this weather? Can't we take them by surprise?'

'Against a dozen men – have you any idea how long we'd last?'

Laughter rang up from the camp just then. The pipe player struck up another tune, something faster this time. There was movement down there beneath the awnings, a few figures staggering about drunkenly. It looked as though they were dancing.

Nico's voice cut through the turbulent air like a knife: 'I think I see her.'

'Where?'

'The woman they're dancing with. She has red hair.'

'You're certain?'

He was squinting hard to make out the figures nearest the fire, staggering together to the rough music of the pipe. Even through the storm he could see the flash of the woman's crimson hair, pressed between two jeering men.

'Bastards are playing with her,' Nico growled.

'Easy,' said his father.

They were handling her roughly, squeezing and slapping her.

'We need to do something. We can't just lie here and watch.'

'What did I just say?'

'I know, but—'

The woman shrieked and tried to get clear of the men. They were both shoving her back and forth between them and grabbing at her hair, but a third man was rising now with a coiled whip in his hand, hollering to take their hands off her, that she was no good to them broken.

'Trust your mother to cause a damned argument.'

'You're all right with this?' Nico spat. 'Looking on and doing nothing?'

'No. That's why we're going back down into the trees and waiting for nightfall.'

'You don't give a damn what happens to her, do you? You never did.'

The sudden pain in his arm was so fierce it took him a moment to realize it was his father's fingers gripping it like a vice.

'You're talking about the mother of my son,' Cole said with his voice shaking, and it was like the night in which he had deserted them all over again, the rage in his eyes, the unexpected violence.

'Let go of my arm.'

'Are you going to do as I tell you?'

'*Let go of my arm!*'

Down below, one of the men knocked his mother to the ground with a savage slap of his hand. A whip cracked out like a gunshot.

Nico broke his father's grip. For an instant they both glared at each other, locked in conflict, and then Nico was surging up and over the crest of the hill before Cole could gain another hold on him.

'Hello, the camp!' Nico shouted down at them, and the men stopped what they were doing to look up at his staggering approach through the drifts of snow. Other guards rose into view. Dogs darted out from between the wheels to growl at him in warning.

Sweat was beading Nico's forehead by the time he approached the circle of wagons. He was on the verge of trembling. Still his anger spurred him onwards.

'I'm lost in this storm,' he declared, trying his best imitation of a Q'osian accent. 'Have you shelter and some food?'

Cloaked and armoured men stood in his way, cautiously watching his approach and the hill behind him. Nico hoped they could not see his fear through the flurries of snow.

'Let him through, let him through,' came a voice from within, and the men pulled back the barking dogs by their collars and opened a path for him.

He fought against an urge to look back up the slope. Stepped between two wagons into the sheltered circle within, finding his fears replaced by something else instead: a roaring sense of his own audacity.

Under the flapping awnings more guards stood around the fire, coolly watching him. They all bore the pale skin of northerners, save for a darker fellow in a fur coat, plump and bearded, coiling a whip in his hands while he appraised Nico with poorly concealed mirth.

Nico looked towards his mother, lying sprawled on the ground now, holding her bruised and tear-streaked face.

Yet it wasn't her.

The woman was a stranger to him. Her hair wasn't even red, more a light bronze that was simply catching the reflections of the firelight.

With his heart sinking he glanced around at the rest of the captives tied to the wheels, not seeing his mother amongst them.

'Listen,' he said to the men, holding up his palms. 'If it's a bother, I'll be on my way again. I didn't mean to trouble you.'

'Nonsense, nonsense,' cooed the swarthy fellow, hooking the coiled whip to his belt as he pranced towards him. 'Shelter and food you shall have, my lad.' He moved with surprising lightness for his size, a large man busily working with small feet. He stopped to throw back Nico's hood for a better look at him, and gasped with delight at what he saw, pursing his hands together against the thatch of his beard.

'Wonderful,' he sighed, and gave the merest of nods.

Nico was turning when something cracked him smartly on the head. He went down hard, rolling onto his side, feeling the awful cold reality of it all suddenly rushing through him like nausea as his bravery fled him.

He blinked up at the fat bearded face leering down with wicked eyes and gold-capped teeth. Turned his head to see the captive women staring across at him through the legs of the dogs, while darkness tried to take away the remaining light.

'You'll make a fine addition to our collection, my boy,' crooned a voice just above his head, and for a horrible instant Nico couldn't tell if it was one of the camp dogs slobbering over his bleeding scalp, or the fat slaver instead. 'A fine addition indeed!'

CHAPTER TEN

Coya

'Try the garlic sashwoon if you haven't yet,' suggested General Creed, Lord Protector of Khos. 'Melts in the mouth like butter.'

'Sashwoon, General, in the midst of a siege?' replied the Dreamer Shard in surprise. 'I'd almost forgotten how much you Khosians love having meat with every meal. Even if it is more likely to be rat.'

'Please,' said Creed. 'Call me Marsalas. And maybe we should keep a lid on the rat talk, at least while people are trying to eat?'

'Why? I bet every plate of meat around us is rat.'

'Because Shawnee here isn't just a fine waitress but the daughter of the proprietor, Olaf. And Olaf's a mean old bastard when it comes to his cooking.'

'Well I see she hasn't denied it yet.'

Shawnee stood there waiting to take their orders on the flat roof-top of the restaurant. 'We have some dog on the menu too, if rat isn't to your liking.'

The Dreamer Shard sighed. 'I'll have some spiced root stew, thank you.'

'Coya?'

From across a gulf of space a heavy voice reached out to him, drawing him from his thoughts. Coya pinched his lips together, turning away from the view of the harbour to face his dinner companions for this evening.

'Yes?' croaked his voice.

'What will you have, man?'

General Creed was staring at him across the linen dining cloth, which flapped at the corners in the breeze like everything else on this windy rooftop. Coya blinked, taking a moment to figure out what he was being asked here, and why they all seemed to be staring at him, and then he saw the wooden menu being displayed in Shawnee's hands, where tonight's meagre specials were chalked on a square of slate.

'Oh, the usual, Shawnee,' Coya said with a flicker of a glance towards the waitress, his appetite still gone. 'Peling soup, but no rice balls this time.'

The waitress smiled. She seemed happy to see him here once more. Shawnee was looking older these days, her pretty features grown lean and tough over the long years of the siege. He had known her for all the time he had been coming here to The Commons on his occasional visits to Bar-Khos, this fine establishment of Minosian cuisine on the edge of the city's western harbour. Run by Shawnee's always-bickering Minosian parents, it was a welcome reminder of home and his own wife's cooking.

'Marsh isn't dining with you this evening?' Shawnee asked him in a wistful tone.

Coya cleared his throat, feeling the awkward silence of the others around the table. By his side, where his bodyguard would normally have been sitting, stood an empty chair instead.

'No, Shawnee. Not tonight.'

She was sweet on the man, Coya recalled. Indeed, only a few nights ago, sitting at this very table, Marsh had talked of sleeping with Shawnee in the same way that Marsh spoke of all his other sexual conquests, in an unrelenting patter that would not be stopped until he was finished.

'Oh,' she said, slowly raising a hand to her throat in realization.

'And some wine,' mumbled a voice from his other side.

It was the Lord Protector's field aide, Bahn Calvone, sitting with a cigarillo burning from his fingertips, looking at no one. 'Some black wine.'

'Yes. Of course.' The woman hesitated for a moment, and then she hurried away with her head down.

Perhaps Coya should have suggested a different establishment for their meal tonight. Yet with the loss of Marsh, he had needed to be somewhere homely and familiar.

They were seated on the flat rooftop of The Commons since the main dining room below was packed beyond capacity, and both Coya and Creed had refused all offers of special treatment; indeed, the general appeared desperate just to be treated like everyone else tonight, for all that the guns could be heard pounding away at the opposite end of the city, firing at the Mannian forces still preparing for their first assaults. It wasn't as cold up here as it should be either. Heat rose from the heating tubes running throughout the clay roof, fed by warmed air from the building's hearth fires below. Around the edges, a waist-high parapet and rows of potted vinebrush helped to baffle the winds coming from the north. With the lines of smoking oilstones strung overhead, emitting a soft golden light as they burned from within, it was cosy enough.

Tonight marked the first night of Kamasat, the four-day-long festa leading up to the end of the old year and the beginning of the new. A night when it was custom to have a meal with old friends. All across the southern districts of the city, the streets and rooftops were alive with people braving the elements; lights and chatter and fires lit for warmth. The Bar-Khosians were not a people to let a ten-year-long siege dampen their festas, never mind a bitter winter.

'You all right?'

It was Shard, leaning closer in her chair.

In the packed space of the rooftop, the Dreamer cut a striking figure tonight, dressed in a one-piece leather suit with black and white pica feathers sprouting from the high collar of her open coat. A silver mask covered one side of her dark, Contrarè features.

His old friend Shard looked weary to the bone this evening. Since arriving with him in the besieged city she had been carrying some kind of sandworm in her guts. Some creature from the Alhazii deep desert, famed for its mind-altering bile, which Shard had hoped would temporarily heighten her powers in her duel against her arch rival – and ex-lover – Tabor Seech, a Dreamer working for the Empire. But the sandworm's secretions had nearly poisoned her to death, and following the defeat of the enemy Dreamer, Shard had been quick to drink down a concoction of her own devising, some smoking demon's brew – or so Coya liked to imagine it – which not only killed off the worm in her guts, but had almost finished her too.

Now she was a shadow of her former self, walking like Coya with the aid of a stick and with a long period of recovery most likely still before her. A Dreamer unable to perform any of her miracles when they needed them the most; when he needed this damned crossbow bolt out of his head.

'I'm fine,' Coya told her.

'Any word on a new bodyguard?' Creed asked with a glance to the stairs, where the temporary guards he'd assigned to Coya were waiting below.

'I'm told they're sending a Volunteer from the local garrison for now. They say she's one of their best.'

'*Hmpf.* You should have chosen a Khosian if you wanted the best.'

Creed cut a striking figure too in the tabled space of the rooftop, even with his great bulk dressed down in casual wools and his long hair tied back in a knot. From their meals the other patrons kept glancing around in fascination, watching the table from the corner of their eyes and this extraordinary gathering of glamour.

Mostly though, people were watching the sky over their heads; the very same ceiling of clouds that Coya and his companions were so earnestly trying to ignore. But another series of booms sounded overhead and they all craned to look – just like everyone else on the roof – at the lightshow in the air.

Creed had said it was an innovation of the Mannians, a tactic of demoralization only recently tested against the people of Lagos before their destruction. Some kind of moving imagery, projected from the brightest lights imaginable – War Wicks, the general said they were called – and cast against whatever haze was in the air. An illusion then, though it looked real enough up there, resembling nothing less than a giant ghostly form hanging in the smoky pall above the city; a shape that seemed to coalesce now and then so that it could be seen more clearly for what it was – a winged demon soaring high over the huddled rooftops.

One of the city's skyships was still trying to circle the beast, firing guns whenever it flew close enough. Spooked like everyone else who laid eyes on it, they seemed to be ignoring the signal-lights from the Ministry of War that flashed at them to cease fire.

'It's an effective show, I'll give them that,' remarked Coya, provoked from his glum silence.

Creed grunted. 'It's an annoyance, nothing more. They're trying to soften us up before they start their ground assaults against the

wall. They think this kind of nonsense will have us quaking in our
boots like children.'

'You see that?' said Shard. 'They're using triangulation. You can
just about make out the three beams of light converging.'

Sure enough, through the hazy night air Coya could see a trio of
beams spearing up from three differing locations in the north.
Where they met was where the beast took form.

'They call the whole thing a Sky Scribus,' said Creed, and he
looked to Shard again with obvious fascination. The more time he
spent with this young Contrarè friend of Coya's, the more he seemed
attracted to her. 'You're certain you can't do anything to stop it?'

'Marsalas, I can barely pull my clothes on right now without
help.'

The general pursed his lips as though to hold back his next
words.

Beside him, his field aide blew out a cloud of smoke and lifted his
head skywards at last. Lieutenant Bahn appeared even more
exhausted than Shard in appearance. In fact he looked as though he
hadn't slept in a month, his eyes raw wounds in the slack facade of
his expression.

Coya had been told about this lieutenant, so favoured by the
Lord Protector, who had turned up unexpectedly after being missing
in action. How Bahn had been captured after the battle of Chey-Wes
and imprisoned for some time by the enemy, until somehow he and
others had managed to escape.

The man had been debriefed by Khosian Intelligence and cleared
to return to his role as the general's aide, at Creed's own insistence
– a most sensitive position if ever there was one. Yet there was something strange in the way he refused to hold anyone's gaze tonight.
The way he seemed lost in some inner turmoil. If Marsh had been
here right now, Coya would have exchanged a meaningful, possibly
paranoid glance with his bodyguard concerning the lieutenant's
condition.

Just then Bahn saw that he was being watched and sputtered out
a lungful of smoke, coughing. He wiped his mouth then tossed the
remains of the cigarillo into an ashpot on the table. His hand was
shaking.

There were rumours, Coya knew, of what the Mannian priests could do to a person's mind, given enough torture and drugs.

I should have this fellow looked into myself. Just for peace of mind.

'Bahn,' declared the general. 'Since when did you smoke, man?'

'I don't,' answered the lieutenant, even as he took another cigarillo from a box and poked it between his lips. 'Just need a little something to keep me alert right now.'

'Still not sleeping right?'

The man shrugged, downplaying his weariness. His hands were still trembling when he tried to spark a match. He looked chilled in the thin clothes he was wearing, as though he had dressed without giving any mind to the season at all – save for a single notion on his way out the door, a scarf wrapped around his neck. Observing his struggle to light the match, Shard leaned across the table with her thumb extended, and suddenly a flame appeared from the end of it, tiny and trembling.

Bahn squinted, as though not quite sure if it was really there or not, then leaned in so that his clammy features were lit from below by the flame and the flickering table candle in its glass jar.

'Neat trick,' he muttered around a mouthful of smoke.

'I thought you could hardly pull your clothes on without help?' barked Creed, his eyes twinkling, the old dog.

'This?' said Shard, blowing out her thumb. 'This is just showing off. I can do this in my sleep.'

More booms rumbled over their heads, close enough now that glasses rattled on the tables. A squadron of skyships were sweeping after the giant figure as it soared above the city beating its wings hard. It grew fainter the further south it came towards them, the trio of light-beams tracking its course all the while, until it turned and circled back towards the north.

It was impossible to fully enjoy a meal when your cutlery was clinking to the sounds of such nearby action. Yet here they were, waiting to dine like the patrons already doing so around them, citizens long inured to living life under fire. Once more the talk resumed around the tables. Shawnee reappeared at the steps with a platter of wine bottles and brought them over. She smiled at Coya again, but he could see that she had been crying.

Look after that wife of yours.

The words rang in Coya's head like a never-ending echo. The last words Marsh had spoken before sacrificing his life for him – thinking of Coya's wife, of all people.

How many times had Marsh joked about Rechelle being the only woman he would ever love, the wife of the very man he had sworn to protect from harm? Coya had always wondered how much truth lay behind his companion's humour. How much of it had to do with the man's inability to ever settle down with a woman, interested only in brief and meaningless liaisons.

'Wine?' asked Creed, enjoying the opportunity to serve others for once.

'Thank you, Marsalas,' answered Coya, and his friend's easy manner was enough to startle him, to stir some emotion into his dry blinking eyes.

Creed was the most relaxed of them all tonight. A Lord Protector buoyed by their recent victories of Chey-Wes and now against the Mannian General Mokabi and his forces in the south. Confident too that they could hold off the newly arrived Imperial Expeditionary Force as long as they stood firm. He was a welcome bastion in what seemed to Coya, for all the general's own assurances, like a gathering storm.

'To the fallen,' Creed toasted, then downed his glass in one swallow and instantly refilled it; perhaps he was not so unshaken after all.

It was all business and war tonight, hardly a celebration with friends. Not that Coya would have expected anything else under the circumstances. Earlier that day they had attended the daily service held for the dead at the Temple of the Lonely Lights, in which Marsh and those others killed in the blast had been added to the latest list of the fallen, their names sung out in remembrance.

In the burnt wreckage of the Council Hall, nothing had been found of Marsh that was recognizable as his own, nothing left to bury or cremate. His lifelong guard and companion had been vaporized on the spot.

Just gone. Vanished without a trace like he'd never existed at all.

'Tell me,' asked Coya, swallowing to clear his throat. 'Have they found any more survivors?'

'Too few,' grumbled Creed. 'We were lucky your man put him in the water when he did. I doubt any of us would have made it out alive if he hadn't.'

In his mind Coya glimpsed it again, the Council Hall and the Pool of Enlightenment . . . Marsh and the envoy engulfed in water and flames while a carpet of fire spilled out across the floor towards their legs; heat roaring at him like a living thing.

'It was hardly luck, Marsalas,' he croaked.

'No. Your man was fast as lightning. He will be honoured for his sacrifice, I assure you. If not for him, most of the Council would have been killed.'

'We should have seen it coming,' said Shard, possibly trying to steer the conversation away. 'Liquid incendiaries carried in the belly, ignited by an accelerant on his nails. The kind of thing we should be expecting by now.'

Her words only rumpled Creed's expression.

'There's no way to protect against everything,' he said with a dark eye to the winged demon in the sky. 'Not when they keep inventing new ways to kill and torment us.'

'That's why we need to attack.'

They all turned to Bahn in surprise that he had spoken so firmly. His gaze lowered, the ragged lieutenant took another draw from his cigarillo.

'You said it yourself, they're just waiting for the ground to firm up out there before they attack. Well it hasn't rained in days. The plain's draining out at last. We should open the northern gates and attack them instead with everything we can, finish them once and for all. Otherwise we're just waiting for our fates to be decided for us.'

General Creed rocked back in surprise. 'You're the last one I thought would suggest taking the fight to them. Normally you wail on me to use caution in these matters.'

'Wail on you, General?' Bahn asked without a trace of humour, inclining his head as though insulted by the remark.

Creed's expression stiffened. Seeing it, Bahn blinked as though coming back to himself. 'It strikes me as the very thing we need to do now. Attack them with all our fury.'

'Clear your head, man,' snapped General Creed. 'You sound like the Michinè on the hill, all wrapped up in appearances. Like the appearance that we hold the lesser hand here. Yet we are the ones hunkered down in a walled city with all the shelter and supplies we need to see us through winter, and enough fighters to hold off the enemy. For once, all we need to do is wait and we will prevail.'

'Still. What if they have more tricks up their sleeves just waiting to throw in our midst?'

'Tricks?'

'General, they would hardly be outside the wall if they did not have confidence they could take the city. That implies factors that we are unaware of. If we attack now, we take the initiative from them.'

His words were enough to silence them all. Coya watched on with interest. Creed was an aggressive general by nature. He had proven as much at Chey-Wes, when he had driven the Khosian wedge through the imperial forces even though they were vastly outnumbered. Now his lieutenant was presenting him with a reason to attack once again.

'Fine wine,' Coya remarked with a smack of his lips, hoping to change the subject, and indeed it was enough to draw Creed back to him. 'I wanted to ask you about something else, Marsalas, before our food arrives.'

Creed refilled their glasses once more, buying some time to gather his thoughts.

'Go on.'

'I understand your intelligence people have a Diplomat in captivity?'

'Yes?'

'I would like to take him off your hands, if at all possible.'

'I'm told he's already been interrogated thoroughly, Coya.'

'Still. I want him.'

Creed shrugged, barely interested in the matter. 'Then I'll see what I can do.'

A gust blew in to play with the candles on all the tabletops. Diners held hats to their heads or steadied flapping napkins. A bell was ringing down in the harbour, another ship heaving off into the night and the wind-lashed sea, and from their table at the very edge of the rooftop they all stared down at the hectic scene.

Coya took in the forest of ships' masts within the shelter of the harbour's walls, and the two forts at each end where bursts of anti-skyship shells were arching out over the black water, trailing reflections below. It was amazing that ships were heading out even now, risking attacks from the imperial Birds-of-War swooping down on them further out to sea, where indeed in the inky blackness a hulk was burning like a candle.

Siege or not, trade with the other Mercian islands needed to be maintained if Khos was to survive. Down at the dock a series of ships were unloading in a frenzy of work crews and carts. A trio of low-prowed longships caught Coya's eye, sleek vessels of the old fashion bearing flags from the nearby island of Coraxa. While the crews shipped their oars, armed figures clambered up gangplanks onto the dockside to form themselves into a ragged formation of fighters bristling with weapons. Red Guards ran towards them in alarm.

'Look,' rasped Creed, rising from his chair, and a number of patrons turned to watch him striding to the parapet. '*Redeemers!*'

'Ah,' nodded Coya. 'I was wondering when they might make an appearance in the city.'

Shard was craning around him for a better look. 'Who?' she asked, for she was the only one here not native to the Free Ports.

'Redeemers,' Coya answered. 'From Coraxa. They wander the hills there, having renounced everything for the chance at redeeming themselves. Helping out villages from bandits. Patrolling the roads for highwaymen. Many of them are old Volunteers with rusty blades and guilty consciences.'

'Redeem themselves from what?'

'What does anyone wish to atone for?' said Creed. 'Things they can no longer live with.'

'Seems a strange way to make things right. They don't heal people, or feed the hungry?'

'Coraxa has those too,' grumbled Creed, and his big hands clenched the painted edge of the roof's parapet. 'These are the fighting kind, though. The kind we would normally need most of all.'

'Normally?'

The Lord Protector was unhappy about something. Coya could see his jaw muscles bunching hard. Down on the dock the formation of figures had spoken with the Guards, and they were marching now, several hundred of them, the foremost ones already leading the way into the street directly below the restaurant.

'Redeemers live to give up their lives in the good fight,' said Creed, raising his voice above the crash of their boots and their throaty shouts. 'They're naturally drawn to lost causes.'

In the cobbled street below, citizens were darting out of the way as the formation stamped along it. Coya glimpsed spears and staffs and all manner of armours, though mostly the men and women seemed clad only in goatskins and other furs, their hair sprouting wild and long. Some even seemed entirely naked, painted blue or black from head to toe, oblivious to the cold.

Creed inclined his head so the corner of his eye glinted just behind the sheen of his hair. He glanced momentarily at his lieutenant, then spoke to Shard. 'They come here now because they are under the mistaken impression that Bar-Khos is doomed.'

CHAPTER ELEVEN

Diplomat

From a distance it looked like any ordinary shipping crate of wood: a stout box four feet long in each dimension, squatting on the back of a moving wagon.

Closer though, it was clear the box was made from fire-hardened tiq, strong as steel, and reinforced with multiple bands of iron. Small holes had been drilled along its top as though to allow for ventilation. On one side, a small bolted hatch was home to an even smaller bolted hatch only large enough to slip through a skin of water, or morsels of food.

Whatever creature lurked inside the box remained silent as the wagon trundled its way into a cobbled yard, overshadowed by one of the city's looming seawalls where gulls were flecks of white shrieking in the updraughts. With a shout, the driver drew the wagon mules to a stop before a large brick building that stretched all the way back to a canal of briny seawater, marking the southernmost limits of the city in the district of All Fools.

Four Specials in their dark leathers climbed down from the back of the wagon. Two drew their blades. Two more hefted long poles with loops on their ends. A fifth figure in civilian clothing clambered down from the front seat, cloaked and sporting a thick beard.

Before them, the building of the inkworks was so large that only one ruined half of it was occupied by the wreck of the small imperial skyship poking from its collapsed roof. Shutters hung aslant and broken over the many remaining high windows. At one of its front entrances, a loading bay was open to the tangles of daylight inside, and a motley group of guards stepped out to greet the new arrivals and their dangerous cargo. The guards carried spears and a few loaded crossbows. Without delay they surrounded the wagon while the Specials fanned out around its rear.

An expectant hush fell across the scene, broken only by the hobnailed footfalls of the bearded fellow approaching the crate. A jagged knife appeared in his hand. The man threw the bolts and tugged open the larger hatch then stepped back quickly, wrinkling his nose at the hot stench wafting from its black interior.

'Out!' he snapped at the reeking animal squatting in the fetid darkness within, prompting it to shift around in its chains, with a dirty five-fingered hand warding off the sudden intrusion of light.

Between the fingers, a glint of a blue eye took the measure of the man.

'Easy,' advised the fellow. 'No sudden moves now. These men would like nothing better than to poke you with their steel if you give them the chance to.'

Shackles rattled – the prisoner slowly sliding forwards out of the box. A pair of grimy naked feet emerged, the skin of the ankles rubbed raw by steel cuffs. Then came legs, bushy genitals, a torso, and finally the bruised blood-caked face of a young man.

His expression was guarded as he lowered his feet to the ground as if he was lowering them into steaming water. Tears streamed from the young man's eyes at the sting of daylight, yet still he craned his neck to look up at the cloud-dappled sky, the first sky he had seen in an endless time.

But then the loops were dropped around his neck and the poles yanked to tighten them, and the prisoner winced, brought back to earth.

'Welcome to your new home, *Diplomat*,' spat the bearded man from a safe distance of six feet.

Yoked in place there, the prisoner's icy eyes took in the half-ruined building, then stared once more at the circle of men standing warily around him, shifting their feet uneasily.

'*Yah!*' he barked with a sudden jerk of his chains, and grinned at their involuntary flinches.

*

'Ah,' declared a figure stepping out to meet him, stooped over a walking cane like an old man, for all that he looked barely older than Ché. 'You made it then. Can you walk?'

Behind him the wagon and its men clattered away. Someone draped a cloak over Ché's naked form and he grasped it gratefully about his body, ignoring the cold bites of the shackles against his chilblained skin.

It was so long since he had been able to stand fully without banging his head on the ceiling of his cell – that tiny pitch-black cell where Khosian Intelligence had been holding him for all this time; an airless black hole in which he thought he would lose his mind. Gasping from cold and exertion, he stood there swaying as he eyed the bent form before him, seeing the man's head bandaged under a cap from which sprouted locks of blond hair, framing lively eyes that danced through their own shadows of pain.

'Coya Zeziké,' Ché said in surprise with his rasping file of a voice.

'You recognize me! I must say that is a little unnerving, coming from a Mannian Diplomat.'

If only he knew of the numerous files held on him in imperial Q'os, this famous Delegate of the League and descendant of their philosopher-prophet. Ché had seen the man's sketched likeness in the books of the Section back in the Empire's capital, marked as one of their Most Desirable targets in all the Midèrēs.

Yet where was Marsh, his bodyguard, the seemingly invincible lifelong protector of Zeziké, the man with eyes in the back of his head, marked as an Extreme Hazard in the books, due to all the Diplomats he'd slain in defence of his charge?

'Your bodyguard, Marsh,' Ché said, showing off now. 'I don't see him.'

Coya pursed his lips and lowered his head, saying nothing.

Dead then. Not so invincible after all.

A feral grin spread across the Diplomat's lips.

'Diplomat Ché,' clipped Coya in return, straightening himself while a breeze cleared the hair from his pinched expression. 'Caught in Juno's Ferry after the evacuation of Tume, though you claim to have deserted your own side. You also claim to be willing to help the democras in return for your release. Well, you've been released into my charge. Now, do I have your word you will cause no harm here, nor try to escape?'

His word? What kind of naive fool was he dealing with here?

'Remove these chains first. Then we can talk.'

'For now, I think, we'll keep them on you. If you will talk, you must do so with their burden.'

The Diplomat lifted his chin to the wind and took in the large building he stood before and the nearby seawall looming over the scene.

'What is it you want of me?'

'For now, information only.'

'Concerning what? I already told them everything I know.'

'Hardly everything. You are an enemy assassin, working for the Section in Q'os, who has disclosed only what he has needed to disclose under duress. I would like to know more than what you have already given to Khosian Intelligence.'

It was true Ché had held some information back, even as his captors had tormented him for more. But his reason had nothing to do with any lingering sense of loyalty to the Empire, and everything to do with self-preservation. Ché had feared they would execute him the moment they thought he was of no further use.

'If I do, you can guarantee my life?'

'Of course. And in return, you will give your word that you will not try to escape from here.'

Ché took in the armed guards around him in their sweeping cloaks, and their companions watching from the flat rooftop above with longrifles in hand, and more guards stationed at the front gate of the property.

'You have my word then.'

'Good,' said Coya, as though that was all it took to satisfy him. He turned towards the building's entrance, taking an awkward step with his cane. 'Come, it's cold out here. There are some friends of yours waiting inside.'

'Cripple, I have no friends.'

Coya winced, then glanced over his shoulder.

'Well, I can certainly see why.'

*

According to the sign above the front entrance, the building was some kind of inkworks.

It was the size of a firing range within: a large, high-ceilinged space of stone columns rich with dust and daylight. Around the vast space echoed the footfalls and voices of men training over on the far side, where the building lay partially in ruins, and was filled almost entirely by the hulking body of the imperial skyship that had crashed through the floor above and the ground floor they stood upon, so that the nose of the skyship was buried in the ground, surrounded by rubble and the remains of stone pans stained a dark blue.

Tracks of inky footprints spiralled across the floor, leading Ché's gaze to the figures practising with their weapons. One by one they stopped what they were doing, and turned to stare at him through the dusky light.

Ché tensed where he stood in his manacles and leg irons, suddenly spotting the familiar faces amongst the men on the far side. Without noticing, he began to scratch at one of the scaly rashes on his arm in sudden, guilty nervousness.

Rōshun. People he had once called his own.

Wild was there amongst them, and young Florés and Aléas, and Fanazda too with his dark sleeked hair and wicked eyes, playing with a dagger in his hand and glaring at Ché as coolly as all the others.

Ché cast a weary sigh, turning to Coya Zeziké in accusation. But the fool only smiled and shrugged a shoulder, as though it was nothing at all.

'When I read your debriefing I was surprised to find you were once a Rōshun apprentice, before you became a Diplomat.'

'Sure, as an imperial infiltrator, brainwashed into thinking I was someone else.'

'Yes, I read that too. It's hard to believe your people are capable of such things.'

'Look, you're not listening to me. I betrayed these people, you understand? I betrayed the location of their order to my handlers and they were nearly wiped out because of it. They must have an inkling of that, I'm sure.'

'Oh, they know, all right. But they say that you saved their Seer on the night of the attack. And Ash, too, claimed to have been saved by you here in Khos. They are willing to let you live if it means you can help us with information. Their leader, Wild, has assured me of your safety.'

'Wild? Wild will be the first one in line. What am I doing here, man?'

'Hush, Diplomat. I told you why you are here. A little cooperation on your part, and you might even earn your freedom.'

A gust of wind blew through the entrance and the dusty air of the space. It tugged on the sheets of silk that covered many of the missing sections of the walls, no doubt cut from the gas envelope of the wrecked skyship itself. The silk sheets were stretched thin enough that they bled with daylight, against which the Rōshun were gathered as dark silhouettes, skilled assassins every one of them, even the very youngest.

Perhaps it was only fitting to have it end at the hands of the Rōshun. At least there was a symmetry to that, a sense of form.

They'll knife me in my sleep, Ché thought with grim certainty. And even as the thought occurred to him Fanazda met his gaze, and the dark thin man slowly drew a finger across his throat.

CHAPTER TWELVE

Dreamer

All Fools, they called this southernmost district of Bar-Khos. A sprawl of streets and alleyways choking the throat of the Lansway, notorious for a decade now as being the closest district to the siege front.

Along its southern limits, All Fools was bordered by a brackish canal that cut across the laq-wide bridge of land from coast to coast. The canal separated the city from the walls of the Shield beyond – and beyond them what remained of the Imperial Fourth Army, chipping away at the city defences for ten long years. Enemy shells were known to occasionally make it as far as the district. As a result, people only lived there if they absolutely had to. Indeed, much damage had been wreaked there during the sky raids of the recently defeated imperial offensive. All across the district stood burnt-out ruins as testament to the infernos that had raged through the streets.

Yet now, like a shift in magnetic polarity, the siege front had entirely reversed itself, with the enemy offensive shifting to the north. Ironically, All Fools had become one of the safest districts in the city. From here most of a city and a good high wall stood in the way of the Imperial Expeditionary Force's big guns.

The Dreamer Shard was reminding herself of this crucial fact as she lounged on a mattress, listening to the faint rumbles of war emanating from the opposite end of the city.

Shard was safe here on the dusty upper floor of the half-ruined inkworks, this expansive brick building located right next to the canal. Safe enough to relax for a single morning, to take her mind off all that concerned her and all that still needed doing.

If only Blame would stop acting like a lunatic long enough to climb into her bed.

Dressed in a thin silk slip, Shard was propped against a bundle of pillows with a heavy quilt covering her body, trying to stay warm in the chilly air despite the fire burning fitfully in a brazier, pulled as close to the bed as she dared. Flames gnawed on logs the thickness of her arms, crackling with heat and light. Beyond the dancing circle of firelight lay the ruined upper floor of the building, cast into darkness by the many canvas tarps covering the windows; a darkened expanse of broken stone and empty shelving, echoing with the sound of a single pair of running feet coming closer.

Out of the gloom swept a naked figure, huffing and puffing as he jogged past her bed and the inviting heat of the brazier. The young man wore only a scarf around his neck and a cap on his head, and a pair of thin sandals that slap-slapped against the stone as he went by.

'You'll catch your death like that,' she called after her rook assistant. 'Why don't you put your coat on, at least!'

Blame's sprightly voice bounded back to her through the shadows.

'Because you told me not to, remember?'

'I meant so you could get back into bed with me. Not suffer from exposure and die.'

'I'm fine, as long as I keep running.'

They'd been up all night again working in the Black Dream, that otherworldly medium of the farcrys; both trying to break through the imperial communications blockade covering the city. Lethal work. Blame had almost died when he'd become snared in an enemy feedback trap. Then Shard had nearly been fried in an ambush. With dawn rising and still no progress made, they had dropped out of the Black Dream with their tensions too high to contemplate sleeping, and so instead had decided to wind down in their own particular fashion.

Blame had been smoking those laced hazii sticks he liked, good strong hazii weed infused with rush oil. Relaxing yet energizing at the same time, the perfect combination for a young rook caught in the middle of a war.

Off he went, skirting the edges of the rubble that filled much of what remained of the floor, Just looking at his naked backside vanishing into the darkness made her shiver, and Shard pulled the quilt tighter about her neck, wishing she had the strength to fashion a glyph in her mind so she could cast some warmth into herself, like she had during much of her recent journey through the Windrush forest with Coya.

Shard had never been much good with the cold. Not even in Sheaf where she had been born and raised, a port city on the southern continent blessed with a mellow climate; not even with the second-skin that was her glimmersuit covering her entire body. The draughty inkworks was hardly helping either, with its broken windows lining the walls covered only by canvas sheets, and the great gaping hole in its roof blocked by more of the same. Though in her corner here, wrapped up well with the brazier's heat reflecting off the two walls, she should have been comfortable enough.

'We should take more time in our lives to run like this,' huffed the dim form of Blame, all energy and inspiration this morning, as though he was conscious that this could be his last day alive. 'We forget when we grow up how exhilarating it is, just to run *free*.'

'Sure,' Shard drawled on her back, taking a draw from a hazii stick she had rolled herself. 'We should run everywhere, everywhere we go, just because it's so much more fun than walking.'

'That's what I'm saying!'

Eyes narrowed, Shard tracked the faint form of her lover along the edge of the room, following him to a huge shape that occupied the far half of the building; a shape that towered high above him, bedraggled with ropes and netting and shreds of torn silk. It was the small imperial Bird-of-War that had crashed into the building, shot down some time during the previous sky raids, spearing at an angle through the roof and both storeys.

Once more Blame stared up at the ruined hulk as he panted past, too shocking a sight to ignore even on his sixth time around. He darted close to the ragged edge where the floor had fallen away, then headed back her way.

The inkworks had hardly been her first choice of quarters in the city. In fact she hadn't chosen this place at all. Coya had been responsible for finding them this space in which to live and do their work in relative safety from the enemy, doubling up with the team of

Rōshun operating from downstairs. She could still hear some of them down there, buoyant after their return from another night mission against the enemy forces to the north. Drinking and letting their hair down, those who had any to let down.

Shard wondered what that dashingly handsome young Rōshun called Aléas was doing right now, the one with the long blond locks and cocky manner. A young man who still refused to acknowledge even the most blatant of Shard's flirtations.

Maybe he doesn't like women with half their faces burned off, came the awful words in her head.

Shard frowned, feeling the white veil against her skin which masked one side of her features. She lifted a hand so she could study it in the dim glow of the fire, and gazed at the second-skin of her glimmersuit shining like water, rainbow colours catching the light.

Maybe he didn't like women covered from head to toe in what looked like a suit of oily water. Though most men seemed attracted to it.

'You still cold?' Blame asked as he panted towards her.

'Freezing. Hypothermic.'

'You should try running on the spot for a while.'

But Shard had a better idea. She slid her stockinged leg free from the quilt so that it stretched across the mattress like an open invitation. 'Better if you came back to bed and warmed me up, don't you think?'

He glanced at her on his way past again, and she tugged the quilt from her chest too, the cold air snapping her nipples into points beneath the thin silk. 'My breasts are so cold I can't even feel them any more. Are my breasts still there, Blame?'

His head was shaking as the gloom engulfed it. Shard followed the slap of his sandals more than the vague suggestion of movement, passing fast below the high windows. His breath was a dry rasp from across the room.

'Can't. I'm thinking.'

'What about?'

'Last year. What I did during Kamasat back at the Academy, when it was nearly Year's End.'

Back when he had been a mere student there, he meant, wintering over at the Academy of Salina as some of them did.

Before she had brought him to this city of death as her only surviving rook.

'We got high and drugged the Chancellor with poppy tea, and
rigged ropes to lift him and his bed out of his bedroom window in
the middle of the night, and all the way up to the top of the obser-
vatory dome.'

'I remember,' she drawled, for she had seen it herself. As resident
Dreamer and expert rook, Shard lived at the Academy all year round
and did not like to ever leave it. 'Even with their hangovers, everyone
turned out to see him up on the dome.'

'You remember how they woke the Chancellor with their calls?
Hah! How he saw where he was and leapt out of his bed?'

Below, a chorus of voices rose up to greet a newcomer coming in
from the night.

'Yes. He nearly slipped to his death, poor fellow.'

Shard jerked as a wail rose from the ground floor below. For the
briefest of instants she thought that one of the enemy's Shades had
made its way into the building, but then she recognized the sounds
of a fiddle striking out to join with voices rising in raucous song.
They were mostly young men down there, many of the Rōshun
merely apprentices by all accounts. It sounded like their Kamasat
party was only just beginning.

Maybe she should try her luck below, see if she couldn't catch
Aléas in a particularly drunken condition while Blame ran off whatever it was he needed to up here.

Shard lay back with a wistful sigh. She was still weak from having
flushed the sandworm from her guts, but her libido was starting to
return to its usual hungry vigour at last. For some reason the flickering firelight was making her think of the Windrush forest, home of
the Longalla, cousins to her own people in the south, the Black
Hands. Shard thought of half-naked Contrarè dancing around a
blazing bonfire; the dazzling gaze of Sky In His Eyes snaring her
own.

Sky In His Eyes . . .

Even now the man lingered in her thoughts, like a promise unful-
filled.

'I'm almost a corpse here,' purred Shard. 'You could do anything you wanted to me and I couldn't stop you, couldn't even lift my little finger to protest.'

Shooting through the circle of light, Blame flashed his handsome sideways grin at her, the same one that had won him this job in the first place. 'Stop it, woman. You're making me hard again. Have you any idea how sore it is to run with your prick whacking about in front of you like a stick?'

'Well, you know I have just the thing for that.'

'You're a succubus. A succubus intent on killing me with her endless needs.'

Yes, she was rather hungry for him right now.

Little wonder though, considering the rising tensions of their situation. Behind them lay a week of running skirmishes in the Black Dream which they had barely survived, always outnumbered and surrounded. And still they were no better off than before. Worse even. For the Imperials continued to block every farcry in Bar-Khos, even the one belonging to the Alhazii Embassy down by the docks, the imperial rooks smothering them with projections of noise so they couldn't be used at all. There was no way for anyone in the city to reach the outside world.

Shard had never seen such a successful blockade before within the Black Dream, that mysterious medium linking every farcry in the world, and allowing communication of thought to be carried between them.

So far casualties were mounting on both sides. Young rooks of the democras, scattered across the Academies of the Free Ports, rallied in their attempts to break through the blockade while the enemy seemed willing to throw everything they had into maintaining it, as though determined to see Bar-Khos cut off in every conceivable way. Already it was the largest battle ever seen within the Black Dream. For the very first time, the young rooks of the Free Ports – who had invented the very craft of *rookery*, of slyly manipulating farcrys using cloned homegrown versions of their own – were finding themselves evenly matched by their Mannian counterparts.

The Empire had finally caught up.

In the inkiness of the Black, you could see them shooting like stars across the firmament, mental projections of rooks dogfighting in their straight lines and rapid zigzags, marking their deaths with startling cascades of light that often crashed against the sphere of the blackout itself – a shell of white noise, hanging around the small cluster of suns that were the city's few working farcrys.

Trapped within, Shard and her rook assistant Blame could only continue their efforts alone. But here inside the blockade they were always heavily outnumbered by enemy rooks who could pass through the shell of white noise at will. Sometimes Shard and Blame fled from dozens of enemy rooks, firing off every defensive and offensive glyph they could at the little sparks of brilliance swarming to cut them off. Their close calls were too many to be remembered now. They hardly seemed worth the slow but steady trickle of casualties they were inflicting on the enemy forces. But every venture into the Black Dream gave them another chance to try their breaching glyphs against the barrier, another chance to break the code that was allowing the imperial rooks to pass through it.

Something had to give, eventually. But for once, Shard was not so certain it would be the enemy.

Yet again she wondered if her ex-lover Tabor Seech, traitor to the Free Ports, and his personally trained stable of mercenary rooks, had a hand in this sudden improvement in the Empire's rooking effectiveness. Seech had been hired by the Mannian General Mokabi, but Mokabi was now dead, his campaign against the walls of the Shield thwarted. And following their recent duel upon the walls, she had thought Tabor Seech himself to be gone.

But maybe she had been wrong.

Are you still alive? Are you still out there, Tabor?

Nothing. No thrum of intuition either way.

Clack clack clack—

She heard a dull tapping sound growing nearer. But only when the stooped form of Coya emerged from a gap in the inner wall did she give it any thought, seeing his cane rapping across the floor.

'Ah, Shard,' Coya declared upon seeing her on the mattress, and quickly Shard pulled the quilt over her breasts and drew her stockinged leg back under its cover.

Coya blinked at what he had just seen, then sniffed at the sight of Blame trotting across the floor in all his nakedness, clearly high as a kite.

Her friend was hardly the type to let such a thing dissuade him.

Clutching his cane, Coya sat himself down on the corner of the mattress nearest to the fire, making himself at home, his only remark a single eyebrow raised a fraction higher than the other.

'Chee?' she asked him, playing along, and propped herself up in the bed with the quilt held over her chest, knowing he was as versed in sarcasm as any other Mercian. 'A pipe? Some hot breakfast to warm your cockles?'

'My cockles are just fine, thank you,' Coya grumbled, flashing another glance towards Blame, who was heading straight towards them.

'Hey,' breathed Blame, flapping past.

'Hey there,' said Coya.

Coya looked back to the flames of the brazier, hands extended to catch their heat, dark shadows under his eyes. He was still grieving for his bodyguard Marsh, she saw, burnt to ashes in the explosion that had ripped through the Bar-Khosian Council Hall.

He showed no sign of the crossbow bolt carried in his skull, save for the bandages covered by the wool hat that he wore, tassels dangling from each side of it like plaits. She had done what she could for him when he had first been wounded in the Windrush. If her strength ever came back to her, and if Coya survived without dropping dead until then, she hoped to do more.

'Is there something I can help you with?'

'Yes,' he said with a slap of the mattress, as though just recalling why he was here. 'That Diplomat I asked for has arrived downstairs. I wondered if you couldn't have a look at him. Check him out as it were, see if he has any schemes lurking in that head of his.'

She should have known. Coya Zeziké, fellow member of the Few, troubleshooter and trouble maker; here to drag in the war on his heels.

There was no hiding from it. Not in this city. Not even if she hid under the quilt until he was gone.

'What are you doing, Shard?'

'I'm hiding under the quilt until you're gone.'

'A bad time is it? Resting here in your comfort while soldiers risk their lives on the wall?'

It always flowed this way with Coya. Always he asked for more.

Shard sighed and popped her head above the quilt. Coya was still staring at the flames, looking glum and lonely. Missing his sick wife as well as Marsh, she supposed. Her annoyance faded. For an instant, Shard wished there was something she could do for him to alleviate his mood. But Coya hated the pity of others even more than their scorn, and so she clamped down on the emotion for fear he might catch a glimpse of it.

'Coya, your Diplomat will just have to wait. I'm stretched thin as it is trying to get our farcrys working again. Not to mention tracking down an enemy farcry we think might be operating in the city.'

'An enemy farcry, here in Bar-Khos?'

'Yes, possibly. We're still trying to zero in.'

Coya chewed over the news unhappily.

'Look,' he said. 'All I'm asking is that you check him out when you next get the chance.'

Clearly surrender here was the only way to get rid of him. 'Fine, soon as I have the time. Now is there anything else?'

He looked up just then, blinking, as he registered the tone of her words, and seemed to remember his manners. With an effort, Coya clambered to his feet, grasping his cane as though it was the helping hand of another.

'That's all,' he said, turning to leave. 'Oh – there is one other thing. I don't suppose you have news on those mythical charts of ours yet?'

The Dreamer bit down on her bubbling impatience. 'I tried some free-dynamic question and answer methods last night, about all I can manage right now. I can say with a fairly high degree of certainty that the charts are somewhere in the city.'

'They are?'

'I believe so.'

'Well, that is good news at least. Now all we have to do is get our hands on them.'

'Hey,' said Blame again.

Coya took a step towards the hole in the wall and the stairwell beyond.

'You all right?' she asked after him.

'Better now, Shard. Goodnight, *Walks With Herself*. Goodnight, *Young Man Yonder*!'

And then he was gone.

Shard snuggled deeper into the warmth of the quilt, calling out even as she did so.

'He's gone,' she told the distant form of Blame. 'Now, for the love of Mercy, will you climb into this bed before my nipples get frost-bitten?'

CHAPTER THIRTEEN

Nico

Nico was on the burning pyre again. Smoke rose to obscure his vision, yet he could tell he was in the imperial arena of Q'os, staked to a bonfire on the sandy floor for all the thousands of spectators to watch from their seating, and the jeering soldiers closer by. He struggled against his chains as flames rose up around his legs, scorching his skin wherever it touched, though no matter how hard Nico fought to be free he knew there would be no escape from this. These people would not be sated until they watched him die in fiery torment.

Once more the madness of those moments seized him like a deranged and foreign spirit. As the flames rose ever higher around him Nico gibbered in terror, crying out aloud from agony and despair, seeking mercy from the Great Dreamer.

Help me now! he screamed.

Please, someone, help me!

'Hey, take it easy. Don't move.'

Nico blinked against the blinding light of day, rolling his head back to take in the grimy faces staring back at him. He was rocking on a hard wooden bench at the back of a moving wagon, facing women apparently manacled and chained together, huddling beneath blankets in their ragged clothing.

'You were shouting out in your sleep.'

'What – where am I?' he blurted, and he struggled to his feet only to find them bound together. With a curse he pitched over and fell hard.

He was drooling, he realized, as he lay there on the floor of the wagon gathering his thoughts. When he tried to wipe his mouth dry he found his hands bound together too, by thongs of leather, and then it all came rushing back to him, the slavers in their camp and how he had walked in thinking to save his mother, only to become another captive himself.

Sweet Mercy, what a fool he had been.

'I told you not to move,' said the woman's voice again. 'You might have a concussion, with that lump on your skull.'

'With my thick head I doubt it,' Nico grunted, shifting over onto his back. Above all the jostling knees a pretty girl was frowning down at him, blonde haired and fine featured, her cheeks pronounced like ripening apples.

'Hey,' Nico gasped up to her.

Her eyes glittered within two purple bruises. She offered him a hand and with a firm grasp helped him back onto the bench beside her.

He winced, gripping his head. This headache would surely be one to remember. Tentatively he probed at his scalp until he came to the lump crusted in blood.

'That was reckless of you, walking into the camp like that on your own. These people look on others as prey.'

Nico squinted at the girl pressed against him, her chains rattling and clinking as their shoulders brushed together, their legs. Hazel eyes dazzled him, flecked with gold in the sunlight, and it took an effort of will to look past her to the front of the wagon, where the driver swayed back and forth, and beyond him to another wagon on the road ahead, where a woman's bronze hair shone in the daylight.

His mother wasn't here. He could only assume she was further ahead on the road with another slaver party.

'I thought my mother was amongst you,' he said in a hush.

'Trying to save his mother, do you hear that?' the girl declared to those closest to her, and his companions brightened for a moment, impressed by what they heard.

'Well, I wish one of my sons was trying to rescue me right now,' declared a lean, short-haired woman sitting opposite him. 'Those good-for-nothing layabouts probably haven't even noticed I'm gone yet.'

'At least your sons still live,' rasped another woman from further back.

Her grim voice silenced them all. Past her, the dark ribbon of the road wound its way through low wooded hills. Nico stared at the other wagons behind them, drawn by steaming teams of oxen, wheels clattering over furrows or locking in the cloying mud, squirming this way and that as dogs trotted alongside. A whip cracked and an ox bellowed in complaint.

Armed riders accompanied the line of wagons, a dozen hard men with black scarves tied across their faces and grey cloaks over their armour; mercenaries of the Empire, here to protect their cargoes of pleasure slaves being brought to the front for profit. The riders were watching the surrounding countryside closely for sign of the Khosian enemy, and Nico looked out at the snowy hills too.

The Breaks, they were called – this last range of hills before the plains of Bar-Khos. Hills which his father knew well.

Where are you? Nico brooded bitterly, hoping to glimpse his father somewhere up there on the forested slopes, a movement blocking a crack of light between trunks.

But he saw nothing, only the stark emptiness of deep winter, the monotony of snow and the bare limbs of the trees. It was still early, the sun slowly rising in the sky. Nico had been unconscious all night long. Plenty of time in which Cole could have acted.

In his head he reviewed all that he knew of his father, wondering how much he truly knew him after all. Could it be – and here Nico was barely able to contemplate the question – that his father was the kind of man to desert his wife and son *twice* to their fates?

But no, surely that was nonsense? Cole had returned with him to Khos and the war, wishing to be reunited with his family. He could have run for it at any time.

All Nico had to do was sit tight and wait. His father would come for him.

At least the storm had blown itself out. Though even with the glow of sunlight on his face it was cold sitting there bound and unable to properly move. The other captives in the wagon huddled against each other for warmth, seven women in varying degrees of sullen misery. They were young mostly, the daughters of farmers and shepherds and foresters by the looks of their hardy clothes and calloused hands, no doubt captured along the Chilos in surprise raids.

To Nico's eyes the Khosian women looked bizarre sitting in their everyday winter clothing secured by heavy chains of iron. It was as strange a sight as when he had first seen slaves on the reaver island of Cheem; people shackled like strongboxes, like prized possessions that had to be stopped from running away with themselves.

The scent of the women's animal fear wafted all around him, as strong in his nostrils as his own stale sweat. They were obviously still in shock at their present enslavement. Yet their heads lifted even as Nico's did, scenting the sea upon a sudden oncoming breeze.

The land ahead was tilting downwards now as the hills dropped towards the plains around Bar-Khos. Suddenly they could all see it before them in the far distance, down there in the haze: the besieged city standing on the southern coast of the island, the plains before it darkly covered in imperial forces and a thousand smoking camp fires.

The sea lying beyond the city was like a slate flecked with chalk. Across it thrust the striking feature of the Lansway, spanned by the walls of the Shield and reaching out towards a smudged impression of the southern continent. But it was eastwards that Nico's eyes turned in eagerness – east past the marshy delta of the Chilos towards home, their homestead and wild farm not far from the foothills of the High Tell.

Nico inclined his head, hearing thunder rising on the breeze. It was the heavy guns of the siege blasting away at each other, and they dragged his attention back to the city, back to the vast imperial encampment they were headed for.

Another day's slow travel and they would be there.

'Hey, pretty boy!'

Alongside him, one of the cloaked mercenaries reached out from his saddle to grab a handful of Nico's hair, and yanked his head back violently. Nico stared fiercely at the man's leering face, appalled by the meaty stench of his breath.

'Maybe we have some fun with you tonight, heh? Maybe we give old Lolaff some dross in his wine to put him out, and we sample the wares before we reach the city, starting with you. What do you say to that, hey, boy?'

Indeed, considered Nico – what to say to that? But he was reprieved just then by the fat leader of the group, Lolaff, who bellowed out from the back of his own zel.

'Jern, keep those hands to yourself there!'

Reluctantly the guard released his grip, hissing through his teeth as he dropped back.

'Pay him no heed,' insisted the girl by his side. But foreboding descended in a smothering gloom nonetheless. His leather bindings were really starting to hurt. His belly grumbled with hunger. His bladder badly needed to empty itself. And there seemed no way of escaping this imprisonment.

'You have a name?'

'Nico.'

'Call me Kes.'

The others watched with forlorn eyes. Their suffering was a palpable presence in the back of the wagon, a pall of misery that could not be ignored, not even by these cold-eyed men or their leader, Lolaff. Yet somehow they acted as though it was nothing to them; men long inured to the pain of others.

Nico recalled again what he had gone through at the hands of the Mannians back in imperial Q'os. The horrors of these people, these fanatical conquerors, now unleashed here in his homeland.

This living existence was a frightening thing when you saw how truly dire it could get for a person. Kidnapped from your home and forced into bondage like some beast of burden. Born as an innocent child into a family of brutal violence and fear. Burning to death on top of a pyre while you struggled for your next breath of agony. A loved one suddenly dropping dead by your side, like his dog Boon; the fabric of life you shared together gone in a heartbeat, nothing left but impressions in the grass.

The Mannians liked to say that what didn't kill you only made you stronger. But that was childish bravado, he knew now.

Even if you survived the worst that could ever happen to a person, you were likely never the same again. For always you would remain aware of the thin crust of ground upon which your life was really built, and how an abyss lurked just below the surface, waiting to swallow you whole through accident or design. Take a wrong step – or do nothing at all – and suddenly you could be plunging into a nightmare situation too horrible to ever contemplate in your normal days. Yet here it was, happening to you now in all its ferociousness, as real as life ever gets.

Too real.

Waiting, deep down every moment of the rest of your life, for the next terrible thing to happen.

But these tragedies seldom happen, said an inner voice not at all like his own. It sounded just like Ash, his old Rōshun master. *Be glad of that. Be glad these things are so rare in life.*

With the wagon jerking him from side to side, Nico recalled what his father had said a few nights earlier, about remembering the joy of past days together, he and his family playing in the rice fields with the rainbow fish.

Nico breathed in and out like Ash had once taught him, slowly and with attention, breathing all the way into his belly and out again until the dread started to drain from his body. He sought out something good in his mind to reflect upon, and straight away the pretty face of Serèse popped into his head, the hot-headed daughter of Baracha: Serèse smiling at him on a rooftop garden with invisible sparks playing between them . . .

He blinked and saw the pretty features of the girl by his side instead, biting her lip in tension.

Remember your joy, he wanted to say to her.

But what good would that do the young woman when some bastard was forcing himself upon her? What good would it do Nico either, for that matter?

*

Gasps sounded from some of the group. Chains chinked as women lifted hands to their mouths to cover the awful putrid stench in the air.

Nico looked up to see that they were trundling past another burnt-out village on the road. This one appeared to be decorated with the corpses of villagers hanging from trees; men, women and children twisting slowly by their necks.

He stared as hard as the others, people learning a lesson never to be forgotten. What the Mannians did not claim for themselves, they killed.

Imperial soldiers still lounged around the scene of their crime in their cloaks and armour. It looked like they were garrisoned in what few structures remained intact in the village, and a gang of them watched the wagons rolling past with their cargoes of women, hands on the hilts of their swords as though judging whether it was worth taking on the guards. A few called out to the captives, but the women wisely kept their heads down.

On the outskirts of the village a drystone cottage stood alone and partially in ruins. A child was crying within. It was an infant, by the sounds of its wails catching at him like hooks of need, and when his peers heard the sounds too they cursed or prayed aloud in agitation. From the foremost wagon a woman screamed out and tried to launch herself over the side, only to be knocked back by the harsh blows of a guard's baton.

'She thinks it's hers,' rasped the grim woman at the back. 'Poor fool lost her young one when they took her. Every time she sees a child, she goes into a fit.'

'You lousy bastards,' snarled the girl next to him, loud enough for all to hear. 'A curse on every one of you miserable rotten bastards!'

Nico tore his gaze away from the passing ruin, and stared off in the opposite direction instead where things were less raw and monstrous, wishing he could block his ears too. He wanted freedom from his captivity more than ever before, and he peered at the trees on the slopes and clenched his fists hard until he felt the fingernails digging into his flesh, trying to waken from a dream.

Still there was no sign of Cole, and he cursed his father's name like a litany.

Downwards they trundled towards Bar-Khos, with the sound of the child's hungry wails fading only slowly behind them, and even then, long after, lingering in their ears.

CHAPTER FOURTEEN

Nico

That night, after making camp in the lee of a darkly forested slope, an argument broke out between the slaver guards and their plump leader, Lolaff, concerning the conditions of their employment.

It sounded like they were complaining about their pay, but the more they argued the more it became obvious to Nico – and no doubt to the other captives too, shackled and bound against the young trees surrounding the fire – that the real issue concerned them instead. With Bar-Khos and the imperial encampment so close now, the guards wanted their way with the women while they still could. So tonight they complained that their pay was inadequate and that they should be compensated by sampling the wares, and threatened to desert Lolaff if he refused.

But Lolaff had obviously been involved in this business of human trafficking for a long time. Like a jovial but stern older brother, he scorned and cajoled the men in equal measure while he held his ground, thrusting his great belly out with the confidence of a man who holds the purse strings, and all the answers to their complaints.

He did not want his goods spoiled before they had even arrived at the front, he told the men. If they touched the women, he would have them arrested by the first soldiers he could find, and their hazard pay, waiting back in the capital, would be reneged.

As a final warning to the guards, Lolaff made a show of holding up a necklace that he wore, and Nico was appalled to see that it was a Rōshun seal of protection, a tiny leathery thing that inflated and deflated as it breathed. Lolaff was showing them that they could not simply kill him and have their way. If they did, they would have a Rōshun vendetta down on their heads.

While they argued some more in frustration, one of the women started calling out to the dark woods. It was the broken mother who had cried out for the child they had passed in the roadside ruin.

'Shut up!' snarled a guard, rounding on her with his baton.

'But I can hear her!' she shouted, lunging against her chains with her hands outstretched towards the dark trees. 'I can hear her crying!'

Every guard grew still as they peered out at the darkness. The woman was right. There was a child crying up there on the wooded slope.

Uneasily the guards trod to the edge of the firelight and stared up the hill.

'What's a babe doing out here in the middle of the night?' the man Lolaff asked aloud, plucking at the hairs of his beard.

'Couldn't be the same one we passed on the road, could it?' replied a guard over his shoulder.

'Well if it is, it's not wandering about up there on its own.'

Suddenly a dog barked from the crest of the hill, and then another – a whole wild pack of them growling and yelping. The camp dogs went into a frenzy and dashed off into the trees barking their challenges, vanishing in the blackness.

Once more the infant's wail rang out from the slope, though this time further to the right of the camp.

'Jern,' muttered Lolaff from the side of his mouth. 'Send a few of your men out. Find whoever it is that's up there.'

With their argument forgotten for the moment, two unhappy guards were sent out to scout the slope, scampering into the tree line with their swords drawn. The rest remained below, hands on the hilts of their weapons, silently waiting; men who had lived through strange nights before in hostile territories.

Yelps of pain rose up from the first of the dogfights on the hill. Dogs snarled and growled in combat. Off to the right a thud sounded from somewhere up in the trees, exactly like the sound of an armoured body crumpling to the ground. Then there was another thud.

The men shifted uneasily.

'Get some torches,' snapped the guard sergeant Jern, not moving from the edge of the firelight. In a rush the men snatched up burning sticks from the fire then fanned out towards the woods, their swords drawn now too, naked steel reflecting the flames.

Fat Lolaff edged back closer towards the centre. The man was nervously dabbing his lips with his tongue. Nico sucked at his own dry lips, a delicate intuition shaping itself on the crest of his thoughts.

Above them, above the ridge of the hill and the scrapping dogs, the stars were shining in all their brilliant insignificance, while the slope below remained a dark mystery, a forest of unknowns. Firelight struck the bare branches of the nearest trees, and then there was only a velvet blackness, into which some of the guards were stepping boldly with their torches.

For a moment the captives were forgotten about entirely, every guard's back turned towards them. Just as well too, for Nico almost leapt from his skin when someone tapped his shoulder from behind, and a panted voice whispered in his ear, 'Son!'

It was his father, hunkered down in the shadow of the tree trunk Nico was bound to, cutting through his leather bindings with a knife.

'You took your bloody time!'

'Hush, lad, you want them to hear us? Now where's your mother at? Point her out to me.'

'I would if she was here.'

'What?'

'I said she isn't here. I was mistaken.'

'*Aiieeee.*'

Even as Cole cut through his leg bindings, Nico was amazed to see an infant child strapped to his father's chest by a sling of clothing, its tiny head poking out. Cole had to work one-handed with the knife, because the little finger of his other hand was held in the child's mewling mouth to keep it soothed.

'Hurry up, will you? You're taking all day!'

'Here,' snapped Cole, 'give him your pinky to bite on. He's hungry and teething.'

With the women on either side of them shifting in their chains for a better look, Nico held the tip of his little finger between the child's sharp gums while his father finished freeing him. But as soon as he did so the child bit down hard.

'*Ow!*'

From the fireside, Lolaff the slaver turned to look over his shoulder in their direction. The Mannian squinted, but he seemed to see only Nico sitting in the shadows beneath the tree, for he spat on the ground then turned back again, calling out to the men on the slope in enquiry.

Gasping in relief at his sudden freedom, Nico struggled to his feet then followed his father around the clearing, rubbing the sores on his wrists.

In the shadows Cole bent down next to one of the captives – the distraught woman who had lost her child. 'Do you still have milk?'

'*Yes!*'

She sobbed and clamped a hand to her mouth as he handed the babe to her, then cradled the little moving bundle in her shaking grasp.

In moments Cole had cut the woman free too so she was able to stand, then he led her away from the camp.

'Come on,' growled his father, looking back to the fire and the guards. 'We need to go.'

'What about the others?'

'We've no time, Nico. They'll spot us any moment here!'

'*Wait, we can't leave these women like this!*'

'Nico!'

'Give me a blade. Your machete there.'

'I'll give you nothing, boy. You can't damn well save the whole world. Now come on.'

Nico growled and turned on his heels, heading back into the firelight.

Now he was free, a silent fury possessed him. All the hours spent in captivity and the shocks before that – the slave market of Tume, and the poor girl shivering naked on the block . . .

Rage dispelled every doubt and fear, and as he passed between the captive women, Nico picked up a rock from the ground, barely breaking his stride, and with a whip of his arm shot it right at the back of Lolaff's head.

There was a crack and then Lolaff spilled over onto the fire. The slaver howled and rolled his bulk clear of the flames but they followed him, pursued him, dancing across his cloak and his hair so that he wailed in panic and scrambled on all-fours to be free from them. His nearest guards turned about in shock.

After him ran Nico, stooping to grab up an oval rock from the circle around the fire. The stone was so hot that it seared the skin of his hand, but that only made him hurl it all the harder at a guard dashing into his path. The guard went down with a dent in his helm, and Nico stooped once more to snatch up the fellow's fallen shortsword, just in time to fend off the blow of another guard's blade, so brutal it almost knocked him off his feet.

But then his father was there by his side, cursing Nico aloud, and he dropped the guard with a thrust of a blade so that Nico was able to bound past him.

What are you doing? asked a frantic part of his mind even as he ran after Lolaff with the shortsword in his hand, following his burning form as he wailed and scampered into the trees.

Nico stayed right behind him, weaving through the trail of oily smoke. On the run he stabbed at a guard swinging his torch around, feeling the awful ease of the blade slipping through the man's leather armour and deep into his flesh. He kept on running, stronger and more agile than he had ever been in his life. It was as though all that Rōshun training he'd once struggled through was flowing through him again, but through a better conduit than before, a better body, so that the heft of the sword in his grip was as familiar as the weight of his hands, and he knew in every instant what to do with it.

'Nico!' roared his father in anger from behind, but he was beyond listening by then.

For those savage moments amongst the trees, Nico cut down every movement that confronted him, using the burning Lolaff as bait for the surrounding guards' attention, and as a moving human torch to show him where to strike and when.

He lost all sense of time, all sense of himself, in fact. It was only when Lolaff lay before him as a still and smouldering heap on the slope of the hill that Nico came back to himself at last, and then he realized there were no more guards around him. In the sudden darkness, absent now of torches, he heard zels snorting as they were spurred from the camp: the surviving guards fleeing as Cole shouted after them to come back for more.

Nico smelled the reek of blood all over him, though none of it seemed to be his own. The sword was a dead weight in his hand as he stumbled back down into the camp, his feet snared by vines and branches now.

The women stared at him with the whites of their eyes when he shambled into the clearing. They were all on their feet now. The grieving mother nursed the child where she stood swaying, her full breast gleaming in what little light was left from the half-smothered fire.

Nico stared back at them all grimly. He was trembling, the shakes coming to him now that the action was over; an unsettling, debilitating sensation that he fought to control. But his father too was trembling, all of them were, knowing it was over, knowing they were free.

Diplomat

'*Sit down.*'

The young woman's voice was a snap of command that almost had him sitting in the chair before he could control himself.

Ché tensed where he stood in a small upstairs room of the ink-works, fighting the lingering urge in his body to do as she commanded him. He was still bound in chains and he stared hard at the woman, taking in the silver half-mask on one side of her face, and her black eyes matching his own for intensity. Her hair was dark, her fine features obviously those of a native Contrarè.

She was also a Dreamer, Ché realized as his gaze flickered over the subtle rainbow shimmers of her skin; the first glimmersuit he had ever seen. '*Sit,*' she commanded again, more forcefully this time, and he realized she was using her voice in some way that was almost impossible to resist. Ché felt his body sag towards the chair, but he fought the impulse and straightened once more.

The Dreamer was tall and thin and dressed in a suit of dark leather. An array of black and white feathers sprouted back from the high collar of her coat, and combined with her sharp nose gave her the appearance of a pica bird, mischievous and clever. For all her presence she was younger even than Ché, and the more that he looked at her the more he liked what he saw. Here was someone who had gone beyond the ordinary realms of this life, and had made her home there.

'Please,' said the cripple Coya. 'Do as Shard says. She won't bite, despite appearances.'

'You must be Shard.'

'You are well informed, Diplomat,' answered the woman coolly.

Ché had heard of her, of course. She was the only Dreamer in the

Free Ports after all, a tradition that came from the Alhazii Caliphate to the east, where Dreamers were found in larger numbers; a smattering of men over the centuries who had supposedly, mystically, cracked the code of the cosmos. A sect that was shrouded in myth and secrecy.

Now here stood one of them in the flesh, trying to command him to sit in a chair.

She was testing him, he realized. Seeing how malleable he might be to her powers. Bored now, Ché sighed and sat down with his chains rattling.

'He still has the pulsegland in his neck,' she said, fingers cupped next to his face. She meant the gland implanted in his neck, the gland that all imperial Diplomats were given, allowing them to locate each other's locations. 'You want me to do something about it?'

'No,' said Coya quickly. 'Not yet.'

Ché saw them exchange a meaningful glance.

He wants to use me as bait, Ché considered. *He wants to see if other Diplomats will come after me.*

'What about his suicide implant?'

'If he had wanted to, I'm sure he would have used it by now.'

Shard pursed her lips, moving closer. She smelled like earth and leather. 'I see the Khosians debriefed him already,' she said distastefully, taking in the bruising of his face, sensing with her hands all the damage inside him. Ché hadn't pissed for weeks without expelling blood.

'They play rough here in Khos, don't forget that.'

'You say he was cooperative?'

'I believe so. Not that it did him much good.'

She was shaking her head. 'If he's really a plant, beatings won't get it out of him. There's only one way to be certain.'

As she spoke, Ché watched her drag a small table across the floor towards him. Carefully, her young assistant approached to lay an object upon it wrapped in red cloth. Around it he arrayed a series of items: tweezers, callipers, vials of liquid, a clean rag.

'Why am I suddenly getting a bad feeling about this?' said Ché, shifting in his chair.

His stare was fixed on the young assistant's hands as they

unwrapped the red cloth from the object. Within lay something resembling a giant mud-encrusted crab lying on its back, with a pair of pink tails extending from one end which flopped about on the desk like the tentacles of a dying squid. Its four claws clenched as the Dreamer touched them one by one, checking the thing over.

'Relax, it's only a Lie Teller,' she told him. 'In most respects, not all that different from a farcry. I promise it won't hurt you.'

A farcry was something that allowed you to communicate mentally, over any distance, to anyone else with their own farcry. Something entirely harmless in appearance compared to this monster confronting him.

Ché cleared his throat. 'I thought Lie Tellers were only available to the Guildsmen of Zanzahar?'

'And to people with friends in their Guild. Now relax. Take a deep breath and hold it in.'

He did so, if only because she spoke in the soothing detached tones of a professional. Because he felt that he could trust her. He even sat there unmoving as she lifted the living thing and placed it slowly over his nose and mouth like a mask, feeling his heart racing as its legs dug into his face so that it gripped on to him lightly.

His composure only broke when the two tails whipped across his mouth then thrust themselves deep into his nostrils. Ché tried to jump up and tear it from him but suddenly he was immobile, his muscles refusing his every command.

The cripple, Coya, watched on with eyes widening in alarm. Ché's own eyes flicked across to Shard standing over him. He felt light-headed. The pains in his body flooded out of him through the numbing flesh of his face.

Weariness washed through him. His eyes closed of their own accord.

'Breathe easily. Relax.'

Ché slouched back in the chair and felt his head lolling to one side. Through his eyelashes he saw the Dreamer's young assistant leave the room and close the door behind him. The door was shivering, swelling outwards as Ché watched it. Like it was breathing.

'Now tell me everything inside you,' commanded a voice from a long way away.

Ché began to babble.

*

Sunlight kissed the skin of his face with heat. What was this? Ché appeared to be floating on his back in a lake of blood-warm water, the blue sky reflected flawlessly across its mirror surface.

Through his fingers the silky water flowed against his caresses. Ché stared at the high sun overhead. There were birds up there circling in the thermals, slipping and diving around each other in play. For a long time he floated on his back and watched them rejoicing in their airborne freedom, as pacified as a baby in a womb.

Why return when there's nothing to return to? he thought to himself after an unnoticed passing of time, and the response came, as it always came at such moments, from that usually silent witness to all that he did in life – his deepest self, his calm centre of awareness. His oldest friend.

Stay here then. Don't go back.

Ripples washed over his chin and splashed his lips as he shifted his posture, so that his legs dangled below him. The lake water tasted as salty as tears.

With a silent grace Ché allowed himself to slip beneath the surface. The milk-warm water enveloped him. As he sank further into the cooling depths he watched the shimmers of sunlight growing ever dimmer above him. Sadness spilled from his heart. Bitter regrets. What had any of it amounted to, this short life of his – all that violence and pain and the following of a path laid down by others? Where had it led him, these expectations and commands from people who had considered him their property, for no better reason than the higher positions they held in the order of things, a world of titles and powers that he had never consented to, had merely been born into?

Ché had remained on the path of an imperial assassin for the sake of his mother, or so he liked to tell himself; yet his mother had been as much to blame as anyone. She was a true believer, a fanatic, so unthinking in all that surrounded her that she considered the ways of Mann to be wholly natural, the only possible shape the world could ever take. Even her role in it as a Mannian Sentiate, a divine whore, she considered a blessing.

His mind turned away from that tangle of darkness. Turned instead to the Rōshun and his time spent in the monastery of Sato, high in the mountains of Cheem. For a handful of years he had lived with the assassin monks in those cold mountains, training as an apprentice, before his secret imperial conditioning had reminded him who he truly was, and he had fled the monastery to return to the capital of the Empire, carrying all the knowledge he had gained of the Rōshun.

It was only now that he fully realized how much he had lost; the life he had thrown away for a people he no longer considered to be his own, these priests with their designs on the world. With the Rōshun, Ché had experienced more than the bitter infighting he'd grown up with inside the Mannian religious order, that incessant dog-eat-dog competition of his peers at the expense of all else, most of all any real and trusting relationships. Instead he'd experienced something he had always suspected was out there, even if he hadn't quite known how to find it – a different way of living, no less. A way that was as real as his previous life in Q'os had mostly been artificial, a facade of pretence, a dangerous game of power over the less power-ful.

With the Rōshun he had known what it was to have a family, a home, at last. And he had betrayed them all, for what?

The Rōshun hated him now, and Ché felt the horror of that coiling through him like a child who finally appreciates the loathing of his own parents.

They would kill him the first moment they had a chance to, never mind how much Coya reassured him otherwise. Yet Ché didn't mind that. Indeed he deserved such a fate, deserved far worse than their blades negotiating their way to his heart.

It was the look in their eyes that he could not stomach. As though they gazed upon a monster.

Stay here, said his sinking mind in his sinking body. *Don't go back.*

Bubbles spilled from Ché's mouth. He felt them tickling his gums, his lips even, as his lungs emptied of air. It was so easy, he realized now, and wondered what had taken him so long to arrive at this fateful end to his life.

Far above his head, a sound of laughter sprinkled itself across the surface like a shower of rain. It was the sound of his mother's laugh-ter, beautiful and mad.

Ché kicked his feet suddenly to stop his descent, and peered up through the gloom at the slanting spears of sunlight far above. He felt a fresh swelling of sadness for all that his mother's life had been as a Sentiate whore within the order. He felt guilt, too, recalling all the blame he had lain on her over the years without even knowing it, blaming a girl for a life she had never asked to be born into either.

Silence. Only the dull thudding of his heart in his ears.

Again the laughter sprinkled across the surface, though it was someone else's laughter this time, deeper in tone, rueful rather than mad.

Curl, he realized with excitement, thinking of the troubled girl who was so persistently on his mind these days. *I can hear you.*

He sensed that she was near and getting closer.

His lungs burning for lack of air, suddenly Ché's limbs were propelling him upwards towards the surface.

He gasped fresh air and tasted the water on his lips like tears again. The light was too bright to look at.

'Welcome back,' said a woman's voice in relief, and Ché blinked, seeing the Dreamer leaning over him.

'What happened?' he gasped.

'Your suicide implant kicked in while we were questioning you. It tried to stop your heart.'

Curl, he thought in confusion, looking about him. *Where is she?*

But he saw only the Dreamer and the cripple Coya standing next to him in the otherwise empty room, and he remembered it was only a dream, a vision brought on by the Lie Teller.

'Looks like he's sincere. He's no plant, anyway,' she told Coya standing by her side. The cripple blinked at Ché as though he was surprised, and Ché thrust his manacled hands at him.

'Now do you mind taking off these damned chains?'

CHAPTER SIXTEEN

Ocean

Where in hell am I? Ocean asked herself, for what must have been the tenth time in as many hours.

Frustration clenched her hand tight to the little boat's wheel. Hunger gnawed at her belly. After days of fighting against the currents and winds it was hard to even know how much headway she was making, pushed along by the inflatable's squid-jets that were always underpowered due to the clouded sun and the sheer coldness of the water. Already she was rationing what was left of the food, yet still she had seen no signs of land. For all she knew she was drifting round and round on some vast circular current taking her nowhere.

Sleep was snatched in whatever rare few hours she could manage. The rest of the time she fought the surging storm waters from the controls of the wheelhouse, her legs cramped and stiff from having stood for so long, even with the support of her ribbed skinsuit stiffening across her flanks, bracing the weight of her shifting body. Wrapped from head to toe in the suit's warming protection, Ocean peered out through the visor of its hood at the deathly grey sea all about her, heaving and wild, thinking that if this was really the Sargassi Sea of the Free Ports, where she had aimed for, it was hardly the calm and shallow body of water she had expected. Winter had churned it into an icy-cold desolation with no end.

Where am I! she wondered again as another wave crashed across the forward window, causing the whole wheelhouse to flex backwards. But this time, when she glanced down at the directional transponder taped to the control console, its precious yellow light was shining noticeably brighter than before, and turning towards white. Her heart quickened in response.

She had been making some headway after all, for she was beginning to get close. Close to wherever this signal was leading her.

One last effort, Ocean asked of her tired body and mind, standing wedged in the rocking, flexing cockpit of the tiny boat, which so far had lived up to the model's reputation of being unsinkable.

She was lit by the green glow of the console, stooped behind the shaking windscreens with one hand gripped around the wheel and her other clutching at the semi-rigid power lever, keeping it pushed in the red. Ocean squinted through the hard spray raining over the wheelhouse, out past the swamped nose of the tiny craft chugging over its millionth steepening wave with all the temerity of a drowning dog, pushing it beyond all design limits.

Nearly there! she coaxed from the struggling boat too. She kept the power in the red and watched the nose surge over the tilting edge of a sea that was a living thing beneath her, frothing white and throwing wave after wave of boundless energies.

It was like being back on Sholos, she thought as the boat dropped down the outer side of a twenty-foot wave, picking up speed, only to plough into the next rush of breaking water at the bottom. Except this was barely a squall compared to the superstorms on Sholos. On the water moon that was her home, the lower-gravity conditions could whip the small world's ocean into waves that were higher than any ever seen here – into real mountains of water compared to these frothy foothills.

Next to the wheel her map was fixed with lengths of tape, a pale sheetleaf covered by an inked representation of the Midèrēs Sea. She squinted at it, taking in the stark X marking the planned spot of her splashdown amongst the Free Ports, trying to divine some kind of answer to where she really was from her course direction and rough distance from the transponder.

At least the map was something to look at besides the heaving seas. Its names rolled in her mind, made familiar from having studied them for so long. *Cheem. Minos. Markesh. Zanzahar*. Right now she'd be grateful to make landfall at any one of them, never mind if it was a Free Port or not. Any major metropolis would do, anywhere she could sell some gold discs in exchange for local currency, perhaps even a little of the precious moondust she had brought along to properly fund her mission.

With hungry eyes she roamed the inked coastlines of the map. Back on her home moon, in the vaults of Opened Records, there were ancient maps that looked remarkably similar to this inner sea known as the Midèrēs, the Heart of the World. Remarkable not because they had been made from distant observations of this planet of Erēs, but because they had been recovered from the fragmented diamond hardfiles of a buried Sky Ark. The ancient maps did not depict the Heart of the World at all, but rather a sea on the dying planet of Dirt, or Terra, the legendary homeworld from which the Sky Ark had come. Indeed from which they had all come.

People still argued over the meaning of that coincidence. How an inner sea of the far-off homeworld could be so similar to the shape of the Midèrēs, down there on a seeded planet. Some took the mathematical approach, considering it to be only a matter of chance; that in all the living worlds of the galaxy, there were going to be some surprising matches to be found. But others, those of a more gnostic persuasion, tended towards much deeper implications; that it wasn't random at all; that the correlation was instead a fingerprint of the Great Dreamer itself – a dramatic device, no less, of some unfolding cosmic narrative.

In other words, that the similarities held some kind of meaning.

The map's corners flapped about in a sudden, howling gust that twisted the wheelhouse in its maws. Ocean looked up to see the world of water and sky being torn apart by the winds, feeling the sea lifting her up from below.

A monstrous roar turned her head towards a wave rushing in from starboard. She just had time to brace herself before it broke across the length of the boat, tilting it sharply as she was thrown to one side. Only the vessel's trailing storm anchors stopped it from capsizing altogether, but freezing water rose up to her thighs as she grabbed for the wheel, boiling about her like broth. She spat the briny taste of it from her mouth and shook her eyes clear, seeing the little swamp rat Pip squirming through the water for higher ground. He hung there on the wheel, dripping wet, as the water level quickly receded.

Ocean looked ahead over the dropping crest of a wave and saw something out there in the darkness – what looked like a column of fire standing in the distance like a vision.

She lost sight of it as they dipped down into another trough, spotting it again as they came up the other side. With her Patched eyes she focused on the glimmering light like a hawk, seeing that it was a ship on fire. Beyond it, strangely, more fires were flashing up in the cloudy sky.

Another glance to the transponder showed that it was shining even whiter than before. Relief washed through her. Ocean grasped the throttle and pushed it to the limits again, aiming for the distant beacon that was the burning ship.

*

She was amazed, frankly, to find anyone out here on the open sea in this kind of weather, considering the fragile wooden vessels she knew they still sailed here on this world.

Yet it was a ship all right, and it was on fire as it wallowed on the high seas. And what was that behind it now, as she drew ever closer?

Ocean strained her vision as far as she could. Beneath flashes of light in the sky, she saw a shadow of land stretching across her course. The water seemed to be calmer than before. Indeed, as she looked north and then south, she saw how the boat had entered an ever-narrowing bay that was still many lems wide, and peering straight ahead over the rise of a swell, she glimpsed a glittering city perched on the dark coastline, above which the flashes of light were most concentrated.

A butterfly tickled around in her stomach; a creeping sense that she knew now where she was bound.

The city of war!

But how? What was her contact on the planet, Juke, doing here in the besieged city of Bar-Khos, of all places, when he was supposed to have made his way to a safe Free Port from which to guide her in?

In glum silence Ocean powered onwards with the chop diminishing the further into the bay she went. She was in the lee of the land now, for even the winds lessened to occasional gusts. Her heart beat faster as the transponder signal grew stronger, bringing her right towards the burning vessel. It was a large wooden merchant ship, its masts still standing amongst a conflagration of flames in which there was no sign of survivors.

In the distance, other ships were headed this way from the direction of the city. Even as she spotted them a shape soared right overhead, turning to head them off – a skyship, she realized with a shock of awe at seeing such a thing. The vessel was larger than images had suggested, huge in fact, considering it was held aloft by a vulnerable envelope of gas. Onwards it swept with a booming thunder suddenly roaring from its side, its blazing guns puncturing the sea before the ships with spouts of rising water.

And then a second skyship rushed over her head with its guns firing at the foremost one, tearing chunks from its wooden backside and prompting an inner explosion from its depths. Ocean gasped as flames took out the silk loft of gas. Her mouth hung open as she watched the rest of the vessel plummeting to the sea wreathed in fire and smoke.

In its spreading wake the waves swelled outwards, bobbing the boat up and down. When Ocean glanced to the transponder its light was bright white, and the device was vibrating loudly. She swallowed a sudden taste of bile. Cutting out the power to the squid-jets, Ocean snatched the transponder from its sticky-tape mount then clambered out of the cockpit with it, staggering against the gusts onto the narrow prow, the inflated deck sagging beneath her feet.

She stopped, riding the surging water with her legs spread wide, staring hard at the device vibrating in her hand.

She was right on top of the signal, for sure.

With a trembling hand she lowered the device so that it pointed straight down between her feet, right through the heaving hull of the boat.

The device buzzed loudly in her grasp.

Oh Juke, she thought with a sigh of regret, thinking of the young Anwi man she barely even knew, who had travelled here from the Isles of Sky to help her. A young man she had only ever communicated with over a farcry. *What happened to you?*

But it seemed obvious what had happened to him. Bound on a ship for a safer Free Port than this one, only to be bombed from the sky and drowned.

Such bad luck, and before her real work had even begun.

Pissed and hissing through her teeth, Ocean tugged the hood from her head so that her great mass of hair popped open like a small tree catching the wind. Then she clambered back into the cockpit with her face set straight to the city, and got the boat going again, knowing that she had no other choice now, that she had to get out of these elements or she would die.

Bar-Khos, she thought with a bitter shake of her head.

Of all the ports in all the world, it had to be Bar-Khos!

CHAPTER SEVENTEEN

Nico

Down on the moonlit plain it looked as though the end of the world had come to the besieged city of Bar-Khos, or at least some early manifestation of the end.

From the enemy positions beams of white brilliance were striking the city's northern wall, swinging back and forth along a glittering confetti of gunfire and explosions. Wherever the great beams spilled over the top they threw shadows into a night sky filled with battling skyships, and what appeared to be a grotesque shape rearing against the clouds – like the face of some fearsome god of old looming over the city.

Flames rose high across the northernmost districts. Horns wailed faintly in alarm, the sounds of them undulating over the plain where imperial camp fires ranged numerous as the stars – tens of thousands of fighters committed to the downfall of the city. Booms of concussion rattled the windy night air.

Yet for all appearances, Bar-Khos and its ancient walls had withstood countless assaults over the centuries, and it had never fallen. There was a permanence to the stones of that city standing so squarely on the mouth of the Lansway, a permanence that had always ultimately frustrated those who would try to conquer it, not least of all the Empire of Mann during these last ten years of siege.

It could only be hoped that this time would be no different.

'How far?' huffed Nico's father, stepping back from where he'd been pissing across their tracks in the snow.

Nico was still standing there relieving himself. He swung away from the sight of the siege to peer back along their trail, gazing through the darkness with his eagle-sharp eyes.

In the distance a single lantern moved across the brow of a hill; a dim speck of light flitting between the unseen trunks of trees.

'Close,' Nico said. 'A quarter-hour behind us, maybe less.'

Cole furrowed his forehead beneath the wide rim of his hat. He pushed it clear of his eyes to once more inspect the clouds to the north, no doubt gauging the chances of more bad weather arriving to cover their escape. His father knew these hills of the Breaks well, and he could read the weather of southern Khos like a seer. He did not look hopeful at what he saw.

'Quick as you can,' Cole said to the twenty bedraggled women, all squatted down on the trail with their skirts hitched up amidst rising clouds of steam, trying to pee on command.

'It's the fact he's enjoying this,' one of them grumbled, and Nico saw that it was Shandras, the short-haired woman he'd been seated opposite on the wagon.

'All you can manage now, ladies,' said Cole as he slapped Nico's back on the way past in mid-flow. 'As much as you can get on the trail, if you please.'

The women were quiet mostly, making what they could of this brief respite from their harried trek despite the strange request made of them. They were cold in the ragged dresses and aprons they had been captured in, even with the thin blankets they wore like shawls. Nico watched them from the corner of his eye, glimpsing the bare skin of their legs gleaming in the night. The pretty one, Kes, caught him taking a peek and lifted her skirt for a brief flash of her thighs, grinning where she squatted.

Quickly he buttoned himself up with a clearing of his throat, and turned away.

Even now we make space for living, he reflected soberly.

Nico was trying hard not to dwell on what could happen here if they were captured again; though even harder he was trying not to dwell on the recent deaths that lay behind him – the startled faces of men in the dark woods as he ran them through with his blade.

Killing had a way of sticking to you like a bad aura, he knew by now. Even if you never thought about your actions at all, they were still there with you, part of you, like something that needed to be washed off but never could be.

Even his father was acting differently towards him. He stared more directly at Nico now, with a kind of subdued disbelief mixed with curiosity, as though seeing his son for the first time as more than a boy. His tone had changed to something less dismissive than before.

If only the price for his father's new-found respect had not been so high.

Nico looked back along their trail again, seeing the flicker of lantern light moving down through the far trees. All that killing had allowed them to escape, yet it wasn't over yet, not with these pursuers hot on their trail. More bloodshed was still to come.

Sometimes, Nico reflected, it was as though life gave you good fortune only so it could rip it away again with the bad.

*

After killing the slavers in their camp and freeing the captives, they barely had time enough to gather what food and supplies they could before Nico had heard riders fast approaching along the road.

The escaped guards must have made it to the small garrison in the last burnt-out village they had passed, for in a moment Nico had spotted imperial soldiers headed their way, even as he shouted out a warning to the others.

In a rush, Cole had led the panicking group west across the road into the trees and the hills, but it hadn't taken long for the imperial soldiers to find their trail in the snow. Soon they were following the group, using a lantern to light up the tracks they were leaving through the drifts. All night long, their pursuers had slowly been closing the distance between them.

Now the ragged group had paused by the banks of a noisy river, the same Bitter River that eventually ran through the city of Bar-Khos – for Cole had claimed to have a sudden idea.

'We need to rest soon,' said the woman Shandras, straightening her skirts as she rose.

'You're resting now, aren't you?' Cole snapped back at her. He was staring ahead to the western skyline, where something kept drawing his attention on a nearby hill.

'We don't rest soon, we're going to start dropping, I tell you.'

Cole rounded on her with his teeth bared, hissing under his

breath. 'If we stop now we get caught by our pursuers. Is that what you want, woman?'

It was in that moment when Nico realized the pressure his father was under. Cole had taken on the responsibility of these Khosian women as his own, even though he would have clearly left them behind given the chance, would have chosen the safety of his own family over anything else first.

'At least tell us why we're doing this, for Kush sake?'

'I did,' he answered, stepping clear of her. 'We're marking our trail.'

The women were standing now and huddling together for warmth, or gathering the reins of the few zels they had managed to retrieve from the slaver camp. They glanced uneasily at the speck of light following them behind.

'Wash your boots off in what snow you can find,' Cole instructed. 'Then rub some of those winterberries onto your boots, mask any scents still on you.' Cole nodded to a nearby bush covered in shrivelled red berries.

Bronze hair flashed in moonlight cast by a sudden break in the clouds. Nico watched his father glance towards the captive they had mistaken for his mother, before he turned southwards to stare across the noisy river, all the way to the orange glow lighting up the sky above the enemy encampment.

'We don't have time for this,' Cole grumbled to his son, his familiar profile shadowed by the brim of his hat. 'We'll be hard-pressed to catch up with your mother now. If she's reached the front, we'll have a time getting her out of their camp.'

'I know. But we could hardly just leave them like that.'

No? said his father's glance.

Nico was tired of saying sorry for what he'd done, for what he had been certain was the right thing to do. In truth, part of him felt a small measure of disappointment at his father's callousness. The father he had known before the war would never have suggested leaving these women to their fates. He certainly wouldn't have criticized his son for wishing to do so. No, this was the scarred, hardened man he remembered during the worsening days of the siege, become almost a stranger to Nico even before he had fled.

Squabbling wouldn't help the matter though. And he supposed

he was hardly being fair on his father either. Cole had saved that child back there after all, even when it meant risking his chances of rescuing his own son. Beneath the scarred and adamantine shell, the father of his youth was still in there somewhere, an easygoing man of generous heart and good humour, glimpsed in those moments when he forgot himself most of all, forgot about the burdens he still carried that were warping him with their pressures.

'You talked about these hills when I was a boy,' Nico remembered, scanning about their position. He could see a herd of water buffalo huddled under a few trees by the water's edge.

'Used to come to the Breaks with my brother Bahn a lot, when we were younger. Back when I still lived in the city.'

It was always a surprise to hear of his father's upbringing in Bar-Khos, before Nico had even been born. He always imagined Cole as a rugged homesteader and outdoorsman, someone born beneath the open sky.

'We hunted and fished. Camped under the stars. Took mushrooms.' He cast the tightest of smiles. 'Good times.'

Hard to imagine such a thing. His father and Bahn as young lads, high on mushrooms under the stars.

'Whatever you're planning here, I hope it works.'

'It'll work.'

Nico looked up just then, and saw that the clouds had momentarily cleared overhead. The stars were shining full of life up there, and he sensed the whole world spinning beneath the soles of his feet; this planet, smaller than once it had seemed in his mind, yet infinitely larger too.

He inclined his head, thinking he heard a horn calling out through the night air, not from the city but closer. His father was watching the speck of lantern light back along their trail, slowly moving along the Bitter River. Their pursuers were getting close. Nico could see the individual shapes of their zels stepping through the gloom.

Suddenly he heard it again, unmistakable this time – a hunting horn sounding out as though their pursuers had caught sight of them. Shouts carried their way on the breeze.

With a grim calmness Cole fixed his stare towards the west again, where the river bulged and curved around a hill. Nico followed his gaze with interest.

'What is it?' Nico enquired, seeing the pinpricks of golden light bobbing about at the top of the slope. For an awful moment he thought they were more imperial soldiers blocking their way. 'Torches?'

'No. That's where we're headed.'

Like some Alhazii prophet of the deep desert, his father raised his rifle into the starry sky and pointed it towards the west, towards the slope topped with glimmers of light, and shouted, 'This way!' to the straggling group of women.

Cole crunched forward into the virgin snow and Nico followed after him, just like in the old days, son and father out hunting for winter quail in the foothills of the High Tell. And just like back then, Nico could tell from the determined hunch of his shoulders and the long steady lope of intent that his father was on to something.

'Come on!' yelled Cole from further up the gully with a throw of his arm ahead, as though that way lay a salvation known only to him.

*

In his surging, long-legged stride Cole led them upwards through the trees, hissing at the women behind them to be quiet now.

Firemoths, Nico realized, seeing what they were headed for at the top of the hill, those strange lights flickering between the trees. Firemoths swarming in their hundreds in one of their deep winter displays. He had no idea why his father was so earnestly headed for them, but at least the group was gaining height now. With the hunting horn calling out ever louder from their trail below, it seemed the best course left to them.

Behind him followed the *chuff* of hooves through the deep snow. Some of the freed captives rode on their few zels, including Chira, the raw-eyed woman who'd been given the child, asleep now against her bosom. After them came the rest of the bedraggled women, hanging on to each other and the tails of the zels as they struggled upwards in a steamy line, young Kes amongst them.

Now they were free, these hardy homesteaders who had been seized from along the Chilos had no intention of being recaptured.

None complained how tired they were, only gritted their teeth harder and kept struggling upwards, spurred on by the horn calling after them from along the river valley below. But with every glance cast backwards by his father Nico knew what he was thinking. It wasn't enough. Soon they would be overtaken.

Up on the brow of the hill moonbirds were calling out into the night, cooing like doves at the twin moons and each other. The moons lit up the ground, one white and one a pale blue shining through breaks in the trees, adding a cool tinge to the already frozen appearance of the white hills about them.

Clouds of firemoths danced the dark clearings, aglow with their own amber light; congregating as they did on the wintry hilltops of Khos in a frenzied festival of breeding. The group hurried through them, scattering the clouds into lesser ones that were no less fascinating to the eye. Nico was hardly the only one to stare at the shining moths flitting about him. They lit up whatever they flew close enough to, so that the trees glowed here and there with passing dabs of yellow light, and with their wings beating fast they cast flickering shadows that made it all the more eerie and unreal.

It was just like the time his father had woken him once late at night, to bring him out into the crystal stillness of the moonlight to see the firemoths mating on the grove of a nearby hill.

Dusted with combustible properties, the wings of the male firemoths were beating against each other so hard they released little clouds of smoke into the air, which seemed to attract the females towards them. Successful males grappled with their female counterparts in flapping, twisting mid-air dances that were the brilliant culminations to their lives, their wings beating ever faster until finally – climaxing in their most frenzied moments – the wings caught fire in a flash of light and carried away the males to their burning deaths, floating up into the night sky like those glowing paper lanterns people released as prayers.

Nico's eyes stung from the oily smoke of their wings. The sight of them sent a chill through his bones, glimpsing his own fiery death in their final brilliant moments. But there was no time to dwell on such things, for the hunting horn was blaring just below them now, and Nico hurried on after his father.

'What are you looking for?' he asked Cole, who was searching about him as though for something familiar here on the brow of the hill.

'Pampa vines. The firemoths like their resin. It's why they gather in these places.'

'So?'

'They're not the only critters who like the presence of the vines. There – this way.'

Cole veered off in a different direction without waiting to see if they were all following. The infant was crying softly now in the arms of Chira, perhaps startled by the sounds of the hunting horn or the sudden jitteriness of the zels as they approached a large clearing floored by trampled snow. Both zels were snorting now and refusing to go any further. Cole stopped to instruct those on their backs to ride well around the clearing, then led the rest of the group directly across it where mounds rose here and there, a musky smell emanating from the many holes at their bases.

'Shoth sets,' Nico remarked aloud in alarm.

'Aye. Now stay quiet and follow my tracks.'

In a line the escaped captives wound their way between the mounds, knowing that the shoths would be asleep in their burrows. Not all of them though. A hiss sounded not far from Nico and he spotted one of the creatures ambling towards them, sniffing at their human scent. Even in the gloom he could see its spiny fur striped black and white like a zel, and its long snout and body and six short legs.

He froze as the shoth inflated the ring of flesh around its neck and hissed with its rattling tongue. The animals were known as spitting shoths for good reason. The very last thing he wanted was to be spat at by one of these creatures, for the scent was so bad he would gag on it relentlessly, and with no way to scrub it from his skin it would linger for days.

Zels, too, went crazy at the smell of shoths, Nico recalled.

In front of him his father held a hand aloft and clucked his tongue at the lone creature to gain its attention. He plucked a handful of something from a pocket of his jacket, red winterberries, which he scattered on the ground before the shoth, then motioned for the others to keep going. They didn't need telling twice, and in moments they were across.

On the other side of the hill the ground dropped away more gently and they followed it downwards, grateful for the easier going. They could see the Bitter River down there again, ox-bowing around a hill.

They had barely made it to the valley floor once more when a commotion sounded from above – men shouting in alarm as their zels cried out in panic. In the broken silence of the night they heard the hissing of a great number of shoths risen in fury, spitting at the men who had followed their trail through the animals' sets. With a crash, a riderless zel bolted from the trees at the top of the hill and fled across the slope. They could hear more pounding away in other directions.

'Nice,' said Nico with sudden admiration. 'The shoths smelled them coming and woke up. Smelled all that urine they walked through!'

Cole was leaning on his longrifle as the rest of the group caught up one by one.

'When I was young, I rode into a shoth set once without realizing it. They scented me on the wind and were spitting at me even as I saw them. After I was thrown to the ground I never saw that old zel again.'

'My brother was once sprayed by a shoth he surprised in the woods,' panted one of the women. 'I couldn't believe the smell of it. Made my eyes run! Half the family ran out when he stumbled through the door into the kitchen. My mother made him stay outside for a week. He said he couldn't sleep the whole time, the smell was so bad.'

Nico chuckled, and like the others he looked up to the top of the hill where the clamour and dismay of the soldiers was still ringing out.

'They say it takes days of scrubbing to get the worst of it off your skin.' It was young Kes who spoke. Her eyes shone in satisfaction.

'Better get moving again,' said Cole. 'They'll still be after us even with their zels gone. And now they'll be pissed.'

Groans and moans protested at his words, the first collective complaint all night. As though just now their spirits were lifted enough to finally voice how exhausted they really were. They needed to catch their breaths first. They needed to take the weight off feet that were lumps of agony. No one seemed able to move.

Nico shrugged at his father's worried glance. What could they do, whip them into action like a pair of slavers?

'If I remember right, there's a bridge not far from here,' said Cole. 'We can all rest a while once we make it across the river.'

'Five minutes,' said Shandras. 'That's all we're asking.'

'We don't have five minutes. We need to move now.'

Still the women refused to budge, and so Cole swore aloud and snatched up his rifle.

'Nico,' he snapped, and spun around on his feet, fully intent on marching onwards no matter what they had to say.

But then his father stopped in his tracks, and when Nico joined him by his side he froze too.

'Hey there,' said a grinning voice in the darkness, and a stray fluttering firemoth cast just enough light to suggest the form of several armed figures standing in their way.

A dash of white appeared in the gloom between them; someone's teeth emerging in a grin.

*

Through the morning chill they ran, with the long dark night receding in memory, their new companions leading the way ahead.

They were Contrarè, this trio of figures who had surprised them in the darkness at the foot of the hill, a fact that was revealing itself ever more in the brightening daylight as they hurried along the course of the river. Their black hair was back-combed into wild contortions sporting feathers and river shells and sticks of carved wood. Nico could see the bows and hatchets the trio carried, and how their clothes of leathers and skins were striped in the green-grey tones of a twilight forest. Their sharp faces were painted too, slashed red and black in their warrior fashion just like the stories said.

Yet these three Contrarè were well south of the Windrush forest here, closer to the city of Bar-Khos than anywhere else. A remarkably rare sight indeed.

Even more surprising was the appearance of the largest of the trio by far – the big fellow who had greeted them so unexpectedly in the night with his shining grin. The giant of a man bore spiral horns tattooed on his temples and as many facial scars as his father, and when he had spoken his accent was plainly Bar-Khosian.

'You're Bull, the pit fighter,' said Cole in surprise as he ran by the man's side, catching a proper look at him at last. 'I saw you fight in Bar-Khos.'

'I was Bull. Now I'm someone else,' answered the big fellow, panting hard.

They bounded over bare rock now. The Contrarè led the way while the women kept up as best they could, following the river as it coursed towards the south, its waters turning a riotous white and falling towards the plain below, dropping further and further away from their feet. The group had reached the southern limits of the Breaks, and were low enough now that the hills were absent of snow. It felt good to be clear of it at last, not having to drag his feet through the cold drifts. Even better to be able to feel his toes again in his boots.

An hour ago in the pre-dawn darkness, with their pursuers still making a commotion on top of the hill from the effects of the spitting shoths, the looming figure of Bull had startled them into a stunned silence. He had taken one look at the ragged group before offering to lead them to a place of safety, mentioning the same bridge that Cole had spoken of. No one had protested when they heard his Khosian accent. None had even dared to scare off this unexpected boon by asking what they were doing there.

'Better hurry,' declared one of the women from the back of a zel. 'They're getting close again!'

Nico looked back as his father did. Their pursuers had stopped calling out with the hunting horn since their misfortune on the hill. He caught a glimpse of them back along the trail, enough to see that they numbered a score of men or more, only a few riding zels now that their mounts had been scattered.

He dropped behind to give some of the struggling women a hand, telling them that it wasn't far now, they were nearly there.

'That's what you said last time,' breathed Kes with her head down, passing him with a frown.

'It's true, look.'

She did look up, seeing what they all saw now – the shape of the bridge spanning a deep and narrow ravine. The Bitter River was a mere white thread far below.

It was one of those tree bridges found all over the island of Khos: a shockingly huge chimino tree trained to grow horizontally across the entire width of the ravine. The chimino's silver-barked trunk was wide enough for carts and people to cross over easily, and its upper branches had been trained outwards to form a hedge along both sides. Below, limbs the size of lesser trees arched outwards and upwards to catch the light with their mighty diamond-shaped leaves.

Gasping for air they straggled onto a road of frozen ruts and followed it to the bridge. A spit of rain struck Nico's forehead cold and hard, and he stopped and frowned up at the dark clouds drifting overhead, feeling the air grow cooler against his cheeks as a breeze began to stir. His father joined his side, and waited there for the last of the women to pass them by, their faces pale with exhaustion, while they both stared back along the trail for a sighting of their pursuers.

'Let's go.'

It was always the oddest of things to cross one of these on foot. The trunk of the chimino was so wide there was barely a curve to the surface they trotted along, and whenever he looked up from his feet he experienced a moment of vertigo as his mind believed he was running straight up a tree.

Rain started to fall, and inwardly Nico groaned. Within moments fat drops were bursting everywhere, blinding him until he pulled up the hood of his coat. Through the falling haze he could make out women dismounting from the two zels, and Contrarè slapping the animals' rumps to send them galloping off across the bridge. Bull was already climbing down the side of the vast trunk, and a few women dared to follow him without hesitation.

'You think we would have thought of that?' Nico asked his father.

'What,' grunted Cole, 'hiding under a bridge?'

The last of the women were helping Chira down with the infant. With no time to spare, Nico and his father clambered over the hedge of branches and then down the side of the dripping trunk after the others.

Quickly they lost themselves from sight amongst the leaves and the furry vines that hung like loops of hair from the giant limbs. A few squirrels and tree lizards scampered away in fright. Nico was a good climber and he descended easily, scenting the resiny perfume from its bark.

Down there the branches curved upwards into the stronger light found above, forming a cradle of limbs and foliage below. The massive leaves formed a roof from which the rainwater ran off in spouts and watery curtains. Bull and the Contrarè made themselves comfortable where they could and the group did likewise, though some of the women muttered about the great gulf of air they dangled above, with the river threading far below. Others shushed them into silence though – for suddenly, up above on the bridge, they could hear the clatter of a great many hobnailed boots running across.

Their pursuers had finally caught up with them.

In fright young Kes slipped and fell against a limb, dropping a knife she'd been carrying for defence. Nico held a hand out to help her, but either she didn't notice or didn't want it. Instead she gripped the much sturdier tree limb and righted herself, staring down at the blade falling through the air, a glitter of steel spinning in the morning light until it vanished into the river.

'I can't stand it,' the girl whispered in white-faced fear. 'I'll kill myself before they catch me again, I really will.'

'Don't worry,' said Nico. 'They're never going to find us down here.'

The footsteps were loud and numerous and right over their heads now.

'We're close!' rasped a voice from above them in accented Trade. 'I can smell those women's snatches on the wind.'

'Can't see how you can smell anything but that damned animal stink on you, Harko. We ever catch up with these women, they'll pass out from the stench of us before we can do anything with them.'

'Who cares? Wouldn't stop me if they dropped dead on us, my prick's so hard for it right now.'

Just then the baby croaked awake in Chira's arms. Every head turned towards them in alarm. Kes bit her lip and closed her eyes, trembling fiercely. Nico gripped the hilt of the blade he carried in his belt.

'Is that a zel?' came another voice from further along the bridge.

'Where? I can't see anything in this rain.'

'Just running from the bridge there. Kush, we're right behind them, come on!'

Onwards the boots thundered, carrying the voices with them until they were no more.

The Bitter River was a soft murmur far below, barely heard in the chorus of the rain.

Together, the group exhaled a collective sigh of relief.

CHAPTER EIGHTEEN

Coya

On the day of Year's End, with the clouds brewing above the windy plain, the first imperial assaults began in earnest against the city of Bar-Khos – thousands of enemy fighters rushing across no-man's-land with a collective roar, only to be dashed against the earthen slope fronting the wall, blown up and shot to bloody pieces.

Coya was there to see the carnage for himself, having climbed to the high parapet to join the city's defenders: Red Guards and purple-cloaked Hoo, Volunteers and foreign Greyjackets, all wreathed in the gunsmoke of barking rifles and the cannon blasting from the wall's turrets. Only an hour ago he'd been down in the southern inkworks questioning the Diplomat Ché, until a contact had informed him that General Creed was planning a sortie against the enemy encampment, hoping to surprise them during their first wave of attacks. Not liking the sound of such a reckless endeavour, Coya had hurried to the northern wall to seek the general out.

Yet finding Creed was another matter. In the heat of the action, every person he asked on the wall seemed to have a different answer for him.

'He was headed for the north-eastern gate, last I saw him,' answered a Red Guard captain from behind his scarf, and the man pointed off along the wall, in the opposite direction to what Coya had been told by the last soldier he'd asked.

'You're certain of that, Captain?' Coya hollered above all the noise.

'That's what I saw.'

And so onwards Coya hurried along the parapet, flanked by his new bodyguard as soldiers stepped respectfully out of his way.

'You really think this is wise, my lord?' asked the bodyguard by his side as a grenade exploded further along the parapet, scattering soldiers from its blast.

He'd already forgotten the name of the woman, assigned to him only this morning by the local League House to replace Marsh. At least while he remained in Bar-Khos.

Coya cast another sidelong glimpse at her through the drifting haze of smoke. A dark-skinned Khosian no older than himself, her lanky body was encased in the tightest, thinnest suit of rubber that Coya had ever seen. As though she wanted the least resistance whenever she moved; as though really she wished to be doing this work entirely naked.

Soldiers stared hard at her as they passed them by: stared hard at her body and the two pistols hanging from the curves of her hips, drawn even now by her cat-like grace.

Yes, that was it – *Lynx*, she called herself.

Coya tore his gaze from her and stared along the parapet, seeking a sign of General Creed.

Banners were fluttering along the top of the wall, snapping like gunfire above the heads of the defenders. He was heartened to see how many flags were those of the League, flown by Volunteers who had been sent here to aid the city; aquamarine squares of cloth, bearing the sacred Golden Spiral totem of the Free Ports.

'Look at those devils coming in again,' hissed the bodyguard, and once again Coya glanced at the sharp-faced features of the Khosian woman, with her dark plaits swinging from the quick turns of her head as she watched the enemy forces attacking.

He grunted, squinting through the crenellations at the waves of imperial fighters roaring towards them once again, his skin reddened by more than just the chilling kiss of the wind.

Down on the plain the host of enemy infantry thundered towards them, even as the cannon along the wall opened up in another murderous fusillade. Spouts of black earth erupted along the front of the approaching enemy ranks, tearing them asunder and tossing bodies through the air like so many rag dolls – a sight that still seemed surreal to his eyes, like something from a dream. With debris raining down on them the Mannian forces hurtled onwards, their banners waving the blood-red hand of Mann as they grew ever closer. Siege towers loomed in the distance.

It was enough to stop Coya in his tracks for a moment. He leaned on his cane to catch his breath, and gazed between defenders at the oncoming wave.

He would swear just then he could feel the stone flagging trembling beneath his boots. Closer they came, stumbling and hopping over a steaming carpet of corpses that stretched all the way to the earthen slope fronting the wall.

There must have been a thousand dead down there already. Coya thought that was a staggering number of casualties for a single morning's work. And now rifle shots were raining down on the enemy figures too, dropping men in droves just as the reloaded cannon roared fury into their masses. Their ranks thinned even further.

Yet still they kept coming, throwing themselves into their near-certain deaths with a commitment he found wholly stunning. As though their lives were truly worth nothing at all.

This is madness, reeled his mind. *This is insanity writ large.*

He was still finding it hard to comprehend, why men would willingly sacrifice themselves in such a way as this. Not in the defence of their families or some other worthy cause, but purely for the matter of conquest.

It was the Empire's greatest feat, right there before him, Coya realized. How they persuaded people to be nothing more than grist in the grind of imperial ambitions, bringing slaughter to themselves and other peoples.

Scowling, Coya started walking again along the parapet in his shambling, hurried gait. Behind him his bodyguard dallied for a moment, interested in some detail of the attack. He snapped over his shoulder for her attention. 'Aren't you meant to be protecting me or something?'

'Sorry, my Lord Zeziké,' she said, rejoining him with her long-legged stride. 'Just trying to reckon their numbers.'

'Call me *lord* one more time and I'll be putting in for another replacement, you understand me?'

'Of course.'

She was the best that they had on Khos, a League bodyguard for nearly five years now. Or so she had boasted to Coya, right about the time he was deciding he didn't like her; didn't like that she wasn't Marsh.

'Call me Coya for Kush sake or call me nothing at all.'

'Delegate, I'll call you anything you like, if only you'll step into some shelter.'

'Never mind that. I still need to find Creed here.'

But enemy shots were snapping in now, fired by snipers sheltering out there on the plain behind movable wicker walls. An enemy shell exploded nearby, sending debris from the earthen slope over the crenellations. The stonework shuddered minutely beneath his feet. And then without warning another shell hit the crenellations themselves and Coya flinched back, glimpsing pieces of stone and men flying from the blast. Screams rose out, and medicos ran stooped through the smoke towards them. People were lying dead out here. Coya's stomach turned.

Lynx had borrowed a shield from somewhere in the last few moments, and she held it aloft casually to protect them both. Together they hurried towards the shelter of a nearby turret, from the top of which a ballista was hurling bundles of rocks through the air. As they scrambled up steps towards the turret's doorway, Coya glanced down and saw that some enemy figures had somehow made it all the way to the base of the earthen slope, bearing ladders. One of the armoured soldiers carried a banner of Mann, holding it aloft proudly for those behind him to follow. Smoke barked from a hand cannon above and the figure fell in two, shorn through the waist. Others hurried to pick up the fallen flag.

'It's like some kind of simple-minded game to them,' he gasped aloud to himself, stumbling through the open doorway into the turret's sheltered interior. It was just as noisy inside, with riflemen firing away through slots in the curving turret wall. 'Carry the flag to the top of the wall without stopping. Try not to get killed horribly in the process. Kill anyone you can.'

A game that had been inoculated into them so deeply that they mistook it for something real, even when chainshot was taking their heads off. He shook his own head in disbelief. 'I can't fathom it.'

'The whip helps,' remarked his bodyguard. 'And crucifying deserters like they do, or soldiers who refuse to attack.'

Slaves then, no matter how you looked at it. Most of those enemy soldiers probably didn't want to be doing this at all, for all that appearances portrayed otherwise.

Huffing and puffing, Coya carried on to the opposite doorway and looked out along the next expanse of parapet for a sign of Creed. But instead he witnessed the imperial tide crashing against the base of the wall.

Lynx was right behind him, the tall woman breathing down his neck.

'My father was a soldier,' she called out, as men scrambled desperately up the slope with shields over their heads. Some were carrying ladders but the Khosian defenders were picking them off first, experts by now at this kind of siege fighting. 'A lot of it comes down to brotherhood as well. Mostly a soldier doesn't want to let his friends down.'

Did that mean then that it was love propelling the enemy horde against the defences of the city? Love for their friends? That they were all bands of brothers down there getting mangled to pieces together – the best of emotions exploited by the very worst of desires?

'Coya?'

He turned, startled to see a familiar sooty face amongst the riflemen. It was Captain Gamorre, leader of the Volunteer Rangers, who had escorted him into the Windrush forest to negotiate with the Contrarè; that damned fool waste of time in which he'd tried to enlist the natives' aid in the war. The lean, stubble-headed woman frowned and rested the stock of her rifle on the floor, looking concerned. 'You really think this is the best place for you right now, Coya? You want to get yourself killed?'

It was one of the curses of his famous heritage, not to mention his crippled condition – people kept treating him like a precious, fragile thing.

'Captain, so good to see you well! Ah, and the rest of you!'

Heads were turning now from the firing slits in the wall, more rangers in their skins and leathers and camouflaged cloaks, and Coya could see other familiar faces amongst them too: the old grizzled sergeant, Sansun; the lad Xeno with the tattooed head; young Curl the medico, with her hair spiked in a tall crest, helping with the ammunition.

It really was heartening to see them alive and well. For a moment, he almost forgot the carnage on the wall.

'How's that head wound of yours?' shouted Sergeant Sansun.

'No better,' Coya told him. 'Tell me, where are your quarters in the city? You must let me treat you all to a meal when you can get away.'

'We're a little busy here, Coya,' answered the captain grimly, hitching up her rifle again before turning her back to him. But Sergeant Sansun took the bait with a bitter snarl.

'Quarters? They have us sleeping in kennels where they used to keep the goddamned dogs.'

'You're joking!'

'I look like a man who's joking?'

'Well that won't do at all. I have a place in the south you can come and stay. Plenty of room there, if a little draughty. I'll clear it with your people if you need me to.'

And Coya told the old veteran where he was talking about, the inkworks down in All Fools.

'Anything would be better than where we're staying now,' said the girl Curl.

'Well the offer's there if you want it,' Coya said. 'Right now, I don't suppose any of you can point me towards General Creed?'

But none of them had seen the Lord Protector. Coya said his farewells then stepped out through the doorway, bracing himself as if he was stepping out into hail. Lynx stepped quickly to flank him.

Outside on the open parapet, the tops of a few ladders were appearing now along the wall. Defenders shoved them aside with their pikes, firing down at whoever was below or swinging at those trying to scramble up over the edge. They looked like they were beating back a fire, grimly calm and dirty-faced, though those weren't flames they were stamping on but human faces, human hands.

Suddenly a cluster of grenades went off, sending figures reeling this way and that. Lynx ducked in front of Coya with the shield held out and caught a few metallic raps against it. When she lowered the shield, they could see a small group of enemy fighters launching themselves over the crenellations at the defenders, hacking wildly with swords and axes.

A few were running right at them.

Coya stared dumbstruck, having never seen the enemy this close before. He saw one sweating, armoured fellow bouncing in on the balls of his feet just like Marsh used to do, two curved swords in his grasp, moving with all the speed and grace of an expert fighter – but Lynx threw the shield at his face and he went down hard. She fired a shot through the throat of a second attacker, and he pitched over the edge. She took a third with a wicked-looking blade in her other hand, knocking aside his weapon before stabbing him deep in the belly.

The young man shuddered, gaping at him over the woman's shoulder as though it was Coya's fault his life was being taken.

Coya looked away, squeezing his eyes shut for a moment.

'*Is that him?*'

'Who?'

'*The Lord Protector,*' said his bodyguard, kicking the folding soldier to the flagstones. Coya saw her point east along the street that ran by the back of the wall. '*Riding at the head of that cavalry column there.*'

Damn it all, she was right. That fool Creed was already setting off on his sortie, leading a cavalry formation towards the eastern gateway in his great bearskin coat.

There was no way to reach him in time. No way to talk some sense into the man, to repeat more forcefully what his advisers had already stated that morning – that Creed was taking an insane and unnecessary risk by leading a surprise attack like this.

'What a way to end the year,' Coya grumbled to himself, not liking this at all.

CHAPTER NINETEEN

Bahn

'Wet work, eh, Calvone!'

The rider by Bahn's side hollered through sweat raining from beneath his helm: a steaming Red Guard hunched in full armour, his crimson cloak flowing behind him like a trailing flame; a man on fire. Stooping in his saddle, the fellow chopped at the next passing figure with his curved sword – a human blur flashing between him and Bahn before it was gone, trampled beneath the hooves of the zels following behind.

The Red Guard whooped from the thrill of the kill.

'Let's clip their wings, men!' shouted a rider directly in front, and it was General Creed himself with his raven-black hair dashing back over his shoulders, the low sun shattering into brilliance behind the blade he aimed straight and true at the enemy encampment.

Bahn shook his head like a man startled awake. The wind washed over the scarf tied across his face, stabbing at watering eyes narrowed below the rim of his helm. He was hot and sticky with the action of the moment, his whole body jerking up and down to the stride of the galloping, reeking zel beneath him. One hand gripped the reins and a bundle of hairy mane. His other hand held his sword like a thing forgotten, rap-rapping against his leg.

What am I doing here? he asked himself with more than a modicum of fear, for Bahn could truly remember nothing from the most recent moments behind him – no notion at all of how he was outside the city's northern wall on the lathered back of a zel, galloping across the plain towards the imperial encampment, following after General Creed in his great bearskin coat.

Bahn wiped his eyes clear of sweat as the zels surged over the trampled turf, enemy figures scrambling out of their way.

Mandalay was the name of the rider flanking Bahn, he recalled now. Colonel Mandalay of the lancers, veteran of the battle at Chey-Wes. Sure enough, behind them charged three hundred cavalrymen in the thinnest of wedges, leaning into the strides of their mounts with their curved blades catching the light, whooping and lashing out at whoever swept by. They seemed keen to be out here taking the fight to the enemy. Keen to be following General Creed at the very tip of the wedge into the enemy encampment itself, bounding over half-finished earthworks and muddy figures scrambling for cover, ignoring the growing crackle of rifle fire coming their way.

Recollections were starting to shake loose in Bahn's skull as the ground flashed past beneath his boots. Memories from the last handful of days were coming back to him, vague and detached as though they belonged to someone else entirely; too awful to recount in fact, too sickening to believe. Yet Bahn had no choice but to assume them as his own, as unpleasant a thing as climbing into the sodden clothing of a corpse.

In his own way he had talked General Creed into leading this brief sortie through the enemy positions. Supposedly it was to gauge the chances for success of a larger attack against the enemy, while giving them a bloodied nose at the same time – though what Creed was gauging now seemed more fundamental than that, more like whose side the gods of old were really on.

Right through the imperial encampment he was leading them, whipping past tents as they charged down one of the lanes between the efficiently arranged blocks of quarters, startled enemy soldiers yelling all around them. Bullets zipped through the breezy air. The riders were moving too fast to be hit but a zel cried out from somewhere behind, sounding like it was falling. Off to their left some outriders were trying to intercept their path, but a sea of tents was getting in their way. To the right rose the distant wall and sanctuary of the city, much further away than Bahn had been expecting.

Something whipped over his zel's snorting head and he knew a spear had just narrowly missed them both.

Bahn leaned further down over the zel's neck for cover. The heartbeats in his ears were as loud as the thundering hoof-beats of their mounts. His tongue was a dry stick in his mouth. Steel sang as Mandalay hacked at another passing enemy soldier. Behind them a

Red Guard cried out as he crashed from his mount, and there was another cry from a wounded zel.

One strike and he could go down here too, right in the midst of fifty thousand Mannian fighters, a people who rejoiced in tormenting their prisoners. He'd be lucky if he bit into the suicide wafer hanging from his neck in time, the same wafer they had all been given in case of capture. Still, Bahn Calvone felt more alive than he had done in days, weeks even.

Perhaps it was the intensity of the action, the cleansing breath of fear coursing through his blood, that pulled him clear of his fugue condition into this sudden spell of clarity. Whatever the reason, Bahn felt himself once again, and he would have rejoiced in the fact had he not sensed the transitory nature of the moment.

How chilling, in fact, to have these sudden precious moments of lucid thinking, only to know that once his blood cooled he would undoubtedly sink back into that shameful weak-minded condition that had possessed him so entirely since his return to the besieged city, his head fogged as though it was drugged, his compulsions those of a stranger, an *enemy*.

Bahn remembered what he was supposed to do on behalf of the Mannian Empire, and all of a sudden he experienced a desperate need to vomit.

I am a traitor to my own people. My own loved ones!

He thought again of the suicide wafer round his neck. He would have reached for it if an enemy rider hadn't flashed towards him, swinging a sword as he came in alongside him.

Bahn ducked beneath the swinging blade. By instinct he jabbed across his zel's head with his own blade, missing too, remembering all at once how difficult it was to fight on the bouncing back of a zel.

More enemy riders were coursing against their left flank. Ahead of him General Creed struck one from the saddle, the figure falling under the zel of Bahn's opponent and almost unseating him. Bahn swung and missed again. Once more the enemy blade came swinging in and Bahn could only duck beneath it, the steel ringing across his helm with shocking force. Bright stars flashed in his sight. With time slowing to a crawl Bahn felt his grip loosening, his body falling before he could right himself.

Free fall. The awful shock of crashing to the ground in his

armour, his arms instinctively wrapping his head while zels pounded over him like the tumbling rocks of a landslide.

Through his arms Bahn saw the Khosian formation of riders charging onwards between the tents, several of the zels riderless like his own, leaving him behind to his fate. He knew he should grab for the wafer hanging from his neck. Shouts filled the air. Enemy figures loomed and a boot kicked out at him, then another. Hands grabbed hold of Bahn and dragged him to his unsteady feet.

He was surrounded by imperial soldiers, wild of eye, jabbering and grabbing for a piece of him.

Let it end this way, he thought with a sudden rush of relief. Let the enemy cause their own downfall with his bloody death here on the plain, depriving themselves of his betrayal.

But no, here came an imperial officer barging his way into the fray, shouting for the men not to harm Bahn but to take him prisoner instead. Now, at last, Bahn snatched at the suicide wafer dangling from his neck. But they yanked it from his hand and restrained his arms behind his back, so that he stood there panting into the face of the officer. The man was red-faced with barely controlled anger. Bahn spat in his eyes, then roared and struggled to be free from them.

'Come on then, you bastards, finish it!'

In the distance he could hear the Khosian guns firing, cutting though the imperial forces that had been attacking the wall since dawn.

It took him a moment to realize it was more than merely his legs shaking beneath him, that the ground itself was beginning to tremble. Over the din of the siege guns Bahn could make out a rumble of hoof-beats growing louder, coming ever closer. He looked around as they all did.

Sweet Mercy, but it was Creed and the rest of the surviving riders, charging right for him with all the force and momentum of three hundred zels and riders at full gallop. While the enemy soldiers scattered around him Bahn stared in amazement, elation, then bitter disappointment. He blinked back tears as Creed bent low in his saddle, the general's teeth clenched hard and one hand thrust out for him.

For a moment Bahn almost let the Lord Protector rush right past him. But at the last instant Bahn's legs started to pump and his arm went up of its own volition and Creed grasped at it, swinging him onto the back of his zel as though he weighed almost nothing.

'Thought we'd lost your there, Lieutenant,' Creed shouted over his bearskin shoulder.

His throat in a knot, Bahn could only slap the general's back in gratitude, in forgiveness.

Soon Creed was leading them clear of the camp and turning south towards the city. Whooping now in cocky victory the riders tore off across the plain, flanking the many thousands of soldiers assaulting the walls and the main gates.

Smoke tussled in the breeze from a siege tower on fire. Skirmishers cleared out of their way, firing bows and slings without effect. Creed turned them towards the same side-gate from which they had sallied out, the ground before it still clear of enemy forces all the way up to its protective berms of earth.

Ahead, the city's wall and its many towers rose higher. Smoke puffed along the crenellations where rifles fired at enemy riders still giving chase.

'That was damned easier than I was expecting,' Creed was shouting. 'You were right, Bahn. I've a mind to hit them tomorrow again even harder!'

I should tell him now while I still can. Warn him of my betrayal.

But now that they were clear of the enemy positions and returning to the city, Bahn's blood was indeed beginning to cool.

He tried to speak, to raise his voice in the general's ear. But shame smothered him, choking him to silence; that and the deep conditioning of the Mannian priests.

Already his thoughts were growing sluggish, turning once more towards bitterness and spite and envy. Bahn felt himself slipping again into his previous state of waking sleep.

Up there on the parapet, he could see the faces of Khosian defenders cheering the returning cavalry as they wound their way through the snaking berms. Again he tried to speak aloud, but then he glimpsed the gate opening ahead of them onto a busy city street and he stifled a sob, knowing it was hopeless.

Perched on the back of the general's zel, Bahn began to weep quietly, a man sinking fast into his own torpid condition.

My wife! My children!

And then the gloom of the gateway swallowed him up just like the shadows in his mind.

CHAPTER TWENTY

Nico

Under the tree bridge they rested in the fork of two massive branches, a knobbly space that was big and flat enough for the entire group to huddle upon, even to lie down. Chira and some others fussed over the infant child, though most of the women were trying to snatch what sleep they could under furs they had taken from the slaver camp.

The world was a haze of rain out there beyond the boughs of the mighty tree bridge. But here where they had taken shelter under the roof-sized leaves it was dry enough, snug even, considering the conditions.

'You're lucky we ran into you when we did,' said the big man Bull, in a hush. He sat with one of his Contrarè companions lounging beside him, chewing on some jerky, while the other lay on his back nearby, watching the women. In the daylight, Nico could see the mixed blood in the giant's features, the Khosian and the Contrarè, and the spiral horns tattooed on his temples.

'Aye,' said Cole, sitting against a backdrop of cascading water. 'Lucky you just happened to be out there in the middle of the night.'

Bull's companion smiled, and gave a toss of his head that threw his long dark hair back from features painted red and black. 'We Longalla are a curious people,' he answered, and he spoke in a voice rich as the earth. When the native shifted around to face them better, Nico saw the surprising blue dazzle of his eyes. 'We heard the hunting horn calling in the night. We thought we would have a look.'

'Well it's a damned fine thing you did,' said Nico with a glance to his father.

'Please. Call me Sky In His Eyes.'

He spoke Trade well. He was not at all what Nico expected of a forest native of the Windrush. Not at all like the stories he had heard about these dangerous, bandit-like folk of the trees. With his feathers and face paints, his grace of motion, his sheer wild beauty, Nico thought he was the most splendid-looking fellow he had ever seen.

The women too seemed fascinated by the Contrarè men, an interest divided between Bull and the handsome young native with the blue eyes. Nearby, their partner's scowl was something of a contrast to Bull's straightforward manner and the smiling ease of Sky In His Eyes. Lying there in his gleaming warpaint, the man's gaze was fierce and proud as he surveyed them all; a reminder that they were still invaders to these native people, even now, a thousand years since they had settled in the lowlands of Khos.

'Can't say I've seen many Contrarè this far south,' said Cole. 'What is it you're doing down here?'

'We're headed for the city,' rumbled Bull's heavy voice back at him.

'Heck of a time to be headed for Bar-Khos. There's an imperial army in your way right now.'

'Still. We have a great need to get inside. I have a warning I must give to the Lord Protector's staff.'

Cole inclined his head thoughtfully, glancing to Nico then back to the big man facing him.

'A warning?' said Nico.

'Yes. There are Khosian traitors in the city. Conditioned by the Mannian priests to bring about your people's downfall.'

Your people, he said, for all that he had once been a famous Khosian pit fighter, and before that, according to Cole, a soldier of Bar-Khos.

'And you know this . . . how?'

Bull didn't much like that question. He set his mouth in a thin line and rocked backed on his haunches.

'Because I was supposed to be one of them.'

'Oh?'

'I fought in the chartassa at Chey-Wes. Afterwards I was captured. We were drugged, manipulated, by their priests. But some of us managed to escape.' He pulled a face at the memory of it. 'When the others headed back to the Khosian lines, I headed into the Windrush instead, where my people found me.'

So he was a deserter then, just like his father. Indeed Cole stirred at his words.

'My brother escaped after being captured at Chey-Wes. Bahn Calvone.'

'You must be Cole, then,' he said with surprise. 'He spoke of you. How is Bahn – you have spoken with him?'

'Yes, back in Bar-Khos.'

Bull lowered his eyes.

'What is it?'

He would not answer for a moment, and Nico felt a sudden tension gathering in his chest.

'Bahn is one of the people I must warn them about.'

'Are you calling my brother a traitor?' Cole's voice had an edge to it, enough to draw the attention of some of the women listening to the conversation.

'No. I know your brother to be a good man, an honourable man. But they have played with that mind of his. I'm guessing he will not even know what he is doing.'

'What do you mean?' asked Nico, horrified now. He had never been close to his uncle, but Bahn was family, and his family had been through more than enough already.

'After my escape,' explained Bull, 'I suffered from nightmares, terrible nightmares. Until a Sky Hermit took a look inside my head, and saw what the priests had done to me. How they wanted me to betray Bar-Khos.'

Cole straightened with his longrifle and took a few steps away, his back turned to them all. Bull watched him closely.

'Now I can only hope to make it to the city in time to stop the others, before it is too late.'

'You have a way inside?' asked one of the women, and Nico saw that it was young Kes.

'I know a place we can get through the wall. Maybe. The trick will be making it that far, heh. Tonight, we plan to try it.'

'You can take us into the city with you?' exclaimed another woman.

'Well that's getting a little bit ahead of ourselves now.'

'You have to take us,' said Kes, trying to catch his eye with her blonde-haired beauty. 'We have nowhere else to go!'

'It isn't that simple, lass. We'll have to sneak through the enemy lines. I don't see how we can do that with all of you trailing along.'

'But we'll die out here, or worse. Cole, Nico, tell him what it's been like! They have to take us with them!'

But Cole only lowered his head, hand gripping the barrel of his longrifle. 'They helped us already,' he grumbled, not liking it any more than she did.

'So where do we go from here, then?'

'My son and I are heading into that camp, down there on the plain. Where we intend to rescue his mother. What you do from here is your own concern.'

'Nico! Tell me you're not leaving us here.'

They were all watching him now, the women who were still awake, Chira with the child nursing at her breast.

'No. We're not leaving you,' he told them firmly.

And his father growled and walked away.

*

'We have to leave them here,' whispered his father, where he squatted further along the branch with his hunched back turned to the others. 'We've no other choice.'

'How can you say that so easily, Father?' Nico asked him.

'Because it's true. If we want to save your mother we'll have to ditch them sooner or later anyway. There isn't another option, Nico. We already saved these people from captivity. They can wait until nightfall and then head for the nearest town, probably Husson. Take their chances like the rest of us.'

Nico was appalled at the sense he was making. Appalled to find life being reduced to this awful formula of necessity.

Kes glanced his way through a tangle of vines, and brushed the hair from her face with a smile. Chira sat rocking the child to sleep again. A few others sat around talking about what they should do now. Nico took in the frayed and spent condition of the women, their faces dark with grime, a few chewing on what morsels of food they had. As tough as they seemed, their time in captivity had taken everything out of them, and then had come the desperate flight through the dark. Now they were understandably shattered.

'They'll be fine,' said his father. 'So long as they only move at night like the Contrarè have been doing. It's three nights' walk to Husson. I'll give them sound directions.'

Three nights!

'They won't be fine and you know it. Look at them, they're starving and exhausted! And Bull says that enemy patrols are everywhere. We leave them here, they'll be caught for sure. I can feel it.'

'What you're feeling is horniness for that girl over there. Do you want to save your mother or not?'

'Of course I don't want to save my mother. Why would I ever want to save my mother from a lifetime of slavery?'

'Then what is it you're suggesting? How do we save your mother and these women at the same time?'

Of course Nico had no answer for him. If he did, they'd hardly be arguing about what to do.

'Son. We can't tarry here any longer. Once it's dark we need to make our move. If we follow the river down onto the plain we can reach the imperial siege camp by tonight, and start looking.'

A thump sounded overhead, and heads craned to look upwards.

'*Ssh!*' hissed Sky In His Eyes from further along the branch, and the Contrarè man rose to his feet and cocked an ear.

Footsteps clattered above them through the drumming rain; zels snorted in the cold air so that they saw the mist falling over the side.

'Might be those bastards who were chasing us, heading back this way,' someone said in a hush.

'Or a patrol,' voiced another.

'Ssh!'

They listened in silence as the footsteps passed them by.

Nico stared hard at his father.

'I tell you, I have a *really* bad feeling about this.'

*

Nico hated these short days of winter.

Already the sun was falling into the western hills in a blazing stew of clouds, the whole day nearly gone, and all they had done with it was hang around beneath the tree bridge, sheltering from the torrential rain while they caught up with their sleep and slowly recovered their strength for whatever lay ahead.

Cole had told the women about the town of Husson three days' march from here, and how it was likely a good bet for sanctuary since it had strong walls. Some of them had wept, hearing this confirmation that he was intent on leaving. Most though were too exhausted even for that, and simply stared at him with wide blinking eyes, as though he was describing a trek to one of the moons for all that it was possible.

Some of the freed captives, now they had time enough to think beyond their present situation, wished to return to their farms to see if any of their family had survived the raids. But others managed to rouse themselves enough to dissuade them of such notions, pointing out that the countryside was crawling with slavers and enemy patrols. Besides, they said, any family members who had survived would have taken refuge where they could, in forests or hills or in the towns. Something the women needed to do themselves now, since no one was willing to help them reach the protection of the city.

Bull, for his part, would say nothing more on the matter. Most of the time he and the Contrarè kept their own company on a bough a little distance away, resting while they could.

Through the day, Cole dozed too beneath his hat, his scarred face almost hidden by the upturned collar of his coat. Exhausted, just like the rest of them. Nico lay not far from him with his back to a branch, watching the group in the failing twilight. His body was tired but after a few hours' sleep he had felt no need for more. It was a comfort simply to lie there doing nothing all day, with the water dripping from the roof of leaves and the river mumbling far below, listening to their occasional quiet chatter and watching the women pass the time together, most of all Kes.

It was the time of Kamasat, one of the group had reminded them. Indeed it should be the last day of the year – Year's End. Soon, some of the women were exchanging gifts with each other in the traditional Khosian fashion: leaves folded into the shapes of love birds and other animals, morsels of food, songs, kind promises. Their muted celebrations drew a few red-breasted robins to the branches around them, and the birds chirped and flitted about in curiosity at their presence there. For a time it was as though their plight was not so lean and desperate after all.

In the deepening gloom the women became ever-darker silhouettes against the glistening fall of rain, and Nico's concerns for them returned even more strongly than before. Yet for all that he had thought on the matter in hope of finding some alternative, he knew his father was still right. What else could be done if they hoped to save his mother?

A sudden movement startled him. With his enhanced eyes he could see that it was Kes, crouched and stepping towards him where he lay a little distance from the rest of the group. Before he could speak the girl straddled herself upon his lap, the hem of her skirt ruffling all about him.

'Here, handsome,' she said in a breathy hush, and planted a hat on his head that she'd woven from strips of leaf. 'Made you a Kama-sat gift.'

'A gift? I doubt I have anything for you in return.'

'Oh . . . don't be so sure of that.'

Kes grabbed his hands and slid them beneath the hem of her skirt, right against the skin of her thighs. He was growing stiff and she could feel it, for she pressed herself down against him, clasping her hands to his head as they both released a tiny gasp of joy.

She smelled of the sky, the sea, the dark earth from which all things grew and all things returned.

'Leave the old days behind and the new ones ahead,' she intoned in his ear in an excited whisper as she rubbed against him even harder, her mouth gently kissing his neck. Nico glanced to his father, still asleep beneath his hat, and at the others, near lost now in the semi-darkness, wondering if he was dreaming.

Dream or not, Kes was fumbling at his belt and the buttons of his trousers while she kissed him full on the mouth now, the flesh of her tongue darting against his own.

Sweet Kush, this is really happening! She's really crazy for me!

Nico groaned aloud as he slid inside her.

'Hush,' she breathed with a smile. She rocked back and forth now, her fair hair falling against his face. 'The others will hear you.'

It felt wilder than he'd ever imagined. Her body was as hard as a sculpture of wood wrapped in soft skin and clothing, yet it yielded in places against his kneading hands. Nico came with a gasp that she stifled with her hand; too quickly, too suddenly, wanting more. Kes kept on grinding, her legs flexing on either side of him while his grasp urged her onwards. He bit at a bare nipple that bobbed and pressed against his grin and heard her stifle her own prolonged moan above him, and when she shuddered and whimpered in his ear Nico came again, exploding this time with all the might of the pent-up years behind him, smothering a primal growl against the scented press of her breasts.

And still they kept on moving against each other, rocking and panting, seeking more.

*

He was lying there with Kes asleep in his arms when a hand slapped his shoulder. It was his father, stepping past him on the bough.

'You're following the river?' Cole was asking the big man Bull, who stood there with his pack on his back ready to leave.

'Aye,' answered Bull. 'We plan to float down most of the way on a log. What of it?'

His father adjusted the hat on his head, offering a shrug. 'Just asking.'

Darkness had finally fallen and they spoke as dim shapes in the gloom of the branches. At least the rain had stopped for now, though by the look of the clouds it could return at any moment.

Already Bull's two companions were climbing up and out of the tree. The big man took a last glance back when Cole spoke aloud.

'You run across that brother of mine, you go easy on him, you hear me?'

Bull nodded, and with a grunt heaved himself upwards. The women watched him go in silence.

Kes remained still in Nico's arms, though she was blinking at him now.

How do I leave her now? he wondered. Lacking an answer, he bent forward to kiss her gently on her pouting lips.

'I suppose we should be moving out too, then,' said Shandras, without much conviction. The women muttered and started to rise. The baby was mewling softly.

Slowly he clambered free from Kes, then helped her to her feet.

His father was watching them both from where he stood leaning on his upright rifle, and as Nico held the girl's hands before him, he saw Cole release a heavy sigh and drop his head.

'All right then,' sighed Cole's voice as he looked at them all. 'I'll help you as far as I can. That's all.'

'Father?'

'You have two choices here,' Cole declared to the women gathering around him in sudden hope. 'You take your chances striking out for Husson alone, or you try reaching the city wall same way as Bull is trying. And I take you most of the way there.'

What's this?

'But you heard the man!' called out Shandras. 'He said he couldn't take us with him.'

Cole shrugged with a tilt of his head.

'Fellow didn't say anything about following them.'

CHAPTER TWENTY-ONE

Dreamer

What a luxury, to spend some time alone with her thoughts away from the bustle of the inkworks.

Shard the Dreamer sat in the wooden outhouse at the back of the building, where a field of trampled earth ran all the way down to the canal. In the cold night air she jiggled on the wooden rim of the privy for warmth, blowing hot breaths into the cups of her hands – still too weak even to ignite a simple heating glyph about her body.

I need to get out of here, came the cold clear words in her head. *I need to get back to my home and my work at the Academy while I still can, before I end up buried by this war.*

She was tired of this war already. Tired of her weakened condition. Tired of risking her life every night trying to break through the Mannian's blockade of the city's farcrys. In her mind she pictured the slopes of the Painted Mountain overlooking the green island of Salina, and the bright buildings of the Academy perched on their terraces, where wisdom and art, curiosity and innovation, were entwined by an ethos of open learning for all. She wanted to be there more than anything else in the world.

Shard straightened with a start as the door banged closed in the neighbouring privy, separated from her own by thin lengths of driftwood. She saw a flicker of lantern light through the cracks. Heard a rustle of clothing and a woman sighing loudly from the other side of the wood.

A sob crept through the thin wood, followed by another.

She couldn't stop herself as she leaned forward to peer between the ill-fitting planks. She saw a figure dressed in black leathers. A young woman with hair that was a wild vertical crest above her skull.

It was Curl, the medico apprentice who had accompanied them on their expedition into the Windrush forest to enlist the Contrarè.

The girl had arrived here a few hours earlier, accompanied by other surviving rangers of that expedition and replacements she did not know, claiming that Coya had offered them new quarters in the inkworks. Weary and cold, they had made themselves at home even as the Rōshun grumbled from the far side of the room.

Shard liked the young woman. She recalled the intelligent curiosity she had expressed towards Shard's craft during their travels. Her quiet strength, for all that there was something vulnerable about her too. And so it was awful to see her burying her face in her hands and crying into them, sobbing with shuddering breaths.

There were times in life when Shard felt truly at a loss as to what to do in the presence of other people's emotions. Should she respect Curl's privacy, or offer her support in some way?

She really didn't know.

Just then the girl banged the wall with a fist and startled Shard back from the gap. But she was only venting her distress, for she banged it again and again, growling in frustration.

What has distressed you so? Shard wondered, and she reached out with her mind to sense the life-force pulsing around the young woman. In a surprising flash of intuition, she sensed the faint second life-force within her.

Curl was with child.

Air hooked in the back of Shard's throat. No wonder the girl was so miserable. What a time to find yourself expecting a child.

The Dreamer blinked, surprised even more by the sight of Curl producing a leather bag from a deep pocket, dripping tears as she opened it upon her lap. A smaller bag of white cloth sat within it, next to a wooden pipe. Slowly, Curl peeled open the smaller bag like the petals of a flower to reveal a mound of white powder within, which she began to scoop into the pipe.

'Oh my girl,' Shard breathed aloud without thinking, and Curl twitched in shock and looked around to spot the eye watching her through the gap.

Instantly Shard sat back and held her breath, pretending she wasn't there.

This is ridiculous, she considered, after a long moment's silence.

'Sorry,' Shard ventured. 'I heard someone crying. Are you all right?'

'Shard?'

'Yes. Guilty.'

A sniffle. More silence.

Really, what to say? What to do?

The girl was in need of help, and a hot flush of frustration overcame Shard's inertia. It propelled her to her feet with sudden intent, so that she hitched up her trousers even as she opened the door with a kick of a boot, then stepped outside into the darkness.

With a tug she pulled the other door open, to reveal the startled features of the young medico. Curl's mouth gaped open as a gust suddenly filled the space of the privy with the white powder that had been perched so delicately, so preciously, upon her lap.

'That stuff will do your child harm in those doses. It's really a very bad idea, you know.'

'*You bitch*,' Curl shuddered, staring down at the now-empty bag. The powder was sticking to her hair and her face so it resembled some kind of desperately applied make-up. 'What would you know anyway?' she asked between breaths.

'About dross addiction? More than I ever wanted to.'

'Addiction?'

'Your hands are shaking. Dead give-away.'

Shard managed a smile and held out a friendly hand for the girl to take. 'Come. I can help you. I can help you both.'

*

At the back of the inkworks, a set of wooden steps was fixed on the outside leading up to a door on the first floor. Holding hands, Shard led Curl up to the door and inside.

Back in her work room, her assistant Blame was nowhere to be seen. He'd left a kettle boiling on one of the little stove burners, and muttering through the clouds of steam Shard lifted it from the flames and put it to one side, wondering where he'd got to.

She set about preparing a special hot brew for the young woman. Hugging herself for warmth and comfort, Curl sniffed around the tables at the back of the room – an office, once upon a time – where most of Shard's portable exotics were arrayed like the fleshy, pulsing, bleeding exhibits of a freak show. She recalled how fascinated Curl had been with the idea of the Black Dream. How her interest had longed to delve deeper.

'How long have you known you were pregnant?' Shard asked across the room.

'I didn't, not for certain.'

Curl was facing one of the sink tanks, puzzled by the snaps and splashes in the briny soup. 'How could you tell?'

'Call it a Dreamer's intuition. Here,' Shard said, bringing a steaming mug to her. 'This will help with your dross cravings, a little.'

The girl blew across the dark liquid for a moment, frowning, then tried a tentative sip. She gagged. 'That's really appalling.'

'You intend to have this child?'

'I – yes. Of course I do.'

'Then you can't take any more dross. I can give you a supply of this tea to help you with that.'

Suddenly a smattering of concussions caused the building to shudder on its foundations. Battles raging in the air.

'I'm frightened,' admitted Curl. Shard reached out to grasp her cold hand again, and to rub it soothingly.

'The father,' Shard tried. 'Is he around? Can he help you?'

Her expression changed, as though she'd just swallowed something sour and unwanted. A stiff jerk of her head. A tear spilled clear.

'I would not ask for his help. Not ever.'

'Have you no one in the city?'

'I did,' she rasped, squeezing her eyes shut. 'But they're gone. Lost in the sky raids.'

'Then you must come with me, when I finally leave this city.'

Curl sniffed. 'What do you mean?'

'Come back to the Academy of Salina, and I'll show you all the Black Dream you want to see. You can learn, and develop whatever talents you like, while you raise your child.'

'Really?' she croaked, and her tears were flowing freely now.

'Really.'

'But—'

'Curl. It's going to be all right, you hear me?'

CHAPTER TWENTY-TWO

Diplomat

Ché was cursing to himself when he returned from the latrine escorted by a guard, and made his way back through the darkened inkworks towards the stairs, his skin red raw where the heavy manacles chaffed against it.

The damned cripple still refused to free him from the chains. Not yet, Coya had told him. *Not until I've had the chance to question you more thoroughly. Not until you've proven you can be trusted.*

And when would that be? Ché wondered grimly. How much more could he offer to prove his sincerity?

Lanterns glimmered at the far end of the inkworks where some of the Rōshun were hunkered down for the night. So far they had refused to speak to him, unhappy, it seemed, at whatever deal they had made with the cripple to not cause him harm. Besides, they appeared to be occupied with other things right then. Like squabbling with the new arrivals about keeping to their own space – these Volunteer rangers who had arrived earlier that day.

As Ché clanked and rattled towards the back stairs, a figure cleared his throat from the nearest shadows. A match flared, and Ché saw the face of Fanazda in the sudden flaring of light, staring at him with his black eyes as he lit a cheroot; just waiting there for him.

The veteran Rōshun said nothing for a moment, puffing away with an expression of sly humour.

Ché ignored the man and shuffled onwards.

At the back of the space more lanterns dispelled the darkness. Some of the rangers were bedded down there, tired and grim from fighting at the northern wall.

Ché froze, spotting a familiar face amongst them. A pretty girl with her hair formed into a spiky crest.

Curl!

He hadn't seen her in a few months. Not since they had both fled the fall of Tume after their brief night of passion together; not since she had found out who he really was, a Mannian deserter, her hated enemy, and had alerted the Khosians to arrest him.

The girl spotted him too in that moment, and when she did, her face flinched with obvious horror.

'What are *you* doing here?' she cried out, causing her companions to follow her wide-eyed stare to his shackled, hobbled form.

'Curl,' he said, too stunned for thought. But she only backed away from him, then hurried off.

'Curl!'

In his mind he saw once more the awful expression contorting her features as she first laid eyes on him.

She really hates me!

*

Ché didn't know if the Rōshun Fanazda was only toying with him or not. He remembered the fellow's dark wit, back when Ché had been a young apprentice and Fanazda had taught the craft of silent killing with a knife. But he remembered too how there had been something vicious about the man, something hard and unforgiving.

In his work as a Rōshun, Fanazda's speciality was slitting people's throats while they slept. Sometimes he had described those slow deaths to the apprentices in a way that no other Rōshun ever would have. Thinking back on it now, having grimly killed his own fair share of people as a Diplomat, Ché realized that the man truly enjoyed it.

If anyone was going to make a move against him, it was Fanazda.

On the upper floor of the inkworks, in a side gallery filled with dusty boxes and crates, Ché feigned a stumble against his tired guard and managed to steal the man's knife from his belt without him noticing. Both cursing each other, Ché retreated to his sleeping furs in the corner and stashed the knife beneath them where he could reach it quickly, then lay down to sleep.

He lay there for a long time, staring up at the darkness of the high ceiling overhead, sore with his bruising and his raw skin, thinking of the girl Curl. His mind turned and turned. Sleep was impossible, for all that he was bone weary.

Eventually he got up again, slowly gathering his chains in his hands. His guard was snoring nearby on a chair. Ché shuffled past the man in his clinking leg irons, and found the stairs to the roof and followed them upwards.

On the flat roof of the inkworks, he stood watching the columns of smoke rising from the north of the city, where imperial shells were falling through the darkness. The glow of burning buildings flickered against the cloudy overcast. Brilliant beams of light tilted across the sky.

Up on the roof, a few rangers were sitting around a brazier of glowing coals, sipping chee and talking quietly, keeping themselves apart from the snipers stationed around the edges – looking south towards the silent, looming walls of the Shield. They scowled at the sight of him, knowing who and what he was now, and Ché scowled back. In a perverse way he was starting to enjoy this constant animosity towards him. He had always been an outsider in life, deep down anyway, where his antagonistic peers and arrogant superiors of the Mannian order would never notice. Such hostility now was familiar ground for Ché, ground upon which he felt sure-footed, even bolstered.

But then he noticed the figure of Curl sitting alone on a far corner of the roof, and such notions fled him.

'Still chained like a dog then. That must be getting tiresome, I bet.'

The voice came out of the darkness by his side. A figure sat perched there on the low parapet surrounding the roof, nursing a steaming mug of chee.

'Wild?' Ché ventured. Through the gloom he could just make out the fellow's great swooping moustaches and his familiar sharp features.

The veteran Rōshun took a noisy sip from his mug.

'How's life?' he asked.

Ché glanced towards Curl again with her back turned, feeling torn.

'Just like how it looks,' he told Wild. 'You?'

'Not much better, I suppose, when all's accounted for.'

'You joined the war, then. I didn't take the Rōshun for the kind to choose a side. Nor you.'

With a grimace Wild stared at Ché with his quick, dangerous eyes. At once Ché knew his mistake.

'I lost a home when you led the Imperials to Sato. I lost friends and brothers. Oshō was like a father to me.' Wild meant the old leader of the Rōshun order, one of many slain during the assault on their mountain monastery. The man nodded, certain of what he said next. 'I will see some justice in this world, some rebalancing of the scales against the Empire, before I taste the dirt in my mouth.'

'Any of that retribution include me?'

'You? No, lad. I gave my word you would not be harmed. Coya insists you're more valuable to us alive than dead.'

For now, his tone implied.

Still, Wild seemed friendly enough.

'You're about the first person here hasn't wanted to spit in my eye.'

'Oh, I still hate you, Ché. But hatred tends to blind when you need to see most clearly. Best to loosen yourself from its grip, I always thought. Just like the old farlanders always taught us.'

'Ash, Baracha – where are they?'

'Dead, we think. Somewhere on the other side of the Shield.'

Ché looked to the south where the dark walls stretched across the isthmus. *Dead*, he repeated in his mind, and didn't quite believe it.

The thunder of heavy guns drew his gaze northwards again, towards the glow of fires across the north of the city.

'You think these people are anything but doomed?'

'I wouldn't be here if I thought so.'

'Still. The Rōshun should have a way out. Just in case.'

Wild said nothing. It was so strange to see the man here after all this time. He didn't seem any different, no older at all; as though it had been only yesterday since they had last spoken, Ché still a young apprentice and Wild an easygoing instructor in cali, the Rōshun fighting style.

It was Ché who was different now; another person entirely.

Wild was reading his expression with bright eyes.

'So the Mannians played with your mind, made you think you were someone you really weren't. That's your story, is it?'

Ché tensed in his chains.

'They just *made* you do it?'

How to explain it to the man? That for Ché's whole life he had never had any choices in what he did. That being born into the Mannian order, the priestly ruling elite of the Empire, meant being born into a world of fanaticism, of dogma and expectations.

A scrape of boots, and Ché turned to see Wild stepping off towards the stairs without another word.

Ché stared after him for a moment, then returned his attention to Curl.

*

When he tried to approach Curl, two of the rangers rose in his way. But Ché just shoved through them and kept on walking until he was standing behind her, his chest rising and falling fast.

She jerked around, startled to see him there. She'd been crying.

'Please,' said Curl, wiping her face clear. 'Not now.'

What to say to her, now he had a chance to speak?

'I only need a moment. Then I'll stay out of your way. I promise.'

She turned her back to him, shoulders hunched; looking small and cold and vulnerable in her longcoat and dark leathers. Ché glared at the two rangers behind him until they backed off a little, then sat down beside her on the parapet. He stared at Curl hard, all his feelings surging up inside of him like a sudden nausea.

It was strange that he wasn't more surprised to find her here like this, in the same place he had ended up too. Ché didn't believe in signs or any other such nonsense. Yet here they both were again, as though it was truly meant to be.

The pain in the girl's eyes was still there, fresh as ever. He knew that Curl was a refugee, one of the few to escape the island of Lagos, where the Empire had put her people to the torch.

He'd shared only a single intimate night with this young and beautiful medico, this girl who had caught his eye back in Tume, during a game of Rash – of all things – while Ché had been disguised as a civilian. Yet something of Curl had remained with him long after their physical parting.

In Ché's darkest moments down in that stone hole where the Khosians had imprisoned him, the girl had been one of the things he'd thought about to stop himself from going mad, from biting through the veins in his wrists. Her startling blue eyes as they'd made love on a stranger's bed; her smile like warm sunlight flooding the gloomy spaces of his mind.

Nothing more, really, than a brief, bright spark of connection in a life that had long ago ceased to have any meaning for Ché; the life of a state assassin, a life barely lived at all.

'They let you go, then,' she said quietly. 'I was hoping they would lock you in a dark cell somewhere, and let you rot.'

'They did. A very dark and cramped cell.'

'So you're on our side now, is that what we're supposed to believe?'

Ché blew air through his lips in exasperation.

'Curl. I don't know what side I'm on. I'm not on any side. But I'm not a Mannian, a believer in the faith. I hardly ever was. Just because I was born into it, that doesn't make me one of them.'

'So you're innocent. You have no blood on your hands.'

'Innocent?' Ché piped with surprise. He thought of the people he had killed during his short career as a Diplomat. He thought of a big bronze water boiler whistling with steam, while a terrified boy hammered from inside it as he was boiled alive. 'No. I'm hardly that.'

'Get away from me; I mean it!'

'Look. I just wanted to tell you—'

'Tell me what?'

His mouth hung open as he stared at the fear and anger in her expression. He saw how Curl held a hand across her belly, as though soothing it, cradling it. Ché blinked, feeling the brush of some vague intuition.

'*Tell me what?*' she demanded to know.

'I just wanted to tell you, I'm . . . *sorry.*'

She tightened her mouth at that. Tears fell from her eyes, but she wore them like proud scars now, not deigning to wipe them away as she rose to her feet to confront him.

'You're sorry?' came her small, twisted voice. 'Just stay away from me. Do you hear me? *Stay away!*'

And with that she strode off across the roof for the stairs, leaving Ché to wonder what else he should have said to her. Yet he knew in his heart there were not enough words in the world to fill the gulf of space between them.

'Curl!' he called after her like a love-sick fool.

But she was gone, and the remaining rangers cast their dark accusing looks at him, the greatest villain in the world.

*

That night, Ché dreamed again of the same deep lake that he'd dreamed about under the influence of the Lie Teller. He floated on his back in the milk-warm waters with his eyes closed against the sun, and the longer he lay there the freer he felt from his cares.

Ripples breached the surface before him. He thought it was a fish at first, but then the tiny head of a baby bobbed out of the water and smiled directly at him.

How bizarre, reflected Ché.

More ripples washed against him as Curl broke the surface too, her crest of hair flattened wet against her skull. She grabbed the baby and they both giggled, turning in the water.

'*Curl?*' he said aloud to catch her attention.

The girl's eyes were black coals burning with malice. She came towards him, lifting a hand clear of the water. Sunlight glinted off nails that were as long and sharp as talons. Smiling wickedly, Curl slowly drew a claw across the skin of his throat.

He gasped at the sudden stinging pain of it.

Ché sprang awake, feeling the pain for real across his throat, realizing that he could barely breathe.

He blinked his eyes open and stared up at the darkness of the inkworks, too shocked to move. The iron taste of blood filled his mouth. It was all he could smell.

Over his sleeping furs crouched a figure with a length of steel in its hand, dripping blood in the lantern light.

'That sound you hear right now,' hissed the voice of a man he knew at once to be Fanazda. 'That's the sound of the air bubbling from your lungs and out through your slit throat.'

It was the truth of it, for Ché reached up and felt the bloody mess of his throat. Mortal fear seized him as his clawing fingers tried to close the open wound.

The knife, you fool, get the knife!

But even as his bloody hand snaked for the knife under his furs, he knew that it was no longer there. Fanazda had it in his grasp.

The Rōshun lowered himself towards his face, breathing fast.

'That's the sound of you dying, Ché.'

Do something!

Gasping mutely, Ché swiped his manacled arms to grab at something, anything, though he only succeeded in knocking over a mug of water sitting on the floor. He could feel the hot blood gushing from the livid rent in his neck.

Ché floundered while Fanazda gazed down at him in panting rapture. It was luck that made him grasp the steel mug again; desperation that caused him to hurl it across the room.

From across the space the voice of his guard spoke out, and then footsteps were approaching.

'What's going on over there?'

Fanazda vanished into the shadows.

Ché's vision was fading. It pulsed with blackness around the edges. More figures hovered over him, someone shouting at the top of their lungs. Ché could only gasp and shake and try to stop his life from spilling out through his fingers. His limbs were growing numb. He knew he was a dead man with only moments to live.

'Let me through,' snapped a woman's voice, and he knew it was the Dreamer from the power he heard in her words, just an edge of it, enough to scatter the faces gathered around him in the sudden lantern light.

Ché shut his eyes and felt the Dreamer's hands clamp down over his own. He heard her saying something in words that seemed to make no sense to his fading hearing.

He slipped away from her, away from them all. Now that it was over, now that all his fears and memories would soon be gone from him forever, Ché was almost relieved that it was death he fell into. He released the last of his breath in a long and bubbling sigh, and allowed himself to sink deep, deep, beneath the warm waters of the lake.

CHAPTER TWENTY-THREE

Coya

The Broken Wheel was a large and sprawling establishment perched on the foundations of an old wagoners' warehouse, where once trade wagons had deposited their cargoes brought there from far beyond the city. It was not a single building, but rather a series of structures added gradually over the years, thrown together with sheets of tar-paper and scraps of wood of every kind and size, from pale pine to the darkest of tiqs, from old wagon planks to bits of driftwood washed up on the coast, so that for all the obvious skill with which it had been built, the notorious taverna resembled something of a greatly oversized beach shanty.

Open every hour, day and night, it remained popular with a clientele just as motley as the patchwork components of its outer shell. All kinds of folk frequented the Broken Wheel. Some came to relax, others to make use of its many pleasures for sale or hire, or to gamble on the regular pit fights staged in the basement below. Others still to talk their illicit trades and deals.

At any time of the day, a person could see burly wagoners still dusty from the roads of Khos – leathery-skinned crews running freight between the city and the island's heartland towns – rubbing shoulders with professional gamblers, stocksmen, fight followers, street girls, thieves, hustlers and dross runners in a miscellanea of Khosians and foreign nationals. The taverna was located in the western limits of the besieged city, where the northern wall and the southern coastline came close together, pinching off an area of ware-houses, stock pens, and reeking, bubbling tar pits known either as the Flats or the Stinks, depending on who you were speaking to, whether they lived there or were neighbours to it. A working district, where most of the Bar-Khosian freight operations were run as well as much of its smuggling.

The Broken Wheel was notorious for all these reasons, but most of all because of who owned and ran it – the Tuchoni criminal family known as the Javalli Clan, respected throughout the city's underworld.

The Javalli were nomads of the road who had settled down, mostly, into an urban life of larceny and fencing stolen goods. Though these days their main activity was smuggling large amounts of dross to the southern continent, with the help of a clan of Sea Gypsies, their historical blood cousins – dross being a substance that was illegal in the Empire, unlike in the Free Ports.

Even the local population of the district looked upon them well enough, here where most folk made hardy livings and tended towards a healthy disdain of the authorities. For the Javalli were unlike many of the other criminal gangs in the city, such as the notorious Caw-Caws or the Dockside Hoods, who were little more than thugs extorting the citizenry with brutal tactics of intimidation. The Javalli understood the importance of community relations. Instead of being a blight upon their area, they gave back to their immediate community by way of festas and food given out daily, ensuring both friendly relations and a certain protective shroud against the law.

For Coya Zeziké, they were often his most valuable contacts in the city.

*

His head was throbbing tonight, even with all the hazii cakes he'd eaten.

Coya stifled a yawn, feeling the weariness of the day weighing down his body. He'd barely returned to the little house he was staying at in the south of the city, just through the door in fact, when the housekeeper had handed him a message in an envelope, brought there by courier earlier in the day.

Coya had sighed as he glanced at the note. It had Vay Javalli's signature scrawled upon it, and nothing more. Her way of saying they needed to meet. He'd thought of going to bed and sorting out this business in the morning. He should have done. Yet something had told him it couldn't wait, and he had told his bodyguard to find a rickshaw so they could head up to the Broken Wheel.

And so here he was, waiting for Vay Javalli as he yawned away in the vast and crowded basement room of the Broken Wheel, with another series of explosions going off somewhere above ground, pummelling the district surrounding the rickety building. More enemy Birds-of-War he supposed, sweeping up from the south to hit the area with dropped munitions.

For the last few nights they'd been striking the western limits of the city, in lightning raids launched from the imperial-held Lansway to the south, targeting the granaries and the thousands of penned animals, trying to destroy what was left of the city's winter food stocks. He hoped they wouldn't be at it all night long again. He wanted to get back to his bed.

Coya scowled as the ground trembled from the aftershocks. He could feel the vibrations strumming through the crowded wooden tiers which filled much of the basement space of the Broken Wheel, and which half encircled the wide pit in the floor; tremors rising up into his dully aching joints. Dust trickled from the floor beams overhead, and he followed it as it fell past swaying silk lanterns into the miasma of smoke below, where excited men and women thronged around the deep pit in the floor, yelling down at the pair of fighters locked in lethal combat there – if they could even be called fighters.

Even now, Coya could hardly fathom what he was seeing down there. From the top tier of seating, he gazed down into the pit at the naked imperial soldier fighting for his life against the advances of a lone slin, its flopping head inflating and deflating as it leaped on him with its scrambling goat legs. The gamblers screamed louder around the pit.

Coya could just make out how someone had stitched shut the slin's gills along its bare flanks, no doubt to stop it from releasing its blinding, noxious scents into the room. Yet he could still smell the creature, even from here on the utmost tier, the odd foul whiff like burning hair.

He looked towards his bodyguard, Lynx, sitting a few arm's lengths away, flexing her spine in that animal way she had of stretching whenever she felt like it. She was so focused on the fight that anyone could have been sneaking up to kill him, especially here in this packed basement, which he thought was precisely the kind of place a Mannian Diplomat would favour for an attack. But just as he was reflecting on how useless she was as a bodyguard compared to Marsh, Lynx suddenly rose and stepped down to block the path of a figure climbing up to join him, a thin fellow in a waxed longcoat.

Below them a shrill shriek rose up from the pit before ending abruptly. The crowd roared.

'Doesn't look much like you're enjoying the show,' ventured the man, staring up at him.

'It's all right,' Coya told his bodyguard, seeing that it was the old smuggler Passon, one of his contacts here in the city.

Passon stopped on the tier beneath him, which thankfully was as empty as the one at the top. He removed his hat, and took out a pocket rag to mop at his sweating bald dome. It was hot in this basement with all the people crowded together, and Passon was a man well advanced in years, red-faced and slightly wheezing; clearly a fellow wringing out the remains of his useful working life before old age rendered him infirm.

'How in all the world did they find a slin and an enemy soldier?' Coya asked with a nod to the pit.

Passon shrugged, his mind on other things. 'Heard they were captured on the wall. Don't ask me how they ended up here.'

Bribery or the return of a favour no doubt. The Javalli had contacts all over the city, including within the middle ranks of the military.

More explosions shook the high ceiling above them. The concussions were coming closer now, dislodging even more trickles of dust onto their heads, though only Coya and Passon seemed to pay them any heed. Old Passon looked up with his watery eyes at the sounds raging above the surface, as though they invoked memories from his past. Coya remembered that he hailed originally from the Green Isles in the far west of the Midèrēs. The famed Green Isles, where they had fought against the invading Mannian Empire just as the Free Ports were doing now, and had been ruthlessly destroyed for their resistance.

Passon had lived through the worst of those times. In his lifetime he had witnessed the most terrifying tragedy of them all, the downfall and enslavement of his own people.

More than anyone, here was a man who knew how the city's survival was anything but guaranteed. That not every story had a happy ending. The very worst could still befall them.

'I got those news-sheets for you,' Passon said, handing Coya a leather-bound package. 'Including your favourite. An edition of the *Holy Times*, straight from the imperial capital.'

'Why, thank you, Passon,' said Coya as he eagerly unwrapped the package. 'What do I owe you?'

But when he looked to Passon the old smuggler was already stepping down to the floor. Passon merely threw a hand over his shoulder in farewell.

By his side, Coya's bodyguard watched as he unfolded the printed pages of the *Holy Times*.

'You read the news-sheets from Q'os?'

'Know your enemy,' he told her. 'Now, hush, let me read in peace.'

It was hardly the right lighting to read by, let alone the best setting. Yet Coya managed it by holding the paper up and peering at it closely while he tuned out all else.

According to its date the news-sheet was more than a month old, if he was figuring his imperial calendar correctly. The front page of the *Holy Times*, and indeed much inside of it, was dominated by a single story, a recent spate of attacks within the Empire's capital of Q'os.

Democras fanatics slay sixty in latest terror campaign.

He blinked incredulous at the headline a few times before scanning through the text of the story. It described how the recent state funeral of Sasheen, deceased Holy Matriarch of Mann, held after her body had been flown home from the battlefields of Khos, had been blighted by a series of bombings and shootings in the streets of the imperial capital.

The *Holy Times* blamed teams of masked fanatics from the democras, heavily armed and thoroughly trained men prepared to die for their cause. Scant evidence was provided though. A suicide note supposedly found on one of their dead bodies. Slogans shouted out as they'd shot people in the streets, hailing the virtues of the democras to anyone who was listening. It seemed that after the slaughter they had made it back to their safe house, only to be surrounded and killed to the last man, not a single one left alive for interrogation.

Yet as a member of the covert network known as the Few, Coya was sharply aware that the remarkable details of the attacks were largely words of fiction. No such operation had been launched from the Free Ports, or ever would be. Hence why no demands had been made by the masked attackers. It was all a depraved show, the main act being the public murder of citizens.

These men were not fanatics from the Free Ports at all, but skilled provocateurs of the Empire acting as such against their own people. The whole thing was a stinking set-up, right down to the bodies found in the safe house – which were likely not those of the real culprits at all.

Coya frowned, chewing his lower lip without realizing it.

Clearly it was becoming the standard operating method of the Empire, this manipulation of the masses through spectacular acts of violence unleashed amongst them. Helped along by the parroting of the capital's press, who always ensured that the lies became solidified as official truth.

In reality, the result from these attacks was that the citizenry of Q'os were in an even fiercer fervour to see the Free Ports defeated in the war. With such personal affronts they could cloak themselves not as aggressors, not as ruthless conquerors, but as distraught and angry victims of foreign barbarity.

War bonds would go through the roof.

'You look piqued,' said Lynx. 'Anything of interest?'

For a reply Coya rustled the loose papers of the news-sheet noisily, then turned his back on her.

If only the people of Q'os really knew, he reflected. If only they were aware of the measures their rulers were willing to take in order to manipulate their collective opinions, to control every aspect of their thoughts.

In the heartland of the Empire, everything that people knew about the contemporary world came from the news-sheets, which were owned and run by wealthy figures within the ruling priesthood of Mann. And for some reason that was forever beyond him, most people naively believed whatever they read on these tissue-thin pieces of paper.

They truly believed that even now they lived in some form of real democracy, something like the League of the Democras itself. Because they were told they did, because it was self-evident, because they took part in elections in which they were allowed to select between the two primary colours of the Mannian order: between the white purity of the truly devout candidates and the blood-red of the all-out fanatics.

For a creed which outwardly prided itself on the notions of individuality – at least the individuality to exploit and rule whomever they could – in reality the herd instinct reigned absolute within the lands of Mann, the people corralled within bounds they did not even see. The populations of the heartland lived under a kind of mass delusion in which everything they believed about themselves and the wider world was largely an *inverse* of the truth, shaped as much by the omission of things as by what was intentionally stated.

They had been taught that black was white and up was down. That they were the good guys and everyone else was the bad, the envious, the downright crazy.

It was the work of Nihilis himself, or at least his lasting influence upon the empire he had founded as the First Holy Patriarch of Mann. Nihilis had been a man able to manipulate reality itself by the clever hijacking of language. He had sponsored the first official dictionary of Trade, the common tongue of the Midèrēs, so that he could subtly change the meanings of the words themselves – the conceptual framework of thought itself. Even his chosen name of Nihilis was an intentional inversion of what he truly represented – a belief in nothing, from a man who ended up founding his own faith.

Coya had read the First Patriarch's little *Book of Truth*, and his even more revealing *Book of Lies*.

Lies were the very foundation of the Mannians' world.

'Those explosions are getting closer,' Lynx remarked, gazing up at the rattling ceiling.

He ignored her, but her voice piped up once more in his ear. She really did seem to have trouble staying quiet. 'Who are we waiting for anyway?'

With pursed lips Coya set the paper down and glared at his new bodyguard, but she only blinked back at him with an innocent frown.

'What?'

*

Down on the floor, an uproar rose from the crowd as yet another naked enemy prisoner was led towards the pit in chains.

People called out in shock at the great size of the man, for he was truly a giant, nine or more feet tall and towering over the armed toughs who escorted him; one of those northern tribesmen used as shock troops by the Empire. He was wearing nothing but a loin cloth, and tattoos covered much of his muscled body. A stained bandage was wrapped over the long and matted hair of his head.

Passon had said these prisoners had been captured while assaulting the wall. It was hard to imagine anyone bringing this particular one down.

'Impressive fellow,' noted Lynx, and Coya saw that her mouth was partly hanging open as she marvelled at the hulking form of the man.

The giant remained composed as they escorted him through the gamblers and drunks, thieves and street girls in heavy chains, with the tips of spears prodding at his back. As they led him to his fate he did not struggle or resist, but rather stepped to the rim with his head held high. While they freed him from his chains, the giant took in the circle of gaping faces around the rim with a slow and steady scrutiny, rubbing at his chafed wrists. Someone handed him a studded gauntlet, and he tugged it on.

The man was breathing fast, his chest rising and falling. He looked down into the pit at the slin quivering in anticipation.

With a snarl he raised both arms then leapt down upon the beast.

'Crazy bastard too,' breathed Lynx heavily.

Screaming, the crowd pressed in around the rim for a better look. Even Coya leaned forwards over the pages of his news-sheet.

Through the haze of hazii smoke he could see the two figures locked in struggle, the smaller slin easily holding back the arms of the giant. Most of the crowd seemed to be waving the enemy northerner on, though it was the slin that Coya found himself rooting for. As monstrous in appearance as it might be, this creature had been captured in its far homeland and brought all the way here against its will, only to be thrust into the calloused midst of a war in which it had no part.

Give it a swift death or give it freedom, Coya thought. But not this.

A figure climbing the crowded tiers below caught his eye, and Coya sat back, folding the news-sheets closed on his lap.

'Easy,' he said to his bodyguard, who was rising at the sight of Vay Javalli stepping up through the spectators towards him, as people hurriedly cleared out of the way.

'Lynx,' he said to his bodyguard. 'Give us some space here.'

For a moment he watched the bodyguard's lithe form stepping away in her skintight suit, graceful as a cat, and then with a huff Vay Javalli sat her own lean body next to his, clad in a quilted Tuchoni longcoat buttoned to her throat.

'So what are they up to in Q'os these days?' asked the swarthy Tuchoni woman, taking a glance at the paper in his hand.

'Only the usual smoke and mirrors,' grumbled Coya, slapping the pages down beside him to give her his full attention.

Coya met the brilliant shock of Vay Javalli's black eyes, overshadowed by the vertical crest of hair on an otherwise shaven head. A wise and knowing humour pinched her middle-aged features, which were leathery and wind-kissed from exposure to the elements. Her ears were pierced through with many silver hoops.

'You don't look yourself at all, my dear Coya,' said the leader of the Javalli criminal clan, for she knew him well enough from their years of acquaintance. 'Where's Marsh then?' she asked with a glance to his bodyguard sitting beyond earshot, who was gazing back intently.

Coya could only shake his head and purse his lips until the realization came to her.

'No! I thought Marsh would outrun us all.'

Down on the floor the crowds yelled their encouragement. The northern tribesman had the slin up against the wall of the pit now, and was pounding away at the creature with a studded fist, yelling out with every strike.

'And your wife,' enquired Vay in an effort to change the subject. 'I hope she's well?'

But his infirm wife was the very last thing he wished to be talking about just then either.

Coya inhaled and made a grimace of a smile. He reached out a hand to settle it on her trousered knee, and gave her a delicate pat; like he did sometimes with his mother.

'Good to see you in good health, Vay. But it's late, and I'm tired. You wanted to speak with me. So let's be hearing it.'

'Very well. This might be something you're already expecting, or it might not be. Either way, I thought it prudent you should know, soon as possible.'

'Know what, Vay?'

'That we have a Visitor in the city right now.'

He swayed back, checking to see if anyone was listening.

'A Visitor?' he echoed in a hush. 'Here, in Bar-Khos?'

'Just arrived by boat, she claims. She came to the Broken Wheel herself to speak with me. Told me she'd been asking around, and had heard what line of business I'm in. Seemed to believe I would have the connections she needed.'

'Connections?'

'She wants to sell seven lirs of pure moondust at the going rate.'

Coya blinked in surprise. 'That sounds like rather a lot.'

'It is. Enough to make a person wealthy as any king. Moondust is rarer than Royal Milk. That pet Dreamer of yours will tell you as much. Seems this Fallen One intends to use it as her stake here, just like the ones before her.'

This was news of the most surprising kind.

He knew the secret of moondust. It was a secret known to members of the Few, along with a smattering of others around the Midèrēs – that the name of the substance was more than mere whimsy, it really did come from one of the moons. A moon that was populated just like Erēs. Those who brought it here were known as Visitors, or Fallen Ones – that untold number of people who had tumbled from the sky over the centuries, mostly hermit monks seeking isolation, and explorers, and the downright crazy, having travelled from the moon of Sholos on a one-way trip.

The Visitors usually hid their true identities, but not always. Some had made themselves known to the Few over the years, though without explaining how they knew of the Few's existence, or so much else about their world. It was even claimed that his own distant ancestor, Zeziké, was a Visitor himself. Which, if true, meant that Coya's blood was partly from another world.

'Why here?' said Coya. 'Why come to Bar-Khos in the middle of a siege?'

'She did seem somewhat harried. As though she was asking herself the very same question.'

'Describe her to me.'

'*Tall*. Black-skinned like a farlander. Called herself *Ocean*. My people thought of jacking her for the moondust but I stopped them, for their own sake. She looked like she could handle them with a snap of her finger.'

Vay Javalli tilted her head as though dislodging one last titbit of information. 'Altogether, she had a very strange manner about her.'

'How so?'

'Like this was truly the first time she had ever seen *anything*. That was how I realized she was for real.'

Coya ruminated over the grip of his cane, not liking what he heard.

'We must bring this woman into the fold,' he decided. 'You have a means of contacting this person?'

'Of course. I've agreed to act as her middleman for the moondust, so she intends to return here to discuss our business tomorrow. Perhaps you could be there too, say noon?'

Coya chewed it over.

'It's almost dawn now,' he said. 'I should head back and get some sleep first. You sure she will turn up?'

'If she wants to leave this city she will. I'm arranging passage for her on a fast skud. One of our regular smugglers.'

'Where does she wish to go?'

'Anywhere in the Free Ports but here.'

Lanterns shook over their heads from explosions growing more distant now. Vay Javalli stood and flexed her back with a rustle of beads. Down below, a chorus of jeers drew their attention back to the fight, and Coya saw that the slin had somehow knocked the massive tribesman off his feet, so that he lay sprawled across half the earthen floor shaking the daze from his head. A sheen of blood was visible on his pained white features, and then the slin was upon him, tearing away with a frenzy.

'Vay, how in Erēs did you get your hands on a living slin?'

In reply she gave her tight-lipped smile. A Tuchoni with a bad habit for sugar, she did not like to display her rotten teeth to anyone.

'When you're the number-one supplier of dross in the city, you gain contacts in the most surprising places.'

Coya never liked to be reminded of the main business she was in, the smuggling of dross to the southern lands of the Empire. Dross could be a particularly addictive substance. Though he could hardly complain about it either. In reality, given that much of the known world's supplies of dross and other narcotics were secretly controlled by the Empire's intelligence agency, the Elash, her work was as much about covert intelligence gathering as anything else.

They clasped hands firmly – scarred palm against scarred palm – and as always in such instances, in a flash of vision, Coya was reminded of his initiation into the Few. How he had stood cold and naked in a total black nothingness with the Truth Stone heavy in his hand, while a voice asked him question after question about his deepest self; how every truthful answer had caused the Stone to grow ever hotter in his clenched fist, only lies seeming to cool it down. Until Coya had cried out from the pain of it, like holding a red hot coal in his grasp, burning so fiercely from the shaking truth of his words that it would leave an indelible scar upon his palm, an impression of a coiling spiral: the divine geometry of the Golden Spiral. A reminder that the truth was always more painful to bear than deceit; that truth required courage and faith.

'To the spirit of the thing,' she told him sincerely.

'To the spirit,' he intoned, and both scars on their hands flared like flames caught in their grasp, confirming their continuing fidelity to the cause.

Vay turned to go, then turned back at the last moment with a finger outstretched in query.

'One other thing,' she remembered, just as the crowd's passionate yells rose around her.

The tribesman held the slin aloft above his head, moving fast for all the great size of him. Blood sheeted from his head and body.

With a mighty heave he launched the creature head first into the wall, where it tumbled to the ground visibly broken.

In victory the tribesman threw his bloody arms aloft, inciting a jubilant roar from the onlookers that nearly lifted the beams from the ceiling in their momentary celebration of the enemy.

Vay shook her head in amazement.

'Those prisoners we've been tossing into the pit have been saying some strange things,' she shouted over the din, leaning closer. 'They say their people are getting ready for something big out there on the plain. Lots of explosives being brought into the heart of their encampment for no good reason. Mines being laid all over the place. Something about getting ready for a Khosian attack. What's wrong, you look pale? Have you heard of an attack being planned?'

Coya nodded stiffly. 'The Lord Protector just tried a little sortie against the enemy encampment. Now he fancies trying for an even bigger one. I don't think his people can talk him out of it.'

'What can it mean?'

'Only one thing,' Coya realized aloud, snatching up his cane as he rose to his feet. So much for getting back to his bed. At the very least he had to warn him, had to tell Creed what he suspected.

'They know the general is planning another attack. And they're setting a trap for him.'

CHAPTER TWENTY-FOUR

Nico

'Now I recall why it's called the Bitter River,' came a woman's voice through the darkness. 'The water tastes *awful*.'

'Like rusty iron,' agreed another.

'Like blood!'

It was certainly an apt name for the river, Nico reflected. He too had forgotten how bitter its waters were to the tongue, though that didn't stop him from swallowing down a mouthful every now and then to quench his thirst. He knew from his time living in the city – which the river eventually passed through on its way to the sea – that it was harmless enough to drink, even good for certain ailments.

'Never mind the taste,' said Kes. 'It's freezing! I don't think I can survive another hour in this water.'

The sound of her voice in the gloom caused Nico's throat to grow tighter. He was finding it hard to think of anything but their recent love-making in the tree, reliving the sensations of his body against her own. But Kes was right. Unlike the mighty Chilos not far to the east of here, warmed all year round by the steamy, bubbling lake that was its source, the Bitter River ran off the snowy watershed of the Breaks instead. Its temperature was cold enough to put off anyone from putting more than a toe into it, for fear of dying from exposure.

Yet here they were in the freezing winter's night, the whole group submerged in the river while they clung grimly to the boughs of a floating fir tree, their teeth chattering and bodies shaking hard, trying not to curse out from the pain of their ordeal.

Just to step into these waters fully had been a collective trial of shock and willpower. It was so cold that the breath was instantly robbed from the body along with its heat, a kind of all-embracing

suffocation that made it hard not to whoosh noisily for every inhalation of air, and harder still to stop hyperventilating once you got
properly started.

To survive, or at least to increase their slim chances of survival,
the group had smeared themselves with layers of animal fat beneath
their clothing, which they'd gained from the blubbery remains of a
slain river marmuk, helpfully left by the Contrarè next to the river
bank. But it hardly seemed enough now – hardly seemed like anything at all, truth be told – against the penetrating bite of the water.

It would be a miracle if they didn't all freeze to death tonight.

The damned rain was hardly helping either. For all that it provided cover it was also making them wetter and colder than they
needed to be, big fat drops crashing from the clouds onto their bare
heads and across the thrashing surface of the river, splashing water
into their faces and eyes. At least the noise of the rain seemed to have
lulled the child to sleep at last. The infant lay in his swaddling,
perched clear of the water across a few branches of the tree, and
sheltered beneath a few more, whimpering occasionally in his sleep.
In the darkness, Chira was still clucking her tongue softly by his
side, comforting herself as much as the sleeping child.

The fallen tree they were all clinging to was a mature Khosian hill
fir, bearing clumps of green needles that had purpled in the winter
frost, short and spiky things which kept poking Nico's face and
going for his eyes whenever he moved. He hoped its foliage would be
enough to keep the group hidden from sight, for the river coursed
across the plain now with the tree drifting along it, and in moments
they would be floating through the enemy encampment itself.

Directly ahead, the plain was covered in the tents of the Imperial
Expeditionary Force, arrayed beyond range of the northern wall of
Bar-Khos where cannon coughed fire into the night, exchanging
shots with the enemy's forward artillery. The distant wall itself was
brilliantly illuminated by blinding beams of white light cast from
the imperial positions, beams that roamed this way and that along
its face, revealing swarms of enemy forces trying to storm it.

Yet more beams of light slanted upwards over the besieged city
itself, and they flickered and flashed with colours which seemed to
form themselves into shapes hanging there in the sky above Bar-
Khos. Nico wiped his eyes clear, seeing a giant face with pits for eyes

leering down at the city's population, flickering in and out of existence against the curtains of rain.

'Holy Kush,' swore his father from ahead, even as others muttered in the darkness.

What were they going through in Bar-Khos right now? Were the children gaping from their windows or dreaming terrible dreams from their beds? Were the dross heads all lying up on the hill of Steziy Park, freaking out at the face looming in the sky like the old High King's ghost himself, returned to slay the great-grandsons of revolutionaries?

Nico blinked, surprised to see a fire burning in the sky off to the west of the Bitter River. But then he made out the dark form of the ridge upon which it was perched, and realized they were passing Beacon Heights, a well-known hill visible from the city, topped with a watchtower and shrine.

Just ahead of him, Cole hissed for sudden silence. They were entering the enemy encampment.

On either bank the tents squatted in their thousands, many of them dark though many more lit warmly from within; shapes moved behind walls of thin cloth. It was too wet for open camp fires tonight. Few figures moved about, save for those hurrying from one tent to the other.

A cough sounded out from the river bank, then a harsh clearing of a throat. Nico craned his head for a better look. A soldier was having a piss over there, cloaked and helmeted, swaying wearily against the air at his back. The fellow looked up at the tree as it floated past him on the river, but paid it no more mind than that, for he spat and eventually turned away.

Onwards they drifted undetected through the heart of the enemy encampment. Zels snickered from their enclosures along the banks; herds of penned cattle brayed in the rain. Still there was no sign of Bull or the other Contrarè ahead of them.

They were nearing a wooden bridge that spanned bluffs on either high bank. The bridge was lit by lanterns, and crowded with wagons loaded high with cargoes as drivers yelled and whipped at their teams of zels. All of them were headed in the same direction, crossing to the eastern side of the river with a long line of others waiting behind to do the same. Along the tree, everyone ducked their heads as they passed underneath. For a few precious moments the bridge sheltered them from the downpour, and then they were out the other side and getting rained on again. More bridges spanned the river here, minor rope bridges filled with lines of soldiers hunched and hurrying across them. Again they were all headed to the eastern side.

Curious, thought Nico, wondering what was going on.

The river slowed, growing wider, its banks lower. Time passed as slowly as the water's flow.

Ahead, the brilliantly lit city wall grew ever closer as the Bitter River curved around a wide bend. The water here grew shallow enough that Nico could feel the slippery rocks beneath his boots. Across its surface bobbed the reflections of distant lights, punctured by ripples. Faintly they illuminated a figure crouched on a sandbar along the inner left bank – another armoured soldier. Drifting closer, Nico could see water dashing off the young man's helm, and how he wiped at his eyes as though he was weeping.

With a slow inevitability, the top of the tree snagged itself against the sandbar right at the soldier's feet, prompting him to look up.

Sure enough, Nico saw red-raw eyes and the stripes of tears on the young soldier's cheeks. He was holding a knife loosely in his hand for some reason. Before him, a branch full of fir needles suddenly quivered, and the soldier leaned forwards to peer closer.

It was Nico's father, the length of his body submerged just beneath the surface, hidden beneath the branch, shaking it.

'Hey,' whispered Cole over the rain, shaking the fir needles again, his tone a playful one. 'You want something to cry about?'

'What?' asked the startled man.

All at once the water erupted as Cole lunged out at him like a crocodile at its beached prey. In an instant he dragged the man back into the water with him, where he broke his neck with a rough twist.

Nico flinched at the sound of it.

With kicks of their feet they freed the tree from the sandbar and carried onwards downstream towards the city, leaving the young soldier floating just behind them, face down in the water, as though he too was now part of the group.

'You think that was funny?' Nico asked of his father.

'What?'

'*You want something to cry about.*'

'Looked to me like he was going to kill himself anyway,' said Kes. 'He had a knife in his hand, did you see it?'

No one answered. The corpse following behind them was spectacle enough.

Laughter roared from one of the passing tents on the eastern bank. The troops were all hunkered down in their shelters, no one in sight now. Nico lost track of the passing time, falling into a kind of trance of hyper-alertness until suddenly, with a jolt, the tree stopped once more against the flow.

His feet kicked at loose rocks.

Damn it, he thought. The river had become too shallow to go any further.

'Shit, shit, shit!' cursed Kes, realizing their predicament as the other women's voices rose in alarm. Nico tried to quieten them.

'This tree's going no further,' Cole declared, and he rose to a crouch to survey the shallow stretch of river ahead. Nico drew up alongside him.

'We're still in the middle of the enemy camp here!'

With a struggle Nico tried to rise from the water, but he could no longer feel his feet. His legs were vague appendages barely under his control. Shivering uncontrollably, he peered over a snarl of branches and through the haze of rain towards the northern wall of the city rising ahead of them, still terribly distant.

'Look,' said Kes from the other side of the trunk, and Nico saw it too: the jagged shape of another tree up ahead in the water, snared on the opposite bank.

'It's Bull,' he said to his father. Nico was still amazed by just how well he could see at night now, as though everything was struck by moonlight, including the outlines of Bull and his two Contrarè companions, hunkered down in the branches of their own beached tree.

They were making no attempt to move, he could see, and little wonder. On either bank facing their position, a fire sputtered in a covered brazier accompanied by a few sentries standing watch in the rain. Storm lanterns hung on poles, casting their light across the water. Just behind both sets of sentries, more lanterns flickered from within sandbagged positions that were dug into the rising ground, facing each other as they overlooked the shoals of the river.

'They're still there. Those lanterns are lighting them up. They can't move for fear of being spotted.'

'What do we do?' asked Kes, and her voice shuddered with the shaking of her body.

'The city doesn't look so far,' said another woman. 'We could make a dash for it.'

They wanted to try it. He could feel it in the air – their longing for the sanctuary of the city that might just be within reach now, if only because hope was foreshortening the distance. But in their silence hung the unspoken truth of the matter – they would be spotted in no time. Such dilemmas lead people to inaction, and so it was with the party now. No one moved. No one offered any ideas, any further options.

They were growing even colder now that they had stopped moving. Each panted breath sounded loud in the crash of the rain. Teeth chattered and steam rose from exposed skin. Near the back of the tree the child whimpered in his sleep.

It was hard to tell how much time had passed in floating down the river. Nico guessed that dawn must be only a few hours away.

'We can't just lie here in this river!' said one of the women. 'We'll freeze to death! I'm already freezing to death!'

They all knew it. Either the elements would finish them one by one or the child would wake up and start crying, giving them away. Nico cast a desperate look about them, but all he could see were the shallow banks of the river and the tents lined along it, where the odd stooped figure moved through the torrential downpour. Zels were snickering up there somewhere just beyond sight. For a moment he thought about stealing some of them and making their escape that way. But then he shook his head inwardly, frowning at such fantasies. He knew he might make it alone, but never with the entire group following behind.

Nico breathed deep into his belly. He was reminded of his brief Rōshun apprenticeship, and their methods of going naturally with the flow of any situation, knowing when to act and when to wait in stillness, allowing space for things to happen. Yet the freezing river was hardly a conducive place to wait around for an opportunity to present itself.

He needed the old Rōshun Ash, and his impeccable talent for getting out of trouble.

'I'm not getting caught like this,' said Kes, shaking her head vehemently. She glanced along the river towards the city as though judging whether she could make it. 'I'm not lying here till the sun comes up and every soldier in the camp is lining the banks for a piss.'

'Nor I,' agreed another.

They were close to panicking here, Nico sensed. And if some of them bolted they would give the others away, and that would be that.

'Keep your heads,' Nico said along the tree. 'It's the only way we all stand a chance of getting out of this.'

'Oh, it's that simple?' said Kes, this girl he had so recently been entwined with, clearly close to breaking point.

'Kes,' he said, reaching out a hand to grasp her own. 'Stay calm. It doesn't end like this.'

'No?'

'No!'

Nico swept forwards through the water to join his father's side. Grabbing on to a branch he lay there in the river with the cold waters rushing through his clothing, shivering and fearful.

'It doesn't, does it?'

'What's that?'

'End like this. I can't see a way out of here.'

His father only grunted.

On the bluffs ahead overlooking the river, sentries in grey cloaks stamped their feet around the smoking braziers. More smoke rose from the dugouts behind them.

'If Bull and the Contrarè fear to make a move,' he whispered to his son, 'we hardly have a chance with all these women.'

'But we can't just stay here!'

His father was shivering, he noticed. When Cole spoke, it was in a file-rasp of exhaustion.

'I said I'd take them as far as I could. Looks like this is it.'

'*I'm not leaving them here!*'

'Nico. Sooner or later it's going to be everyone for themselves anyway. Think straight. Your mother is likely somewhere in this camp. The pair of us can cut loose on our own. We can pass as camp followers while we look for your mother.'

'No, not yet. I'm not moving until we absolutely have to. We have to give them as long as we can here.'

Cole hissed into the sodden night.

'And how long is that?'

'As long as we can!'

CHAPTER TWENTY-FIVE

Bahn

This is it, chimed a voice in his head that he no longer believed was his own. *This is the day*.

A rooster called out from next door's yard. A dog barked from somewhere down the street. In his cloak and full armour, Bahn Calvone stood facing the tall mirror of his marital bedroom surveying the reflection before him – the scuffed boots that he had once kept meticulously polished, the tarnished helm tucked in the crook of his arm, the sword and hand cannon dangling in their sheaths from his belt. Never before had he felt the weight of it all on his body like he did now, the pull of steel and leather like an anchor fixing him to the spot.

Do it.

Bahn blinked in the pale light of dawn gathering at the window; in the shadows thrown across the room; in the faint mist of his panted breathing.

Do it!

He grabbed for the double-barrelled hand cannon and yanked it from its holster, pointing it straight at the mirror.

Bang, he thought, and then Bahn shifted the gun and pressed the barrel hard against his temple, where beads of sweat were running.

Bang!

Bahn flinched from a sudden din below – his wife Marlee heating water on the kitchen stove. Little Ariale must be awake already, having coughed through much of the night. His son was probably stirring in his bunk too. Always the last to rise.

They were the centre of his world, his whole sense of meaning. But he couldn't think of his family just then. He knew that if he did the weight of all he carried would crush him down into a weeping heap on the floor; and then the grief would kill him.

The heavy gun dropped with his hand and Bahn felt the pain flaring in his side again. He had bruised his ribs the other day when he'd fallen from the zel, even wearing his armour. And now he was expected to go out and do it all over again, this time on foot.

Beyond, in the world at large, the enemy artillery was fading away as the first assault of the day began against the city wall. Rifles crackled from the defences. Boots could be heard marching through the streets in quick-step formation.

It was New Year's Day.

Time to go.

*

Smoke was pouring in black clouds over the wall and the heads of its defenders, tossed by the winds from a siege tower burning somewhere on the other side. Within moments it had fogged the street with a scented, eye-stinging haze, making the faces around him grimy from soot, causing soldiers to clear their lungs with ragged coughs.

Through the overhanging pall, Bahn could see flocks of birds wheeling up there in anticipation above the nearby wall, waiting for the first lull in the fighting so they could descend in their winter-starved hundreds to feast on the dead. Behind them the early sun rose low in the sky, obscured by the haze, and Bahn squinted at the sight of it as though glimpsing an omen; a black sun in a blackened sky.

Slowly, a tug brought him back to the world of people around him.

Bahn looked down to see his wife tying a scarf about his neck above the low collar of his armour, her mouth talking without sound. But then his ears seemed to pop, and suddenly he could hear what she was saying, something about wrapping up warm in his present condition. Indeed he could suddenly hear everything around him again, like the whole world dumped right on his head: the awful racket of the fighting on the wall while the Khosian artillery boomed away; the commands being shouted along the lines of soldiers waiting in the streets below; packs of war hounds growling to be set free from their leashes. A small army was gathering here behind the wall.

'Where are you, my love? Where have you gone?'

'Still here,' he heard himself reply.

'Barely. You're on the far side of the world these days.'

'I'm here. Right here.'

'My dear husband you're in no condition for this. You should have told the Lord Protector as much, that you're not yet fully recovered. He would never expect this of you if he knew what a fog your head is still in.'

Behind them, staff-sergeants were striding past the lines of fighters forming along the street in long columns. They barked at the civilians to get clear; wives and lovers, sisters and mothers, friends and perfect strangers seeing the soldiers off to battle.

'I'm fine,' Bahn lied to her face, and she scowled and thumped him lightly on his breastplate.

He didn't tell his wife that he'd volunteered for this mission, having asked to be by Creed's side today. Let alone that he'd helped spur on this second raid against the Imperials, on foot this time and with greater numbers, by backing up Creed's plan against the protests of the Lord Protector's closest advisers.

Instead he jerked as something hot settled against his cheek. His wife's hand cupped in tenderness. For an instant the connection of her touch seemed to break through Bahn's numbness, reaching some deep inner memory of himself, causing him to blink quickly, startling tears from his eyes. But then once more he felt himself falling away from her, away from all that he loved – an awful sensation, like something from a dream, like that first moment of panic when your foot fails to meet resistance on the ground and keeps on going, pulling the rest of you with it, pulling you down through a bottomless crack in the substance of everything.

'Oh my love. My husband.'

She was holding him now, her arms spread around the bulk of his armour, her soft body crushed against his stony silence. The winds gusted over the fighting on the wall, while the cannon roared and a man screamed his life away. Around them the staff-sergeants blustered at the men forming up in the street. Officers were already taking positions at the heads of their squads.

It didn't feel like New Year's Day, with its usual sense of hope and fresh beginnings for the future. More like the end of all things.

Where are my children? Bahn wondered all of a sudden, and then he recalled that they were being looked after by Marlee's sister while his wife came to see him off.

'No heroics this time, you hear me?' Marlee hissed into his ear. 'If they need someone to sacrifice themselves for the greater good, then you let it be someone else this time. Think of your family!'

Not at all the kind of thing his wife would have once said to him, daughter of an old soldier and as proud a Khosian as they came. But then she had recently almost lost him to this war, just as she had once lost her father to it, on the very first day of the siege. That which did not kill us shaped us.

There was Creed now, riding up with his retinue of bodyguards, his chosen men, only to quickly dismount and take his place at the head of the column.

'I have to go,' said Bahn, and when he pulled himself free from his wife he felt the whole weft of his emotions tearing off with her, leaving him standing there as an empty shell. It was so hard to hold her gaze for any longer than a heartbeat.

He turned and stepped away through the crowds.

'I'll wait here for your return,' his wife called after him in hope.

But Bahn said nothing, already gone.

*

By word of mouth alone, Creed had requested two thousand volunteers to assemble here at dawn. Two thousand fighters to join the score or so who already knew of the raid to come, men and women willing to take the fight to the enemy outside the city gates, even as the Mannians' first assaults began against the wall.

And so here they had gathered in the brightening light, in the streets nearest the wall with only a block of buildings in between, to be counted into line. More were still arriving, but they were being turned away now, for there were enough already. People wanted a crack at the Mannians, it seemed. Bahn found himself stepping past a noisy mix of Red Guards and purple-cloaked Hoo, Volunteers and

Specials, foreign Greyjackets and wild-haired Redeemers in their furs, young and old, men and women alike. Their weapons were too varied to list, but everyone was being handed a pair of bog shoes to bring with them, unwieldy things of wood and leather strips, like rounded snow shoes but not as large.

Chanting cloudmen moved along the columns blessing the troops; robed monks dabbing at foreheads with sky-blue paint, right over the third eye. Go in peace. Go with the blessing of your people, they intoned.

Their administrations were a stark contrast to the screams of the enemy forces assaulting the wall, visible over the rooftops of the buildings; the imperial shock troops high on narcotics and their near-to-death experiences, launching themselves from siege towers and ladders at the Khosian defenders thronging the parapet above. The monks' chanting was like the gentle thrum of bees in the hedgerows as they made their way along the lines, though a voice was booming out now to drown them – the voice of the Lord Protector, towering at the very head of the column, shouting over the heads of the gathered two thousand.

'Are you ready?'

'*Hoo!*'

'Fire parties, keep your wicks smoking. Burn everything you can! The rest of you, no mercy for these rapists and plunderers, these scum of empire.'

'*Aiyee!*'

'Clear your heads this morning,' hollered General Creed. His words rippled back along the crowds, passed on in Mercian fashion by the raised voices of people repeating them for others. 'I need you sharp out there. Sharp as razors. Our aim is to wreak the greatest harm and misery upon those forces gathered outside as we few thousand are able. And our method will be a simple one. We will *maim*, rather than *kill*. Chop their bastard limbs off them! Let them bleed, not die.'

The assembled soldiers began to mumble to each other in query. What was that?

'Dead soldiers need no shelter, nor food, nor treatment. Wounded soldiers are a drain on them all. A drain too on morale. We all know this well enough, from the injuries they have inflicted upon us over the years. Today, let us reap of that bloody harvest!'

'*Hoo!*'

'Will we allow these invaders to enslave our people, as they have enslaved all others before them?'

'*No!*'

'*Then let us show them our fury!*'

And with that Creed was off, trotting along the street with his bodyguards flanking him; a great bear-coated figure waving everyone onwards as the whole column set off after his lead.

Hand on his helm, Bahn dashed between two of the bodyguards before they spotted him, and joined Creed and his few aides. The street was lined with civilians, braving the sporadic shelling as they shouted out in gratitude and for good fortune. Some asked for the names of passing fighters so that they might be remembered.

'Just like Chey-Wes, eh, Bahn?' remarked General Creed with his long hair flowing.

'I suppose so, General.'

Yes, like Chey-Wes, when Creed and his smaller Khosian force had taken on this very same enemy army. Though back then the Khosians had used the cover of night to attack, and surprise had meant everything.

Back then, Bahn hadn't been carrying the fate of Khos at his waist either. He could feel it even now against his armour, or so he imagined, the press of the leather tube containing the charts to the Isles of Sky, tucked into his belt and strapped in place.

He had managed not to betray their existence to his Mannian handlers, yet he had also failed to hand them over to his own commanders. Stuck in a limbo, this was the best he could do with them.

Let them fall where they will.

Creed turned left into a street that led right to the wall, and they all followed him at a trot, four thousand boots stamping the cobbles. They were in the north-east quarter here, and ahead in the wall a small postern gate was being opened at their approach. Daylight shone through a portcullis and tunnel from the other side.

Yelps sounded from the war hounds as their Red Guard handlers ran to flank the column, forming up just behind Creed and his retinue. Weapons jingled. Already men were panting and sweating, and they had barely even begun.

The fighting had yet to reach this far eastern section of the wall. From the high parapet the defenders stared down at them with open mouths, cloaks drifting in the wind, only now aware of the impending sortie heading outside.

'We'll give you cover as long as we're able!' called down a voice from the parapet, and Bahn sighted a puff of pipe-smoke and then the lean form of Halahan himself, the Nathalese commander of the foreign brigade known as the Greyjackets. The fellow had one foot propped up on the parapet as he watched their approach.

'Make sure that you do,' Creed shouted back.

Through the open tunnel of the postern gate the wind was howling like a living thing. It shot out at them as they came nearer, an icy force that tore at cloaks and scarves and faces as though trying to turn them back from their audacity.

And then the mouth of the gateway swallowed Bahn and Creed and the rest of the bodyguards in its shadows, and in the fierce blast of the wind he could hear nothing at all, not even the racing thunder of his own heartbeat. He could barely see either, and through a screen of tears Bahn focused on the square of daylight growing nearer, and General Creed's form bounding ahead.

Suddenly they were trotting out into the light of morning again, out onto the open plain facing the city.

To their right, the silver waters of the Bitter River ran through another portcullis in the wall. The distant enemy encampment lay sprawled on either side of the river, well beyond effective range of the Khosian guns. To their left, the enemy forces were ranged along the earthen slope of the wall: towers, smoke and masses of running figures. Other enemy figures ranged closer towards them – skirmishers reacting to the sight of their sudden emergence from the wall. Shots rang out from the parapet behind and they started falling.

Bahn had drawn his sword some time in the last few moments. They all had. The ground here beside the river was boggy with all the recent rain. In a hurry he followed Creed's example and strapped the big bog shoes to his boots. Everyone else was doing the same.

Creed led them north-east, away from the assault and the safety of the wall, headed straight for the enemy encampment. It was hard to run in the bog shoes without feeling like a fool. Bahn could only hear individual sounds now, coming to him one after the other: the amplified pants of their breathing; the jostle of equipment and armour; the splash of boots on the soaking ground; the dim percussions of gunfire behind; the awful snarl of the war hounds bounding ahead.

A trio of League skyships soared over their heads, joining them on the raid to offer what covering fire they could. But it was the figures rushing at them as they neared the river that seized Bahn's full attention now – imperial light troops in leather armour, wielding swords. The Khosian war hounds were quick to dart in at them, going for their limbs as they tried to drag them to the ground.

Bahn glanced over his shoulder to make sure the small army was still at his back. Two thousand figures followed behind on their unwieldy bog shoes, looking ridiculous in their wide-legged bounds with water splashing from every footstep. Yet they covered the marshy ground much faster than the approaching enemy forces, and they started flanking them easily.

Creed launched himself right into the enemy midst with a heave of his broadsword, and just like that he hewed off an arm with an easy lop of the blade. Barely pausing for breath, the general grabbed at the arm of another fellow who had been wrestled to the ground by one of the hounds, and he lifted his butcher's blade again to chop through the man's arm just below the elbow.

The enemy soldier screamed.

General Creed, Lord Protector of Khos, turned to his bodyguards likewise hacking away at the limbs of their imperial attackers, then to the column of fighters snaking back all the way to the city wall, and with a heave he tossed over their heads the severed bloody arm as though an example to them all.

'*Make them bleed!*'

CHAPTER TWENTY-SIX

Nico

At first he thought it was a lantern shining in his face, but then Nico cracked open his eyes and saw that it was the faintest hint of pre-dawn in the clouded sky.

With a stiff neck he lifted his head from the branch he lay across to blink down at the shallow river water rushing beneath him. Instantly Nico recalled where he was: perched on a felled tree in the middle of the Bitter River, right in the middle of the enemy camp.

Sudden dread stewed in his stomach.

He must have dozed off for a time, despite Cole's fierce warnings to them all not to fall asleep while they were this cold, for fear of never waking again. Yet something had snapped him awake.

Quickly the young man looked back along the fallen tree, where everyone was still grimly hanging on, propped up as best they could out of the water, huddling together for warmth. Near the back he spotted Chira nursing the baby, who had stayed miraculously quiet throughout the long hours of waiting.

No doubt for many of them it had been the most miserable night of their lives, frozen stiff and exposed to the elements, wondering when one of the enemy would spot them lying there in the water. At least it had stopped raining, though with the steady encroachment of dawn, they would soon be clearly visible sprawled across the branches of the tree like this.

It was time to make a move, no matter how desperate their chances. There was nothing else for it.

He turned to see Kes lying sprawled over the half-submerged trunk, nodding off too. In front of him, even his father seemed to have fallen asleep.

Splash!

Nico lifted his head at the sound, as did his father. Up on the right-hand embankment, two figures were hacking down the sentries hunched around a brazier. It looked like Bull and one of his companions, while down in the river stood the third Contrarè, firing his bow at a sentry just above him so that the man toppled from the bluff and into the river, creating another violent splash.

'Kush,' cursed Cole, shifting where he lay, with the river sloshing around his boots. 'They'll wake the whole damned camp up. We have to move.'

With dawn approaching, the Contrarè too must have given up waiting for an opportunity to present itself – a change of guards or some other unexpected diversion – and had decided to create a way out for themselves.

But sure enough a shout went out from the sentries on the opposite bank, raising the alarm. His braids and tassels flying, the Contrarè fellow in the river sprang to the bank and scrambled up to join the others, who were charging now at soldiers hurrying from the doorway of the dugout.

'Everyone,' said Cole snatching up his rifle, and then he shook his head, not knowing what to say to them all. 'Just make a bloody run for it, before they're lining the banks.'

Even as he spoke a pair of women thrashed off through the water, though both fell sprawling after a few floundering steps. The others were trying to rise too, but they were in the same condition as Nico, their rubbery legs having divorced them.

Like the most ridiculous of drunks, like dental patients escaped on ether, the group staggered clear of the floating tree only to fall crashing into the shallow river on their hands and knees, flashing expressions of pained surprise. In their panic, they made their way towards the bluff on the right-hand bank as though it offered hope in this hopeless situation, for at least the Contrarè were killing Mannians up there.

A crack sounded out from a sudden puff of smoke on the opposite bank; a spout of water flew up next to Cole's thigh. Up came his father's rifle as he fired back in the same instant, toppling an enemy figure.

Another crack sounded and the women floundered faster for the side, falling and crawling just as much as they ran. On the stilts of his legs Nico made it to the bank and glanced back, fearful of what he would see.

From the far side enemy soldiers were leaping down into the water with their curved swords drawn. But it was the sight of Kes that stopped his heart in its next beat. The girl was still close to the snagged tree, unable to stand without her numbed legs giving out on her, so bad that she was giggling at her own uncontrollable antics, giggling in a hysteria of fear as the enemy soldiers splashed across the river towards her.

'Kes!'

Nico drew his sword and took a step back into the current, but a hand gripped his arm like a vice and yanked him back up onto the bank; his father, shouting curses into his face as he took another shot.

Other women were struggling clear but Kes was still out there, crashing across the river before falling again. She was giggling as she staggered to her feet, stuffing a fist into her mouth to try to stop herself, silly with panic. He remembered her saying how she'd rather kill herself than get caught again. She glanced back at the enemy soldiers. One of the figures fell as Cole fired his rifle.

'Kes!' he screamed again, and he ignored his father's shout and leaped back down into the river. 'Come on!'

The girl locked eyes with Nico, terrified and alone. And then a crack sounded from the far bank and Kes's face exploded outwards, and he saw the bloody mess for an instant before her body toppled into the Bitter River in a splash of red froth.

He was so horrified he couldn't move. But then his father was yanking him up towards the bluff and the dugout after the others, and there was no time to focus on anything except the moment itself, and the next one after that. Soldiers were emerging from between the nearest rows of tents, already dressed in full armour, flanking them and leaving nowhere to go but up. Bull had emerged from the dugout with a naked sword in his hand. But a volley of gunfire made him duck back inside.

Something whisked past Nico's head – crossbow bolts streaking in as they ran. Three strides ahead of him one of the women fell dead with a bolt sticking from her back.

'You lousy bastards!' Nico screamed with tears blinding his sight.

Gunshots zipped through the air. Streaking bolts and arrows. One of the Contrarè was lying face down in the dirt, not moving. Nico leaped over him. Women were crowding into the dugout for shelter, and his father shoved him towards the doorway and fired back with his rifle as Nico tumbled inside. He almost tripped over the dead body of an enemy soldier, and then he glimpsed the women taking cover in the cramped space with the Contrarè, ducking down from the gun slit, dripping wet with their soaked clothes and hair stuck to their skin.

Bull roared in the doorway as bullets splintered the wood all around him. He took cover as gunfire blasted outside in a rippling fusillade, and then Cole came spilling inside with a burst of breath and shots ripping chunks from the dirt wall over his head, cursing them for all that he was worth.

'We're trapped!' screamed Chira like it wasn't obvious to them all; the woman crouched in the far corner, clutching the bawling infant to her chest as though she would never let go of the child again.

*

He couldn't stop seeing it in his mind, the moment Kes's face had exploded into a bloody ruin; her thin body crashing into the river.

It was his fault, he knew. He should have helped her get clear of the tree instead of just leaving her there to fend for herself. But it had all happened so suddenly, like a nightmare made real.

Even now he half expected the girl to be sitting there when he looked for her amongst the women huddled down in the dugout, throwing him her sly lopsided grin. And each time he failed to see her, Nico felt the same sickening stab of remorse.

How did anyone ever get used to such things in war, their companions ripped away from life right beside them while they carried on? And this startling, guilty grief that he felt was born from the loss of a single companion, one person he had barely known, for all that they had so briefly shared. How did soldiers cope when it was one comrade after another torn away by violent deaths, people they were as close to as anyone in their lives?

How had his father coped, at least for as long as he had? It was little wonder he had been turned into a shadow of his younger self from his years fighting beneath the Shield.

Cole was peering along the barrel of his rifle, perched through the gun slit in the sandbagged wall that directly overlooked the river, looking for someone to shoot at on the opposite bank while he chewed on a stalk of wheatgrass.

The sun had long ago risen into the sky, yet the enemy attacks against the dugout had lessened over time. No longer did they try to toss grenades inside or rush them with sheer numbers. The enemy seemed content enough to take the odd rifle shot from afar, though even those were waning, so that now the silence in Nico's ears had been ringing for long moments uninterrupted.

'They've stopped firing,' someone remarked.

'Maybe they're getting ready to storm us again,' sighed Shandras, and she struggled to her feet with a bloody shortsword in her hand.

In a corner, Bull snapped awake where he sat slumped against the wall. His surviving Contrarè companion, Sky In His Eyes, stood watch near to Nico at the doorway with an arrow nocked in his bow, eyes squinting towards the nearest tents.

'No,' said the Contrarè. 'I think not. I don't see anyone out there.'

Neither could Nico, for that matter. It certainly was quiet outside. So quiet that he took a step around the doorway of sandbags to take a peek for himself.

Around the dugout lay a score of dead enemy soldiers, sprawled in all contortions where they had fallen during their assaults. From the doorway he could see down into the imperial encampment spread along both sides of the river, all the way to the small hill that was Beacon Heights and the watchtower standing at its peak.

To the right, on the eastern side of the river, figures were moving about in the brightening morning light, a bustling camp awakened to a new day. Yet the riflemen along the bank had stopped firing now, and simply lay there watching them across the span of shallow water. While here on the western side, with the imperial flags snapping in the wind, the camp looked entirely deserted.

There wasn't a soul in sight

'You know, I think they're actually gone.'

'What?'

'Don't ask me how, but I think half the camp down there is empty.'

'Yes,' agreed the Contrarè man by his side. 'I thought I was going crazy.'

'You are,' snapped Cole, stepping over to join them even as the women were struggling to their feet for a look.

But Cole stared in surprise down at the tents below them.

'Must be a trap,' grumbled his father. 'Some game they're playing with us.'

'We're hardly so important they'd clear out half the camp for us.'

Suddenly they heard a din in the distance, over the murmur of the river.

'You hear that?' his father asked.

Nico had pricked his ear to the air, his mouth hanging open to better hear.

He frowned in surprise.

'Sounds like battle.'

'Must be the action at the walls,' said Shandras.

'No. Listen. It's getting *closer*.'

The others strained to hear too. The sounds were unmistakable now – gunfire and the thunder of pounding boots, thousands of boots upon the plain, coming closer towards them in a rising tide of screams and panicked shouts.

'It's the Bar-Khosians,' Shandras gasped. 'They must be attacking the camp!'

Her words were enough to spur Nico to action. He drew his sword then stepped out through the doorway, feeling the heat of the sun against his head even as a lean wind scoured his skin.

'*Nico!*'

Still there was no sign of anyone. *Bang* went a gun from the other bank and Nico ducked low, hopping over bodies towards the cover of the nearest tents. When he swept aside a door-flap he saw that the tent was empty inside, and when he turned about his father was following after him, firing a shot across the river while Bull and the rest of the group shambled from the dugout.

Smoke was rising now above the tents to the west, from fires raging through the encampment. Khosian skyships drifted over the haze, firing down upon the enemy. The sounds of battle were definitely coming closer.

'Maybe they've all gone to the fighting,' panted a woman crouching down for a breath.

But Cole shook his head. 'No. It still wouldn't be this empty. There isn't even a camp dog in sight. And those troops across the river haven't made a move against us.'

'Whatever's going on,' gasped Bull, 'our best bet for getting into the city is linking up with that Khosian force over there.'

For a moment Nico was hardly listening. He could see Kes's body still lying in the river.

He shook his head to clear it, then met his father's steady gaze. Cole had been right. They had done all they could for these women. His mother was out there in this camp somewhere, having to bear who knew what at the hands of these people.

Now it was time to find her while the camp was in disarray.

'What are you doing, man?' asked Bull.

He watched his father dragging a dead enemy soldier into cover. Cole said nothing as he pulled off the man's cloak, then tossed a helm into Nico's hands.

'We're going after my mother,' Nico told them all, trying on the enemy helm for size.

'Bull's going to see you safe, all of you,' Cole told them. 'Isn't that so, big man?'

Bull straightened in his skins and glanced to his Contrarè companion, who shrugged minutely.

'Please,' said Chira. 'I want to live. I want this child to live.'

The man exhaled long and hard, snorting steam like the animal he most resembled. Unexpectedly he held out a hand to Cole and his father took his grasp, wrist to wrist in the old soldier's clench.

'Good fortune,' Bull told him.

'Yes,' added one of the women. 'I hope you find that wife of yours, wherever she is.'

His father nodded, surveying them all, swallowing down some sudden emotion.

CHAPTER TWENTY-SEVEN

Halahan

The Lord Protector was showing them bloody mayhem all right, Colonel Halahan of the Greyjackets could see from the high parapet of the wall.

Tents were burning throughout the southern outskirts of the enemy encampment, where Creed had led his fast-moving force on their surprise raid, flanked by a trio of skyships spitting down covering fire.

Yet still the imperial assault upon the wall continued unabated. Thousands of fighters rushed at the defences in rolling waves that one by one crashed against them in riotous havoc. It was almost as though the Mannian commanders barely cared for Creed's latest counter-attack.

Halahan carried an uneasy feeling in his guts. A sense that something wasn't quite right here.

He was almost expecting it when he heard the shouts of alarm rising from behind. The Nathalese man plucked the pipe from his mouth as he turned around to peer back into the city.

Strange, he thought, gazing along Renunciation Street to the wagon and zel-team thundering towards the wall as though out of control, soldiers and civilians leaping out of the way.

The driver looks like he's whipping them on.

Halahan grunted, swinging his longrifle from the crenellation to peer through its scope along the city thoroughfare.

The wagon driver was indeed spurring on the team of zels to run faster – a fellow clad in a Red Guard cloak with the hood swept back from his head, one hand clutching at the reins and the other lashing the lathered zels with a whip.

'That's Tensin, isn't it?' remarked a voice by his side. One of his men, one of his Greyjacket snipers, checking out the sight through his own rifle scope. 'Officer of the Tower Watch?'

'Aye, but what the devil's he playing at?'

Colonel Halahan lowered his rifle and stepped over to the edge of the parapet, right above the north-eastern postern gate.

Guards were stepping out onto the cobbles now, raising their hands for the approaching wagon to stop. But it charged onwards without slowing, and a sudden dread flooded Halahan's stomach as he looked on, seeing the heavy load of powder kegs sitting in the back of the cart.

'Jet,' he said to the Greyjacket still aiming his longrifle, his voice less steady than he'd heard it in years. 'Take out the driver. But be careful with those bloody powder kegs in the back.'

The rifle jumped with a crack and the driver cast up his arms, tumbling from the wagon in his red cloak and armour.

Yet still the wagon came thundering onwards, the blindfolded zels charging in panic for the gates.

If a bullet breached one of those kegs of powder the whole lot would go up in the middle of the street. Yet if they didn't take down those zels . . .

'Open fire!' Halahan yelled at anyone within earshot as he lifted his own rifle and shot at one of the lead zels, though the creature only staggered in its harness and kept running. Other shots rang out.

Too late, he spotted a second figure crouched out of sight in the back of the wagon, squeezed between the stacks of powder kegs. Jet saw him too and fired off another round, but by then Halahan was screaming for everyone to get clear of the gates. He shoved Jet through the doorway of the gate tower, still yelling at everyone to get clear, and pushed him through the busy space to the doorway on the other side, roaring at everyone's startled expressions.

'Get out! Get out!'

Halahan was still shouting as the wagon exploded behind them, beneath them – a sudden eruption of noise and heat that lifted the whole gatehouse into scattering blocks of debris, sending Halahan flying through the air with his arms and legs flailing.

The old Nathalese veteran crashed against stone and felt the impact of broken bones inside of him. He blacked out for a moment, and then he came to with a dizzying sense of vertigo, a coalition of pains competing for his attention.

It was no time to be lying around in a daze. Halahan cried out as he rolled onto his back. Grit rained down upon him. Dense black smoke robbed him of air.

All at once, awful screams were breaking through the ringing in his ears. He saw Jet staggering about covered in blood. Other figures moved about in the bank of smoke pouring over them.

He coughed up blood, nearly passing out from the pain that shot through his ribs.

I'm dying, Halahan thought without panic, knowing what it meant to be coughing up his own blood. *After all these years, the bastards finally finished what they started.*

He could be honest with himself now, he supposed. Lying there in the timeless dimension of the moment, Halahan knew that he'd only been half alive since fleeing his homeland of Nathal all those years ago; since fleeing the ashes of all that he had known. Only half alive for all that time, and most of that had been occupied by the infinite grinding patience of his vengeance, which would never be stopped so long as he breathed – his need to draw blood from these Mannians who had conquered and enslaved his people.

Yet he didn't regret it, his years of grim and single-minded determination to get his revenge – this man who had once so long ago been a preacher of peace. Only half alive was still a lot better than what many of his people had suffered, and were still suffering.

Halahan could hear the roar of the enemy on the other side of the wall as though they were getting closer. Volleys of gunfire were ringing out. Officers bawling orders along the wall as though they were suddenly under attack.

He found he could still move if he gritted his teeth and focused on his hatred for the enemy. He groped towards a rifle lying there amongst the debris and clutched it tightly. Gasping, shaking his eyes clear of sweat, he clawed his way through the rubble to where the tower and parapet had been blown away in a great bite, dragging the rifle as he went, coughing a trail of blood. Wounded men moaned and cried out.

Below him the explosion had replaced the postern gate with a smoking crater in the ground. The wind was howling through the gaping chasm in the wall, and with it came enemy figures leaping and hacking at any defenders still on their feet.

Sweet Mercy, he thought. *They've breached the wall!*

The enemy seemed uncommonly silent in their assault, until he glimpsed their white robes and masks and knew that they were Acolytes, the fanatical warrior priests of the Mannian order. With a grunt of effort he propped the rifle before him, wiping clear his eyes before taking a glimpse through its cracked scope. He fired off a shot, a loose one, feeling lucky, and dropped a masked Acolyte on the run.

Halahan cracked open the rifle and replaced the spent shell, his head clearing as he inhaled the familiar, bracing whiff of gunsmoke. He nestled down into the stock and fired again, another loose one, another fallen enemy figure.

'*Good shot!*'

It was Nilsetti, the crazy ex-teacher from Serat, one of his oldest and toughest Greyjackets, crouched down and taking a shot with his own gun. Beyond the man, the parapet was alive with action as far as Halahan could see. Enemy forces were throwing themselves over the crenellations like never before.

Another explosion sounded out from further along the wall. Black smoke rose from a fiery core.

Another bomb.

'That's the main northern gates down too,' Nilsetti shouted. The Seratian squeezed off another shot then looked down at Halahan, who was struggling now to slot in another shell, fumbling at an action he had performed a thousand times and more. 'They've taken us, man!' Nilsetti was yelling at him. 'We've been betrayed by our bloody own!'

A wave of noise was rolling towards them over the dying echoes of the second explosion: more of the enemy charging for the fallen gates. The Imperials were flooding through the gateway below now, though defenders were forming across the road to block their way, staff-sergeants in red cloaks bawling them into position, Red Guards locking shields and drawing swords, even as Acolytes sped in with their own blades flashing to crash against them.

Other figures darted in from the side streets too – wild-haired men and women in skins and furs. Some whirled blades on the end of tethers as they charged straight into the enemy attackers. Redeemers, Halahan saw, placing themselves at the very fulcrum of the action, laying down their lives to stem the flood.

He was too stunned to take it all in. He could barely believe it was happening. All these years defending Bar-Khos, and now the enemy forces were flowing through the breached gates into the city.

At last his shaking fingers slid home the shell. Colonel Halahan cocked the rifle and took aim. It was impossible to miss now, like shooting into a stream choked with fish. Halahan took a man in the back then reloaded once more, wheezing for air, wondering how many breaths he had left in him, how many shots, how much fight.

CHAPTER TWENTY-EIGHT

Nico

'The slave pits,' Cole whispered into the soldier's ear, and relaxed his grip just for a moment, just enough for the red-faced man to take a gasp of precious air. 'The slave pits for the new arrivals, the pleasure slaves. *Where are they?*'

'North of here,' rasped the imperial soldier. 'Near the river. Just . . . follow the stench.'

Nico hissed at what he heard. 'We must have floated right past them on the way down the river.'

But his father was too busy strangling the man to comment, the soldier floundering and growing limp in his arms. He held him like that for a long time, dripping with sweat, then dropped him like a sack of spuds.

'You didn't have to kill him,' said Nico, staring down at the young man's features.

'You think I enjoy this or something? You rather he woke up and told the whole camp where we're going?'

Behind his father, through the tent wall, figures were hurrying back and forth along a busy thoroughfare, jostling and noisy. Nico adjusted the imperial helm on his head and glanced out of the flapping doorway.

'This is all starting to feel heavy, don't you think?'

'That wasn't heavy enough, what we've just been through on the river?'

'Yeah, but then we got this far, maybe close enough to rescue my mother. And now my guts are in a stew.'

His father's smile was a grim one. It was getting to him as well, the tension.

'Come on, you fool. Let's go and see if she's there.'

*

Dressed in the cloaks and helms of imperial soldiers, Nico and his father had crossed the river using one of the many swaying rope bridges strung across it, leaving behind the seemingly deserted camp and the nearing sounds of battle. On the opposite bank they found that the encampment was thronged to bursting, its tents and thoroughfares alive with activity.

It was as though much of the population of the western side of the camp was now here instead, temporarily anyway, crammed into whatever shelter they could find.

Even now scores of soldiers were staggering back across the nearest bridge with officers yelling at them to hurry, while others kicked stragglers into positions along the embankment. Over on the opposite side, smoke was streaming from the many tents on fire, creating a haze that was carrying towards them on the wind. The clashes of fighting were close now. Through breaks in the smoke he thought he glimpsed Khosian standards flying tall and proud.

'*They're routing,*' Nico whispered to his father as they hurried along.

'No, it's too orderly for that. They're pulling back for some reason.'

His father didn't like it, whatever was going on. Cole bunched his jaws and kept his head hunched low in his imperial helm, leading Nico northwards.

Zels whinnied from their pens or from the harnesses of wagons they dragged through the mud. Men held on to caps and leaned against the gusts with their cloaks sweeping around them. Under thrashing awnings, cooks stared from their cauldrons at soldiers waiting cold and miserable for their breakfasts. Cole and Nico hopped between hot sparks flying from the strikes of a blacksmith, under lines of washing flip-flapping about their heads. They hurried past the tired stares of men lying in their bedrolls in their small tents, smoking roll-ups and pipes, and the even wearier faces of men waiting to use the latrines along the river bank, backs turned to the gusts.

Clearing a busy road, his father suddenly stopped in his tracks. 'This is it,' came his raw voice in the wind.

They were facing an open patch of ground, covered in mounds

of earth and square tarpaulins lying stretched out here and there. Flanking the open space were pens of cattle, except where the river glittered in the morning sun, and off to the right where large tents stood with a few figures moving amongst them.

'What do we do?'

'Start looking.'

Casually they sauntered onto the ground as though they both belonged there, Nico headed for one of the tarpaulins while his father headed for another. With a glance towards the nearby tents, Nico stooped down and tugged at the edge of the tarp.

Underneath was a pit in the ground, covered in a tight lattice of wooden poles. Startled faces blinked up at the sudden intrusion of daylight. Nico baulked at the fetid stench rising in the waves of warm air. Flies were buzzing down there. Someone coughed in the gloom.

'*Reese!*' he hissed down, taking in the dull grimy faces of women squinting up at him. '*Mother!*'

No one spoke.

'A red-headed woman,' he tried. 'Please, have any of you seen her?'

Down in the gloom a woman reached up and clutched his hands between the wooden poles, squeezing in desperation.

'Red hair,' she gasped, eyes shining in her grimy face. 'Called Reese?'

'Yes!'

'If I tell you, will you get me out of here?'

Nico grimaced and tried gently to free himself from her grip. He looked up to his father, crouched down at one of the other pits. Beyond Cole, at the row of tents, a soldier brushing his teeth with a covestick was watching what they were doing.

'*I can't!*' Nico said down to the poor woman. 'They'll see me. Please, what can you tell me?'

'I'll do anything!' she rasped as she lunged upwards, her face pressing against the poles, her blue eyes screaming.

A hand grabbed at his shoulder, yanking him to his feet.

'Keep moving,' said his father by his side, and his voice was even grimmer than before. 'She's over there by the tents, lashed to a punishment post.' And his father nodded to what it was they were headed for, a post of wood taller than a man, propped at the edge of the field.

As hard as he stared Nico couldn't see her there; as though he couldn't bring himself to see her there. Yet the closer they came to the post the more he seemed to focus on the details of the woman hanging like a carcass of meat: the naked flesh streaked with blood, the hands bound high over her head, the wild red hair.

'Holy Mercy of Kush, it's her.'

'Hold it together now.'

'Look at what they've done to her!'

'I know.'

'I'm going to kill – *shit!*'

'What?'

But his father saw him too now: the soldier sauntering over from the tents with the covestick still in his mouth. At once, Cole and Nico both picked up their pace, but the fellow quickened likewise to cut them off.

'Let me do the talking,' said Cole.

'I will not. The only accent you can do is Khosian.'

'You men need something?' asked the soldier as he blocked their way, waving his covestick at them as emphasis to the dangerous curiosity in his eyes. 'Lost, maybe?'

'That woman there,' said Nico before his father could speak up, adopting the best Q'osian accent he could manage. And he nodded over the man's shoulder towards the punishment post, towards what was hanging there in naked shame.

He could see the individual stripes on her back now. The vivid, livid lash strokes across his mother's skin.

'You've whipped her, I see,' Nico said, and his voice sounded thick in his ears. His father stirred at the sound of it, still saying nothing.

'A crying shame too,' said the soldier. 'Bitch needs to be broken in though. Went and bit off a fellow's nose on her first night here. You interested in buying her or something, lad?'

'Yeah,' Nico growled and shoved past the man, no longer able to hold himself back.

'Hey!' called the soldier from behind.

'*Mother,*' Nico croaked as he came around to face her, cradling her head and her battered face. '*Mother, it's me, Nico.*'

Reese stirred for a moment, her eyelids fluttering. He saw a gleam of eye in all the bruised swelling around it – his mother grimly holding on.

He wanted to be sick. Trembling uncontrollably, Nico held her cold body against his own, taking her weight. With his knife he cut her free so that she sagged in his arms, and in a rush he wrapped her in his Mannian cloak.

His father appeared by his side and swiftly hefted her over his back. 'I'll take her.'

Behind them the soldier was lying face down in the dirt, his covestick drifting along a spreading outflow of blood from his slit throat.

Nico felt nothing, looking at the body in that instant. Nothing but a simmering satisfaction.

Whumpf!

The air trembled with a sudden shockwave, making them both turn towards the south, towards the distant wall of the city, where a spout of fire and debris was rising high above one of the gates.

Cries of alarm rose from the surrounding pens of cattle.

'You there!' someone called out from the tents.

A man was striding towards them with his sword drawn.

'Let's go,' said Cole, turning with Reese across his back, and together they started running across the field towards the river, headed for the sanctuary of the Khosian forces battling their way through the enemy camp on the other side.

'Stop there!'

The soldier gave chase, and another two further behind him, burdened by their armour and their drawn blades.

Not looking back, his father kept his head down as he ran, sweating and puffing with the weight of Reese, though he chanced a look to the south again and the city wall, where a pall of black smoke was now rising.

'I think they've blown open the city gates,' he gasped.

But Nico was more focused on the soldiers in pursuit. He cursed as the ill-fitting helm slipped over his eyes once again. Grabbed it off his head and tossed it behind him, dropping the nearest man with a lucky shot to his kneecap.

A few steps ahead Cole was charging down the river bank towards the slow flow of the water, sunlight dazzling across its surface.

'Keep going,' Nico called after him. 'I'm right behind you!'

And Nico drew his sword in one swift stroke and turned to hold off the enemy, no longer feeling afraid now, only enraged.

CHAPTER TWENTY-NINE

Bahn

In the thick of the fighting, Bahn Calvone paused with his hand cannon pointed at the Lord Protector's spine, his finger twitching on the trigger.

'Sweet Mercy,' growled General Creed in disbelief, so quietly that only Bahn heard him from a step behind.

The Lord Protector had stopped to look to the south, drawn by the thunder of explosions just like Bahn and everyone else – Creed's bodyguards and the two thousand sweaty, bloody fighters who had accompanied the general on this sortie through the outskirts of the enemy encampment. Even the nearest Imperials themselves were turning to look, so that everyone stared towards the city wall where twin columns of smoke were rising, and the Khosian horns blared in alarm.

'They've blown the gates!' wailed a young Volunteer as though they couldn't see the calamity for themselves, couldn't hear the victorious roar of the imperial forces storming towards the breaches.

Red-faced and panting, General Creed lowered his blade and stood there in the windy gusts of the plain stunned to silence. Bahn too lowered the gun in his hand. With confusion tearing him in two he stared open-mouthed at the masses of fighters and their war banners gathering before the smoking gates, knowing they would be pouring through into the city beyond.

Bahn fought hard to think of his wife and his children, there in the family home in the north of the city – but when he did a flash of white pain speared through his mind.

Marlee! he thought in defiance, and the sudden shooting pains in his head nearly dropped him to the ground.

He blinked through his tears, seeing the gun in his hand, the snub double barrels he had just been pointing surreptitiously at Creed's spine, with the intention of shooting the Lord Protector dead. It was only when he focused on the gun in his hand, and what he needed to do with it, that he was able to see and hear clearly again, and his confusions dimmed to a background chatter.

'How in the sky did they blow the damned gates?' growled Creed, and Bahn could see the general's face had drained of blood.

In the distance, the sounds of battle along the walls were reaching a fevered pitch. Closer though, in the camp itself, all seemed strangely silent, save for the snap of flames from the tents they had set ablaze, spreading quickly on the wind.

Bahn blinked, taking in the figures of the nearest enemy troops now running away, scampering off through the encampment in the direction of the nearby river.

'They're running!' rose the shout from various throats. 'Why are they running?'

And suddenly it was as though all two thousand fighters were standing alone there by themselves, with not a single enemy figure remaining.

Gusts blasted through the enemy encampment, blowing open the flaps of empty tents. Men glanced around nervously. Officers looked to the general, his hair swept from his head and pointing towards the city wall even as he stared after it, consumed by what he saw.

'I'm dreaming,' Bahn ventured aloud, clutching at straws.

'We all are,' growled Creed. 'We're dreaming this whole stinking war and this is the latest nightmare.'

But Bahn meant it – he felt like he was wading through a delirium. Numb in body, and now increasingly so in his mind, he peeked out from far inside his head at the bleak and lonely world all around him.

'We need to retreat,' called out an officer in black leathers, and it was Major Bolt of the Specials, veteran of Chey-Wes. 'We need to get back to the city, right now, General!'

Creed stirred, leaning over to spit out his distaste at what he was seeing. If the Lord Protector was frightened, only the paleness of his features showed any sign of it. He glanced to the last enemy figures disappearing from sight through the camp, then back along the trail of writhing bodies left in the wake of his own forces; hundreds of fallen enemy soldiers with an arm or leg shorn from their bodies, maimed and bleeding out onto the earth right next to their severed limbs – a whole road of them leading all the way back to the smoking north-eastern gate, which was now swarming with imperial forces.

'Your orders, General?' shouted a Red Guard colonel, pushing through the gasping fighters with his helm missing from a bleeding scalp.

'Quickly now,' shouted Creed over the heads of his fighters, and thrust his sword aloft. 'With me, damn it!'

At a run they set off south through the deserted outskirts of the camp, Creed and their fluttering banners leading the way through the rolling smoke. Bahn stayed close to the general, his gun shaking in his hand. Off to the right, their three skyships were engaging a pair of imperial Birds-of-War. One of the enemy ships was trailing flames. He could see burning figures leaping from it.

A man stumbled to the ground in front of him, a young Red Guard carrying Creed's standard, and then Bahn tripped too on something and went down almost on top of the fellow. Reaching back for his fallen gun, he glimpsed what he had caught his foot on – a thick wire mostly buried by loose earth.

Bahn grabbed the thing and gave it a tug, and gasped as it popped from the ground in a line that ran towards the nearby Bitter River.

What was this?

Buried mines?

At once the world erupted in a blast of dirt and hot air that rocked the earth beneath him. Everything inside Bahn was squeezed hard. Coughing grit, he looked out from the cover of his arms as another explosion shook through the ground, sending a fountain of black earth rising skywards, bodies flying like limp dolls in every direction.

Bahn could only huddle down further, flinching from every shock of air jolting through him, the earth bucking like a living thing beneath him. He snatched a glimpse of fighters hurling themselves to the ground with their own arms over their heads; others running back the way they had come; yet more spinning through the air, through the morning sky right over his head. And then a cloud of smoke and grit rolled over him like a burial shroud and turned day to night, the whole world coming asunder like his own heart.

Where was Creed in all this mayhem? Could he have been blown to pieces like the rest of them – Bahn released from his awful task by this Mannian trap instead?

But it seemed not, for a hand was suddenly pulling at his cloak, and Bahn recognized that indomitable strength hauling him to his feet.

Marsalas Creed was snarling something as he dragged Bahn through the choppy haze. His hair flew wild around eyes squinting fiercely in all the gritty hail coming down, and the Lord Protector surged through the maelstrom like a man defying a tide; like an old pit fighter coming back from a knockout with all he had left.

In a wedge of bodyguards Creed led them away from the erupting earth, charging between the blazing tents of the encampment towards the only ground that wasn't exploding around them – eastwards towards the river, and the distant flashes of imperial troops still fleeing from the vicinity. Deafened by the concussions, they rushed past tents blazing in the rising winds, leaving the dead and wounded where they fell. Bodies lay scattered everywhere. No one could hear Creed shouting for everyone to follow, yet fighters formed around him and his young standard-bearer anyway, the raised shields of his bodyguards clattering with debris.

'Mines, General!' someone was hollering into Creed's ear. 'They've laid the camp with mines. It's a trap!'

'I can see, can't I?'

Before them glittered the Bitter River, flowing across the plain towards the city wall, the early sunlight striking across it in glassy scales of brilliance that played in Bahn's eyes, captivating him.

'*Where are you, my love? Where have you gone?*' Marlee had asked Bahn as she had seen him off.

He should have said something to his dear wife, something meaningful, while he still had the chance. But instead offering only forgettable platitudes of farewell.

Bahn blinked in the sunlight bouncing from the river, seeing a line of gunsmoke suddenly rippling along the opposite bank.

'*Get down!*' someone was yelling as they ducked or fell from the incoming volleys of shots. Though Bahn only stood there gaping, hearing the rip of bullets going past him, tearing through tents and flesh alike. Others were braving the fire too: a short-haired woman in the skins of a Volunteer ranger, bearing a longrifle. He saw her crouching down at the river bank, a captain by her insignia, waving her companions onwards, shouting with spirit at the riflemen crashing to the earth around her feet and returning fire.

A familiar face startled him, and then Bahn glimpsed it again. It was the young street girl turned army medico known as Curl, her achingly beautiful features so out of place here in all this ugly violence, the crest of her hair bobbing high while she tended to a wounded man.

Maybe the girl was a portent of some kind, seeing her here in the midst of the fighting again, just like he had at the battle of Chey-Wes. A reminder of the man he had once been, before this living death that had become his existence since that battle, when he'd been captured by the Mannians and slowly replaced by a shadow formed only to do one remaining thing with his life, to destroy all that the real Bahn had ever loved.

Shoot me now! he shouted in his mind as he stood there opening his arms wide, waiting for an enemy bullet to strike him dead.

But it seemed he was invincible just then, bullets narrowly missing him while other people were shot through. And then once again Creed's hand grabbed a hold of Bahn and yanked him into a crouch, where the Lord Protector was hunkered behind the shields of his bodyguards. Creed paid him no mind, too busy waving battle signs to some officers lying in a crater behind them with their men. Through the smoke, the remains of their forces were flooding towards the river over the churned earth, channelled by what were obviously mines going off on every other side of them. Mines that most of all were blocking their means of escape to the south, their route back to the city.

Faces all around him glanced this way and that, framed by frantic motions. Everyone looked grim, sick, just getting through the next moment and the one after that. Even Creed had lost his usual shine. He looked flattened, like the day he had been told his wife was dead.

Oh Holy Mercy what have I done?

A bodyguard fell back against Bahn's boots, his skull pierced by a bullet. Bahn stared down at the dead man.

'Signal our air support,' Creed was hollering to a few soldiers hunkering down next to him, clamping their helms to their heads. They held the chunky wooden box of a Sun Writer between them, and Creed slapped the nearest signaller on his shoulder to gain his startled attention. 'Tell the ships to start laying down covering smoke along the river, in both directions.'

'Shouldn't we call for a pick-up?' Major Bolt yelled at him. 'We're pinned down here. And anywhere we move is likely to be mined.'

'Three ships will hardly carry us all, Major.'

'At least we can get you out. At least we can deny them that!'

Bahn saw the general frown in an uncommon display of annoyance.

'The smoke, dammit!' he shouted to the stunned signallers. 'Signal for the smoke!'

Quickly the message was flashed to the nearby trio of skyships, which were turning back now from a burning enemy ship.

In a line they flew towards them, the foremost diving fast with its skul sails sweeping wide, a huge thing when seen above the rows of tents. A Sun Writer flashed from its prow, and then it was so close that Bahn could make out the crewmen on its decks, its marines firing down with rifles and crossbows. But then a series of rockets shot up into the air from the opposite side of the river, trailing white ribbons of smoke. They all missed but for two of them, which pierced the gas canopy and blew it away in a flash of fire.

Down the ship came, spilling crew over its tilting sides. With a mighty crash it splashed into the river and then exploded from within. Bahn turned from the wash of heat. When he looked back he saw something dropping from the sky, and then something else. He wiped his eyes of tears and saw the smoke barrels raining down from the remaining two skyships, barrels that landed along the banks of the river belching a thick yellow mist stretching out in the breeze.

Creed was ruminating on something and looking south towards the distant city wall, where anyone making a run for it along the bank was being hit by concentrated gunfire or blown up by more buried mines. He turned northwards, taking in the nearer rise of Beacon Heights and the fighters already streaming that way along the bank, more and more of them as they tried to flee the worst of the gunfire, following the river in their efforts to stay clear of the mined and deserted encampment.

Again Creed shouted his orders to the signallers. 'Flash another message to the ships. Tell them we're heading for Beacon Heights. We'll make a stand there while they lift us back to the city.'

Major Bolt wasn't happy with the idea. The man looked northwards to the Heights, frowning at the fighters being picked off as they ran along the bank.

'You think we can make it that far?'

'Some of us might. What choice do we have, man?'

*

Beacon Heights was a small ridge of limestone cliffs that rose from the plain like the serrated edge of a knife. A Khosian watchtower straddled its highest point, though the tower now lay in the hands of the enemy, as seen by the white imperial flags flying from its top sporting the red hand of Mann.

Even so, the hill looked like sanctuary to the remnants of General Creed's forces, shot and cut to pieces during their desperate flight along the river bank, for all that the skyships had laid down their cover of smoke. Out of the thinning violet clouds, five hundred survivors staggered onto the base of Beacon Heights just ahead of the imperial cavalry hot in pursuit, struggling upwards onto its steepening flanks as the enemy zels began to falter on the rocks.

No one was looking at anyone else now, each person intent only on the ground ahead through the tunnel vision of their exhaustion. On Bahn's right a tall Volunteer was carrying a comrade over his shoulders, talking to him as he surged upwards with great gasps of strength born of fear. But his wounded friend was missing most of the back of his skull, and clearly dead. To Bahn's left, a storm-haired Redeemer yelled out in sudden pain and pitched over, a quarrel bolt sticking out from the furs on his back.

Bahn didn't even think to return fire with the gun that he carried. He was intent only on General Creed ahead of him, who had stopped on an out-thrust of stone to survey their chances above, ringed loosely by his four surviving bodyguards and blasted by gusts that were brushing patterns through the furs of his thick bearskin coat.

Shouting out commands even now, Creed was somehow maintaining the sheerest thread of order through his remaining officers and his own towering presence. Somewhere along the way his young standard-bearer had fallen, replaced by another fresh-faced soldier just as teary-eyed as the last one, the standard itself a flapping torn rag by then. Next to Creed crouched one of the signallers with the Sun Writer, flashing again to the pair of skyships circling overhead, which were heavily engaged with two enemy Birds-Of-War.

'Major Bolt,' Creed was saying as Bahn caught up with him at last, almost reeling from his lack of breath. Fighters kept on scrambling past him headed for the top. Others fired back down at the enemy forces giving chase, or threw rocks and grenades, forcing them into cover.

'Major, we'll need that watchtower for ourselves,' shouted the general to Bolt with a gesture to the ridge above them. 'Take some Specials and rangers up ahead with you. See if you can take the garrison.'

He spotted Bahn bent over gasping for air. But Creed only looked away to the city behind him, more visible now that they were above the plain.

'Can't tell if they're holding them back or not,' he said, with the emotions barely suppressed in his voice, or perhaps it was only Bahn hearing it that way, five years of knowing this man as his field aide, knowing how he must be raging within.

You can do this!

Gunfire could be heard from further up. A few squads of Specials were making their way onto the ridge in crouched runs, tossing smoke grenades ahead of them and braving the enemy shots from the watchtower, while a line of rangers provided them with covering fire.

In the brief moment of respite, Bahn gazed at Bar-Khos smoking on the plain, wondering how he was meant to save his family now.

What of the promises that they would be spared?

He pictured Marlee and his son, running for their lives through the northern streets of the city; little Ariale in her mother's arms, crying in fright at all the noise.

Even as he thought of young Ariale, his precious daughter, Bahn turned to the sound of an infant child crying nearby, just beyond another out-thrust of limestone. He thought he must be imagining it, but then a group of ragged Khosian women hurried into view, and he saw that one of them was bearing a bawling babe in her arms.

Bahn frowned, wondering what they were doing here.

'Bahn, you bloody bastard!'

A figure was stepping out from behind the group of Khosian women, looming over them in his massive bulk. For a moment Bahn was distracted by the fellow's Contrarè skins and beads, but then he saw that it was Bull, his old Red Guard companion from the earliest days of the siege. A man he had considered to be dead.

Bahn almost smiled at seeing his old friend alive again. But then he looked at Bull's troubled expression, and a chill ran through his spine.

He knows! He knows what I am about!

Of course Bull knew, how could he not when he'd been a prisoner of the Mannians too; had been there when the priests had messed with their minds.

The Lord Protector was moving again, working his way up the slope with his men towards rangers waving them on from the ridge above. Bahn started moving too, not looking back as Bull called after him.

The last time he'd seen the giant of a man, they had just broken free from the pit in which the Mannians had imprisoned them after the battle of Chey-Wes. It had been raining hard, in the middle of the night, and Bull had held off the enemy while the other prisoners made their escape. A truly heroic act, in Bahn's eyes, one which most likely had saved their lives.

Yet now he fled from the man.

'*Bahn!*'

White smoke from a grenade obscured Bahn's world for a moment, changing the tone of the sounds about him. He lost sight of Creed and then he tripped on something on the slope – a dead Red Guard lying across his path.

As Bahn staggered to his feet he looked down to see Bull appearing through the pouring mist, fixing him with a dangerous frown.

He knows!

He tried to yell at him. Tried to tell him to keep back. But then Bull jerked to a stop, frowning in pain. The big fellow looked down at his stomach which had suddenly ruptured in a splash of red, reaching splayed fingers towards the wound there. Bull looked up again in shock, in betrayal, as he took in the smoking barrel of the gun in Bahn's hand, aimed directly at him.

Bull toppled to the ground and rolled back down the slope, his great body scattering figures left and right.

What remained of Bahn swirled around and surged onwards up the slope, not daring to look back at what he had done as he reloaded the gun.

CHAPTER THIRTY

Nico

Nico knew that when you found too much happening at once, it was always best to surrender to the natural instincts of the body; to simplify everything down to the next step you were taking, the next breath.

So he ran behind his father doing only what needed to be done and nothing more, existing only in the vibrations of the moment.

They had rescued his mother, draped now over Cole's back, and they weren't stopping for anyone.

Back there on the opposite bank of the river, where Nico had held off the imperial soldiers on the slippery grass while his father bore Reese across to the other side, Nico had fought with the same speed and recklessness as he had at the slaver camp, as though swordplay came naturally to him now, something he had been born to do. His blade had snaked hissing through the air, following moves that were drawn from the Rōshun blade discipline of Cali, a super-aggressive fighting style favouring lightning-fast kills against multiple opponents. Before he'd known it, four soldiers were sprawled on the bank either dead or dying, giving Nico the chance to leap into the freezing river so he could swim for the other side, desperate to catch up with his father and mother.

By then, all kinds of havoc had broken out further down the river. Explosions threw fountains of earth high into the air above a rising chorus of yells and gunfire. Clouds of drifting smoke from the many tents on fire down there obscured their view, but Nico glimpsed a skyship falling from the sky, and two more climbing away from it, dropping barrels over their sides trailing a yellow mist.

Back on the western bank the tents were just as empty as before. But when they had heard the shouts of men approaching, Nico and

Cole had quickly hidden inside one, sheltering down out of the gusts. Frantic figures had run past them following the bank of the river – Khosians, they realized, hearing their voices shouting out in desperation. Quickly they ditched their imperial cloaks. When they stepped outside again they saw they were in the midst of a full-scale retreat of friendly forces, all of them headed north for Beacon Heights.

There was nothing else they could do but join them, for all that these friendly troops were under fire and surrounded. At least the surviving pair of skyships were throwing down smoke and fire for cover. Through the yellow mist, Nico and his father made it to the slope of Beacon Heights, and struggled up it like everyone else towards the watchtower on its ridge, Cole heaving from the weight of Reese on his bent back, raining sweat. Shots and arrows pursued them, along with the distant horns from the city wall calling out in alarm.

Nico lost sight of his father for a few moments beyond an out-cropping of rock, and when he rounded it he grunted in surprise. There up ahead, in a cloud of thinning smoke, were the women they had rescued from the slavers, Chira and Shandras and the rest of them, hurrying up the slope towards a man rolling to a stop on the ground.

His father came to a halt above the fallen figure, surrounded by gasping women. He crouched down to check the man's pulse.

It was Bull, lying there on the ground in their midst with a bloody, ragged hole in his midriff, his dead eyes staring wide with shock.

Oh no.

'*Hecheney-naz-hai!*' shouted Bull's Contrarè companion, Sky In His Eyes, kneeling beside him, leaning on his bow like a staff. The native was trembling with anger. He looked up the slope as though towards the source of his outrage, then took off at a running lope.

'It was Bahn,' said his father to Nico with a sick look on his face. 'I saw it myself. He shot Bull dead.'

'*Are you sure?*'

Cole glanced up at his son, snarling. 'You don't think I know my own brother when I see him. Here, take your mother. Get her to the top.'

'It's true then? Bahn's a traitor?'

'Take her I said!'

His mother was lighter than Nico expected when he hoisted her over his back. All skin and bones, it seemed.

'Get to the top,' Cole repeated before setting off with his long-rifle, darting up the slope close on the heels of the Contrarè.

Already the women were scrambling upwards again, helping each other over the rocks. Shots were still coming in from the enemy forces below, slowly working their way onto the Heights behind the retreating forces. For all his new-found strength, Nico was still gasping for air as they neared the top. His feet slipped on loose shale and his mother groaned.

Up on the ridge the wind was howling. It tore at the cloaks of the surviving Mercians as they ran towards the stone watchtower, tossing the black smoke that poured from its shattered gateway. High above the battlements a Khosian flag was being hoisted.

In a flow of fighters Nico jogged along the narrow ridge until he entered the fallen gate of the watchtower. The wind was screaming through the gloomy passage. It pushed him into an inner courtyard enclosed by a high arching roof, speared through by shafts of light from arrow slits around its walls. Already the space was crowded with fighters and the echoes of their voices, men dragging the bodies of dead enemy soldiers out of the way while medicos tended to their own wounded.

In the throng, he caught a glimpse of his father ducking past the Contrarè man and running for some nearby steps. Huffing and puffing, Nico hurried after him.

*

Daylight washed Nico's eyes again as he stepped up onto the battlements of the watchtower.

It was getting crowded up here too. Nico hefted his mother on his shoulder and coughed from all the yellow smoke drifting on the wind. Through its winding tendrils he spotted a few dead imperial soldiers lying on the flagging of the roof, and then he noticed that everyone was gaping at the sky. He followed their collective gaze to the skyship diving fast towards the Heights, dropping more smoke barrels for cover as it came.

Rockets shot up from the Mannian encampment below, streaking wildly this way and that, though missing it entirely. Along the vessel's port side cannon fired at the camp, even as the skyship levelled out with its skul-sails flaring against the headwind, forward thrusters burning hard to slow its descent, the ship drifting down like a leaf onto the narrow ridge.

These skymen really knew how to fly under pressure.

A few voices whooped aloud at the sight of such a daring landing, whooping even louder as the ship cracked open its two hull doors for the fighters already running towards it, whilst others grabbed at mooring lines being cast by the crew.

Nico tore his gaze away from the sight to search out his father.

Over by the far parapet towered the Lord Protector himself, flanked by shields and with his dark hair flowing past his famous features. General Creed was studying the landed skyship as he snapped instructions to his people, standing there larger than life. Across the way, Nico spotted his father at last. Cole was staring over the heads of the soldiers, alert as a panther focused on its prey.

Bahn! he thought in surprise as he noticed his uncle at the back of the crowd, leaning against a crenellation.

He pushed towards him as his father did. For a moment he couldn't quite fathom what he was seeing, but then it came to him with a jolt – his uncle Bahn was aiming a hand cannon at the back of General Creed's head.

'*Brother!*' he heard his father yell out, and Bahn was visibly rocked to see Cole barging his way through the crowd towards him.

His uncle was weeping from red-raw eyes, the tears clearing tracks down his grimy features. Bahn opened his mouth wide as though to say something, though it might only have been a silent cry for help.

'Is this a dream?' Bahn finally managed to shout over the din of the milling soldiers.

'What?'

'Is this a dream, brother. Am I dreaming all of this?'

Cole shook his head slow and forcefully. 'No, Bahn – this is all happening, believe me.'

His uncle winced at the words. He turned his attention back to the gun aimed in his shaking hand.

'Bahn!' yelled his frantic father, unable to get through a group of

Volunteers. He aimed his longrifle at his brother over the shoulders of the crowd, shaking his head at him. 'Don't, Bahn – what are you doing, man?'

Around them his voice was drawing the attention of others. Panicked, Bahn gripped the gun with both hands to steady it, his eyes and nose running, his features contorting with pain.

He fired.

A second shot crashed out even as everyone was ducking from the first one. Bahn stumbled where he stood, blood blooming on the side of his neck. Shocked, Nico swung his head to his father's smoking rifle, then round to General Creed, who had disappeared behind a wall of shields and panicking soldiers. Faces yelled back in anger and fright. Someone grabbed Bahn while another knocked the gun from his hand.

Cole was gasping down at his dying brother when Nico finally squeezed his way through, cradling his brother against the angry clutches of the surrounding soldiers.

With care, Nico lay his mother down against the parapet, shaking with emotion from the sight of his father weeping so openly in grief.

His uncle's face was draining of colour as he blinked up at his older brother. His mouth was moving. His hand tugged at something in his belt without the energy to draw it free. Nico strained to hear what he was saying.

'Hush,' said Cole, protecting his brother with his body against the jostle of men. He lay a hand on Bahn's and helped him pull out a leather tube from his belt.

Nico stared in dumb surprise. It looked just like the leather tube holding the charts to the Isles of Sky. The charts his father had given to Bahn before they had left the city to fetch his mother, with instructions to pass them on.

What had Bahn been doing with them all of this time? What was he doing with them out here?

'Stay with us!' his father hissed, and he clutched the tube between them and clamped his other hand over the bloody wound in his brother's neck, trying to keep him alive.

But he was fading fast.

Bahn gasped and looked up at a Cole for an instant, frightened at what was coming at him headlong in a rush – death itself. And then the air rattled from his lungs, and he seemed to deflate in his brother's arms, and his gaze faded to nothing.

Cole dropped his head in silence, drawing his son's tentative hand to his shoulder.

'He's killed him!' men were ranting all around them now, and they started kicking and tearing to be let loose on the assassin, trying to get through the line of cooler heads to stamp on the fallen Bahn. A boot lashed out and connected with Nico's head, sending him spinning to the flagstones with the senses knocked clear out of him.

'He's shot the Lord Protector dead!'

CHAPTER THIRTY-ONE

Coya

Coya was sitting in the back of a small carriage, en route from the Broken Wheel to the siege front, when another massive explosion rumbled across the city from the northern wall, its shockwave rippling through his belly with the heaviness of dread.

He was too late, he knew, seeing the thick columns of smoke rising into the brightening sky. His suspicions had been right after all. The trap was sprung already, and somehow this was part of it, some terrible Mannian scheme unfolding before his eyes.

'Faster!' Coya shouted to the driver of the carriage with a double thump of his cane.

The fellow whipped the lathered zel onwards. But as they turned into the Avenue of Lies the zel clattered to a sudden stop right in the middle of the crossroads, confronted by a crowd of panicked citizens pouring all around them, faces whitened with fear.

'*Erēs Preserve Us*,' Coya recited aloud as he gazed north along the Avenue of Lies, seeing how one of the pillars of smoke was rising from the ruins of the main gates in the wall. 'They've breached the gates.'

'Can't go any further than this,' said the driver quickly, nervously, stubbornly.

'I need to get closer,' Coya said to his bodyguard. 'Find out what's happening with Creed.'

'What we need to do is get as far from here as we can.'

The carriage rocked as Coya stepped down onto the cobbles amongst the flow of people. It rocked again as his bodyguard Lynx jumped down lightly from the other side. 'Stay here!' Coya told the driver. 'I doubt we'll be long.'

But Coya had only taken a few steps when he heard the driver whipping the zel into a run, and saw him taking off along a side street away from the danger.

'Fool didn't even ask to be paid,' spat Lynx in disgust.

Coya Zeziké stood crookedly in the middle of the crossroads with both hands resting on the grip of his cane, listening to the horns as they sounded their Call to Arms to soldiers and citizens alike. The sounds of battle were loud here, crashing like a wave along the parapets of the wall just beyond the rooftops of the district, where figures struggled in combat through smoke and fire. Right ahead of him, at the end of the Avenue of Lies where the fog of war shrouded the blasted gates, rose the greatest din of all.

Coya wondered if this was it, impossibly – the downfall of Bar-Khos happening right before his eyes.

Past him trotted a hundred Red Guards headed for the wall. From the opposite direction a courier zipped by, wide-eyed and kicking her zel for all it was worth.

Still Coya stayed in the middle of the road, wanting to see what was happening at the gates before proceeding. Like an island of stubborn resistance he stood there peering ahead as people rushed around him, citizens either fleeing from the action or running towards it with whatever weapons had come to hand – hammers and axes, pitchforks and bows.

What a way to start a new year, he thought, scowling.

He nearly leaped from his skin as another startling explosion blasted from the distant gateway. Glass shattered all along the Avenue. People ducked their heads and ran onwards in panicked, bouncing strides.

It was a bomb going off, Coya realized with a taste of bile in his throat. Somehow the enemy had set off a bomb in the vicinity of the ruined gates, catching out those who ran in to reinforce the defending forces there. Screams of the wounded filled the air.

'Come on,' said his Khosian bodyguard beside him, her voice strained. 'We need to get out of here before this gets even worse.'

He had forgotten she was standing there, this replacement to Marsh, this stranger in her skintight suit that kept drawing his eye. Coya ignored her, straining to see what was happening at the far end of the thoroughfare. It was so odd to witness the Avenue of Lies like this, the main commercial artery through the city becoming a siege front in the battle.

A wall of smoke and grit was rolling down the street towards them.

'Master Zeziké,' tried his bodyguard again.

'Call me Coya. I've asked you that already.'

'Master Coya. *We need to leave now.*'

Figures were running back along the street. Armed citizens fleeing from the blasts, waving back those still coming towards them. He couldn't hear what they were shouting.

A hand gripped his arm. It was his bodyguard, trying to pull him away, but Coya snarled and yanked his arm free. Frowning fiercely, Coya peered along the Avenue towards the approaching bank of smoke.

He squinted, spotting the flash of a white cloak in the rolling haze. And then he saw others too, figures clad in white armour and masks, running full tilt along the street and cutting down anyone within reach.

The hairs rose on the back of his neck.

Acolytes. The fanatical warriors of the Empire howling in their drug-induced frenzies, come to enforce the Mannian promise of order and prosperity with the points of their blades.

'We need to leave *now*!'

His bodyguard was pulling at him again. It almost annoyed Coya, the obvious way in which she handled him with care, knowing all too well that Marsh would have picked him up roughly by now and bundled him to safety. But then Coya glimpsed the fear in the Khosian woman's expression, and his wits came back to him at last.

'Of course,' he said to her. 'Lead the way.'

The street to the south of them was choked with people suddenly flocking from the buildings, along with Red Guards trying to get through from the opposite direction. Seeing the bottleneck, Lynx led him into a side street where others were filtering too, holding a pistol in her hand now. With the heels of her boots rapping against the cobbles, she hurried in her long-legged stride towards the far end with Coya shambling along as fast as he could.

He gasped, spotting more flashes of white in the junction ahead. Already some Acolytes were charging into the side street, hacking and cutting at anyone that moved. A few ran at Lynx, howling like wild animals as they came. Lynx stopped and turned side-on with her pistol raised. She shot the first masked Acolyte through the forehead, then drew a stubby machete from her belt and hefted it into the side of a second attacker as she ducked from his swing.

She was even faster than Marsh, Coya saw with surprise.

'We're trapped,' Coya panted.

Ahead of them though, the Acolytes spreading out from the junction were coming under sudden attack. A plant pot burst against one of their heads, showering those around him with a rain of dirt and breaking his neck with an audible crack. Jeers rose from the nearby rooftop of a corner taverna, where men staggered half-drunk as they started heaving what they could down at the enemy forces below.

'This way,' said Lynx, and she darted through the side door of a shop with Coya right behind her.

Through the dim and reeking space of an animal emporium, Lynx led him towards the light of the open front door, past cages of trilling paradise birds and craning desert tortoises. A mug of hot chee still sat steaming on the front counter, and Lynx snapped it up and drained the whole lot before she reached the doorway.

'*Hello hello!*' someone croaked out, and they both jerked around to see the big green parrot sitting on a perch in the front window, flapping its wings.

Lynx flung the empty mug to the floor and stepped outside, looking left and right. '*Come again! Come again!*' the parrot squawked after them.

Out in the daylight again, Coya saw the enemy figures closer than he'd ever wanted to see them, battering the door of the taverna while a flaming bottle of alcohol crashed down into their midst in a splash of fire. The drunken Khosians roared from the rooftop.

Red Guards were clashing with a line of Acolytes in an opposite side street. Lynx led him south away from the scene, her thin shoulders hunched low as she reloaded her gun, plaits swinging as she looked about her.

In another side street people were being attacked by enemy forces as they fled from a Temple of the Grove, crowding out of its forest of living, leafy pillars in a collective panic. Swords flashed in the daylight. Men and women spilled to the ground and did not get up again. Coya wanted to cry out from the pain of what he witnessed, from the sick horror boiling in his stomach. He was barely looking at where he was going when he shoved into the back of his bodyguard.

'*Shit!*'

More Acolytes were flooding from the east into the next crossroads ahead, so close he could see the whites of their eyes behind their masks. Citizens yelled in fright and scattered from their way, fleeing in every direction. Lynx shouldered one of them aside before he could floor her, but then Coya took a shove from another desperate man and crashed down onto the cobbles hard.

Winded and shocked, Coya groped for his cane while he wondered if this was the end of him, here in the Shield of Khos on the very day of its downfall, so far away from his wife and home. A gunshot cracked out. A figure leapt right over his head. It was madness, too much to take in at once. Everything seemed to be slowing down. Odd, how life grew more unreal in equal measure to how intense it became; as though this dreamy hyper-state was closer to reality than anything else. Coya could hear the rasp of his own breathing like a panicking stranger panting down his ear. Something came to his hand and he grasped it, knowing it was his cane. At last he managed to suck down a lungful of air.

Struggling up, Coya caught a glimpse of a boy spilling from his feet on the other side of the street. In the next moment, through the passing legs of running figures, he saw the boot of an Acolyte stamping down on the youth's skull as though it was a ripe melon.

Fear propelled Coya onto one knee.

Past his face snapped a white cloak reeking of gunsmoke – another Acolyte, cutting off the screams of a grey-haired matron fleeing for her life, right there in front of him. Lynx was spinning in mid-air to cut through an enemy's leg below his knee. She turned towards Coya but another Acolyte was on her instantly, screaming the insanities of the fanatic. They were all over the place, white cloaks flapping with splashes of blood. A man took a sword from behind right through his abdomen. Another fell at the chop of an axe through his neck. It was all Coya could do but wheeze for air while giving witness to the butchery, his heart perched mid-beat in his chest, each image searing itself in his mind right down to the living tissue.

An Acolyte reared over him, bloody sword in hand, and Coya knew right then that he was dead.

He wished he could muster some bravado in his last moments, spitting into the bastard's face like Marsh would have managed. But instead, Coya found himself thinking of Rechelle and how she would be broken when she heard of his death, for she adored Coya as he adored her; they were completed by each other, lessened when apart.

I'm sorry, he said to his wife with all the regret in the world.

Yet as so often happened in Coya's life, good fortune struck right when he needed it the most. Maybe it was true what people had always said of Coya's lucky touch, that he'd had all his bad luck when he was born a cripple, and only had the good to make up for ever since – because suddenly a runaway zel crashed into the howling Acolyte, bowling him off his feet as the animal reared up in the harness of a driverless carriage.

Suddenly there was Lynx by his side, hauling him bodily up over her shoulder just like Marsh would have done.

Lynx staggered for the carriage with Coya's head hanging from her back. He heard her fire her pistol and then she stumbled, almost dropping him, but she stayed on her feet and stepped over a dead Acolyte to the carriage, and tossed Coya into it.

When he looked up he saw his bodyguard reloading her gun, face pinched with concentration. She seemed to be paying no mind to the hilt of the knife sticking from her side.

For an instant Lynx looked right at Coya, this woman of whom he barely knew anything, save that she was dying. Over her shoulder a white-masked figure was rushing at her back.

With a teary grin, Lynx lifted the pistol high and fired it over her head, scaring the skittery zel into flight. Coya rolled back as the carriage bounced off along the cobbles. People flashed by the open flapping door, their screams fading only slowly in his ears though lingering on in his mind, imprinting themselves for as long as he lived.

CHAPTER THIRTY-TWO

Nico

Nico's eyes were closed, though he felt the skyship shuddering and swaying as it dropped height, and heard the main thrusters roaring as loud as a flood following in their wake. Through whips and crackles of the wind, a great many voices muttered prayers to the World Mother, to Mercy, to Luck, to the Way of All Things.

'You all right?' said a voice over his head.

'I'll live,' he heard his mother reply. 'I just needed some water. How about you?'

'What do you mean?'

'I don't know. You can hardly look me in the eye, Cole.'

'Knocks you on your ass, watching your brother die like that.'

'You sure that's it?'

'What, I need more?'

Nico managed to open his eyes by the slimmest of cracks. His head was throbbing and his vision swam, but he could make out his father crouched over him where he lay, and his mother too, awake and talking now; both parents together once again like something from his dreams.

In the fierce winds his mother's red hair danced as vibrantly as a flame, captivating his delirious mind. She had a hand cupped to Nico's skull where a hard lump was pulsing, and she looked down at her son with a battered, grimy expression of concern.

'You think he's concussed?'

'Maybe. He took a good crack to the head.'

Nico recalled Bahn dying in his father's arms while soldiers grabbed at the fallen man; then being knocked out by a kick from someone's boot.

'I can hardly believe it's really him. All this time I thought he was dead.'

'Yeah, what was your thinking there, letting him run off like that to train as a Rōshun?'

'Oh, that's rich. If we want to start passing around some blame here . . .'

Cole sighed like a man regretting his words.

'Please, I brought him back to you, didn't I? That has to count for something.'

'You think I'd be talking to you otherwise?'

Nico blinked to clear his vision, clouded by a sickening wash of colours that resonated with his throbbing skull. He seemed to be lying in the hold of a skyship with his head propped against something soft. The hull door on this side of the ship was missing, which explained all the air blasting in and threatening to freeze them to death – along with the fact that his head was perched right next to the edge. Other figures were sitting with their legs dangling right over the side. It was the only place for them in the crammed space of the hold, where fighters swayed on their feet against each other.

Cole and Reese stared at each other over his still form.

'How was it, back there?' he asked her.

'Like a nightmare I never want to talk about,' she said. 'Thank you, for getting me out.'

His father dropped his head with his eyes closed, and Reese lay a comforting hand on his shoulder. A cold tear splashed the back of Nico's hand from her welling eyes.

'Reese,' said Cole in a strangled voice, then he shook his head suddenly lost for words.

'I know, husband. I know.'

He was weeping silently, clamping a hand over his face while his body shook hard. She squeezed his shoulder like she used to all those years ago.

An explosion rocked the ship, causing everyone standing to stagger from side to side. Hail seemed to scatter against the hull, and then Nico realized what it was – enemy guns firing up at them.

His head lolled further to one side, so that from the corner of his eye he could see the northern wall of Bar-Khos sweeping past below. Figures were swarming all over its facing slope of earth, clambering up ladders, launching themselves onto the parapet and into the fierce fighting. A gate was lying in smoking pieces and more enemy forces were flooding through the breach, spreading out into the city beyond.

People crowded towards the open doorway for a better look, muttering in dismay.

Fires were raging down there in the northern city streets, their rising pillars of smoke whipped up by the passing of the ship. Citizens could be seen fleeing ahead of imperial forces, who were hacking down everyone in sight. Screams rose up on the wafting hot air of the flames. Guns fired from rooftops, people hurling what projectiles they could at the enemy below.

'Sweet Mercy on them all,' he heard his mother say.

Nico could only stare in wonder.

The ship tilted as the nose levelled off. Rooftops rushed by not far below. They were passing over scenes of gathering resistance now, roadblocks being built across the streets while defenders formed up behind them. Khosian cavalry swept eastwards towards the Avenue of Lies, scattering civilians from their way.

And then everything was replaced by the white stones of the Stadium of Arms, and Nico saw that the ship was landing inside the great stadium even as another ship was taking off.

'Hold on,' his mother said down to him, seeing the flicker of his eyes. 'Just hold on.'

Nico looked up at her brilliant green eyes and at his father's worried frown, and knew that no matter what happened now, for good or bad, at least he was home.

CHAPTER THIRTY-THREE

Coya

These things have happened before, Coya Zeziké recited in his head while he held a long breath then released it. *These things will happen again.*

It was a mental calming exercise, taught to him by one of his childhood mentors of the Way. An aid for restoring context to a frightened mind. Yet Coya felt soothed not at all by the cold stoicism of the words.

Another skyship was settling on the sandy floor of the amphitheatre that was the Stadium of Arms, its great loft almost filling the space.

At once, dozens of figures were staggering out of the vessel's hold, carrying or supporting the wounded towards medicos already desperately at work down there – more survivors from General Creed's doomed raid against the enemy encampment.

For the last half hour, skyships had been bringing them in from their desperate position out on Beacon Heights, yet there was no sign of the Lord Protector down there, no sign of him strutting about in his usual towering manner shouting commands this way and that. Only chaos and despair around a body covered in a sheet, lying on its own square of dirt.

Coya swallowed hard, still amazed by what he was looking at. Still shaking.

For as long as he lived he hoped never to live through another day like this one.

He had made it here to the Stadium of Arms in something of a daze, hardly realizing he was galloping past the famous Bar-Khosian landmark until soldiers had leaped into the street to stop the runaway zel and its carriage. Eyes wide at finding Coya Zeziké lying in its back, they had hurried him inside, away from the enemy forces flooding from the north and the citizens fleeing past in their thousands.

Just in time, Coya discovered, to witness the body of the Lord Protector being carried from a landed skyship. Marsalas Creed, his old friend. Shot in the back by one of his own, some of the survivors were saying, in the very trap that Coya had suspected was being prepared for him.

Still in a daze, Coya made his way through the throng to see the body for himself. He forced himself to bend and lift a corner of the sheet.

It was Marsalas all right, lying there unmoving on the ground with the awful emptiness of death; an inanimate thing where once there had been life. The Lord Protector wore an expression of peace on his bloodless features, as though he had been glad, in the end, to lie down from the burdens of his life. An illusion, surely, Coya had thought bitterly, for Marsalas had never stopped fighting for life, his own or his people's, just as much as he had lived for the fight.

But it was a poor time for grief and recollections. There was a city falling out there.

Waving off the attentions of those around him, Coya hurried to the busy steps of the amphitheatre and climbed past bloody tiers filled with the wounded. He was shaking badly now, unable to stop himself. He saw a flash of Lynx again; her face in those last moments. He pictured her fighting the white-armoured Acolytes with her final breaths until they cut her down. Panting and gasping, Coya pushed upwards until he reached the top, where a high stone walkway circled the arches and columns above the tiers, hoping for a better look at the situation outside.

It was about as bad as he might have expected, he realized grimly, seeing imperial infantry already engaging troops outside the stadium walls.

They were wasting no time with the Khosian forces at the wall, it seemed. Instead, enemy units were obviously rushing through the blasted gates and heading deeper into Bar-Khos – heading here to this strong point at its centre, where the nearest reinforcements were the fortified garrisons strung along the waist of the city, and the Shield to the south.

With citizens still fleeing through the neighbouring streets, imperial infantry were converging on the Stadium of Arms in ever greater numbers. He saw Khosian soldiers falling back to the entrances below, overwhelmed by missile fire from the enemy. Around Coya, riflemen were blazing away in hot reply. Their volleys forced the enemy forces into cover too, vanishing into surrounding buildings from where they started firing back. Though some Acolytes were simply ignoring the hail of fire, and making frantic charges for the lower-floor entrances, trying to throw explosives before they were shot down.

At least help was trying to get through to the stadium, in the form of a column of cloaked Hoo fighters to the east, fighting with shields and their long charta spears and collective shouts of '*Hoo!*', and reinforcements of Red Guards to the south. But their progress was being slowed by ever more Acolytes rushing to fill the streets in their way.

It was shocking to see so many imperial fighters in the heart of Bar-Khos. Clearly it was going badly for those thousands of friendly forces defending the wall if so many of the enemy were getting through. A murderous din of battle could still be heard coming from the north – more gunfire and explosions than Coya had ever heard before, like a dozen lightning storms all crammed down together over the city. Smoke rose from streets of burning buildings.

Yet there were so few soldiers to be seen retreating now from the north. They must be trapped up there, outnumbered and encircled, those thousands of Khosians and foreign volunteers who were the majority of the city's defenders.

Without them the city would surely be lost. Especially if the enemy overran the Stadium of Arms, which anchored Bar-Khos's defences both north and south. Standing at the very heart of the city, the structure had been built centuries ago with fortification in mind, intended from the beginning to stand as a central bastion of defence should the city ever fall to its enemies. Yet even here, with a garrison of a thousand fighters at hand, the situation was becoming truly desperate.

Everyone who could fight was being pressed into action, even the ragged survivors of Creed's ill-fated raid. As the latest arrivals stumbled clear of the landed skyship down on the stadium floor, they were being hollered at by staff-sergeants to help defend the perimeter defences; exhausted men and women leaping from one scorching hot pan straight into another.

Still trembling with emotion, Coya stood on the high walkway clutching his cane in a white-knuckle grip, barely aware of the busy reports of riflemen as he took it all in. He was no good to anyone here, he realized; just a useless spectator in the way. He needed to find some way out of this place so he could rejoin Shard and the others down in All Fools, before it was too late. But still he couldn't move. In the end it was the sight of a familiar face amongst the nearest defenders that finally roused him.

Coya hurried along the walkway as fast as he could, calling out as he did, 'Sergeant Sansun!'

'Take some cover, you bloody fool!' shouted Sansun, turning amidst a cloud of gunsmoke in the buckskins and leathers of a ranger.

Coya swayed back into cover, suddenly noticing the intensity of enemy gunfire striking the white facade of the stadium in puffs of rock dust – almost as though the Mannians were firing harmless pellets of salt at them. Yet to his left a rifleman fell back with a cry of pain, and elsewhere an explosion suddenly ripped a chunk from the outer facade, sending other defenders hurtling backwards.

'We must stop meeting like this,' Coya called through the racket to the ranger sergeant. 'Good to see you still in one piece!' But Sansun seemed unimpressed by his words.

'Can't see that lasting for long, can you?' replied the Minosian man, breaking open his fuming rifle to reload it. The lines of his face were dark with dirt; his hair singed to bare spots on one side. Sansun flinched at another explosion, his fingers fumbling as he tried to slot a fresh shell into the gun.

'We're not alone here,' Coya told him, though mostly it was a reminder to himself. 'We have the entire democras at our backs, remember that, Volunteer.'

'You think I've forgotten? Home's just about all I can think about right now.'

The sergeant's words prompted Coya to glance across the faces of the rest of the squad, crouched along the parapet. He spotted the young sniper Xeno, firing down at the enemy like he was shooting fish in a barrel, mouth open in excitement. And the medico, Curl, dragging back a fallen casualty.

'Where are Captain Gamorre and the others?'

'Dead.'

'I'm sorry to hear that!'

Sansun put the rifle to his shoulder then peered at him over the stock.

'You need something, Coya?'

'Yes, I need to get south, into All Fools.'

Sansun lifted an eyebrow high, the only response he needed to give. The sergeant looked back to the sandy oval floor of the stadium far below, where the emptied skyship was taking off with its tilted thrusters roaring away, flooding the open space with its din and smoke as the vessel lifted past them into the sky.

'Only way out of here just took off without you.'

Coya Zeziké pulled a desperate frown, his gaze a wild thing tearing this way and that. He turned back to the view outside.

People had been caught out by the swiftness of the Mannians flooding through the breaches, so that now the flat rooftops of the city swarmed with citizens taking refuge where they could, seeking places to hide or brazenly hurling down what missiles came to hand at the enemy. Massacres were unfolding amongst the reds and greens of winter roof-gardens. Other buildings were being set on fire beneath the people's feet.

Over the crackle of rifle fire, through the uproar of the shouting, Coya could perceive a dim wash of sound coming from the fallen districts of Bar-Khos: a shrill yet subtle chorus that was the collective screams and cries of thousands of trapped people.

He rocked on his feet, hunching deeper into himself the more that he witnessed.

'Don't think. Just shoot,' shouted a rifleman to a younger fellow beside him yelling in panic.

Towards the south, just beyond the Red Guards trying to fight their way through, a hasty last-ditch line of defence was being thrown up across the streets by soldiers and citizens alike. Buildings were coming down – the Khosians collapsing them strategically, Coya realized, using them to choke the streets with barricades of rubble. Behind the barricades, the district was teeming with people who had already fled from the north.

'I need to make a dash for our lines there,' Coya shouted to Sergeant Sansun.

'A dash? You really think you're up to it?'

'Question is, are you?' Coya retorted, and he rapped his cane against the ranger's boot in challenge.

*

Downwards Coya hobbled with Sansun and his squad of rangers following after him; down through the crowded tiers of seating, with the whole wide world sounding like it was coming down around his ears.

Don't think, Coya recalled the soldier's advice to his freaking comrade up above. *Just shoot.*

On the ground level, a mob of startled faces filled the wide arcade of supporting archways that ran below the tiers of seating. The noise here was a physical force upon the senses, jolting and jarring, nearly overwhelming him. Medical crews bawled for supplies and help as they tried to cope with screaming casualties. Dogs barked at walls that shook with explosions from the other side. A pair of Greyjackets ran past carrying a heavy box of ammunition, only to drop it onto the ground so that shells spilled everywhere.

Yet even in the chaos, people stepped aside for Coya when they saw him approaching, startled to see him there amongst them in such moments as these.

'Coya Zeziké!' someone cried out for the tenth time in as many seconds, though this time Coya turned to look with faint recognition.

Towards him sprang the portly form of Koolas, the independent war chattēro, whose reports on the siege were read throughout the Free Ports.

'Not now, Koolas, my dear fellow. Can't you see we're all rather busy?'

'What do you make of our situation?' asked the war chattēro, a pencil and notepad in his hands. 'Can the League send relief forces in time to save us?'

'Koolas, please, this is hardly the time for an interview!' yelled

Coya, and he was gladdened to see Sergeant Sansun pushing the fellow aside.

They hurried past a burning brazier where a tall Ground Marshal was surrounded by officers all shouting at him at once. At the edge of the circle, a bald and heavily scarred fellow caught Coya's eye, for he had one of the officers shoved up against a column, a young Michinè nobleman by the looks of him, and the scarred man was yelling into his face with a passion and waving a leather tube at him.

Coya stopped even as the man saw him there and released the officer.

'You!' he shouted, coming at him waving the leather tube like a sword. 'Coya Zeziké. You're just the person to take these off my hands. None of these bloody fools will listen.'

'And you are?'

'Cole Calvone. I have charts here to the Isles of Sky, if anyone will damn well take them.'

Maybe Coya was hearing things. Maybe in his distress he was creating phantoms of impossible hopes.

No, he realized. It was simply his good fortune holding out again, impossibly so. Coya almost muttered a silent thank-you to the cosmos.

'My dear man. Did you say something about charts?'

CHAPTER THIRTY-FOUR

High Priest

A kind of glee played across the ancient features of Kira dul Dubois as she gazed down upon the burning districts of Bar-Khos, blazing brightly beneath the murk of the morning sky. As a priest of Mann and true believer, it seemed like the culmination of her life somehow, wickedly and delightedly so, to be standing there within the enemy city, watching its downfall.

The flesh is strong, she recited in her head, stirred by the triumph of her faith.

Kira had always known the truth of the First Patriarch's words, that the reign of Mann would have no end if only they could some day defeat the Free Ports – for Nihilis had always understood the true threat of the democras, this League of people who had been on the rise even longer than the faith of Mann. He had always known how their foundations of equality and cooperation made them the very antithesis of the Mannian faith, and even a danger to it.

And now here was another validation of his prophecy, happening before her very eyes. From this victory over Bar-Khos, the Empire would go on to seize the rest of the weakened Free Ports. And then, finally, they could turn to the long-standing matter of the Alhazii Caliphate, and the completion of this project of conquering the known world, so that they might shape it in their own image.

Mann would finally reign supreme.

Kira watched on from the high tower of the mansion, over the roofs of other villas that rambled down from this cliff-top district, trembling from the cold and from the excitement of what she was seeing. Beneath the hood of her cloak, the old crone muttered quietly to herself, and wrung her withered hands together like two sticks of deadwood – proud that they had played a part in this destruction.

Upon the breeze came scraps of smoke and cries of panic. From here, near the sea cliffs of southern Bar-Khos, the whole northern half of the city seemed overrun by flames and imperial forces.

It was a sight of savage beauty, for sure. Enough to have drawn her from the sanctuary of her warm room to this windy rooftop to gain a view. Enough even to draw pricks of emotion to the old woman's eyes, for there was a reckoning in what she saw here; a long-overdue rebalancing of the scales.

Kira inhaled the scent of burning wood like sweet incense on the wind, taking in the dull shine of the sea and the many ships now fleeing from the western harbour, loaded with citizens escaping while they still could.

It had worked, this plan of theirs to employ the Khosian traitors in breaching the gates of the city. And Creed too, the Lord Protector, had been slain. Now the future was clear. Mann's destiny was to conquer this world, for there was nothing left to stop them.

She had come a long way since her days as a young initiate in the underground cult of Mann, back in Q'os. Clenching her numb hands together, chilled to the bone, Kira swayed backwards and felt the whole course of her life rushing through her.

Such a long way to come, she thought with a little vertigo, a little dizziness, recalling the girl she had once been all that time ago. An ignorant and hungry street hustler, who might never have left the slums of the Shambles if her best friend Sool hadn't gone and joined the cult of Mann, prompting Kira to do the same.

Had that really been her, the same person, so audacious yet naive?

Kira had been beautiful back then. She remembered her beauty as she felt the dry rasp of her hands and the stiff, aching arthritis in her bones. She had become the lover of Nihilis himself, she and Sool together; lovers to the founder of the underground cult who would become, after the coup of the Longest Night swept them into power, the First Patriarch of Mann.

She hadn't lasted long as his lover, not nearly as long as Sool. Yet Kira and her family had gone on to the heights of power and wealth within the burgeoning Mannian Empire. It had almost been easy, so long as she never stopped for long enough to think of the blood on her hands.

It had been Nihilis who had sent her to this doomed city of Bar-Khos, in order to oversee their covert operations here; a man who had pretended to be dead for decades now. An ancient, twisted creature who she increasingly despised, despite her devotion to the faith he had founded.

Kira blinked long and slowly like a sated vulture, her eyes reflecting the burning districts below. Gunfire echoed like Alhazii firecrackers in the warrens of streets zig-zagging out from the heart of the city. She looked around, seeing yet another skud lifting off from one of the neighbouring mansions. No doubt more Michinè nobles making their escape.

She was close to the Bar-Khosian Council Chambers here, standing on a prominence of white rock, though by all accounts they were largely empty now, only Chonas the First Minister and a handful of his people remaining behind. Soon she would go there herself, when the time came to accept the Bar-Khosians' unconditional surrender.

A scuff of boots announced the arrival of her bodyguard, Quito, at the top of the stairs.

'There's news,' said the old Diplomat. 'I thought you should know.'

Kira sighed and hoped he wasn't about to spoil her good mood.

'Go on.'

'One of our teams picked up a signal in the southern district of All Fools. From the pulsegland of our rogue Diplomat. The one who deserted after Chey-Wes. It seems he's been moved there by the Khosians.'

How delightful. The young Diplomat who had slain her daughter Sasheen as she had retreated in battle, following Kira's own instructions.

Now a traitor to his own people.

'He's in the open?'

'Alarum thinks we can get to him. Though he doesn't think we can spare any people.'

'*Forget what Alarum thinks. Strike the Diplomat dead.*'

CHAPTER THIRTY-FIVE

Diplomat

Horns were calling out when Ché finally awakened. Squinting at a harsh stream of light that poured through the inkworks' broken windows, the young Diplomat cocked his head to listen more closely, hearing the alarms sounding all across the city, frantic and desperate in their calls.

Nearby, his guard's chair was empty and the man nowhere in sight. Voices sounded loud and hot-tempered down in the ground floor below.

Something was happening, he sensed. Something big.

Ché tried to rise and felt the discomfort flaring across his neck. He groped at his throat and found bandages there, covering a stitched wound that itched more than it was sore.

The Dreamer had saved him then, miraculously, on the night he had wakened with his throat cut.

Should have let me go, thought the young Diplomat, and sank back against the furs with a sigh.

But then he recalled Fanazda's cruel face looming over him with the bloody knife, and his helplessness as he lay there bleeding out, and Ché growled and threw the furs aside, and struggled awkwardly to rise against the heavy weight of his shackles and chains.

An empty wine bottle lay next to the guard's chair. Ché stooped to grab it up, feeling light-headed as he straightened so that he breathed deeply to steady himself. Gripping the bottle by its neck, Ché shuffled for the stairs with cold murder in his eyes.

*

Down on the ground floor of the inkworks, people were hurrying back and forth carrying wounded figures between them, trailing

271

blood all over the place, their raised voices echoing throughout the space as they yelled to clear the way. Ché noticed the Rōshun on the far side, hunkered down in conversation, and elsewhere a smattering of Volunteers, Red Guards and other soldiers, looking ragged and bloody and defeated. Civilians were crowded there too amongst the racks of urns at the back. Every face looked white with shock and disbelief.

Thunder sounded in the air today, like every other day in this damned city, though the cannons rumbled louder than he had yet heard them. Indeed they sounded close by.

Coya was shuffling across the room with his head down, his sweaty features burning with emotion. But the cripple didn't even see Ché standing there, and he hurried on towards the stairs not looking at anyone, shaking and gripping a leather tube in his hand.

With a start Ché spotted the girl Curl coming in through the front entrance, sagging with exhaustion. Other rangers followed behind her. Yet she was the last thing on Ché's mind just then – it was Fanazda he was after, and when he spotted the lean Rōshun dunking his head in a barrel of water, Ché headed straight for him, smashing the bottle against a passing table so he was left gripping its jagged neck.

'Easy,' said a voice as someone grabbed Ché by the arm.

Wild stepped in front of him, almost close enough for their chests to touch. His big moustaches were twitching in humour, as though he did not entirely disapprove of Ché's choice of action. Still, Wild's next words said otherwise. 'Wait!' said the Rōshun. 'This isn't the time for this.'

'Get out of my way, or I'll kill you too.'

'Listen to me! The northern wall has fallen. They've taken half the city already. People are acting crazy enough as it is.'

'I don't care if the Seventh Horde is headed our way. He's getting cut. Right now.'

It was then that Fanazda spotted him standing there in his chains. The man flinched in surprise before he masked his expression with his usual mocking sneer.

'*Fanazda!*' Ché roared across the space of the inkworks, causing every head to turn his way.

'Don't be a fool!' rasped Wild. 'You think you stand a chance in those bloody chains?'

Ché thrust his arms out with the iron links snapping tight between them. 'Release me, then.'

'Ché . . .'

'If you have any sense of honour at all, Seratian, you'll take them off me.'

'I'm being lectured on honour by a deceiving low-life Mannian, am I?'

'I was once a Rōshun too, Wild. *Now step aside.*'

'Fine, have it your way then,' snapped the man, and he stepped aside, motioning to one of the guards. He told the man to fetch the keys to Ché's chains, and while they waited Wild called the Rōshun over, who gathered now in interest.

There were ten of them in all. Ché studied the familiar faces amongst them, including the many younger Rōshun who had been apprentices at the same time as himself. Aléas was one of them, one of their sharpest blades even as a boy, chewing a match and gazing at Ché with all his usual nonchalance.

But then Fanazda was fast approaching, and Ché straightened with the broken bottle in his grip.

The man stopped a dozen feet away, confident and relaxed with a hand resting on the hilt of a sheathed knife, tapping away with a forefinger. He wore a tall imperial sky-officer's hat slanted haphazardly on his dripping head – salvaged, no doubt, from the wreckage of the crashed Mannian skyship on the other side of the vast room. Ché supposed that Fanazda must be pushing forty by now. Yet he knew too that the man was one of the fastest knife fighters Ché had ever known.

Wild addressed the semi-circle of his peers. 'Looks like there's a score to settle, never mind that the city's falling round our ears.'

'Have we time for this, Wild?'

'Fellow had his throat cut,' Wild answered, though he was staring hard at Fanazda. 'We'll make the time.'

The guard returned with the keys and Wild snatched them off him, bending to unlock the leg irons first.

'I don't care what Coya says. Anyone still has a problem with our

Mannian companion here, now is the time to settle it. Here's your chance to see how well a Diplomat fights for his life.'

'What are you saying?'

Indeed, thought Ché. What was he damn well telling them here?

'I'll give you a count of two hundred to do what you like to him. Knives only!'

The Rōshun stirred, a few smiling. Wild stood and cast aside the leg irons. His eyes were glittering.

'However, after the count of two hundred, if he still lives, you leave the man alone. Anyone lifts a hand towards him after this – well, he forfeits his life. That includes you, Fanazda. Are we agreed?'

'Aye!'

Ché was scratching at the stitched wound across his neck as Fanazda drew his knife, and started loosening up for the fight to come. He waited for Wild to remove the manacles, but the man leaned in close instead.

'That's all I'm taking off,' Wild told him quietly. 'Your legs are free so you can make a run for it. My advice to you now is that you do precisely that. Get out of here, while you still can. The snipers are gone from the roof. Get outside and lose yourself in the crowds.'

Over the man's shoulder, Ché saw that Curl was looking his way across the room. He had no intention of fleeing from this place, not yet.

'Stay out of my way,' he growled. And it was only then that Ché realized – like some bizarre dream – that he was naked.

On the hard stone floor of the half-destroyed inkworks they stood facing each other – Ché against Fanazda and four other Rōshun who had stepped forward with knives in their hands, a few younger ones amongst them.

'You want a piece of him?' shouted Wild, retreating out of the way. 'Come and take it.'

For a moment no one moved save for Fanazda. And then the others started spreading out around him.

'*One!*' Wild called, standing in a shaft of daylight. '*Two!*'

Ché's heart was pounding in his throat. His muscles were stiff from his long imprisonment, his head light from the simple exertion of moving around. He wasn't going to last long in manacles against five Rōshun. Mere seconds, he reckoned. He would have to make this fast; single out Fanazda, take him out, then fall back into whatever defensive position he could manage.

Ché pictured it in his mind, rehearsing what was to come; mentally preparing himself for what he needed to do.

'*Ten*,' shouted Wild. '*Eleven!*'

'You first, Fanazda,' Ché declared, pointing the broken bottle towards his opponent. 'You get the first try.'

He hardly needed to urge the man on, though. Fanazda hopped in lightly on the balls of his feet, the knife held like a natural extension of his hand, thinking this was going to be easy.

'*Fifteen. Sixteen!*'

Suddenly Ché crouched low as Fanazda stepped in within his reach. Fanazda feigned to the left, then his knife snaked at him on a whisper of air so fast Ché could barely see it.

Ché was faster though, even now in his ragged condition. He grabbed the blade in mid-air like he was snatching a river trout, trapping the steel in the grip of his palm even as it cut through the flesh. Fanazda had time to flare his eyes in surprise, before Ché stuck the broken bottle right into his neck, once, twice, three bloody times.

He hopped back as the dying man crashed to the floor grasping at his wounds.

'*Twenty-two! Twenty-three!*'

Ché kept hopping backwards until he was right next to Wild. It was gallant of the man, he thought, not to resist as Ché got behind him and pushed the jagged glass right up against his neck.

The remaining four Rōshun froze. They looked to each other uncertainly while Fanazda gasped his life away on the floor. Others were rushing to the fallen man's aid, including Curl with her medico bag.

'Don't stop on my account,' Ché prompted Wild, and he pulled the fellow back until Ché felt the wall pressing behind him.

'*Thirty. Thirty-one.*'

Over Wild's shoulder he watched the Rōshuns' hesitation.

'I'll do it!' he shouted, pushing the broken glass harder against his neck. 'I'll kill him if you take a step closer.'

'Not so hard, Diplomat,' Wild muttered from the corner of his mouth. '*Thirty-five. Thirty-six!*'

Ché couldn't help but look towards Curl just then. The young woman was gaping at him in horror, her hands bloody.

What else could I do? he implored with his eyes. *The man tried to kill me in my sleep!*

'Forty-one. Forty-two. Forty-three.'

It was the longest wait of his life.

CHAPTER THIRTY-SIX

Dreamer

'You've heard the worst then, I take it?'

It was Coya, stamping into the room all hot and blustery. Shard looked up from the wooden crate she was packing, as did her assistant Blame, busily grabbing things from the table surfaces.

'What, that the city is on the verge of being taken?' Shard drawled in reply, feigning a bravado she did not feel.

She didn't think she'd ever seen her friend so stunned before, or so ragged. Coya resembled a version of himself who had been dragged through a hedge then left in a ditch for a day and a night. His usually immaculate clothing was a mess. His eyes were blasted open; like a man who had stared hard into the abyss only to find it glaring back at him.

'You won't believe what I have here,' he rasped in a throaty voice. 'There might still be time yet.'

He slapped a leather tube on the table before her, then opened it up and pulled out the sheets within. Coya was trembling as he flattened them out for her to see.

Shard gazed down at a map of the Great Hush, marked by the route of an expedition.

'That isn't what I think it is, is it?'

'Yes, Shard, the charts to the Isles!'

For just an instant, she wondered if they were fakes that Coya had put together in some vain hope of saving the city. But one glance at him told her otherwise.

The breath caught in her throat.

'How in all Erēs did you—'

'Never mind that. What do we do with them right now is the

question? Surely we can force the Caliphate into imposing a ceasefire in the siege.'

Her mind was already racing with the implications. She looked to Coya. He looked back at her, hopeful, excited. Even Blame came over to study the sheets in stunned amazement. She watched him trace a finger down a pencilled coastline all the way to the Isles of Sky.

'Huh,' he said in wonder. 'They're not even islands.'

Indeed not. It was clear from the maps that the legendary Isles were actually the peaks of mountains.

The Alhazii Caliphate would agree to almost anything in return for keeping these charts – and therefore the location of the Isles – a secret. If it meant preserving their monopoly, the source of all their power, they could certainly be pushed into helping the democras in this war.

Skies above, Coya was right. There might even be time to save Bar-Khos if they acted quickly enough. They could take these charts to the Alhazii embassy down by the harbour and show them what they had, before thrashing out the beginnings of a deal with Zanzahar by farcry. With the Caliphate on their side in this war, the Alhazii could force the Mannians into a ceasefire here, under threat of cutting off their black powder.

'Damn it!' Shard growled.

'What?'

'The city is still under a communications blackout. We have no way of reaching the Caliphate.'

'You can't break through?'

Shard raised an eyebrow in annoyance. Coya whooshed the air from his lungs, frowning, looking about him in frustration.

More explosions boomed to the north like waves crashing against the foot of a cliff. The building rattled.

'We need to leave the city,' she said. 'Get out from under this blackout.'

'There's no time, Shard! Can't you hear them out there? We're barely holding them back at the barricades as it is.'

Coya inhaled deeply, then matched her gaze with the steady clarity of his own. 'Think, damn you. Put that oversized brain of yours to good use for once.'

'I am thinking!'

'Well think harder!'

Shard bit her lip in frustration. 'None of this would be a problem if I still had my strength. I could Dream my way through their blackout easily enough, and reach the Caliphate directly.'

'So what do you need? How do we get your strength back in a hurry?'

'We can't. I'd be doing it already, if there was a way.'

'Shard. Please. There must be something!'

'A miracle, you mean? Some fellow Dreamer here to flood me with vitality again? Or maybe I should go looking for a jar of Royal Milk in my pockets? Maybe I'll even find a few shots of moondust to blow the breath of the cosmos through my veins?'

Coya craned closer over his stick with a sudden wily look in his eye.

'*Moondust*, did you say?'

Her forehead furrowed in puzzlement as he tapped the tip of his cane against the floor.

'I think I might know where to find the very thing.'

CHAPTER THIRTY-SEVEN

Nico

So incredibly vivid, the inner world of dreams at times. So real that it was hard to tell you were even dreaming at all.

Yet what was that? What did it suggest, about the mind, about reality itself, when a dream could be as real as anything ever experienced in the waking world, for all that it was only a construct of your imagination?

What did it mean, if you could be fooled into believing in existence so easily by your own mental workings?

Maybe the cloudmen of the Way were right in considering all things to be part of the Great Dream. Maybe there really was a Great Dreamer casting all of this into being from its own cosmic musings.

In his fevered mind, Nico knew that he was dreaming. He knew that he lay on a hard stone floor with a bandage wrapped around his throbbing head. He could even hear the constant background murmur of people in the large space all around him, and the dull concussions of war in the distance. Yet he did not wake himself, preferring to remain where he was in the stirrings of his dreams – high in the mountains of Cheem on a sunny day, where he had trained briefly as a Rōshun apprentice, brought there by the old farlander Ash.

For a spell he had been fishing in one of the cool mountain streams with his friend and fellow apprentice Aléas, within sight of the Rōshun monastery, talking and joking.

But then Nico found himself scrambling up the boulders of the stream alone and breathless with anticipation. Rounding a bend of grassy banks he came to a large pool and stopped with a gasp, seeing the shocking, thrilling gleam of a young woman's flanks in the water.

It was Serèse, daughter of the fearsome Alhazii man Baracha – bathing there by herself and turning slowly his way. Before she could see him, Nico threw himself into the long grasses, trying to stifle the excited rasp of his breathing.

His eyes were magnets locked to the attraction of her bronzed and naked skin. Serèse stood in the water with her fingers trailing across its surface, a twisted lustre of black hair hanging between her perfectly pouting breasts, her thighs shimmering in the reflected sunlight, taut as paper. From her narrow hips her pelvis curved around the soft bulge of her abdomen, pointing to a dab of dark pubic hair that was drip-dripping into rings of spreading motion between her slightly parted legs.

A groan rattled from the back of his throat like his final breath of life.

But then Serèse turned her face fully towards him, and Nico saw how it was a bloody ruin. He looked away in horror.

Behind him men were shouting now. A bonfire was blazing down there in the lower valley, tall and bright. Nico glimpsed the white cloaks of Acolytes flitting between rocks below, headed his way – hunting him, he realized, so that they could burn him alive on the flames of the fire.

Again he groaned aloud, though this time in dread.

'Nico?' Serèse enquired with a start, looking up to his position with the sunlight pooling around her in a million flashes of brilliant white, a vivid contrast to the bloody red remains of her face.

'I think he's dreaming,' a distant voice was saying.

And then Nico remembered once again where he really was, and slowly parted his eyelids to see his mother's concerned and bruised features hovering over him, framed by the red sheen of her hair.

Such a relief to see her there alive and well after all his worries. It was possibly the best feeling he'd ever had in his life. Though his mother didn't notice him looking up at her just then, focused instead on the young medico crouched over him inspecting the lump on his head – a pretty girl with a splendid crest of hair, dressed in dark leathers.

'I lost him once before,' his mother was saying. 'I couldn't make it through that pain again.'

'It's no problem. I don't mind having a look.'

'You must be too young to have any children yourself.'

The girl frowned, burdened by her thoughts for a moment.

'You'll understand when you do. I loved this one from the first moment I saw him.' And Reese looked down at him with sudden tears, and she flashed a startled smile to see Nico looking back at her.

'Son?' she asked, leaning close to dab a damp cloth to his forehead. 'Can you hear me?'

'Mother,' Nico croaked, his mouth dry. 'Where are we? What happened?'

A hand patted his own – the young medico, standing without meeting his eye. 'His skull's fine,' she announced, and she brushed the same shaking hand across her grubby forehead. 'If he is concussed, it's only minor. But he should stay off his feet for a while.'

'Thank you,' said Reese after the woman's retreating form. 'Thank you for looking at him.'

Nico coughed to clear his throat.

'Where are we?' he asked again, and his mother leaned over to clear the curls from his eyes, studying him with intense interest.

'We're in Bar-Khos, down in All Fools. How do you feel?'

'Like I just got kicked in the head.'

'I think you did. But you're fine now. You're safe.'

'Where's father?'

'Taking a shift at the barricades.'

'Barricades?'

She paused in indecision.

'Much of the city has fallen. We're holding on here in the south, but just barely. They're trying to get everyone out by ship.'

Ah yes, the war, the siege.

Nico peered through the low flickering lamplight, finally noticing the trickles of dust falling loose from the ceiling every time a nearby explosion rocked the building.

The pain in his head was considerable when he made an effort to sit up. He ignored it though, just as he ignored his mother's complaints that he should lie still, and not move.

'I'm not going to just lie here, Mother, while the Mannians are banging at the front door.'

There – it was better now he had his back to the wall. Nico could see around him at last. He waited for his head to stop spinning. They were in some kind of industrial building, high and long, and half ruined at one end by what seemed to be a crashed skyship rising vertically through the roof. People were crowded around the edges of the space, soldiers and citizens alike, most of all here at the back, where small camp fires warmed the air between racks of clay urns.

Silk sheeting soughed in a breeze. On the far wall, the aquamarine of a tattered League flag caught his eye. For a moment Nico peered at the Golden Spiral at its centre. He had been taught how the spiral with its ever-flattening tail was a shape of sacred geometry, describing a divine ratio played out all around them in the natural world: the shells of snails, the curls of waves, the spirals of galaxies in the night sky. A reminder, even here and now, that the world's infinite complexity arose from an underlying architecture of beautiful simplicity.

As Nico gazed upon the scene, he saw a pair of Red Guards helping each other to their feet. The soldiers looked barely older than he was. They both sported bloody bandages on their heads, and one limped as the other gathered their swords and helped him towards the open doorway at the front of the building, where the dark of night competed with the flashes of falling shells.

'Have you lost your wits?' Reese protested as Nico struggled to his feet, and she stood up too, her red hair flaming in a beam of lamplight, scowling at him like he was ten years old again. 'What are you doing?'

'What I need to be doing,' Nico growled back at her.

He felt a little unsteady on his feet for a moment, but the sensation passed. 'Where's that sword I had with me?' he asked her, bending to pick up his winter coat spread upon the floor.

'Sword? I've no idea. You can't be thinking of going out there in your condition. You might be concussed!'

'We'll all be dead if we don't hold them back.'

He stilled her with a sudden embrace. She held him tightly, her face wet against his neck. 'It's good to see you, Mother,' he said into her ear. 'Now I have to go. I'll be back as soon as I can, I promise.'

But as he stepped clear he saw that she didn't believe him. Indeed, his mother looked as though she would never see him again, her face pale and stricken as Nico shambled away, headed for the front doorway and the sounds of battle, wondering only where he could get his hands on a weapon with which to fight.

*

'Excuse me,' Nico said as he brushed past someone on his way across the busy floor – a young, short man hurrying the other way, shackled and accompanied by a guard.

But the fellow only replied with an icy stare, as though he was a knife-edge away from gutting Nico where he stood.

Danger! cried his body and mind all at once. *Death!*

But Nico ignored the warnings, too far gone to feel anything but anger. He straightened where he stood and glared back hotly. He was in a mood to fight anyone just then.

'Curl!' called out the man as a figure suddenly caught his eye. It was the very same medico who had been having a look at his head, pretending she hadn't heard him.

Nico passed a water barrel and drank from it until his thirst was sated. Tempers were running high in the packed space of the building, which was cold and draughty for all the fires that were burning. Tense voices argued back and forth. A pair of Volunteers were shoving at each other over what seemed like morsels of food.

Coming in from the cold, a Red Guard started shouting over everyone's heads about the Stadium of Arms being captured, and how the barricades were barely holding.

A sword, Nico thought. *I need a damned sword.*

'Nico?'

He looked up with water dribbling from his chin towards a figure bounding towards him, barely believing his own eyes.

'Aléas!' he shouted to his approaching friend. 'What are you doing here?'

The young Rōshun threw him his lopsided grin, then broke through Nico's surprise with a firm embrace.

'Same as everyone else. Just trying to survive the end of the world.'

He looked well for all that his cloak was travel-stained and his clothing ragged. Only his long blond hair was its usual combed neatness. Less than a fortnight had passed since they had last seen each other, yet it felt like months to Nico just then, a whole lifetime ago, since he had set off in search of his mother.

'Come on,' said Aléas. 'Some of the other Rōshun are here too. They'll be gladdened to see you.'

Nico wasn't so certain of that. It was hardly as if he had made many friends in the brief time he had known the Rōshun.

'Later, when I get back. I want to check on my father first.' And his glance outside at the flashing darkness told Aléas all he needed to know. 'Why don't you come with me? You can fill me in on everything I've missed on the way.'

'Can't, I'm afraid. Big meeting soon, about some important mission we're meant to be going on. I've been asked not to wander far.'

Nico glanced over his friend's shoulder but saw only dark forms in the firestruck shadows. 'The big Anwi man,' he asked, recalling the fellow who had accompanied them from the Isles of Sky. 'He's still with you?'

'Juke?' Aléas scowled. 'The man took off not long after you did. Said he had somewhere important to be. I haven't seen him since.'

'And Ash. Baracha. Did they ever make it back?'

A blink; his only show of emotion.

'No. They never did.'

The booms of explosions rattled the building, sending more dust trickling into the air. A man cried out in his restless sleep.

'This really is a sorry state of affairs to find ourselves in, huh?'

'It truly is.'

'I'm headed for the barricades. Just come with me for a little while. It'll be like old times again.'

Aléas looked towards the open doors.

'Well maybe I can skip out for half an hour. Make sure you don't get yourself killed again.'

'Good man! And listen, I've lost my sword somehow. Can you get me a blade?'

The young Rōshun stiffened with mock sincerity. 'You're really asking if I have a spare blade?' With a smile he opened up his cloak wide like a pair of wings, to reveal the glitters of blades hanging there from his belt, his side, his outer thigh, his ankle.

'Take your pick.'
Nico reached for the biggest blade he could see.
'Just not that one. No, not that one either.'

CHAPTER THIRTY-EIGHT

Nico

Through the dark and crowded streets of All Fools, Nico and Aléas hurried towards the sounds of war.

Ahead lay the rest of the city like a heap of coals smouldering in the night. Brilliant explosions dazzled their eyes, flames soaring high. But they were nothing compared to the lightshow in the starry sky, seemingly beamed from the enemy positions in the north – sheets of lightning flickering more rapidly than any thunderstorm imaginable, flashing so fast that they created the strangest of visual effects here on the ground. Every time he glanced at Aléas running through the shadows, his friend was flickering in and out of existence while moving in the jerkiest of motions.

'Damned lights are giving me a headache,' said Nico through gritted teeth.

His head throbbed as the cobbles shook with another tremor.

To their left rose the Mount of Truth, its crest festooned with signal flashes and cannons firing down on the enemy-held streets to the north. Skyships circled around it laying down even more fire.

A cart hammered along the busy street with its driver whipping at a pair of zels, loaded down with wounded figures. Children were screaming in fright from a nearby house.

The fiery buildings in the distance burned like so many bonfires.

'You frightened?' Nico asked his friend.

'More tense than anything. You?'

'Feels like a snake's in my belly.'

'Yeah, I hate this part before the action. Before your blood is up.'

It was funny to hear Aléas speak like a grizzled veteran, for he was the same age as Nico, eighteen years old. He recalled that the young man was originally from imperial Q'os.

'You all right with this, taking on your own people?'

But Aléas only scoffed at his question.

Mortar shells were falling across their line of sight, concussions felt through the soles of their boots. Flames bloomed from the rooftops.

No wonder people were crowded in so tightly here. All Fools was the southernmost district of the city and furthest from the enemy, stretching across the throat of the Lansway between both harbours. Its streets and alleyways were filled with people who had fled from the falling north of the city; desperate figures hunkered down together for warmth under what blankets or cloaks they possessed, praying for a way out, or standing watching the falling shells, or shouting, or walking about in a daze. Soldiers stumbled past drooping with exhaustion. People gabbled noisily from the rooftops over their heads.

'Almost reminds me of festa,' Nico said, for that was exactly what he was thinking of just then, those famous week-long carnivals of Bar-Khos, his favourite times in the city; the streets and rooftops hosting a thousand, never-ending parties in defiance of the siege.

Was it all gone now? Would any of that ever happen again, when citizens were fleeing by ship from the harbour even now, and those waiting out the night here were likewise awaiting their turns to flee?

'Reminds me of my first Rōshun vendetta as Baracha's apprentice,' said Aléas. 'In the city of Calretti with the Mannians at the walls. We stole inside disguised as Calretti defenders, going after one of their Rice Tyrants in his Forbidden Palace. I was sick with fear the entire time. I mean physically sick from it. Baracha couldn't stop laughing.'

'Ash was no better. At the worst of times he'd find something that was funny.'

Nothing else to say to that; their lingering silence a kind of respect for the two men most likely dead now, lying out there somewhere beyond the looming black walls of the Shield to the south.

'You ever think about it? What comes after this?'

'A hot bath, I hope.'

'I mean death, Aléas. What happens when we die? I mean, when they brought me back to life, I could hardly remember a thing about who I was. But I could remember, just for a while, impressions from when I'd been dead. Death wasn't just a nothingness. I still existed in some way.'

'Or you had some crazy dreams before they woke you up.'

Nico shook his head. He knew it had been more than that. Dreams, he reflected. Maybe he had been dreaming in death just as he dreamed in life.

'You think the Great Dreamer is twisted enough to kill me twice in as many seasons?'

'Why not?' answered Aléas, straight-faced. 'The cosmos seems to like its surprises, the more dramatic the better.'

'True, but now that we've said it, doesn't that kind of cancel it out?'

'Cancel what out, that you might die here? You really think it works like that?'

'I think, Aléas, I have a strange feeling right now, and it's only growing stronger the closer we get to those fires. Like I could be going to my death all over again.'

'Relax, you're just spooked. Anyone would feel that way after everything you've been through. Just keep your head down when we reach the barricades, you'll be fine.'

The scenes grew worse as they neared the roar of battle. Buildings were ablaze in solid lines here, and crowds had gathered with sloshing pails to fight the fires, though their efforts were hampered by the shells that were still falling. In the middle of the street a pair of snotnosed children cried out for their parents with arms outstretched. Not far from them stood an old woman in her woollen nightgown, biting the knuckles of one hand as she stared at the chaos all around her, her wits blown to pieces. Monks hurried back and forth, humping water or helping carry the wounded clear, tending to those already dying.

With every footfall Nico's heart-rate grew faster.

'There it is,' said Aléas, but Nico had already seen it ahead – a barricade sealing the end of the street, with more barricades extending across streets on either side of it, in a line of defence that ran right across the southern districts.

It was larger than he'd been expecting as they came nearer. A rampart of rubble and beams that rose a full twelve feet in height, flickering in and out of sight with the rapid flashes of lightning in the night sky. Defenders scrambled along the slope with their heads down, occasionally backlit with yellow eruptions of fire, moving in the same jerky motions as everyone else through the constantly flashing light: Red Guards, Volunteers and a good number of civilians.

Above their heads a skyship blew up like a midnight sun, momentarily washing everything with its brilliance.

'Stay cool,' Aléas shouted, taking the short bow from his back and notching an arrow. 'Don't lose your head!'

At a jog they approached the barricade with the defenders' shouts and gunshots assailing their ears. A shell landed across the street, blowing off the roof of a building in a rain of debris – shocking in its proximity. Hunching low, Nico looked for a sign of his father amongst the figures ranged along the top of the defences, but he couldn't see him. He supposed Cole could be anywhere along the front line here.

A block of masonry provided cover as they both hunkered down behind it. The slope of the barricade looked like a dangerous place to be right now. Most of the defenders at the top were lying with their arms over their heads as bullets struck around them. Only a few riflemen were brave or reckless enough to fire back.

So what now? Nico thought to himself.

Aléas read his expression, and slapped his arm with a grin.

'You having fun yet?'

*

Really, he'd been expecting to do more than simply hunker down like this, jumping at every explosion, just waiting for something to happen – waiting, indeed, to be useful. Nico had been ready to take on the enemy hand-to-hand if needed, yet there was no fighting to be done, not here and now anyway.

Maybe they should head further along the defensive line, where the Imperials could be heard assaulting the barricades in a clash of shields and swords. But with all these mortar shells coming down it was hard to get the body moving again; it seemed like madness to leave the shelter of their cover.

He was just turning to Aléas when a sudden white heat blinded him, and Nico threw his hand over his face before an even greater blast knocked him clear off his feet.

Screams sounded through the falling dust. Coughing and spitting grit, Nico looked up to see the large bite of rubble now missing from the middle of the rampart.

Aléas was squirming on the ground trying to recover his shortbow. Someone's severed legs were lying not far from him, bloodied and bent out of shape. Across the street another blinding explosion went off inside a half-ruined building, warming Nico's face with its heat while the cobbles shook. Even as he looked on, the building's brick shell sloughed away like a discarded coat, leaving the bare bones of its structure engulfed in an inferno. Soldiers tumbled out through windows and doorways, frantically tearing off their burning cloaks.

Nico gripped the bucking ground, gagging at the scents of roasting meat carrying across the street, terrified out of his wits.

'Aléas!'

Overhead a lone, sputtering flare sailed into the air, casting its green light across the battlefront. Nico pulled himself into cover again while the flare hung for a moment in a sky stitched with angry tracer fire. Everything around him seemed angry now – the rippling shocks of air blasting back his hair, the cracks of gunfire, the yells and curses, the flames, the popping grenades, the ground itself rumbling as though enraged at being awakened.

It was easy to fall victim to your fears here, easy to simply burrow down under your arms while you tried to hold in the contents of your bowels with what little will remained amidst the panic.

Those men and women dashing about on their feet must be harder than Sharric steel and braver than fools. Indeed, they must be crazy in a way – crazy like those cloudmen in the tales of the Way, cackling in the face of death. How else could they get themselves moving in all this lethality?

He looked to Aléas, likewise cowering behind a nearby block of stone. His friend was staring back at him with wild eyes.

'*I can't move!*' yelled Nico.

'Nor I!'

Another explosion struck the top of the barricade, throwing aside bodies and debris. The defenders were sliding back down into better cover, though Nico swore aloud as he glimpsed the lone figure still up there at the top, a woman standing erect as though immune to the blasts.

'They're coming!' the woman roared over her shoulder, and in a burst of fire he saw the pair of axes in her hands and the animal skins covering her body. She was a Redeemer, making her last stand here in the falling city of Bar-Khos.

'You hear me, they're coming!' she roared again at the defenders behind her, but nobody was moving to help, too many still falling back or carrying the wounded clear.

Pinch it off, said an audible voice in Nico's head, and he knew right away that it was the ghost of Ash, his old Rōshun master.

What do you mean?

Your fear, boy. Pinch it off!

But how?

Easy. Like this.

And just like that it vanished, the crippling terror inside him, and Nico was cool as the running waters of the Bitter River.

'Come on!' he shouted to his friend, surging to his feet. Not looking back, Nico scrambled up the slope of the barricade on all fours past soldiers and armed civilians, drawn onwards by the lone woman's calls.

A harsh wind struck his face as he cleared the crest of rubble. Nico stumbled until he gained his footing. He narrowed his eyes, taking in the smoke blowing towards him across the dark open plaza of a marketplace on the other side. Bodies lay everywhere, though like a high tide they were denser near the foot of the barricade. He spotted movement out there. Enemy infantry, dashing between the remains of the market stalls, keeping their heads low as they neared the barricade, the odd defender taking a shot at them.

Freeing his blade, Nico hopped over to join the woman's side.

She was about his mother's age, with her hair knotted in a dark tail that reached all the way down her back. She stared grimly into the marketplace.

'I hope you can use that blade in your hand, lad,' she said with a glance to his civilian attire, then nodded to the approaching figures. 'Those are more assault squads headed our way.'

The enemy was close now, close enough to see the contours of their armour and the puffs of steam from their mouths. One of them fell to a rifle shot and then a squad of them was rushing for the barricade, a good twenty or thirty soldiers with their shields held high.

'Hurry up, they're attacking!' yelled the Redeemer over her shoulder.

A grenade burst at the foot of the outer slope, and Nico crouched down as another one went off even closer, throwing up debris and white smoke. Behind the smoke came figures scrambling up the slope, yelling their Mannian battle cries. Nico hefted the sword in his grasp, readying himself to use it. Rubble shifted by his side, and he was heartened to see Aléas leaping up to join him. The young man flashed a grin, then in the next moment shot an arrow through the throat of an enemy soldier clambering towards him.

Suddenly another archer appeared next to Aléas – the Contrarè man Sky In His Eyes, firing his bow too. Nico gaped, wondering what the Contrarè was doing here in the midst of all this.

It was no time for pondering such details though. A host of imperial infantry were rushing up the rubble right at him, shields held above their helms, shouting each other on. The Redeemer howled and leapt down into their midst, cleaving about her like a woman possessed. She was singing to herself, he could hear through the din – singing the song of her impending death as she cut down as many of the Mannians as she could.

Nico kicked at a soldier's helm and swung his blade at another, chopping clean through the man's forearm. Along the top Aléas and the Contrarè man were shooting arrow after arrow in an unspoken duet, leaping about even as they fired, both of them clutching a handful of arrows so they could shoot in rapid succession – two, three, four arrows flashing into the enemy ranks faster than most people could shoot one.

Nico reared back with a desperate parry of an enemy blade, kicking aside a shield so he could thrust his own sword through his attacker's neck. How easy it had become, this killing of men. Grimacing, Nico snatched a glance back to see more defenders rushing to join them now that the shelling had momentarily ceased. From further down the street, a column of old Molari were rushing to their aid: retired veterans with their chartas and shields.

'When did you learn how to fight!' Aléas shouted when he saw Nico's new-found skill with the blade.

But even as Nico opened his mouth to shout something back a gun cracked out from below, and Aléas staggered and fell to the rubble, his bow clattering over the side.

'*Aléas!*' Nico roared, and impaled a man so fiercely that his blade stuck in the soldier's armoured stomach. With the strength of rage Nico heaved up a lump of masonry and cast it over the side, buckling an attacker's shield and dropping the man behind it. He grabbed up another block and threw it at an enemy head, denting his helm. The fellow with the sword stuck through his stomach was still staggering aside, so Nico grabbed the hilt and kicked him clear of the blade.

Yelling out, he leapt upon the enemy with a fury.

CHAPTER THIRTY-NINE

Diplomat

'All right, all right, keep it down, the man's got something important to say!'

Around the room the chatter faded as the sergeant shouted out for order, striding through the gathered figures with shoves and slaps of their backs, rangers and Volunteers alike.

In his wake stood the cripple, Coya, ruminating over his cane as he surveyed the lantern-lit men and women with his reddened eyes, waiting patiently for their attention. Soldiers quietened further at the sight of him, this famous League Delegate of the Free Ports. Near the far end of the space, Rōshun emerged from behind the tattered silk sheets that formed their sleeping area to gather themselves quietly, sombrely, as though they had been expecting this late-night address from Zeziké.

At last only the soft murmurs of the civilians could be heard from the back of the inkworks. People crowded between racks of clay urns, trying their best to rest with the building shuddering at every nearby explosion, with the gale of violence so close by.

Something's up, thought the ex-Diplomat Ché, from where he sat on top of a barrel with his back to the wall, in his manacles, in his exile, watching them all from afar. He was dressed in some clothes at last, dead man's clothes no doubt, too big for his small frame, and he was busy picking the lock of one of his manacles, using the pin of a brooch he'd stolen from a sleeping civilian. But as Coya Zeziké stepped past he caught the spirited gleam in the man's eye, something of hope and sudden chances, and Ché sat up straighter, his shackles clinking.

A few heads turned in Ché's direction; a few hostile stares from the rangers he'd been watching surreptitiously for a sight of Curl amongst them. He glimpsed the girl now, chomping through a loaf of bread in hunger, though she feigned not to glance back at him.

'Thank you, Sergeant Sansun,' announced Coya in a voice that projected strong and clear across the crowded space, dispelling the echoes of war. 'You all look as tired as I feel, but allow me a few moments of your time. I'm afraid the Stadium of Arms has definitely fallen. Our barricades are barely holding back the enemy forces who now occupy much of the city. Thankfully, many of the citizenry were able to evacuate the northern districts as they fell. They're crowded around the harbour districts, waiting for passage out on whatever ships can take them. Which means the longer we hold out here, the more people can make their escape.'

'And what about us?' shouted a Volunteer. 'Are we expected to die here in Khos, or are we getting out too?'

Voices rose loudly at that, and Coya held up his hand to try and settle them.

'A dozen volunteers!' Coya shouted over them all, and his voice rang through the space like struck steel. 'That's how many I need to save this city. To save Khos!'

Silence. Looks of disbelief.

Ché sighed as the manacle on his wrist snapped open, and he slipped it off and rubbed at the chafed skin for a moment, taking in the scene. In moments he had unlocked the other one, and he hopped off the barrel onto his feet, feeling light and free without his iron burdens. Beside him, his guard was wholly intent upon the gathering.

'I can't disclose the details to you right now,' Coya was telling them all. 'But we might stall this war in its tracks, if only we can make contact with the Alhazii Caliphate. Yet our one hope of doing so lies with the Dreamer, Shard. And right now she needs some help.'

'What kind of help,' asked a veteran ranger with obvious suspicion, plucking a pipe from his mouth.

'Some people I know. The Dreamer has ascertained that they're trapped behind enemy lines, holed up in a taverna called the Broken Wheel. We believe a person rather crucial to our efforts is with them.'

'So you need us to go and get this person.'

'Yes. With her aid, our Dreamer might be able to get a message through to the Caliphate, and end this war. The Rōshun here have already agreed to help in this venture. Now we need a dozen riflemen to provide cover. Are you interested?'

'You didn't answer me, Coya Zeziké,' shouted the Volunteer. 'When do we get to leave this bloody city?'

Coya stirred above his cane unhappily. 'We leave when our work is done here, not before. Sergeant, if you please.'

The ranger sergeant nodded, and started dragging his heel across the floor, drawing a line in the dust.

'A dozen volunteers,' he hollered. 'Step over the line if you're willing.'

'You're going, Sergeant?' called out one of his companions, and when Sansun nodded, his squad of rangers stepped forward one by one to join him on the other side of the line.

Ché straightened, spotting Curl amongst them, the girl hesitating before she crossed the line. The sight of her drew him forward, pushing his way through the crowd on an impulse he barely comprehended.

Every head turned to him in stunned surprise.

'You want to know if I can be trusted or not,' Ché said to Coya. 'Well, this is your chance. I can help you here, especially if you're going behind their lines.'

'He'll run for it the first chance he gets,' said someone from behind.

But Coya held up his hand to silence them. For a long searching moment he gazed into Ché's eyes, reading what he could like a diviner of men's intentions, until at last something prompted him to decision. 'You already gave me your word you would not try to escape. But if you do run, one of these rangers will shoot you through. You understand, Diplomat?'

Ché nodded.

'Good. Then get ready to leave, all of you. A skud will be arriving soon to pick us up. And thank you. Tonight we show these Mannians that we're not finished yet. Where there's a will, there's always a damned way.'

CHAPTER FORTY

Diplomat

First chance I get I should make a break for it, Ché was thinking to himself on the deck of the skud, thrilled that the choice was there for the taking at last.

His shackles were gone. He even had a sword hanging from his belt. Slipping away in the darkness of night should be the easiest thing of all, and then he could leave this city and the war behind for good, and set out on his own course.

Ché resisted a rare urge to smile as the skud lifted off into the starry Khosian night, its thrusters burning like tiny twin suns too bright to look at, fighting to free the weight of so many people from the colossal pull of the world. Upwards the gas loft surged, lifting the rest of the skyboat with it, swaying sluggishly as they climbed away from the darkened inkworks below.

In a lather the boat's captain, a small rotund woman armed with a tongue like a living lash, tramped along the small and crowded deck scolding the passengers to move fore or aft, spreading out their weight more evenly. Once satisfied they'd achieved some measure of trim, the captain called back to the pilot at the wheel. Suddenly the skud swung fast towards the north-west, spars creaking and twisting, silk loft ripping above their heads. Figures leaned into the turn and grasped the rails for balance; six Rōshun crouched along the sides in their dark robes; a dozen rangers to fore and aft.

All were silent as they peered ahead at the darkened districts, lit here and there by flaring fires. An inferno was blazing high above the heart of the city where the Stadium of Arms was engulfed by flames. Around it raced skyships locked in battle, tearing through a night sky that flashed with sheets of lightning cast from the Mannian War Wicks out on the plain.

Closer still, explosions were walking a track through the southern districts, following a line that was likely the barricades of the
Khosian defenders, the only thing now holding back the imperial
forces. Across it all zipped a webbing of rifle fire, shots tracing
courses through the night like ghostly green meteors, as silent as
everything else against the roar of the thrusters as the skud sped
towards the north-west.

It was bitterly cold on the open deck. The wind whipped and
probed at his body, leaching any heat it could find. Ché blew into his
hands, whitened to the bone.

Idly he scratched at the healing wound on his neck, and found
himself gazing up at a night sky he hadn't seen properly in countless
weeks, at the running river of stars that was the Great Wheel, that
brilliant blaze of distant suns glowing like lanterns within flecks of
luminous colour. Powerful emotions stirred within him.

In one single outflow of breath, Ché expelled all the tensions
from his body; a whole lifetime of burdens he hadn't even known he
had been carrying, released upon the wind.

He was free of the Empire and the Mannian order. Free of the life
he had been born into, the life of an imperial assassin. All he had to
do now was wait until a chance presented itself, and he could be free
of these Mercians too.

Yet at the thought of fleeing into the night, Ché glanced along
the deck towards the young medico, Curl, where she sat with a few
of the rangers. Even though he barely knew her, he cared for this
troubled Lagosian girl. He couldn't explain these disproportionate
feelings he held for her. Yet if he thought of harm falling upon Curl,
his stomach tightened into knots.

In the flashes of light across the sky he saw her watching him for
a moment, before the silhouette of her head turned to observe the
city ahead.

Smoke billowed up into the skud's path, biting at their throats
and eyes. Low and fast they sped over the Khosian's defensive lines,
where imperial ground forces clashed all along a winding barricade.
Gunfire raged just below for a moment, and the cries and screams of
battle. A few bullets clattered off the skyboat's hull.

And then they were racing onwards, into the occupied parts of

the city, the boat turning ever westwards over streets filled with rushing enemy troops, until the captain called out a hushed command.

'Stop thrusters!'

Suddenly the skyboat was drifting along in creaky silence, ruffled
by a wind that filled the side-skuls and bore it along. The sounds of
battle fell behind. Everyone on the deck quietened. They were passing into the deserted western districts of the city now, areas of
warehouses and industry.

Ché cleared his throat as an acrid stench caught at the back of it.
Others were doing the same.

'It's the Flats,' someone explained. 'All the stinking tar pits in the
area.'

'Hush now,' hissed the captain.

On the wind the skyboat passed over imperial forces in the streets
below, looting what they could from the unlit buildings, piling anything valuable onto the backs of wagons. No one spoke as the skud
drifted on over vast pens of braying cattle, around which more
troops were stationed, visible next to bonfires in the streets. Their
laughter rose up to them in the wind.

The moons were not yet risen, the boat seemingly invisible in the
night sky. Soon they were past the imperial positions and sweeping
out over open tar pits where all was dark, the bitter stench so thick
they could taste it in their mouths.

Just then he heard the cripple Coya murmuring something to the
captain. Slowly the skud turned to a different heading with soft
blasts of one of its thrusters. Coya wore a pair of Owls so he could
see through the darkness. He murmured again to the captain for
another adjustment in course.

Ché strained to see through the darkness too, and saw that they
were approaching the largest building in sight, a tall structure
wrapped in gloom like the dwellings around it.

'That's it,' said Coya. 'The Broken Wheel.'

'Looks deserted,' ventured one of the rangers at the front, the
young lad Xeno with *This Boy Kills* tattooed on his skull, peering
through the scope of his longrifle.

'No, they're there, all right,' said Coya.

'How can you be so sure?' asked another.

'One of the Rōshun managed to get through with a message. He told them to stay tight, until we could come and get them.'

Lookouts strained through their Owls, searching for a sign of the enemy in the gloomy district around them. The thrusters stopped panting away as the skud drifted right towards the building. In a hush a few crew members lowered a land anchor from its winch. They heaved and strained until the anchor snagged on the eaves of the wooden roof below, threatening to tear up the boards as the vessel came to a halt in the breeze, squirming like a fish on a hook. Sweating now, the crewmen began to winch the boat downwards, but the gears squealed as they were turned, setting everyone's teeth on edge.

'Easy, easy,' snapped the captain. 'Get some oil on those gears first.'

Ché could feel the tension in the air, could almost sense the quickened heartbeats of those around him. The city looked empty here, but there were structures not far to the south with lights inside and imperial flags flapping. Soon the crewmen had winched the skud low enough to throw some netting over the port rail.

All at once, the half dozen Rōshun were pouring over the side and down the netting smooth as water, every one of them wearing Owls. Around the rail, the rangers stationed themselves with their rifles aimed and ready.

'Smells like blood,' Wild hissed up from the flat rooftop below, crouched down in his black robe. Behind him the other Rōshun were shadows moving within shadows. 'Smells like a massacre happened here.'

'There's some bodies on the street below,' added the young ranger sniper, squinting through his scope. 'Looks like they were thrown off the roof, or they jumped.'

The deck was quiet save for the heavy breathing of the men.

'Could be a trap,' said Ché, inspired by the tautness of the moment.

Faces looked at him in disgust.

'Could be a whole company of imperial troops down there, lying in wait for you.'

'Well, there's only one way to find out,' said Coya, and he

surprised them all by hitching himself over the rail with stiff, awkward jerks.

'You'll need to be quick,' said the captain from the wheel, glancing to the night sky in the east. 'One of the moons will be rising soon. When it comes up, we'll be as visible here as though it was daylight.'

Already Ché could see a soft glow on the eastern horizon. He looked to Curl, climbing over the side with her medico bag slung on her back, helping Coya down the netting.

Time to move.

'Break your neck,' said one of the watching rangers as Ché followed the others over the side.

CHAPTER FORTY-ONE

Nico

They looked about ready to drop, these people crowded across the slope of the barricade, panting and steaming as they caught their breaths from the ongoing action at the very top, where others took their turn for a while, fighting off another imperial assault with desperate yells and crashes of steel and shot.

In the rising moonlight the defenders' ashen features blinked with exhaustion. People were too stunned to look at each other as they gulped down water or anything stronger at hand to settle their nerves, their shaking bodies. Bruised and battered, many of them bled from poorly bandaged injuries; soldiers and civilians thrown together into this improvised last-ditch line of defence.

They had been strangers to Nico when he'd joined them that evening with the enemy shells exploding all around them, though now some of those who had survived the endless night of fighting were familiar to his eyes, and he to them.

Over there he spotted the lanky young woman who'd been bringing them water and stale bread throughout the worst of the action, singing the whole time in old Khosian against deafening blasts that had most of the men cowering under their arms and cloaks while she trod past them. Even now, face blackened with soot, the woman struggled along the rubble offering water from a skin to those who needed it, wiping a strand of hair from her tired yet dogged expression.

There, just beyond her, sat the cock-eyed cartwright still wearing the leather apron of his craft, next to the young hood from Cherry Hill sporting a tattooed head of Caw-Caw motifs. They were both watching the old Michinè fellow bent over his fallen son, the nobleman openly weeping like no Michinè they had ever seen.

Brindle Valores was his name. The man had joined them only a few hours earlier, bringing with him his disgruntled son and a dozen house guards to the fray. Now the tears ran down his white-painted face.

During the most desperate moments in the fighting, the fellow had helped Nico regain his footing while shouting words lost in the battle's storm, baring his teeth as though a defiant grin was precisely what the situation required. Khosian flares had been going up all along the winding barricades that crossed the city, signalling where reinforcements were needed the most, where the line was buckling against the relentless waves of enemy forces coming at them out of the night. With their own section of barricade close to being over-run, the Michinè nobleman had counter-attacked with his surviving house guards and his son. They had beaten off the attackers, but not before his son had taken a spear through the belly.

Now the enemy was retreating once again up there at the top, replaced by sporadic rifle fire that forced the defenders back down into cover. It sounded as though the shelling and ground attacks were moving further along the line for now, seeking softer sections to exploit.

Upon the slope, Nico thinned his stare against another flare and spotted a familiar silhouette stepping down through the hunkered defenders, boots sliding on the shifting debris. Behind Aléas came another figure, the Contrarè man Sky In His Eyes who had been causing so much havoc with his bow.

Aléas was holding a hand to his side when he sat down next to Nico with a wince. His wound, where a bullet had entered and exited his side, narrowly missing his vitals, was bleeding again through the bandages and his tunic.

His friend was tougher than he looked, Nico was reminded. Though he hid the admiration from his voice with a tone of annoyance.

'You should go and get those stitches looked at, Aléas. Before you bleed to death.'

'I'm fine,' said Aléas, taking a drink from a water skin as the Contrarè man settled down next to them.

Sky In His Eyes looked now to the street behind them where the dead were stacked like stiff boards of wood. Grimly his stare took in the upturned faces, covered in a fine layer of ash cast from the infernos to the north, and the monks chanting and waving burning incense above them.

Half the defenders seemed to be either dead or missing now. Nico wondered how they would ever hold back the imperial tide at this rate. And then he saw the same question hanging on many of the haggard faces around him too – on the expressions of those fellow citizens who had gradually knotted around him in the thick of the fighting, inspired in some way by the certainty of Nico's actions, so that they'd followed him wherever he made a stand and even now remained close by.

'You were a force to be reckoned with, saving your friend here,' said Sky In His Eyes. 'These people around you . . . they gain strength from your own.'

These Contrarè spoke oddly, Nico thought. They were so open with their sentiments, as though there was no guile in what they said.

'I lost my head, is what I did,' Nico answered him truthfully, remembering the moment with a grimace. 'You and that bow-work however . . . We could do with a few more thousand Contrarè like you, that's for sure.'

But Nico's words caused the man to flinch in his skin.

'Yes,' he said with regret. 'And I am only here by accident. You should know, not all of my people still argue about supporting your cause or not. Some have engaged the invaders anyway. Even now, they raid the imperial lines of supply to the north. They cause what havoc they can, where they can. And perhaps soon the rest of the tribe will join them. And then they might even come here.'

'More help than we deserve, I reckon,' Nico admitted. 'My father once told me much about our dealings with the Contrarè over the years. You have little reason to favour us Khosians at all.'

Surprise tilted the Contrarè's head to one side, and he took a moment to gather his words. 'It always helps to share a common enemy. Where is your father, anyway? He was here a moment ago. Ah, I think I see him.'

Sky In His Eyes raised a hand as the figure of Cole stepped away from a group of soldiers and limped towards them, his longrifle cradled over his arm. He had come upon Nico during the last lull in the fighting, shouting out for anyone with spare ammunition.

Cole nodded to the Contrarè, looked to Aléas, then frowned at his son.

'We should head back to the inkworks while the pressure's off here,' he told Nico, wiping his grimy face with an even dirtier hand. 'Grab something to eat. Let your mother know we're still alive.'

'I told you, I'm not leaving this fight.'

'Nico. She'll be worried sick by now.'

'Then you go.'

'Aaiee . . . You're as stubborn as she is, you know that, boy?'

It sounded like a compliment, not a criticism, just then. Nico looked to the crest of the barricade again where the odd rifleman was taking a careful, sparing shot with whatever shells he had left. The battle rumbled away further along the line.

'*Hecheney*,' Cole said, catching sight of the Contrarè.

'*Hecheney*,' replied Sky In His Eyes.

'Must feel a long way from the Windrush.'

'Like another world away.'

Nico gazed back along the street, drawn to the sight of the Redeemer woman sitting on a lone block of stone. Still alive, even now, after flinging herself repeatedly at the enemy forces. Somehow invulnerable in her madness.

In the pale moonlight, the woman was tearing out handfuls of plaited hair with awful slow tugs that were making a bloody patchwork of her scalp. Her body was trembling, eyes spilling with tears. Working herself up for her own end, her own bloody salvation.

'Any news from along the line?' he heard himself ask his father.

Cole took off his hat to wipe his brow, following Nico's stare to what the Redeemer was doing to herself in the middle of the street. 'Same gruesome mess as here,' he grumbled. 'General Tanserine is anchoring the line from the Mount of Truth. It stretches from there all the way to the south-eastern docks. The enemy need only break through at a single point, and it's all over.'

'What about in the north?'

'Most of the northern wall fell fast once they got inside. Some sections are still holding out, though. Other forces have fallen back into defensive pockets.'

He flinched – they all did – as a mortar round exploded close by. Further along the line, the sound of fighting was growing even louder – yet it was more than that. Nico cocked his ear to a roar of voices rising above the clamour.

Up above, riflemen were flapping their hands to gain their companions' attention, and people hurried up the slope for a better look.

'Let's see what all the fuss is about,' suggested Nico, scrambling upwards.

*

A man fell back from the crest of the slope, shot through the head by an enemy sniper round. The rest ducked lower, their rifles cracking angrily in reply.

On his belly, Nico peered over the barricade at what had once been a thriving marketplace, and was now only a no-man's-land of craters and debris surrounded by blackened buildings.

To the west another assault was being thrown against the defences, a thousand imperial fighters glimpsed through the ruins as they stormed a section of the barricade further along. To the east, a column of riders cantered this way along a thoroughfare running parallel to the barricade. Angry cries were rising from the defenders as the riders passed by towing a wagon in their wake, which had two beams of wood crossed vertically upon it, bearing what was obviously a naked corpse.

'What do you see?' someone hissed to one of the few riflemen with a scope.

'They've strung up General Creed,' grunted the man.

'*The Lord Protector*,' others were yelling, seeing what they could all see now. '*They have the Lord Protector!*'

Nico squinted hard through the moonstruck night. He could see the imperial banners flying from the column of riders cantering along the far side of the market square, and the bouncing wagon bearing its gruesome display for everyone to see – General Creed's naked body lashed to the cross-beams by his arms and legs, a sheen of long black hair flapping in his wake.

'Must have found his body when they overran the Stadium of Arms,' growled his father.

Birds were fighting over the corpse as it was drawn along at a steady clip. They were big red and black skrakes, and they were tied to the corpse by long leashes of cord. Some hopped into the air flapping and yanking against their leashes to be free. Others, though, hopped onto Creed's head, pecking at flesh, at the sockets of the eyes.

'*Bastards! You bloody bastards!*'

Nico glanced up to see the cartwright standing with his axe raised above his head, screaming out at the passing cavalry. Someone tried to yank the man back but he was beyond reason, and he hopped down onto the other side, screaming out with enough force that he drew a few enemy shots towards him. Even the glinting helms of some of the passing cavalry turned his way.

'That's Romano leading those riders there,' rasped a voice wrung dry of all emotion next to Nico's side. It was the old Michinè fellow, having left his fallen son below, wheezing heavily as he squinted through an old spyglass propped upon a shattered brick, his powdered face streaked and filthy beneath his grey wig. 'I'll swear to it. I'll swear that's General Romano leading from the front there,' he said breathlessly, ignoring a spark of dust from a near-miss – and when he looked to Nico, it was with eyes hollowed out by the totality of his loss. 'Bastard has come out to mock us in our darkest hour.'

Nico focused upon the lead rider of the column, who was looking back at the cartwright yelling from the defences. The white-armoured man rode like a prince, as cocksure as the prancing white war-zel he sat upon. As though he owned the street, the city, the whole damned world.

Nico gritted his teeth together, a deep rage uncoiling within him.

Another green flare rose to the west of them, hanging for a long moment above the barricade where the fighting was at its heaviest. Horns were sounding out from the enemy forces there. Already, reinforcements could be seen flitting through the ruined streets towards them, hoping to break through.

The column of cavalry was picking up speed too. Leaving the wagon behind with a few riders, they formed a wedge as the young General Romano led them on a charge across the far corner of the market square.

'There goes a man who believes in his own destiny,' muttered the Michinè.

Riflemen were yelling out for more black powder as their companions took eager shots at the flashing forms of the cavalry. The enemy riflemen opened up too with renewed vigour, laying down as much covering fire for their general as they could.

A cry sounded out. The cartwright fell back with most of his head missing; a jet of blood describing a perfect Golden Spiral through the air.

Spurred by a sudden impulse, Nico surged to his feet and took off running in the direction of the fighting, hopping over the loose rubble with the grace of a wild animal, never minding the enemy fire as he drew his sword once again.

'Go on, my boy!' shouted the old Michinè after him. 'Give the bastard your steel!'

*

He couldn't explain what he was doing. Only that he was an arc of motion, another Golden Spiral describing itself upon the world.

Across the next street Nico followed the top of the barricade, scattering surprised defenders out of his way. A quick glimpse back told him that his father was giving chase too, along with Aléas and the Contrarè fellow and some of the citizens who'd been sticking with Nico throughout the night. Others too were rising to join them as they rushed by.

Through clouds of smoke the barricade led him across the second storey of a ruined building, and then Nico was out the other side and he saw the fighting before him, the frenzy of violence fierce as a summer wildfire.

Soldiers and citizens were standing shoulder to shoulder along the brink of the defences, trying to fight back the mass of imperial infantry tearing up the slope at them. But the defenders' line was a ragged one. Enemy units were breaking through into the streets behind, where Khosian civilians tried to surround them.

Imperial horns called out as though they were beckoning others to the kill.

Raising their own thunder, the Mannian General Romano led his wedge of cavalry straight at the barricade, surging with spurts of steam and clashes of steel up the outer slope. Explosions lit up the night, and Romano's furious expression flashed like a man possessed, white foam flecking his snarling lips; a mad wolf needing to be put down.

Nico hefted his sword.

He shoved a defender aside, and another, then launched himself and all caution to the wind by leaping off the top.

For an instant Nico glimpsed the surprise on the young general's face, and then they collided and went spilling to the ground in a host of gasps and grunts.

Nico was first to rise, more nimble without the weight of armour. He lifted his sword over the fallen general's head with every intention of severing it from his body – but then a zel charged into him, and Nico went crashing to the ground again, hooves crashing all about him.

He knew he would be dead in the next moment, but he grabbed his fallen sword anyway and rolled onto his back, seeking out the Mannian general. An enemy rider crashed near his feet, an arrow sticking from his throat. Close by, a zel reared in pain at a rifleshot in its flank, dismounting another rider.

From an intuition, Nico rolled aside just in time to avoid a blade slicing down at him.

The enemy general roared in rage before launching another strike, and Nico barely fended it off as he scrambled to his feet, bouncing off the flank of a zel back into the man's range.

Romano cut this way and that, clearly skilled with the blade, clearly outmatching Nico with ease. He was younger than Nico had been expecting, his striking features contorted by rage. All manner of chaos had broken out around them. Helmed faces leered down with flashing eyes. Zels whinnied and spun about, attacked by defenders with spears and charta rushing down the slope. A grenade shook the ground.

He's good, Nico had a chance to think, even as he deflected the young man's furious blows left and right, falling back against the rubble. Any moment now and that blade of Romano's would be sinking deep into his body. In desperation, recalling his Rōshun training sessions, Nico swept the general's sword aside then launched himself right at him, smashing his forehead into the man's nose and breaking it with a crack.

Romano fell back roaring like a wounded bull, and Nico's sword swung up in his grasp like it weighed nothing, and he thrust it into the general's side – only for the man's armour to deflect the point of his steel. Nico stabbed again, at the throat this time, and once again the armour there caught his blade. Another rump of a zel slapped into him. Another rider went down.

Romano's blade sung through the air just over his ducking head, and just for an instant the general was badly over-extended.

Time seemed to slow. Nico's breath was a ragged wheezing thing in his throat. Heartbeats drummed in his ears. In pure desperate instinct, Nico slashed low and fast and felt the blade passing clean through Romano's knee.

Down went the general with a scream, rolling and sliding back down the slope. Nico pounced after him but an enemy rider tried to block his way. A few riders were leaping to the ground now with their shields raised over their fallen general, and even as Nico tried to reach him someone grabbed him from behind, and pulled him roughly back up the slope.

'Let go of me,' he roared, knowing that it was his father and Aléas come to take him from his victory.

Romano too was being lifted away. The man surged in the clutches of his men and raged at Nico with a grasping outstretched hand, the blood spurting from the stump of his left leg.

'Easy, boy, easy,' said Cole into his ear. 'Look, they're falling back!'

'*But he's mine,*' screamed Nico. '*He's mine!*'

'Not today he isn't. Not today, son.'

CHAPTER FORTY-TWO

Diplomat

Broken glass crunched under Coya's boot, causing the others to stop mid-step so that they could glare at him across the space of the darkened taverna.

The oldest of the Rōshun, Wild, straightened with a sigh. 'Place looks deserted anyway,' he said. 'Anyone alive over there?'

Across the room, Curl the medico shook her head next to the many bodies that lay around the bar amongst scattered tables and chairs. 'Most of them are Mannian infantry,' she said. 'Looks like someone made a stand here.'

The stench was worse than a slave pit, Ché thought, wrinkling his nose as he crouched next to the body of an imperial soldier. Inky shadows filled the interior of the Broken Wheel, cast by the faintest of starlight leaking through gaps in the shuttered windows. Ché had to grope for the knife in the soldier's scabbard.

Wild was right, he thought. If anyone had been holed up in this place, they were long gone now.

'Spread out,' croaked Coya, and his voice shook like the concussions of battle still raging to the south. 'There are many rooms. Below us, another large taproom. We must be certain.'

*

'Come on,' muttered the captain of the skud overhead, standing at the rail of her small skyboat while she peered towards the east, where the first glimmer of the moon could be seen rising above the far mountains of the High Tell.

At the stern of the boat, her chief hand glanced up at the moonlight now striking the underside of the loft, then looked back at her with a frown.

What's taking them so long?

A jingle of movement sounded from one of the riflemen, the young man with the tattooed head. He was flapping his hand for her attention.

'Trouble,' he told her, and she looked in the direction of his scope to see a lantern passing between two buildings only a few streets away. Following it came the sudden echoes of loud voices, clearly locked in an argument.

'Imperial patrol. I think they're drunk.'

The captain shook her head, not in the least bit surprised. This whole damned awful week, her luck had been running bad.

The skud strained against its anchor, silk loft rippling softly in the breeze. It seemed as though every person on the boat held their breaths as the enemy squad emerged into sight and headed straight for the Broken Wheel, swinging a shuttered lantern to light their way.

'Shut up!' One of the soldiers roared in accented Trade. 'Just shut up, the pair of you. Jengi, give me more of that Cheem Fire before you finish it all.'

'It's mine, I said. I found it!'

'Am I going to have to pull rank on you, soldier?'

There were a dozen of them. Imperial troops in grey cloaks stamping past the taverna in a ragged group, burdened with chests and bags of loot and bottles of alcohol, too cold and drunk to bother looking up at the skyboat hovering right above their heads.

'Jengi, you bastard, what are you doing over there?'

'Being sick by the looks of it.'

'You believe this? Selfish prick drinks it all down him then throws it all up again!'

The group stopped to gather round their companion bent over and retching against the side of the taverna, shoving at him in angry play.

'Lemme alone!'

One of them belched. Another laughed aloud. They seemed in no hurry to move on.

Let's hope they don't realize they're standing outside another taverna.

To the east the moon rose higher into view, casting its glow like a beacon light against the floating skud.

The captain narrowed her eyes. She could see skyships out there to the north. Imperial Birds-of-War flying over the northern wall and headed this way.

'God damn worse week of my life,' she growled to herself.

*

'Mannians,' hissed Wild. 'Get down!'

They crouched in the ruins of the room they'd been passing through, Ché and Curl and a pair of Rōshun, faces covered by scarves to ward off the stench of the dead.

Ché looked up through a broken shutter at a sudden dance of lantern light passing by on the street outside, hearing a gabble of loud voices. The light moved on a little way, but the voices hung around not far from the window.

'Chinsk, go warn the others,' muttered Wild.

'The moon's getting up,' said young Chinsk. 'Captain said we had to get back before it—'

'I know, lad. Now go and tell Coya we have some Imperials passing by.'

The young Rōshun rose and moved smoothly from the room. It was true what he'd said about the rising moon. The street was brightening outside, the far walls washed by a pale silver light.

'Let's give them a moment to move on,' Ché suggested, and no one disagreed.

A wind was gathering out there, the occasional gust causing the whole structure of the Broken Wheel to groan and flex while it whistled through a thousand cracks. Ché felt the hairs on his arms rising, like a lightning storm was approaching. He blinked in surprise at a soft violet light shining around the sword in Wild's hand.

'Arcwind,' the Rōshun whispered as though that explained it.

Curl was crouched next to him. Ché saw her silhouette jerk as a bottle smashed outside on the cobbles and somebody laughed.

'You all right?'

'Yeah,' she breathed, trembling slightly.

He watched her turn towards him; turn away; turn back again.

'Why did you volunteer for this mission?'

'I wanted to make sure you'd be all right.'

He wasn't certain what to make of her sigh or the lowering of her head. And then he spotted Wild rising slightly from his crouch to stare back through the shadows.

'Who's that?' said the Rōshun in a hoarse whisper. 'Is that you, Chinsk?'

'Who are you speaking to?' Curl asked him.

'Over there behind the barrels. I saw someone move.'

'You've good eyes. I can't see a thing.'

But Ché could see him too now, a small boy hiding down behind some scattered barrels, a pair of eyes gleaming in the gloom. Without warning the child bolted from his hiding place to rush out through the doorway from which they had come.

Ché lost sight of him as he hurried into the central room of the taverna again, where the other Rōshun were emerging from another doorway. He glanced over the strewn tables and chairs all the way to the bar on the far side, before he spotted a shape near some stairs – Coya, standing over his cane, one side of his face struck by moonlight.

The crooked man gestured towards the bar, where a sudden, gentle thump sounded.

In a hush the Rōshun spread out, following Ché across the floor with their blades drawn.

'Put them down,' said Wild. 'It's only a child.'

And then Ché was staring down at the floor behind the bar, where a wooden trapdoor was fitted snugly into the planking.

Ché gave it a soft tap with his knuckles.

Nothing.

'Stand back,' said Wild, grabbing the iron ring of the trapdoor, and then he gave a mighty heave and lifted the whole door up in one go, so that he fell back with it on his ass.

Before a smile could even cross the distance of Ché's lips, a shocking pain struck his ears like stabbing splinters of wood. Then a fierce nausea gripped his being entirely.

Ché doubled over from it, trying to breathe, trying to see through his swimming vision as a figure climbed out of the hole in the floor, not a child but a dark form looming taller and taller above him.

With his guts twisting about themselves, Ché managed to wriggle clear of the bar, and glanced back to see a towering black-skinned woman with a cloud of hair glaring down at the writhing form of Wild. But then his cramping guts rolled him over in agony, just like everyone else squirming on the floor all about him.

Through his tears Ché saw the impossible – someone still standing on their feet, right there in the middle of the room.

It was Coya Zeziké, the damned cripple, hunched against the gale of force washing over them all, leaning on his cane as though it was some mythical taproot fixing him to the centre of the world. Coya even managed a shambling step forwards, breaking the illusion that he was immobile, replacing it with another one in which he had some kind of power here too, some kind of counter-force. As though to ward off her energies he held out his hand, and called out: '*Hold, Fallen One, we come as friends!*'

And just like that the howling nausea vanished, and the pain in Ché's ears slowly drained away.

*

'Tell me now and tell me straight,' Coya said to the tall black-skinned woman. 'Do you have the moondust with you?'

'Right here,' the figure answered, swinging the bag on her back into view.

'Then let us save our introductions until later, shall we?'

She didn't move for a moment, but then she nodded her consent.

She was a good seven-foot tall, this woman who had floored them all by some unknown means. Ché tilted his head at her strange accent, unable to place it. Far-Eastern, maybe.

Behind her, more survivors were climbing out of the trapdoor, where a deep cellar ran under the floor. Six, seven Khosians at least. They would be hard-pressed to fit them all onto the skud.

'Vay, good to see you alive,' Coya said to another woman stepping up and wiping dust from her unhappy expression. The middle-aged woman was a Tuchoni, he saw, with great metal hoops through her ears and a scarf on her head.

'Coya. You have a way out of here?'

'Yes, there's a skyboat waiting on the roof.'

'Then let's go,' said the Tuchoni woman. 'I've had my fill of hiding out in wine cellars.'

The moonlight was bleeding through the shutters now. The wind gusted again and the building creaked all around them. The skud would be squirming up there against its anchor.

As they turned to leave a loud shout came from outside. And then someone cursed as rifle fire broke out in the street.

'We must hurry!' Coya rasped, and he led the way towards the stairs even as the Rōshun swept past him.

'Where's Curl?' Ché asked one of the passing men.

'Who?'

'The medico, man. Where's the damned medico?'

But the Rōshun youth only shrugged as he headed up the stairs after the others.

Ché was swearing to himself in an uncharacteristic panic as he pushed back against the flow of people. More gunfire crackled overhead, sounding like return fire from the skud.

He came upon her in the room where they'd spotted the boy in hiding. Curl was bent low over one of the bodies on the floor; a young girl, covered in blood, gasping as though trying to speak.

'Help me,' Curl rasped upon seeing him, pressing a pressure bandage against the girl's side. 'She's still alive.'

Ché peered down, seeing the blood bubbling from purple lips, and the dark shadows of her sunken features.

'She's dying, Curl. She's lost too much blood. We need to get out of here!'

'*Help me!*'

He cursed again and grabbed Curl up in his arms and threw her over his shoulder. She weighed very little, but she yelled and squirmed so fiercely he nearly dropped her.

When Ché staggered around, he was startled by Wild standing there in the doorway, a shortsword held at the ready.

The Rōshun cocked his head as though vaguely towards an apology.

'Thought you were making a run for it, Diplomat.'

Ché growled. 'Come on, you fools,' he snapped, and barged past with Curl still writhing and shouting in his grip.

The main room was empty now, the last of the survivors and Rōshun already vanished up the stairs leading to the roof. Ché clambered after them with Wild giving him helpful shoves from behind.

A distant cannon boomed its unmistakable thunder. Suddenly the building shuddered to the sound of a near miss.

Men were shouting up there on the roof amongst all the crackling rifle fire. It sounded like the rangers hollering down to the Rōshun to hurry. Another cannon boomed out. This time the explosion rocked the whole building on its foundations, and Ché fell against the stairs with bits of wood falling down around them. Curl yelled in fright.

More frantic shouting came from above. Someone was cursing and shouting Wild's name as the skud's thrusters started to roar.

'They're leaving without us!' Wild hollered as he scrambled up past Ché and Curl, launching himself for the open doorway of the roof.

A moment later Curl and Ché spilled out after him onto the windy rooftop, even as the skud was lifting into the night with its thrusters blazing away.

Figures were still gripping onto the netting that hung from the skud's side, the hull swaying ponderously with all the extra weight. To the north a pair of imperial Birds-of-War were approaching with their cannon booming in unison. The shots whistled in, barely missing the canopy of the skud as the small skyship swung away.

'I don't believe it!' cried out Curl.

'Believe it,' said Wild glowering after them.

Ché said nothing, watching the departing skud sweep south towards the safety of the Khosian lines. He turned his head back towards the stairwell, hearing the crashes and stomps of hobnailed boots in the building below their feet.

CHAPTER FORTY-THREE

Nico

'In all my years, I never thought it could end like this,' declared the old Michinè fellow crouched by Nico's side.

'Just keep passing me those fire flasks!' Nico yelled as he swung back from a hole in the wall, eyes still locked on the imperial forces surging over the barricade with flames suddenly rising up in their midst.

They had taken cover in the blackened upper storey of a half-ruined chee house that overlooked the barricade, he and many of the surviving defenders. Only the old retired veterans known as the Molari remained down there fighting the Imperials hand-to-hand, lashing out with swords and their wickedly long chartas, able to match the heavy enemy infantry with their own ageing shields and armour.

Explosions lit up the sky. The building trembled every few moments, *boom, boom, boom*, as though some kind of giant was stomping around out there. It was hard to hear anyone over the maelstrom of the battle.

'Remember my name,' yelled the old Michinè, trying to ignite the wick of the bottle in his grip with a spark lighter against the gathering gusts of wind. 'Remember the name Brindle Valores if you somehow survive this storm. Remember that I was here, fighting for my city with my only son, Yan!'

'I will!' Nico told him with a voice raw from shouting, and he flapped his hand at him in impatience. 'Now hurry – another flask!'

At last the cloth wick flared up and the Michinè handed him the bottle of spirits, his expression glowing manically in the sudden light.

Nico took a step back from the hole and hurled the flaming flask down at the enemy forces below, where it crashed across the front of the barricade in blossoms of fire that leapt, roaring, upon the clambering men.

By his side the old Michinè, Brindle, cackled and clapped his hands together, then reached for another bottle.

'Keep them coming,' shouted his father, Cole, crouched down with his rifle at a hole in the wall. 'Give them everything you've got!'

'Hey, Nico!'

It was Aléas, calling from the ragged window where he was drawing back his bow; still here, for all that the young Rōshun was supposed to have returned to the inkworks an eternity ago.

'What?'

'You want me to remember your name too, if you get the chop?'

'That would be kind of you!'

'Aye,' shouted a wounded Volunteer from a gloomy corner. 'Philos Janjay is my name. Remember me too!'

Suddenly, around the debris-strewn room, people were shouting their names out to each other like the introductions of drunks; as though at least in that way, they might leave some trace of themselves with whoever lived on.

Aléas was grinning, looking wild with his blond hair standing straight up on end, charged by the energies carried in the strengthening wind; another Arcwind, blowing cold and fierce from the northern Reach. Everything metal around them was sparkling with an eerie violet ghost light, armour and blades alike.

Nico could taste the charge of the winds as they blew through the ruined building. His own curly locks stood straight up on his head too, and everyone else with hair that he could see. It looked as though they were all in the process of falling.

Along the walls of this upper storey, soldiers and civilians were firing rifles or throwing bricks or fire flasks just like Nico, occasionally ducking down from enemy gunfire. Right outside, the imperial forces howled and screamed in the throes of their violence. With shields raised, they milled before the rubble blocking the front of the ruined chee house, and surged in their thousands against the barricade that ran across the street to another row of buildings on the far side, where more defenders were likewise pouring fire onto them.

Through a missing section of wall in the corner of the building,

Nico could see the front of the fighting stretching off into the west of the city, towards the glittering hill that was the Mount of Truth. In the moonstruck darkness it looked as though the Imperial Expeditionary Force had thrown every last man at the Khosian defences, for the enemy massed as far as he could see now, steel glittering like the flitting backs of fish, glowing with the violet light of the charged winds.

Khosian horns were calling for reinforcements all along the line of barricades now. But there were no more reinforcements to aid them, other than citizens wielding fallen weapons, mangled to pieces by the heavy imperial infantry they rushed to stop.

Those citizens still sticking with Nico were those who had proven their mettle by so far surviving the night. In a hail of fresh mortar fire they had sought cover in the ruins of this building, where others already fired down upon the enemy, and here they had remained for the shelter it provided, the chance of living for another few minutes longer.

Another grenade flew through one of the windows. Aléas was quick enough to catch it out of the air so he could toss it back out. He cast a desperate glance his way, and then Nico threw another burning flask into the fray.

As the flames rose high he glimpsed a wedge of movement out there in the crowded market square; a formation pushing through the milling enemy, heading right for the chee house. Nico leaned forwards into the wind for a better look. He saw fifty hulking infantry rushing towards them at a fast though measured trot; a wedge of burly men wearing heavy suits of armour, black as night and covered all over by spikes and blades, bearing small shields fixed to their forearms, full helms on their heads, hatchets or cleavers in both hands.

'Widowmakers,' his father Cole spat from his hole in the wall. 'Experts at close-quarters butchery.'

'That sounds bad!'

'More than you know.'

The thunder of their boots was loud enough to still everyone for a moment where they stood or hunkered down; their hair standing on end while the building trembled around them. Even some of the wounded looked around from where they lay at the back.

Squinting along the length of his longrifle, Cole took a shot then quickly broke open the smoking gun to reload it. 'Better get ready,' he called out with his voice calmer than it had any right to be. 'They aim to take this building, and they don't go down easy.'

No one needed telling twice. The defenders started shooting and throwing everything they could at the nearing force, until gunsmoke was filling the airy room. Across from Nico, a Volunteer manned a pair of repeating crossbows set upon a mount – his shoulders braced by wooden stocks as he fired the crossbows in quick succession at the approaching men. '*Come on then! Come on!*'

A fire flask crashed open at the enemy's feet, but they stamped through the flames without slowing. In a rush, a squad of the Widowmakers made it to the foot of the building under the cover of wicker screens. One of the screens caught fire when Nico hit it with a flask. Then the squad was hurrying back into cover under another screen peppered with arrows.

'They dropped something against the building,' the Michinè yelled out, just as a mighty hand-clap shook the air and rattled the broken glass spread across the floor, and smoke and grit tumbled in through the gaps in the wall.

The Widowmakers were trying to breach the barricaded ground floor of the chee house with explosives. A second squad of them ran forwards under cover of their screens.

'I need shells,' his father was yelling. 'Does anyone have any damned shells?'

'A few,' shouted a Volunteer. 'I think the sergeant downstairs has more. Grab me some too!'

Cole vaulted for the stairs, leaping down them even as Nico called after him.

Another explosion shook the front of the building. It was hard to see with all the smoke filling the room now, but he made out the Volunteer manning the repeating crossbows, pointing the weapons almost straight down now, firing away with the spit flying from his lips. '*Come on, come on!*' Suddenly a flaring white heat engulfed the Volunteer, knocking Nico off his feet.

He rolled onto his back, coughing, singed and smoking, to see that the man had been blown into ribbons of flesh still falling to the floor. In the haze the old Michinè fellow was retching and coughing his lungs up, while people cried out from where they had fallen. A staggering Red Guard was shouting something he couldn't hear. Nico wriggled over to what remained of the front wall, and glanced out over the edge of a gaping hole.

Below in the market square, a few Widowmakers were aiming big tubes mounted on their shoulders at the building. A rocket streaked out from one of them like a screaming firework, and the upper corner of the chee house blew up in another blast of fire and air. Coughing hard, Nico blinked through the falling dust at the still form of the old Michinè fellow lying twisted amongst the rubble, his dead eyes staring back at him.

Brindle Valores, Nico thought to himself. Your name was *Brindle Valores*!

Shouts of alarm were rising through the wooden beams of the floor. And then he heard the awful ring of steel against steel as the uproar rose even louder, knowing the enemy had breached the ground level. Nico squirmed to a hole in the planking and looked down into the room below, glimpsing shapes hewing this way and that in the glow of a swinging lantern, hatchets and cleavers rising and falling fast.

The screams that rose up from the scene were enough to chill his blood.

Father!

On all-fours he scrambled towards the top of the stairs, but others were quicker, and closer: Aléas drew a pair of stubby curved swords, and without hesitation the young Rōshun bounded down the stairs into the desperate melee below.

Another rocket exploded. A body toppled over Nico, and he struggled clear as more of his companions lay dead or screaming. Bloody faces peered at him from the shadows at the back where they'd put the wounded, people unable to move. It was all falling apart, and there was nothing they could do to stop it.

Growling like a cornered dog, Nico drew his sword and scrambled to the very top of the stairs. His blade was glowing with a pale hue, just like the blades of the figures filling the stairwell below him; people fending off blows as they were forced back up towards him. In dry-throated desperation, he looked for his father or Aléas amongst their numbers.

At the bottom they were being cut down one by one, until Nico finally saw the Widowmakers themselves, their spiky black bulks forcing their way onto the stairs; hulking men in helms and armour of overlapping plates, which swords bounced clean off or were snared by the spikes and blades covering them all over, so that they were using the heavy suits offensively too, even as they hacked away like butchers. Sweet Mercy, they even wore leather butcher's aprons across their fronts.

They're dead, Nico thought in horror. *Everyone down there is dead.*

The last two defenders on the stairs fell beneath their blades. And then someone staggered over to Nico's side, a flame flickering in his grasp.

'*Here*,' said the young lad with the Caw-Caw gang tattoos, and he handed Nico a lit fire flask. '*Burn the bastards.*'

Tears streaked Nico's face as he hurled the flask down the stairwell onto the advancing figures. Their sudden human yells were enough to break the spell of their monstrosity. Quickly the lad beside him threw down a flask too.

Black smoke tumbled up the stairwell to engulf them both. Flames caught and billowed on the updraught from the gusting Arcwind. They both dropped to the ground to escape the worst of it, gasping for air. Someone was still firing their rifle out of a window.

'No way am I going out like this!' shouted the young hood from the floor. 'No way!'

And then a rocket streaked into the room and burst the world into a million tiny pieces, sending Nico falling through its shattering crust.

CHAPTER FORTY-FOUR

Diplomat

It was just like Tume all over again, Ché kept thinking in his racing mind; he and Curl trapped behind imperial lines while they tried to make their way to the Khosians and safety. Even the air here stank from all the ponds of tar, just like Simmer Lake up in the Reach, where the city floated on its raft of weeds.

Curl didn't want to hear it though, such reminders of their previous brief time together. Panting from the weight of the medico bag she still insisted on carrying with her, she ran just ahead of him along the darkened alley refusing to acknowledge his chatter in any way.

'Am I boring you?' he panted at her back.

But still she said nothing.

It angered Ché, the girl's continuing hostility towards him. As though everything the Mannian Empire had done to her people was somehow his responsibility. Even his efforts to save her life here seemed to mean nothing.

'Maybe I should have just left you behind back there, like the rest of them did.'

The girl cast a rare glance over her thin shoulder, meeting his stare with the flash of an eye.

'I didn't ask you for any favours.'

'So? The least you can do is acknowledge that I'm talking to you.'

'I'm acknowledging you now, aren't I?'

At the front of their short line, the Rōshun Wild raised a dry chuckle.

Ché cursed mentally in annoyance. For a moment he considered cutting off on his own here, and leaving them to get back to the Khosian lines by themselves. He could escape this city easily enough on his own. Curl would just have to take her chances like everyone else. Wild was more than capable of protecting her.

Indeed what was stopping him?

'Give me one reason.'

'What?'

'Give me one reason I shouldn't just take off on my own here?'

Curl said nothing, just hunched her shoulders a little more, gasping into the blowy night air.

'*Fine*,' he snapped, and stopped running. With the others bounding onwards, Ché turned and started walking back the way they had just come, feeling angry and bad at the same time.

Let them laugh. Let them ignore him. If she wanted it this way, then she could have it.

'Ché!' called her hushed voice after him, and Ché jerked to a stop, startled by the sound of her voice saying his name. He turned to see them both panting back at him.

'I'll be no one's whipping boy in this life, you hear me?'

In the distance a man screamed out from a rooftop, and voices laughed and jeered. Wild shifted impatiently.

'I hear you,' said Curl. 'All right? I hear you. Now stop messing around!'

*

And so Ché found himself jogging along behind them once again, mostly heading south towards the Khosian lines.

At least an hour had passed since their frantic flight from the Broken Wheel, pursued by drunken imperial soldiers whom they had quickly given the slip. Since then, the trio had spent most of their time trying to find a way past the looting imperial forces, sometimes slipping through back yards and houses, sometimes holing up for a spell when they had to.

But now in the southern Flats the streets seemed clear for a stretch, and they were making the most of it, hurrying through a deserted residential district of winding back streets and small plazas. The sounds of battle seemed louder here, echoing between the tall whitewashed tenements that rose up on either side like canyon walls. Wild led them onwards.

'What was that back there?' asked Ché. 'The big black woman with all the hair. How did she drop us like that?'

'No idea,' answered Wild. 'Never seen anything like it. I thought my guts were going to burst.'

'Maybe she's a Dreamer,' said Curl.

'If she is, I didn't see a glimmersuit.'

Ahead in the darkness Ché saw another crossroads where the alley branched into three others. They were starting to all look the same now in this winding warren of tenements.

'Here, Wild, turn right again.'

It was the fourth time he'd told the man to change direction.

'What? I'm telling you, lad, this is taking us round in a circle.'

'I know that.'

Both moons had risen now, their light shining off the white-washed walls and striping the alleys with shadows cast from the lines of washing overhead. The lean wind was standing all his hairs on end as Ché paused suddenly, tying something across the alley from the grills of opposite high windows.

Ché cast a quick glance over his shoulder, then hurried onwards to catch up with the pair again. Wild and Curl had stopped in yet another crossing of alleyways.

'We've been through this place already,' said Curl. 'Why are we going round in a circle?'

'Because we're being followed, lass,' answered the Rōshun before Ché could.

'Followed by who?' she said, turning for a proper look, until Ché stopped her with a grab of her arm.

'*Diplomats*,' he hissed into her ear.

'What – where?'

'All around us,' growled the Rōshun, Wild, as though his throat was suddenly parched, peering along one gloomy alley and then another. 'You certain they're Diplomats?'

Ché was looking to the far end of an alley, where a shape was now darting towards them.

'You ever hear of how Diplomats have glands in their necks that pulse when other Diplomats are close by?'

'Of course.'

'Well mine's pounding away like it's about to burst.'

Wild cursed and drew his curved blade, spreading his feet slightly beneath his black robe. 'They're coming for you, you mean?'

'I doubt they'll be in the mood for making distinctions.'

Wild was breathing in the mindful Rōshun manner, stilling himself, emptying himself, preparing to unleash his body and mind into action.

'How many?' he rasped.

'Hard to say. Half a dozen, at least.'

Wild glanced back at him with apprehension.

'We can't handle that many, lad.'

Four alleys speared off from the crossroads. A figure was sprinting down every one.

'We're trapped,' gasped Curl. She hurried across to a door and tried to tug it open, but it was locked. She looked to Ché as he stepped casually out into the middle of the crossroads next to Wild.

'We can't just stand here!'

Ché held up his hand with his digit finger extended like the barrel of a pistol, and aimed it at the nearest approaching Diplomat.

'Great,' said Wild, backing himself against a wall. 'Man's gone and lost his mind.'

Out of the shadows hurled the nearest figure, trailing a dark cloak that flared behind him like sweeping wings, close enough that Ché saw the whites of the young man's eyes and the glints on his blades.

Timing it precisely, Ché fired the pretend pistol that was his hand, and watched as the nearing Diplomat was jerked impossibly off his feet.

Wild took a surprised step from the wall. 'How did you . . .'

But already Ché was turning towards another alleyway and another Diplomat – a running figure clad in the same flaring cloak as the last one. Ché fired again with his pretend gun, and once more the fellow jerked back as though shot through the neck.

'How's he doing that?' gasped Curl, even as Ché took out a third man with a twitch of his finger.

He swung around to face the remaining figure coming at them, drawing a knife from his belt as he did so. Launching the blade spinning through the air, it struck the man square in the forehead and sent him sprawling to the ground.

Ché turned to Curl and tossed the coil of stitching twine into her hand that he'd taken earlier from her medico bag.

'Magic,' he told her.

But his neck was still beating fast where the pulsegland lay beneath the skin. He glanced up, just as a form leapt across the alleyway overhead, followed by another.

Ché was pushing Curl back against the wall even as something round clattered onto the cobbles behind them. It was a grenade, with its fuse cut so short it was about to go off, no time even to think about it.

A flash of movement swept past them both – Wild kicking the damned thing away. But it exploded in his face, and he was thrown spinning to the ground in a blast of light and heat.

Curl shrieked while the Diplomats overhead howled for their blood.

CHAPTER FORTY-FIVE

Coya

Out of the starry night sky came the skyboat trailing smoke from its fiercely burning thrusters. Downwards it dropped, with its canopy backlit by fiery pulses ranging across the city skyline, cutting its thrusters at the last moment so the flat-bottomed hull first bounced and then skidded across the inkworks' grassy yard, while men ran to grab at the mooring lines being cast left and right.

Quickly a figure hurried from the opening door of its hull, waving aside the gathering people to limp with his cane towards the front entrance of the building, his excited shouts cutting through the storm of the battle.

'Let me through!' he hollered, bearing aloft a leather satchel as though it contained the most precious thing in the world. 'Let me through there!'

*

'I've got some!' Coya called out as he burst through the doorway of the Dreamer's work room. 'I've got some moondust!'

The Dreamer looked up as Coya held aloft the small leather pouch he had taken from his satchel. Her assistant's mouth dropped open.

'Hold everything,' Coya told them both, stamping across to lay the pouch within Shard's reach on the bench.

Thunder rumbled outside just then, a long peal of explosions that rattled the few surviving panes in the windows. Coya gripped his cane for support. His heart was racing so fast he thought it might burst if he didn't snatch a moment to calm himself.

On their way back they had flown over the Khosian barricades again, where he had seen the defences close to being overrun in many places, even as the Khosian heavy guns from the Mount of Truth lay down all the fire they could along the fighting front.

He knew there wasn't a moment to lose if they were to save the city.

Shard looked as tired as everyone else did these days. She glanced at Coya then looked to the pouch on the table, licking her lips.

'This all of it?'

'Only a sample. Our Visitor is downstairs with the rest.'

She glanced at him again. 'Really? Downstairs?'

Her fingers were trembling as she reached across and opened up the bag. All three of them leaned forwards, peering down at the small mound of moondust glittering in the lamplight like powdered diamonds.

Coya saw the Dreamer's eyes gleam with sudden hope.

'Tell him about the imperial farcry we uncovered,' she breathed as she took a knife and delicately dabbed the point of it into the dust, prompting her assistant to jerk from his daze.

'What's that?' Coya asked him.

Blame seemed unable to take his gaze from the tiny glittering pile. He looked like he was fighting the urge to bury his nose in the stuff, so he could inhale the whole lot in one go. 'We found that enemy farcry we were looking for. Looks like an imperial cell is working out of a place you call the Heights.'

Coya frowned in surprise.

'You jest.'

'We had nothing better to do while we waited,' said Shard, and she drew the knife towards her with a tiny portion of the moondust on its tip. 'Figured we'd have one last crack at finding it.'

Shard brought the point of the knife to her lips now, and they both watched her closely as she drew the moondust into her mouth.

'Actually tastes like the real thing,' she said, sounding surprised.

And then the Dreamer rocked back on the balls of her feet, eyes instantly glazing over. The colours of her glimmersuit swirled across her skin. 'Oh my,' she said. 'It is the real thing. You realize what you've just brought me here, Coya?'

'Just what you asked for. Something to boost your powers. Now will it work? Can you break through the blockade and reach the Caliphate with this stuff? Can you tell them about the charts?'

Shard said nothing as she picked up the pouch and made her way to a chair in the far corner. When she saw Coya and her assistant trailing behind her, the Dreamer cast them a scowl.

'Give me some space here. This might take some time.'

Coya clenched his teeth together hard. Time was what they possessed least of all.

'Just do it, Shard, and quickly!'

CHAPTER FORTY-SIX

Diplomat

'I told you we should have split up,' Ché huffed from the iron rungs of the ladder.

Above him, Curl's small, leather-encased form wriggled upwards into the night.

'You're not leaving me alone behind enemy lines,' the girl hissed back down at him.

'It's me they're after, not you.'

'Then tell *them* that!'

They were both climbing the side of a tall chimney stack, which rose like a skysteeple from a brick building they had sought cover in at the edge of the Flats. Ché glanced down below his feet at the Diplomat following them up the ladder. Two other Diplomats, each one far out on either side of the ladder, were climbing almost as fast up the chimney's ragged brickwork.

The figures looked small against the curving side of the stack, this feature in the cityscape that only moments earlier had seemed a viable place to make a stand. It was freezing up here, the cold blasts blowing through his clothes like they weren't there, numbing his hands and nose and cheeks. In the charged winds a purple light was flickering along the length of the ladder.

His skin kept getting little shocks of pain as he grasped the rungs.

'Leave the girl out of this,' Ché yelled down at them all. 'It's me you want. She's nothing to me.'

'You think you get a say in this, traitor?' called back the Diplomat on the ladder. 'We'll do what we like with the bitch, soon as we deal with you.'

'Just try it, asshole!' Curl hollered down.

The Diplomat threw his head back to let loose a long animal howl.

'Faster,' Ché urged her. 'Don't waste your breath.'

His limbs were hollow with exhaustion now. It was shocking how fast Ché had lost his condition, locked up in a stone cell too small to even stand in, let along exercise. Sweat blinded him, and when he swept his sight clear he saw Curl cresting the top of the chimney and hurried up after her, giving it one last effort until he hauled himself onto the foot-wide rim with the wind pressing against him.

Curl was perched there on the circular ledge of bricks with her legs and arms hugging either side of it, hanging on for all she was worth against the desperate pulls of the gusts. From here the buildings on the ground seemed a long way down. Flames and explosions crossed the southern districts of the city in a ragged line.

The wind whistled around the great black mouth of the chimney, from which arose a flutter of warm air bearing the reek of tar. Taking a deep inhalation, Ché felt his sinuses and his head clearing instantly.

'Move away from the ladder,' he told Curl. But she seemed incapable of releasing her grip from the brickwork.

He sighed and slowly rose to his feet, swaying in a crouch with his arms held out for balance. She looked up at him as though he was mad.

'Curl, quickly now!'

With awkward backwards shuffles she worked her way further around the rim. Ché took a handful of steps after her, like a tightrope walker battling the wind.

'Keep going,' he said as he spotted the first Diplomat cresting the ladder with a pistol aimed right at his chest. Ché drew his shortsword.

The gun went off even as he was throwing the sword desperately at the man's head. The throw was too hasty, too loose, but then so was the Diplomat's shot, for it went past Ché's ear while the flat of his blade struck the man's face.

The Diplomat pitched from the ladder in a silent fall to his death.

Ché swept round to see Curl still working her way around the rim. Another Diplomat was struggling onto the top, not far in front of him. A gust blew and they all clung on for a moment to the brickwork. When he glanced back, the third Diplomat was scrambling up onto the rim too, trapping Ché in between the two.

'Your knife, Curl!' Ché shouted. 'Throw me your knife!'

She grunted as she tossed a stubby blade towards him, but she cast it poorly, so that the kife clattered against the inside of the chimney and fell into its unfathomable darkness.

'Thanks!'

In front of Ché, the Diplomat was crouching down with a large fighting knife in his hand; a young man of a similar age to himself, his head shaved close, grinning through the darkness.

'I'm going to enjoy this,' he spat while Ché's boots scuffled for position on the narrow ledge. But then a shot rang out and Ché jerked in surprise, almost losing his footing.

Curl was holding a smoking pistol in her hands. Ché glanced back, seeing that the third Diplomat had vanished from sight.

Now it was his turn to smile at the man before him.

Like two wolves they leapt at each other snarling, his opponent's knife whipping this way and that, trying to snake past the blocks of his forearms.

Whoosh! Whoosh! went their controlled breaths.

Ché felt a slash across his arm. He struck the man's belly with his fist. A hand grabbed his tunic and he knocked it away, but then a sudden pain punched into his side, and Ché hopped backwards along the rim to gain a breath of space. He could feel the sticky wetness where he'd been stabbed.

When he inhaled, the wound sheared him with a white agony. Suddenly sweat was smearing Ché's vision, his heart galloping in his ears.

The man was good; possibly even better than Ché when Ché had still been in top condition.

He snatched a moment to look across at Curl perched on the other side of the rim, staring back across the black mouth of the chimney with her eyes wide with fear.

Emotions flared within him. If he was going to do one good thing with his life, it had to be now.

When next the enemy Diplomat leapt at him with his blade, Ché surged in under the swing to tackle the man bodily with all his force.

They both fell back against the rim of the chimney, and then they rolled off so that they tumbled together into the darkness inside.

As Ché spun through the inky blackness the last thing he heard was Curl's voice screaming out his name, as though she truly cared.

CHAPTER FORTY-SEVEN

High Priest

Dawn was rising over the deserted district of the Heights, where Michinè mansions perched above the sea and the burning city of Bar-Khos. In her basement salon, Kira dul Dubois sat alone before a roaring hearthfire, trying to soak some heat into her frail and ageing body, reading through reports that suggested the battle was all but won.

Soon, the Mannian consolidation of profits through loot and slaves could begin, in a process that would include the inevitable fall of Al-Khos to the north and the capitulation of the entire island, opening up the entirety of its resources. Khos's crop harvests alone were worth an annual fortune. And then there was the Windrush forest, all those laqs of prime timber waiting to be exploited, and yet more slaves in the form of the native Contrarè.

But Kira could leave her own portion of that to agents of her family. She could fly homewards to imperial Q'os knowing that the projected revenues would be enough to restore her family's falling fortunes.

All it had cost was the life of her only daughter.

A knock sounded on the door as someone opened it. Perhaps this was news of the end now, Kira thought, seeing one of her attendants standing there in his civilian clothing in the frame of the doorway. But then she caught the paleness of the man's features and the sick look in his eyes, and a sudden chill ran through her.

'What is it, child?' Kira croaked, shifting in her chair.

'Mistress,' he panted. 'You must come at once.'

'I asked you what was going on, Gendan. Now will you answer me?'

The attendant looked to his feet as he spoke, almost blurting out the words. 'We just heard through the farcry. The capital has ordered an immediate ceasefire. Our forces are to stop their hostilities against Bar-Khos at once.'

It was clear he wasn't jesting. Yet what else could it be but some sick joke?

'The orders must be fake, surely. A Khosian ploy?'

'We've authenticated the messages, Mistress. They're genuine.'

What was this? What lunacy was she facing now?

Scowling, Kira gathered her robe about her and rose stiffly from the chair. The man was silent as he led the way with a lantern up the stairs.

Up on the ground floor of the mansion her people hurried about with an air of tense confusion. They looked to Kira as though she had all the answers and more, but she ignored their tense expression as she stalked from room to room, seeking out the spymaster Alarum, not wishing in those moments to betray any kind of uncertainty by asking where he was.

Kira found the spymaster at the back of the sprawling mansion, where their farcry was set up on a dining table, and where a few of his people sat connected to the thing by long fleshy cords held in their hands.

Standing there in that moment, it was only then that Kira realized what was disturbing her so greatly. The city of Bar-Khos seemed to be lying in silence outside. There were no rumbles of cannon fire, no snaps of rifles, no sounds of battle at all.

'Report,' she snapped, when Alarum finally hurried over to join her in a far corner of the room.

'It's the damned Khosians,' said the spymaster in a hush with his back turned to the room. 'Their Dreamer contacted the Alhazii Caliphate in the middle of the night. She claimed the Khosians now hold charts to the Isles of Sky. They threatened to release these charts to the world if the Caliphate didn't intercede in their struggle here against us. Immediately.'

A soft hiss escaped between Kira's teeth.

If it was true, this was news that would change the order of the world.

'Mistress?'

'Go on, Alarum, I'm still listening.'

'The Alhazii then contacted Q'os. The Caliphate threatened an instant embargo against the Empire if we did not agree to a ceasefire, effective immediately.'

Kira swayed back on her feet as though she stood on the cusp of two worlds; the world that had been and the world now to come.

In her stomach, the sickness was opening into a bottomless gulf.

She knew the Caliphate would do anything to protect the location of the Isles, and therefore their precious monopoly on exotics and black powder. The Mannian order too would do anything to find the Isles, most of all Nihilis himself, the First Patriarch of Mann, who had been born and raised in the Isles before he had been exiled, his memory of their location wiped clean.

'How could they have come by such a thing? Surely it must be a tactic to buy them some time?'

'I don't believe so. Our agents in Zanzahar say the charts were mentally projected by way of proof. They're the real thing all right. Seems the Mercians flew a skyship to the Isles and back while we were engaged in this Khosian campaign. I've no idea how they knew how to find them.'

Her small clenched hands were trembling in anger. 'They flew a skyship to the Isles and back, and you knew nothing of the venture? *Nothing at all, spymaster?*'

Heads turned towards the rising of her voice, but then they kept on turning, twisting towards the curtained windows at the back of the room where a sudden flash of light lit up the back garden like the brilliance of day, and a guard's shout was cut off in mid-yell.

Before anyone could react, the windows of the room burst inwards in a rain of glass and confusion. Kira fell with the weight of Alarum rolling over her. Smoke tumbled into the room, pouring from grenades bouncing across the floor. Someone yelled in fright.

No, it can't be! Not now, not like this! How did they find us?

On all-fours Kira squirmed out from under Alarum in a breathless panic and scrambled for the doorway. Terror rode through her as she heard more yells rising from the front of the house. A gunshot rang out followed by fierce clashes of steel. Behind her in the room an ominous series of hollow thuds was sounding out amongst the desperate shouts of her people. When she glanced back through the smoke she saw figures wearing scarves and goggles, swinging clubs at every skull within their reach.

It was panic that caused her hand to slip out from under her on the wooden boards, so that Kira sprawled to the floor with the breath knocked out of her. There was no way out of this, she realized as she was struck within by a sudden resonance of emotions. Tears smarted her eyes.

Her whole body was shaking as she reached to one of the rings on her fingers and snapped it open, revealing the poisonous yellow powder inside.

How dreamlike it all became, when you were this close to taking your own life.

Kira hesitated, staring bitterly at the poison as though it was the sum total of her life. It was almost impossible to do this act when you had no real desire for your life to end. Yet the alternative would be far worse, she was certain. Captured alive by the Khosians. Caged like an animal and tormented by her captors.

Too late though. For a shoe pressed down against her hand, pinning it to the floor along with the ring.

Kira blinked through her tears, seeing the end of a cane rap lightly against the floor before her. She strained to peer up through the smoke at a crooked form standing above.

'Kira dul Dubois, I presume?' said Coya Zeziké with a dazzling, self-satisfied smile.

CHAPTER FORTY-EIGHT

Nico

The sun's brilliance was a furnace heat against Nico's face, its light snaring in the lashes of his closed eyes, so bright that it filtered through into the constellations of stars spinning in the dizziness of his mind.

He took a peek, and saw the hunched willow tree he'd just fallen from swaying almost imperceptibly in the blue summer sky overhead. Winded, Nico lay on his back in the long grasses trying to catch his breath.

Suddenly the head of his dog appeared – Boon, panting with his tongue hanging out. The dog started licking his face.

'Go on,' Nico told Boon, pushing him away, and the act seemed to prompt some return of his wits. Nico recalled that he was back home on his family's wild farm; back in the forest garden his father had lovingly created over the course of Nico's young life, filled with all its varied flora and fauna. His favourite place as a boy.

He wasn't surprised when his father's handsome features appeared above him, his hat partly blocking the sun.

'You all right,' Cole asked plainly, as though Nico had merely tripped over his feet rather than fallen from the highest branches of the tree.

Looking up at it now, Nico considered it a miracle he hadn't broken his neck.

'*Uhgnn*,' he said instead of what he really intended, and realized that his mouth was full of blood from his bitten tongue. He spat to clear it, and managed to say, 'Juth winded. The branth – broke on me.'

'Aye, I saw it. Come on, get up, you fool. Let's see if anything's broken.'

From the cottage his mother's voice sounded out, calling them for dinner. His father reached out a helping hand and Nico grasped it, feeling the warmth of his touch, its reassuring firmness, as he struggled to his feet.

*

'Nico,' someone gasped in his face, close enough that their breath caused his eyelashes to flutter apart.

It was his father, Cole, crouching over him in the hazy light of dawn.

Nico groaned. His whole head felt swollen. His eyes were puffed into squints. He lay next to the collapsed and blackened ruins of the chee house; a mound of rubble still smouldering with small fires. Wounded people were scattered all around him.

'I'm all right,' he managed to gasp, taking in the brightening sky that hung above his father's concerned expression.

'Can you move?' asked another voice, and Nico blinked in surprise as he saw Aléas squatting by his side.

The young Rōshun's face was badly bruised, and his clothes hung in tatters from his lean frame. Yet he was alive!

'I don't know.' Nico shifted on the cloak he lay upon. He was stiff and sore all over, covered in cuts and abrasions, but he didn't think that anything was broken. Burns covered his arms, and he hissed when he moved them. 'It hurts. Give me a moment.'

Across from him, the ragged form of Sky In His Eyes was sitting on a slope of rubble chewing at a strip of jerky, his skin blackened with soot, his head tilted back to the sunlight as though he bathed in it.

Gulls were circling up there, crying out to each other with their raucous calls.

'Why is it so quiet?' Nico asked. 'I can't hear any fighting.'

'Come and see,' answered his father with gleaming eyes, and offered him a hand.

*

In a world of ruins they staggered through the light of a new day. Four faces whitened by dust and ash, their bloodshot eyes blinking at each other with the dull incomprehension that they were some-how still alive.

Around them the dead lay everywhere they looked. A carpet of corpses covered the street and what remained of the barricade, defenders and Imperials alike lying frozen, grotesquely, in every possible position. Nico covered his nose and mouth, almost gagging from the stench.

A roar of silence raged in his ears, the pounding sounds of the battle gone now. Even the gusting Arcwinds had faded so that the day was eerily still.

'The Mannians started sounding the retreat about an hour ago,' said his father, limping along as he used his rifle as a crutch. 'They pulled back just as the barricades were falling all along the line, then called for a ceasefire. Strangest thing I've ever seen.'

'What do you think it means?'

'The charts to the Isles,' suggested Cole. 'Maybe the plan worked after all.'

Nico shook his head, dumbfounded.

He really didn't know what to say. He was too numb inside for thoughts or feelings.

Stopping in the middle of the street, Nico gazed towards the barricade and the high tide of imperial infantry lying across its crest, remembering the action of the long night he had just survived. The shells raining down with their terrifying randomness, blowing craters out of the street. Citizens fighting desperately with anything that came to hand. Nico attacking the young General Romano himself and hacking off his leg. The Widowmakers storming the chee house before it was blown to pieces.

Madness, he thought, shaking his head.

How did any of us survive?

'I thought you were all dead back there.'

'So did we,' said Aléas.

'Maybe we are dead,' said Sky In His Eyes, staring dazed towards the sun.

When Nico clambered up the barricade to the top, he looked out at the empty squares and streets beyond, blackened and ruined. A few fires were still burning, but the Mannians were gone.

He trod back down to join the others, shaking his head.

'Son!' cried out a voice, and Nico looked up to see his mother hurrying along the street towards him.

Her embrace nearly knocked him from his feet. Reese shook in his arms as she sobbed with relief, and the heat of her emotions was enough to overwhelm Nico's numbness so that finally he felt something; suddenly felt everything.

For a spell they simply stood there holding on tightly, their tears spilling down each other's necks. And then she noticed Cole standing close by, and she drew him into their embrace too, mother, father and son.

CHAPTER FORTY-NINE

Coya

Was it really over, Coya wondered?

Or was he dreaming, perhaps, still lying in his bed imagining that they had won the war, imagining that the Mannians were withdrawing from the city under threat of an Alhazii embargo?

He was shaking with exhaustion, though his body rang with elation too.

'So what happens now?' asked the woman by his side, the black-skinned Visitor from the sky who called herself Ocean.

She towered above him, where they stood on the parapet of the seawall not far from the inkworks, watching the columns of smoke still rising across Bar-Khos into the clear blue sky. Khosian horns of mourning were calling out from the Stadium of Arms, which had been retaken this morning by General Tanserine and his forces while the Imperials retreated through the northern gates, leaving behind them a city burned and blackened, and untold thousands dead.

'Now?' he said. 'Now the Mannians have five days to free all of their captives and vacate the island, or Zanzahar will cut off their black powder.'

'They've agreed to just pack up and leave?'

The woman's accent was lyrical, her voice husky.

'Yes, such is their bind. We're even shipping some of their forces to the southern continent. At least that way we can make sure they're not taking any loot or slaves with them.'

Sure enough, from the parapet of the seawall, they could see the many Mercian ships out there in the Lesser Bay of Squalls, already picking up the first imperial forces from the beaches near the delta of the Chilos, to ferry them south across the bay.

Coya stared with red-raw eyes. He was shattered after all they had

345

just been through, yet his head was still racing too fast for sleep. For long hours he'd been sitting next to a farcry negotiating with the Caliphate in Zanzahar, hammering them down until they agreed, at least, to enforce this ceasefire and imperial withdrawal; all in return for keeping the charts to the Isles a secret.

How much further support could be wrangled from the Caliphate was a matter of conjecture. But for now, it didn't matter.

The Free Ports had won!

Coya took a deep breath and steadied himself against a crenellation, his other hand trembling on the grip of his cane.

'You okay?' asked Ocean.

'Kush, I feel like weeping. Weeping from the sheer release of it all. What a time it has been. So many good people gone. Yet we did it. We actually did it.'

The Visitor was studying him closely, as though he was the most interesting thing to see here – not the smoking cityscape, not the ships in the bay, but Coya, bent over his cane ready to drop.

'You look just like him, you know.'

'Who?'

'Zeziké, your famous ancestor.'

'Oh?'

'Back on Sholos, some like to say he was one of our own. There is a likeness on record that's supposed to be him. And it's true, you both look the same.'

'I've heard of such things. Rumours and vague hints. What else do you know about him, if I may ask?'

Ocean shrugged in her tight skinsuit. There was something poking out from one of her hip pockets, he saw – a little striped rat, twitching its whiskers at the air.

'Not a lot,' she admitted. 'Some say he was the youngest person ever to attempt the crossing between our worlds. They say he was an eleven-year-old boy when he made it here to Erēs. After the landing, he found himself in the Free Ports in the middle of a siege, just like I did here.'

'You know, I'd mostly written it all off as myth. Until right now, talking to one of you in the flesh.'

Coya's ancestor, Zeziké, had lived more than three hundred years ago in the time of the Squabbling States. In his youth, Zeziké had indeed lived for six years during the siege of Al-Coros. The experience had defined the young Zeziké, who one day would become the famed Mercian philosopher and the inspiration for the democras. He had written about his siege years in many of his later works.

Well, Coya supposed – wherever his ancestor had really come from, here or the distant moon – Zeziké had known what it was to live under siege. And not briefly, either, like Coya in Bar-Khos. But for six long years, starving and under threat for most of that time.

Before Zeziké had died in old age, he had written how all of life was a siege. All of life was a struggle to remain free. Always you were under attack by forces beyond your control – people sick with power trying to enslave you, while time itself wore away at your strength, and bad fortune and the spite of others bore down on your spirit.

You had to stand up every day, every little way, for your liberty, because the moment you stopped doing so, you started losing it.

Life was an endless struggle, he was saying. One that made many people embittered and hardened, even cruel. The secret was to go the other way, Zeziké believed. To open up your heart to the suffering of others. To be kind. To be mindful. To find your own happiness anyway, learning how to rejoice in the midst of it all, knowing everything to be a desperate dream.

It sounded like a kind of madness, Coya had once believed. How could you rejoice like that in the midst of a siege; in the midst of constant pressures to submit?

Now, though, he understood.

Coya Zeziké gazed westwards, towards the rest of the Free Ports beyond the horizon. He longed to be home already, home in far Minos with his wife.

'Hell of a city,' Ocean said in her thick accent. 'I only wish I had a chance to see it under better circumstances.'

The tall woman looked up at the winter sun, warm in their faces, then towards the two moons setting in the west, staring hard at the pale blue one, her home of Sholos. A place she would never see again.

She wrapped her arms about herself, surveying the horizon of this strange new world that was now her home. Coya sensed a subtle, primal fear vibrating through her.

'So. Are you ready to tell me why you're here yet?'

A shadow crossed her pensive expression. A rare cloud was passing over the sun just then, and Coya shivered. Casually, Ocean swept a hand over their heads so that suddenly the air formed into a kind of vague translucent lens right above them, a lens that refracted the cloud and the gulls and caused the sun to brighten, so that the air around them grew hotter.

'You're a Dreamer, then?' he asked her.

'In a way.'

She had said very little so far. From the secret records of the Few, Coya knew that the people of Sholos maintained a kind of quarantine around the world of Erēs, both physical and cultural. These Visitors were not meant to be here. They had breached that quarantine. Though even then, the Visitors gave very little information away to the rare natives they confided in, as though still bound by some ethical directive.

'Ocean?'

She was staring at the far moon again, as though taking a measure of how much she should say.

'In your tongue, my kind would be called *God Killers*.'

Coya almost smiled at the grandeur of the title. 'I did not think there were any gods left to kill,' he quipped.

But the woman was deadly serious, and she stared down at Coya as though in pity at his ignorance; perhaps even in envy.

'Surely you have heard of the Hidden Ones?'

Coya stirred.

The Hidden Ones were some mythical old gods from thousands of years in the past. They were said to have secretly controlled entire civilizations from behind the scenes, evil puppet-masters able to assume any form. Until, that was, they had been driven out in some war of the ancients – a conflict that had almost sundered the world.

'On Sholos we share the same stories. Though sometimes we call the Hidden Ones the *Eaters of the Light*.'

'You're not going to tell me they're real, are you?'

Ocean sighed loudly and looked down at the brooding city. Her tall frame swayed on her feet, her big mass of hair ruffling in the merest of breezes. He waited for her to speak, cosy under the lens of air, the bright sunlight striking glints across her dark features as she gazed across Bar-Khos.

'This war you've just had here with the Empire of Mann. It's nothing, trust me, compared to what is to come.'

Her tone sent a chill running through him.

'What are you trying to tell me?'

'What I'm trying to tell you, blood of Zeziké, is what you asked to know. Why I'm here.'

And Ocean pinned him with her deep black eyes that knew so much more than he ever would, and she said:

'Frankly, I've come to save your world.'

CHAPTER FIFTY

Dreamer

The Dreamer Shard had seen miracles spill from her fingertips. Wonders that shook the foundations of her understanding.

As a disembodied spirit she had flown so high that the blue sky had turned to a starry blackness over the sphere of the planet, until the shield that quarantined Erēs had barred her from going even higher. She had communed with dimensional beings in the spaces between the real and unreal, and glimpsed visions of futures that came true.

Yet still the Dreamer ranked these last few days amongst the many marvels of her life. This last-moment reversal of their fortunes; Bar-Khos reprieved along with the rest of the Free Ports.

As she walked across the grassy field of the inkworks, Shard observed the haze still hanging over the silent city. Nothing stirred save for the odd skyship in the air. The ceasefire was holding, two days after she had gotten through to the Alhazii Caliphate aided by the powerful moondust, bearing news of how the democras held the Caliphate's most vital secret in their hands.

And just like that, it was over.

There remained, of course, a mountain of work still to be done; further negotiations with the Alhazii, while the remaining imperial forces on the island were ferried to the southern continent. Not to mention the reconstruction of a battered city. But Shard was glad to be leaving all of that in the capable hands of others. She was going home, as much as she had any home these days, to her precious Academy in Salina.

As she walked towards the waiting skud, Shard was so happy at the prospect that a tumble of ice crystals were falling from the hem of her cloak, leaving a glittering swathe in her wake. A little playfulness on a Dreamer's behalf, on this day of her departure.

'I really wish you would stay a while longer,' said Coya as he walked slowly by her side. 'I might still need you here.'

Shard sighed to herself. She had only just helped to save Bar-Khos and the Free Ports from defeat in the war. Not to mention finally removing that crossbow bolt from Coya's brain, and repairing what damage she could.

Yet still he asked her for more.

'We've won, Coya. All is well. Besides, I'll be a lot more use to you back at the Academy. I can do more from there than I can here.'

'But still.'

She had taken another tiny speck of moondust earlier, just enough so she could maintain a warming glyph around herself without effort. It was heightening every sense that she had.

'You smell that?' she said, sniffing the air.

'Smells like it always does.'

'Yes, like death. I'm going home to my life, Coya!'

He wished to be going home himself, she saw. Coya would be lonely here in the city.

'How long are you staying behind here?'

'Who knows? Until the Caliph's negotiation team from Zanzahar arrive, and we hammer out a deal. And now there's this business with the Visitor to contend with. She's still bereft of any details, but she wants to enlist the aid of the Few.'

'They must be watching, somehow, from up there, to know so much about us.'

'Yes. A strange thought.'

'You'll keep me informed?'

'I will. I think she'll be leaving the Free Ports soon. She seems in something of a hurry.'

Coya stopped, his eyes squinting in the sun. 'Well then, I'll say goodbye here. I don't think I have many more footsteps left in me today.'

'Of course. And don't worry. I'll make a trip over to Minos when I get back. Let Rechelle know that you're well, and headed back soon.'

'Yes, please do.'

Shard looked at her friend in the brilliant daylight, every detail leaping out as the moondust whispered through her blood. Coya was quietly ecstatic, for all that he needed to lie down for a few days; for all that the impressions of what he'd seen here had etched new lines in his youthful complexion; for all that she was leaving him on his own.

'Good work, Coya,' she told him sincerely.

'And you, Walks With Herself.'

They grasped hands for a moment, partial saviours of a city, the spiral scars on their palms burning together. When Shard turned to walk away, she had left a handful of ice crystals in her friend's palm, sparkling like a pile of crushed diamonds; indeed like moondust itself.

'Look after that supercargo for me!' he called after her, referring to the Mannian High Priest they had captured, Kira dul Dubois, who Shard was taking back to Salina.

'Oh, I will!'

On the deck of the waiting skyboat, the surviving Rōshun were waiting along the rail in their dark, patchwork robes. Around them shone an aura visible to Shard's eye, pulsing with deep purples nearest to their bodies, and sky blues further out; the men satisfied with themselves and this vendetta they had brought upon the Empire here, even though they had lost a third of their number. In brooding silence, they watched the captured Mannian priest, Kira, being escorted through the open hull door by a pair of Red Guards, the old crone bound in chaincuffs.

Her aura was like a seething black storm.

Curl was waiting too up there on the small deck, standing at the prow looking north towards the city. The young woman had decided to take Shard up on her offer of coming back to the Academy with her unborn child. Yet there was a sadness about her. A sense that she was leaving something behind here, something unresolved.

In the shadow of the hull, a figure was speaking up to the handsome Rōshun they called Aléas. As she approached, the figure cast up his bow to Aléas as though by way of a parting gift, calling out a farewell in clear Longalla, and as he turned away the breath caught in her throat, for Shard saw that it was Sky In His Eyes, right here in Bar-Khos, today of all days.

'Hah!' he said. 'I said we would meet again, did I not?'

He was pleased with himself as he came towards her, his Contrarè appearance so incongruous amongst all the others.

'I didn't know you were in the city,' Shard managed, trying to sound composed.

It seemed so long ago since this man had come to her aid in the Windrush forest. Sky In His Eye's striking blue gaze roved up and down her, liking what he saw of this civilized Contrarè with her glimmering skin.

'We meet again,' he said, 'even as you are departing. It cannot be.'

Was it too late to change her mind and stay on for another day here?

Yes, it really was too late. The skud was loaded with her gear. And there was no guarantee when she could catch another one out.

'Come with me then,' she said before even thinking about it. 'Come with me to Salina, and let me show you the island.'

'Salina is a long way from the Windrush, Walks With Herself.'

'Well that's the point. Come and see another part of the world while you can.'

'Hah! It is good to see you again. Good to see you are still part of the Great Dreaming. You almost tempt me with your offer!'

Shard glanced across the field towards the figure of young Blame, standing in front of the inkworks laughing heartily at something. Her assistant was staying behind in the city, to liaise with Coya on all things related to communications security during the negotiations. He chatted to another young man, the one they called Nico. Making friends, perhaps.

'Please, come with me,' she said to Sky In His Eyes, and she took a step closer, breathing fast. 'We can spend some time together. Get to know one another.'

His gentle smile was an infectious one, and it crept and stretched upon her own lips until she felt herself blushing.

'You really wish me to come?'

'I really do.'

'Then thank you. I accept your invitation with all my heart.'

*

As the canopy of gas bore the skyboat aloft into the air, Shard felt her own body lightening too as excitement fluttered in her belly.

Crewmen wove through the press to trim the skuls and tighten lines. They shouted people out of their way, not in annoyance but in simple necessity, for they were headed home too, at long last.

Rising higher, she could see clear across the city to the northern wall, and beyond it to the churned-up plain, covered now with the camp debris left behind by the departed Imperial Expeditionary Force.

To the east, along the coastline, smoke rose from the temporary imperial encampment that had been established near the delta of the Chilos, from where both Mercian and Mannian ships were transporting the imperial forces across to Pathia as fast as they could.

But Shard seemed to be the only one looking at any of that right now. The civilians and Rōshun gathered along the rail were intent upon the ground below, upon the inkworks and the figures waving them off from its expanse of grass.

Shard leaned over the rail too, and saw some rangers firing their rifles wildly into the air in farewell to their young medico, Curl.

And there, further back, she saw Blame standing with the young man Nico, both of them holding their fists in the air.

And there was Coya too, her dear friend, staring up from his crooked stance with a hand shielding his eyes.

With a roar the skud's thrusters started blasting on full, and the vessel soared above the city, heading west.

The people below were mere specks now on the grass of the inkworks, the whole of All Fools coming into view. Still they fired their rifles and pumped their fists in the air.

Shard raised her hand to them all, to the whole city falling away below. Ice crystals spilled from her fingertips and went raining over the side, ever more of them as the skud climbed higher, until a blizzard of ice was spreading out in their wake, sparkling in the sunlight as it fell, filling the sky with her happiness at leaving it all behind.

Beginnings

At least they could say it was a good day for a funeral.

In a cloudless sky the sun blazed away too brightly to look at, soaking the air with enough heat that he could almost forget it was still winter here in his homeland of Khos.

For days now this spell of balmy weather had hung across the city. A False Spring, some called these early breaks in the winter, a common phenomenon at this time of year; reminders to everyone that spring would soon be on its way for real.

Nico breathed it all in as he hiked along the flattened summit of the Mount of Truth, leading the way ahead of his father and mother. Below them the city murmured with the sounds of traffic and reconstruction; citizens picking up the pieces of their lives, or burning what remained of them out on the funeral pyres across the northern plain.

'Hurry up,' he called back to his parents, for they were dallying behind him again, his father walking as slowly as he could arm in arm with Reese, not wanting to do this. 'We're going to be late as it is!'

Cole's eyes glinted for a moment beneath the rim of his hat. He was not a man to be hurried, least of all today.

Late for his own brother's funeral, thought Nico with a shake of his head.

They were passing the walls of the Ministry of War now, a tall white-stone building perched there on the brow of the hill, right in the middle of the parkland. Many of its windows were boarded up, and one wing was blackened with fire, but it was still very much in use, if the figures rushing to and fro were anything to go by, and the many Red Guards still positioned in the fresh earthworks around it.

Some trees had been sheared in two by bomb blasts. Others stood black and bare.

The delegation from Zanzahar would be talking inside with representatives of the League, discussing the terms for keeping the charts of the Isles a secret. But Nico didn't care for any of that right then. It was all too abstract for his present mood, this moment in which he was alive and here to mark the passing of one of their own.

Everything was shining with a subtle lustre as he stepped along the gravel trail. It could so easily have been Nico having his ashes scattered today in the wind. During the worst of the fighting he had thrown himself at the enemy like a man possessed. Yet he had survived, when so many others had fallen.

Maybe it was fate, he thought. Maybe it just hadn't been his time.

Or maybe, when you'd already died once before, the odds of it happening again were just that much less.

Remember me! Remember my name!

In his mind he heard the men calling out their names in the smoky chaos of the chee house, hoping to leave something of themselves behind before the Imperials overran them.

Nico recited every one of their names again, recalling each face as he did so.

Already, it all seemed like a lifetime ago.

*

On the southern point of the Mount of Truth, a grassy field sloped down towards the sea and the Lansway and the walls of the Shield in gentle corrugations, like tiers in some natural theatre.

It was a popular spot with the locals for the views that it afforded, and it was here where the family of Bahn Calvone had gathered to scatter his ashes into the breeze, at the request of his last testament.

Nico and his father had ridden out onto the plain on the heels of the departing Mannians, to find Bahn, hoping to bring back his body for a proper funeral. Up on Beacon Heights the bodies still lay where they had fallen, and they had come upon Bahn at the top of the watchtower, lying on his back alone with his dead eyes staring at the sky.

Cole had said nothing as they bundled his brother in a cloak and lifted his stiffened body across the back of a zel.

Now, on the Mount of Truth, with the monk's words coming to an end and their tears still salting the ground at their feet, the mourners watched as Cole cast his brother's ashes into the wind, his expression set into a fierce scowl.

Marlee wept into her hands, a widow like so many others now, while Reese and a sister held her in their arms. The two children were there too, Juno and Ariale, though few others had turned up for the ceremony. Certainly none of Bahn's companions from the Red Guard. Not even his bitter crone of a mother.

Rest in peace, thought Nico, staring at the ashes sweeping away in the breeze, the last remains of a man he hadn't really known, when all was said and done. For Bahn had always been an enigma to Nico, much like his own father.

When he looked around once more at the small gathering, Nico was surprised to see Coya Zeziké standing there in attendance, the young man leaning over his cane with a sad and thoughtful countenance.

The famed League Delegate roused himself as the monk blessed everyone, marking the end of the ceremony with sweeps of burning incense. People stirred and cleared their throats. His father stood with his back turned to them all.

Coya made the sign of the Golden Spiral across his chest, then walked towards Nico over the grass while his two minders remained behind.

'Ah, Nico Calvone. I was told I would find you here today. Bahn was your uncle, I understand?'

'You knew Bahn?'

'I ate dinner with him once, if that counts as knowing a person. I'm sorry for your loss.'

If Coya knew of the circumstances of Bahn's death, how he had killed the Lord Protector, he was tactful enough not to mention it.

Nico's father had already made a report to the Ministry of Defence concerning what he knew of his brother's actions, and how they were the result of torture and manipulation at the hands of his previous Mannian captors. He hoped to clear his brother's name in some small way, though the authorities had cast some scepticism on his accounts. Indeed they had seemed more interested in where Cole had been all these years after he had deserted the army. Only the fact that the war was over had stopped them from putting him in chains.

Even now they were still looking for General Creed's body amongst the many dead. Maybe the Mannians had burned it. Maybe they had even taken the corpse with them as some macabre trophy. Though Nico had heard that a proper Khosian state funeral was still being prepared anyway.

'Forgive my timing,' said Coya, brushing a blond lock from his eye. 'I was hoping you might have a moment to spare. Please, walk with me a while?'

Nico's father was watching them as they both walked away from the funeral. His mother too, trying to rub some heat into Marlee's bones, stared after him with narrowed eyes.

After everything that Nico had been through, it did not seem so strange to be walking side by side with the most renowned Delegate of the democras and ancestor of Zeziké. Coya was smaller than Nico, hunched over his cane. A young man trapped in an old man's twisted frame.

'Here, take a drink of this,' said Coya, holding out a hip flask. It sounded like a command rather than an offering, and Nico stared at him for a moment before he took it, and swallowed down a mouthful. He grimaced. It tasted like Cheem Fire.

'Good. You will now forget everything I say here in about ten minutes' time. Unless I give you the antidote first.'

Nico stared hard at the man. He wasn't sure if he believed him or not, but he was intrigued.

'You were the apprentice of Ash,' said Coya. 'The young man he brought back from the dead. The only apprentice, I understand, who Ash ever chose in all his years as a Rōshun. He thought very highly of you.'

'And I him.'

The tip of Coya's cane stabbed little holes in the turf before their footsteps. 'He was certainly one of the good ones, for all that he was an assassin.'

'He was a spectacular old bastard, is what he was. The world is a lesser place without him. Now, how can I help you?'

Coya glanced behind to see if anyone was close by. 'I heard how you fought in the battle for the barricades,' he said. 'You held people together. You even took the leg of General Romano himself. Tell me. Did Ash ever mention the Few?'

'What view?'

'The *Few*. A secret network of like-minded citizens. Banded together across the Free Ports to fight concentrations of power and outside threats. We ensure the democras has a fighting chance to thrive.'

The man blinked at Nico's incomprehension. Coya looked down to the city, and he cast his hand towards it.

'Don't be fooled by appearances here. This is hardly the end of our troubles. More than ever, we need the likes of you in our organization.'

'The likes of me?'

'People of action. Of experience. Of heart.'

Nico recalled the moment back in the Bar-Khosian gaol cell all that time ago, when he had first agreed to become Ash's apprentice. A decision that had changed the entire course of his life.

'It sounds dangerous, this work you're offering.'

'Not work. A vocation. A cause.'

'Still . . .'

'Join us, and I promise you will see and know things beyond your wildest imaginings, Nico.'

'Well, I have a pretty wild imagination, I should warn you.'

The crooked man stopped and turned to face him, his lively gaze engaging his own. Coya's sudden zeal was like a hot wind blowing right at him. 'I'll even introduce you to a woman from *another world*, if you like.'

Nico could still taste the Cheem Fire in his mouth. His head was starting to feel groggy.

'There really was something in that drink, wasn't there?'

'A simple memory blocker. I have a vial of the antidote right here in my pocket.'

'Don't you think this is all a little sudden?'

'We always do it this way. Right in your face and in the heat of the moment. So, will you join us, Nico Calvone?'

'There must be a catch. There's always a catch.'

'No catch. Only a commitment.'

'To what?'

'To the betterment of all, Calvone. To your heart. To your spirit. To all that's wild and free in this world. To the good fight!' Coya smiled and slapped his arm in play. 'Now do you choose to forget these words of mine, or do you join us?'

Nico's parents were still watching from afar. They had lost him once already, after he'd made a bargain just like this one. His ashes had even been scattered in the back yard.

Yet everyone dies in the end, and that was the scary truth of it.

What mattered was how you chose to live in the present.

'This woman you mentioned,' Nico ventured, turning away from his parents. 'Did you say she's from another world?'

The End

extracts reading groups
competitions books new
discounts extracts
competitions
books
new
events books
extracts new titles reading groups
interviews
discounts
new books events
events new
discounts extracts discounts
www.panmacmillan.com
extracts events reading groups
competitions books extracts new
events
reading groups
books